THE
REALM
BEYOND

THE
REALM
BEYOND

RYAN HOYT

Machete & Quill Press

For my fellow travelers
braving this quest for justice & truth—
the end is within reach

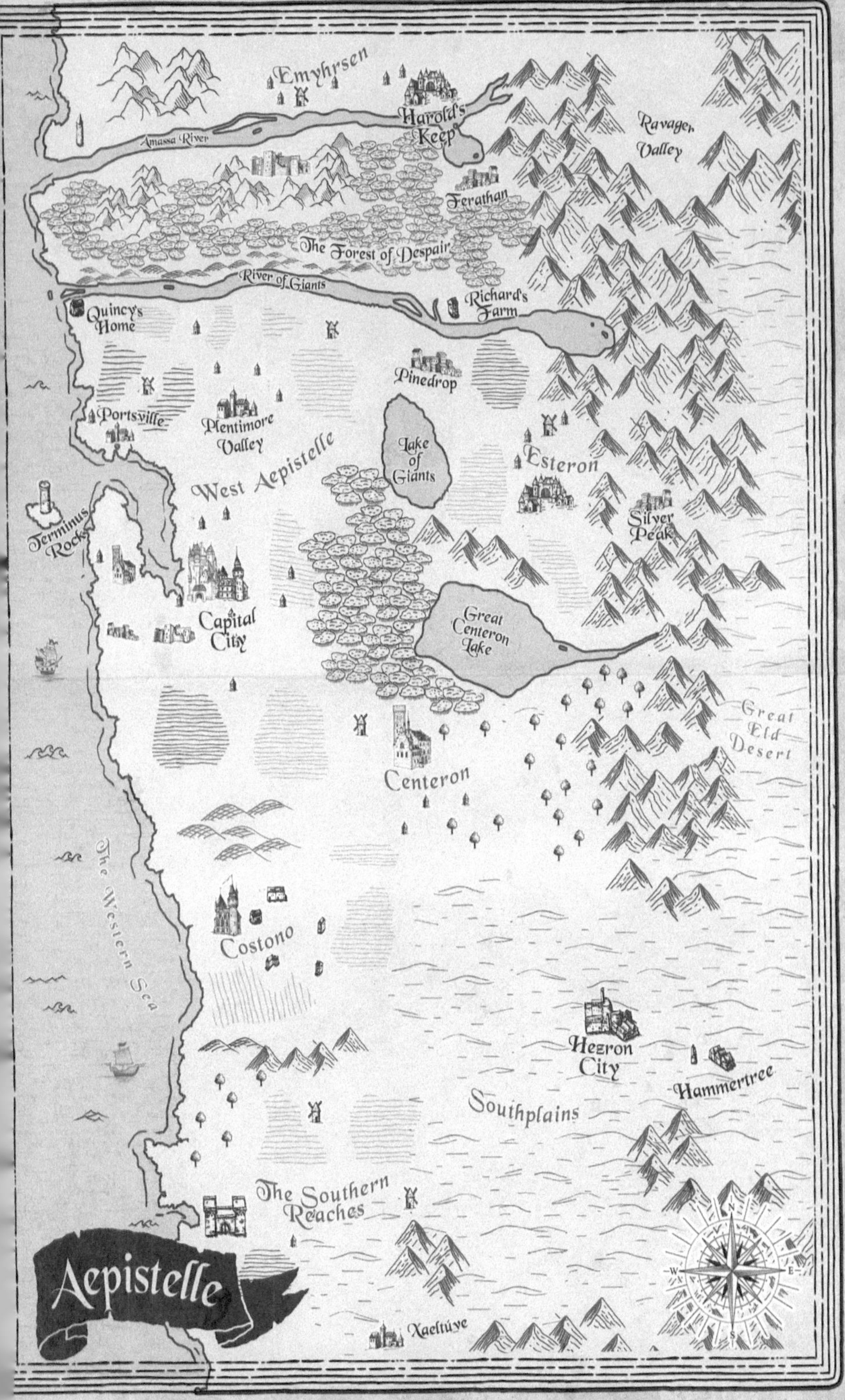

Emyhrsen
Harold's Keep
Amassa River
Ferathan
Ravager Valley
The Forest of Despair
River of Giants
Quincy's Home
Richard's Farm
Pinedrop
Portsville
Plentimore Valley
Lake of Giants
Esteron
West Aepistelle
Silver Peak
Terminus Rocks
Capital City
Great Centeron Lake
Great Eld Desert
Centeron
The Western Sea
Costono
Hezron City
Hammertree
Southplains
The Southern Reaches
Aepistelle
Xaeltuye
N
E
W
S

CHAPTER 1

KIEVE

"Calvertson!"

Kieve Fallbrook's voice reverberated off the brick buildings as he sprinted through yet another damp alley. He had lost track of which streets he was traversing several blocks ago. His throat was parched from breathing hard, raw from yelling his partner's name repeatedly. His feet were killing him. He wore his dress shoes, not the typical boots he used on assignment. This was supposed to be a night off from all things work. All things except his partner, that is. He had just needed to step into the bank on the way to the restaurant with Gemma, and that was when the subject of their assignment showed up. Unfortunate for the robber, because the Royal Mystic Committee's top duo was there.

Gemma hadn't dressed for a night on the town. She had worn her trusty boots, the only footwear she'd brought to Esteron City when they'd been dispatched there earlier that month. She'd taken off in pursuit without hesitation or fear while Kieve had simply stood there, dumbfounded. By the time he had emerged from the bank, his partner and her mark were nowhere to be seen.

Even now he could smell Gemma's perfume. She'd been gifted a custom batch by a practitioner they'd helped register with the Committee at their prior outpost. It had a floral scent with a hint of ocean breeze. All he needed to do was follow his nose through these alleys to know which way Gemma had gone, as the smell stood out in contrast to the trash and dung that lined the narrow corridors.

Kieve paused as he spotted a glimmer at the other end of the alley. It was just like the glimmer they'd seen in the bank when the would-be robber had caught sight of the pair and changed her mind. Kieve's hands went to his belt instinctively, but his twin daggers weren't holstered there this evening.

"Crap," he said before turning back and running toward the other end of the alley, away from the ghastly thing now pursuing him. He was only glad his partner wasn't there to see his cowardice. He glanced back to find his pursuer gaining on him, her unseen feet splashing through the puddles. In seconds, she'd be on him with whatever invisible weapon she might be carrying. He'd never get that date with his partner after all. He faced forward and found his second wind.

"Incoming," a voice called out from above. A resident of an apartment building lining the alley tossed a burlap sack of garbage out of a third-floor window. Kieve sidestepped it, but his ankle twisted. He staggered a few steps before putting his full weight on the foot and regaining his speed. He'd feel it later, perhaps, but that would mean he had survived this ordeal. The mouth of the alley was almost within reach, pedestrians walking on the sidewalk on their way home from work. Surely his pursuer would relent on a crowded street.

The pedestrians parted in confusion, but they hadn't noticed Kieve's approach. Something pushed through the crowd from the opposite side.

The glimmer.

But...

He chanced another glance behind him, only to find the blurred pursuer still there.

There were *two*?

The one ahead of him produced a blade. It seemed to appear out of thin air, inches at a time until it was fully visible. A sword?

No.

"Machete!" he called out, excitement tucked into his exasperation.

The blade lifted up and back, then slashed down. Kieve pounced forward and to the left, kicked his feet out, and slid past the blur with the blade as it arced down and connected with his unseen pursuer.

A line of blood was floating in the air when he looked back at where the blade had connected. A woman grunted in pain. There was another sound like glass shattering, and shards rained down into the alley. The wounded one's momentum kept her going despite the blow. She slammed into the newcomer, and both seemed to fall to the ground.

Piece by piece, the hazy mass wrestling in the alley revealed itself. There were shards of glass sprinkled all around. Kieve reached out and grabbed one, ignoring the way it pricked his pointer finger as he brought it close to his face. It looked like a speck from a smashed mirror.

One figure slammed into a brick wall as more of the invisibility suit fell away and revealed locks of dark brown hair.

"Calvertson?" Kieve asked. He got to his feet and ran at

the form attacking his partner. His shoulder connected, and he slammed down on top of her. More glass crunched, piercing his forearm through his wool coat. Kieve grunted.

"What gave it away?" Gemma asked as she pulled off what remained of the invisibility shroud. Sweat glistened on her forehead and cheeks, but the spark of adventure shone bright in her eyes. She had started off as an academic, yet Kieve had witnessed her rise to the top of the ranks in the Royal Mystic Committee, and it was in moments like these that he understood precisely why. "Look out!"

The mass under Kieve had slipped free, and a foot-long section of copper piping emerged from inside the unseen cloak. Kieve tried to heed Gemma's warning, but his reflexes weren't as quick as his partner's. His shoulder took the brunt of the blow, which missed his head by a fraction of an inch.

"Still have my teeth," he managed as he rolled away from his attacker. The pipe pulled back for another swing as Gemma's own weapon slashed down. Both the pipe and a severed thumb hit the ground in unison.

The wounded attacker cried from the ground between Kieve and Gemma, a deep and painful wail. Gemma reached down and pulled off their invisible mask, revealing a pale, tear-streaked face. The woman appeared to be in her fifties with hair cut down nearly to the scalp.

"Bastards," the woman said through her sobs. "All you had to do was leave me be. The banks don't need the money. Nor do you Committee vipers!"

Gemma's machete disappeared into her own invisible cloak for a moment before the entire cloak crashed to the pavement. Gemma stood there, just taller than Kieve, her machete back in its sheath at her side. Her clothes were matted with sweat. "That thing was way too hot and heavy,"

Gemma said. "Not sure how you'd make a suit of glass more breathable, though."

"You had to go and break both of my suits, too?" the woman said to Gemma. "They were all I had!"

"What about the money you stole?" Kieve asked. "You've knocked more than a dozen establishments that we're aware of and picked countless pockets, I'm sure."

"Every penny I stole was for the cause," the woman spat back. "Nobody was hurt by my actions. Shareholders, perhaps. Bank managers. They still went home with their pay, though."

"Don't forget those tax collectors," Kieve said.

"As if King Davin needs more of our hard-earned money out in Capital City. You lot should be ashamed of yourselves." She used her good hand to pick up her severed thumb and stared at it in shock.

"I'm sorry about your finger," Gemma said. A crowd had gathered on either end of the alley, and members of Esteron City's police force marched toward the scene from the farther end. "I couldn't let you hurt me or my partner."

"The world could use two fewer Committee pawns!" the woman screamed loud enough for the crowd to hear as the officers pulled her to her feet. "All your kind ever does is imprison and kill the innocent. There'll be a reckoning soon. The people have had enough!"

Her voice grew distant as the police escorted her through the front line of onlookers. Some of them looked hesitant to move, as if they weren't sure the right party was being taken to prison, but they relented and let the officers pass with the bloodied woman.

Kieve turned back to Gemma. For a moment, he thought her confident exterior had shattered like the suit she had worn, but then she caught his stare and cocked an eyebrow. "Is there a problem?" Gemma asked.

"Just the way this evening has turned out." Kieve gestured at the debris on the ground. "How did you come across her suit?"

"While you were standing around in the bank lobby, I followed her into a vacant storefront around the corner where she'd set up camp. The spare suit was partly open, piled on her sleep sack. She wasn't moving that fast, so I decided to throw it on, see how it worked." Gemma knelt and picked up a section of the suit. "Thousands of little mirrored pieces, each one angled precisely such that the reflections render its wearer invisible."

"So she wasn't using powers?" Kieve asked. His shoulders slumped. "We didn't need to be involved at all?"

"I mean, we did a better job of catching her than the local crew. It's not a total loss."

Gemma's smooth veneer seemed to wrinkle slightly. There was something she wasn't saying, and Kieve couldn't figure out what it was. They had been partners for nearly three years now, and this wasn't the first time he'd detected doubts in her. The first year especially, she was quite bitter toward the Committee, making him question why she had even joined it. Yet she was good at what she did, and she matched the Royal Mystic Committee's new mission perfectly: showing compassion for those afflicted with unnatural abilities or powers and convincing them to register those defects with the Committee. Distrust was rampant, as was to be expected given the Committee's bloody past, but Gemma had a way of showing empathy and getting their subjects to follow the new requirements. And during their more dangerous and colorful cases, like this one, another side of Gemma emerged—one that thrived on adventure and peril, leaving Kieve to wonder if there was more to Gemma's past than she was willing to tell.

She seemed like someone who had experienced a lot in her lifetime. At twenty-seven years old, she was too young to have fought in the war. Her Capital City upbringing likely hadn't allowed for much adventure. But there was something else about her, something that made Gemma Calvertson one of the greatest assets of King Davin's Royal Mystic Committee.

CHAPTER 2
GEMMA, TWO DAYS LATER

The office building at Fort Braxen on the outskirts of Capital City had been full when Gemma had joined the Royal Mystic Committee. Following the six weeks of physical training, Gemma would have been content with a corner of a dining table in the compound's cafeteria. That she got an enclave of her very own among the basement archive stacks was a miracle, or perhaps it was the sway of her powerful royal benefactor. Sharing the space with a new partner made it a little less special at first, but she'd come to appreciate Kieve Fallbrook and even respect him. In the rare moments when she had time to dawdle, she found herself combing through the case files that the Committee's administrators had tucked away in that dim space. Her blood often boiled at how flippantly the officers had written about which religions' clergy they'd arrested, what kinds of abilities had afflicted the folks they'd executed.

Following Gemma's surrender to King Davin, the monarch had promised that things would be different, that the Royal Mystic Committee would act with compassion toward those it had once demonized, and that Gemma would be among the first to work under its new mission. While Davin had made an earnest attempt to stay good to his word, it had taken considerable effort to get the hardliners within the organization to comply and change the way they'd operated for the past two decades. There were some high up in the ranks who were aware of Gemma's deal with the king, and those folks eyed her with distrust and resentment, even now that she had three years and dozens of successful cases under her belt. Her partner, Kieve Fallbrook, had been a hardliner himself, though his start with the Committee had been only a few months before Gemma's. It had taken patience on Gemma's part and many displays of compassion toward their subjects before Kieve started to see the benefits of the changes. Likewise, getting the people of Aepistelle to trust the Committee was an ongoing effort, one Gemma herself wasn't confident would ever be achieved given its bloody history.

Gemma hunched over her desk, flanked by two lanterns struggling to make up for the lack of sunlight in the subterranean space. She worked hard on the report, providing intricate details of everything that had happened in Esteron City, even though she knew her supervisor would give it a cursory glance at best before filing it away here in the archives. She left out her partner's advances, his misguided attempt to ask Gemma out on a date. Kieve was only two years her senior and handsome enough, and he'd softened his stance over the years on the Committee's new humane approach. However, the roughness he'd shown early on in their partnership still didn't sit well with her. She wondered how much of his change of heart had been a show to win over her affections.

Footsteps echoed in the stairwell. *Kieve returning just in time to not contribute to the report*, Gemma thought. *Again.*

But the man who turned the corner around the book-shelves that stood in for actual walls around Gemma's office was decidedly *not* Kieve. He looked to be around forty, his hard face not unlike others of their ranks. He clearly recognized her, and the creases around his eyes deepened as a warm smile brightened his face.

"Can I help you?" Gemma asked.

"Good afternoon, Ms. Calvertson," he said. There was an unmistakable excitement in his voice, as if he'd been looking forward to this meeting. Gemma noted the tan folder tucked under his left arm.

"Is it still afternoon? Hard to tell this far below surface level," Gemma quipped. She'd stolen the line from Kieve, who had been missing in action since lunch.

"Indeed it is. I should introduce myself. I am Lieutenant Cragen Palignon of Special Operations, head of the Northern Division."

Gemma rose to her feet and slightly bowed her head, as was customary when addressing a superior in the Committee. It wasn't a military branch, so salutes weren't necessary. "Nice to meet you, Lieutenant. What brings you to Capital City?"

Palignon laughed, then pulled the file from under his arm. "I've heard a lot about you over the last few years. Your reputation is one that takes most of our agents at least a decade to earn."

"Can't say I expected word of my exploits to reach the Northern Division," Gemma said.

"Cracking the case of the invisible woman wreaking havoc in Esteron? And the boy with the wings and feathers terrorizing Hazy Gulch? The more bizarre the situation, the more likely that Gemma Calvertson will be there to make sure it's resolved cleanly. You're quick to act where more experienced agents would freeze up, yet each action is well thought out and executed with precision. That's to say nothing of your compassion, which has proven to be contagious among your peers."

Gemma noticed the way he looked at her. It wasn't creepy, but rather as if he knew her and her story well. Her time with Richard and Denny and Arnem. What had come after with Kosar and Syntha. The past she'd hidden away three years ago to ensure her success in the Committee.

"There's something familiar about you," she said. "We haven't met before, have we?"

Palignon looked down at the file in his hands, which was still closed. Gemma thought the man was considering how to answer without giving away too much. That wasn't at all unusual for a member of the Royal Mystic Committee, especially someone from Special Operations, which engaged in many of the more clandestine and classified activities for which Gemma had no clearance.

His voice dropped to nearly a whisper. "We have not met, though we have some mutual acquaintances. It's best if I say no more than that."

Gemma furrowed her eyebrows as she thought about who he could be referring to. None of her old friends were sympathizers of the Royal Mystic Committee. She hadn't heard from her brother, George, since he'd embarked on his journey with Jestan and Naliah to bring the Tzakabyans back to their ancestral lands. Arnem was dead at Denny's hand, and the boy hadn't been seen since. Marzele had disappeared around the same time. Gemma's former employer, Garrod Hannon, had cut ties with her, though he'd been spared punishment for any role he may have played in Gemma's story. Syntha hadn't contacted Gemma since she'd been sent away by King Davin in the Southern Reaches; the young woman had most likely heard of Gemma's new career with "the enemy" and written her off completely. And then there were Gemma's parents, who remained under Quincy's protection on the coast. Perhaps this man was in league with Quincy's mercenaries, but Gemma didn't think it likely.

"Don't try to figure it out, please. It's for your own good." Palignon dropped the file onto her desk. "I've put in a request for you to lead this case. I think you may find it interesting."

Gemma sat, then reached for the file and opened it. "And it's been approved?"

"It's been cleared from the top. Commander Bryne and I are old pals." Grushka Bryne had risen to the head desk of the Royal Mystic Committee not long after Gemma had joined. The man had filled the spot vacated by Sir Marin Allemon, whose death Gemma had witnessed in Emyhrsen.

Gemma scanned the first page. Her eyebrows rose when she read the location. "Plentimore Valley?" She looked up at the man again, studying him for any sign that this was a setup.

"Plentimore Valley," Palignon said. He turned and walked back toward the stairs, then stopped for a moment and faced Gemma again. "The subject of this investigation just might have information regarding a question you've been trying to answer for the last three years."

With that, he was lost to the shadows of the basement stairwell.

CHAPTER 3
GEMMA

Gemma went from one basement to another as she made her way home to her subterranean apartment on Capital City's north side. Despite the dangers of her job, the salary she received was not enough to pay for a townhome in her family's old neighborhood or even a single-bedroom apartment on an upper floor. The best she could afford on her own was a dingy studio under a launderer that had flooded her apartment twice in the two years she'd lived there. She was rarely home, though, and most of her room and board at assorted inns was covered by per diems when she was on assignment.

Gemma dumped the contents of her duffel bag onto the bed she hadn't slept in for three weeks. She opened her closet and pulled out a few items. She brought each one to her nose to make sure they were clean enough, winced at the tinge of sourness plaguing each article, and stuffed them into the bag anyway. Perhaps there would be a laundry service in whichever inn the Committee's pittance would cover.

A growl emanated from her belly. Gemma walked over to

the cookstove, where a pot sat. She pulled off the lid to reveal stringy noodles that had long since dried. She eyed them suspiciously, grabbed a fork, and poked at them. They were rock hard. They *had* been in there for three weeks, abandoned as they cooled off when Gemma had been interrupted by Kieve at the door, coming to collect her for the assignment in Esteron City. She shuddered and dropped the lid back into place. She could eat on the train.

The doorknob rattled. Gemma reached for her machete at her side. "Who's there?" she called, though she suspected Kieve had arrived early.

"It's me, Gemma." The voice had a tinge of an accent from the Southern Reaches. She unbolted the door and pulled it open.

"What are you doing here, Kosar?"

The man pushed past Gemma and moped into the center of the room. He looked around at the mess, then at Gemma's travel bag, and finally at Gemma. "You know you wouldn't have to keep running off into the night if you just stayed with me, don't you? I can take care of you, Gemma. It smells like death in this little crap hole."

"What are you doing here?" Gemma asked again. "When in the last few years have I done something to make you think I have any interest in talking to you?"

His face was dejected. Gemma thought he looked like a little boy, nothing at all like the confident young man she had fallen in love with on a rooftop, who had charmed her on the boat to his father's palace down south and made her feel like she could find safety in his homeland. This doppelgänger carried himself much differently, a product of being lied to by the man he had thought was his father and manipulated by the man that actually was.

Tears filled Kosar's eyes. "I just need someone to talk to.

There is nobody at the castle who I can confide in. Please, Gemma, show me compassion, as I've always done for you." He plopped onto her bed and patted the space next to him.

Gemma rolled her eyes and sat in her only chair at the makeshift table instead. "You have five minutes, and then I need to leave."

"That's how you treat a prince, then? It's the same at home. My father"—by this he meant King Davin, his biological father, and not Governor Herron, who had raised him as his own son—"speaks to me only at mealtimes when there is no one else to talk to but the servants, and he shows more respect to them than he does to me. It's been three years now since I sacrificed everything to take to my rightful place at his side. Three years that I've been showing him my loyalty at every opportunity, only to have him metaphorically backhand me at every step. I called myself a prince just now because that is what I am, but does anyone know it?"

Gemma felt a mixture of pity and disgust, with an emphasis on the latter, and she was quite sure it showed on her face. He winced at her expression.

"Does anyone know I am their prince?" he asked again. "Answer me, please."

"No, Kosar, not aside from those you've betrayed. Those who are still breathing, I mean."

"Nobody in this rotten kingdom knows who I really am because my father hasn't announced it yet. But he will soon. He must. His time in this world is running out. Whatever charms he has been using to appear younger are becoming less effective. His health is starting to fail even if his resolve to rule eternally is not. I'm sure the time is approaching when he will tell the world that he has a son and an heir, when I will be crowned prince of Aepistelle, first in line for the throne. Then people will bow down to me. They will kiss my polished boots. They will fawn over me. Lust for me. And you will be among them, Gemma."

Gemma scoffed, but Kosar brushed it off.

"Or you can lower the curtains on this little act of yours and take your place as my lover once more. As I promised you in the Reaches, I will take care of your family. I will erase the marks against all your friends who are in hiding or in exile. I will show kindness like you've never seen, Gemma. Your affection for me was strong once, and it can be again if you let it. Please, be my princess." He rose to his feet and took three steps toward Gemma. He held his hand out to her. "Be my queen."

A pause.

Silence.

Gemma laughed. Not the laugh of a girl giddy at the prospect of being royalty, but an ugly snort of hilarity. Instead of reaching to take his hand, she covered her mouth to try and stifle the laughter, but it was no use. She let it loose instead. Kosar flinched away from her. He turned and kicked the frame of her bed.

"Ouch!" he yelled, then hobbled to the front door. He yanked it open, turned back to her, and shook his head. "You'll regret this, Calvertson. You'll wish you had never mocked me." With that, he stepped outside and slammed the door.

Two seconds passed before the door opened again. "You know where to find me when you change your mind," he said, then slammed it once more. Gemma's laughter continued as he stomped up the stairs to the sidewalk like a petulant child.

The door opened yet again a moment later. Kieve stepped into the apartment with a look of confusion. "It looks like I've interrupted a good time," he said. "Who was that gentleman storming out of here like a fire mage had just set his britches aflame?"

"That would be Kosar," said Gemma, wiping tears of laughter from her cheeks. She stood and made for the pot of stale noodles to scrape them into the rubbish bin.

"A former lover?" Gemma thought she detected a hint of jealousy, but Kieve put on enough of a grin to hide it.

"It's complicated." She said no more, and Kieve didn't push. "What are you doing here, anyway?"

"You weren't in the office when I stepped in tonight. It's unlike you to leave before midnight."

"Just packing for our assignment," Gemma said. She lifted her bag. "Not even one night to sleep in our own beds before we're sent out all over again."

"*We* weren't sent out, Gemma. Looks like this one is a solo mission for you."

"What are you talking about? They never send us out alone."

"Commander Bryne summoned me to his office and asked for a verbal account of our last mission. He avoided eye contact the entire time and rushed me through the story as if he wasn't listening to a word of it. Then he told me I was to take two weeks off for mandatory rest and recovery."

"Why do *you* get a paid vacation when I'm the one who broke the case? Again?" Of course, Gemma had no desire to take a vacation. She would have chosen to continue working had she been offered the option. Downtime meant being stuck in this dump of an apartment in this dump of a city. Sure, it was only a few miles from the home where she had grown up, but Capital City held nothing for her anymore, no people she cared about outside of her colleagues. Her friendships from her youth and her time at the university had faded over the years due to her commitment to her studies and then her work. Her parents now lived hundreds of miles north. She chose not to visit them, as they neither understood nor supported her decision to join the Royal Mystic Committee, and she could better protect them from the center of corruption anyway.

"Bryne knows you're the real strength of the team," he replied, and Gemma was certain she read hurt in his tone. "Said you could handle this one yourself."

"The weird thing is that Commander Bryne didn't assign it to me. It was a lieutenant from Special Ops."

"Should I be worried about you? I'm happy to tag along on my own dime if you want. I'm not prepared for a vacation anyway."

The noodles finally came loose in one large clump and plopped into the bin. Satisfied, Gemma set the pot back down on the stovetop. "I'll be fine. You should take the train down to Costono. I hear the coastal line has some beautiful views."

"Sounds romantic. It'd be better if you could join me."

"Better yet, you should take Kosar with you. I'm sure you two would have much to talk about. And by *much*, I mean *me*."

"And with that, I'll take my leave. Alone, not with the mopey boy. Be safe, Gemma."

"You know, every time someone says that at the start of an assignment, it turns out to be the opposite of safe. Then again, it's just Plentimore Valley this time. What could go wrong there?"

But Gemma knew that danger lurked everywhere, even in the land of wineries and jolly little folks like her late friend Arnem Wynstone.

Even Plentimore Valley had its secrets.

CHAPTER 4
KIEVE

Kieve had no doubt that Gemma's initial placement in the Royal Mystic Committee had been engineered. Her meteoric rise, on the other hand, had been her own doing. Kieve had witnessed her cunning and skill from the beginning when they'd been assigned to work together to investigate some of the more supernatural and bizarre unsolved cases. But just who had helped Gemma get her job at the Committee, Kieve did not know.

There were only a handful of individuals with the power to secure that position for her. People like Commander Grushka Bryne, who had to have signed off on it at least, or someone in King Davin's cabinet. Davin himself often meddled in the affairs of the Committee. It was his keystone project, after all, the one that would most define his time on the throne.

And there seemed to be more meddling happening now. Kieve had been intentionally left off of Gemma's latest assignment for someone from Special Operations. Their involvement normally meant a case was dangerous and involved violent criminals or extremely sensitive intelligence. While Kieve had seen Gemma hold her own against violent and dangerous people, she didn't have the military background that most Special Ops agents had.

As Kieve walked across town under what few stars shone through the polluted air of Capital City, he feared that perhaps his partner was being set up by someone powerful. Could Davin be shifting the Committee's strategy once again? Gemma had joined when Davin had walked back his vow to crush those associated with magic and religion. Her time in the organization was defined by her compassion for those the Committee once would have locked up or executed. While others had scoffed at the new regulations—Kieve among them, though he was now ashamed to admit it—Gemma had been the poster child for forgiveness and rehabilitation. If the superiors wanted to do an about-face on the policy, they'd have to get rid of Gemma Calvertson or find some way to tame her.

Peers nodded to Kieve as they passed him in the streets around Fort Braxen. The Black Ledger, the tavern they were flowing from, was as much a headquarters for the Royal Mystic Committee as Fort Braxen was. Should anyone want information on the latest missions and intelligence, one needed only to grab a barstool and nurse a drink or two. Then again, one would also stick out like a giant in Plentimore Valley, as the Committee folks were a tight bunch.

Kieve pushed his way through a group of comrades and flagged down the bartender. "Midnight Mash, please," he said. The old woman behind the bar grunted something, walked away, and returned a moment later with a mug of the darkest ale in Aepistelle. The froth was thick and reminded Kieve of marshmallows roasted over a fire. He sipped it, then wiped the frothy mustache off his upper lip and slurped it from his finger. After some small talk with one of his old academy chums, he made the rounds, searching for anyone who looked out of place. Special Ops folks were a different breed in some ways, but they had the same love of winding down after a long day with a beverage or three. Whoever they were, they weren't a regular here, so Kieve knew he'd be able to spot them.

And there he was. "Should have known," Kieve whispered under his breath.

Across the room, sitting with the commander himself, was Cragen Palignon. The man was a contemporary of Bryne's—they had come up through recruitment and training together. Their competitive spirits were legendary, each trying to make more arrests, smash more temple windows, burn more cantrip scrolls and holy books than the other. Bryne had suffered an injury to his leg at some point, leaving him desk-bound, while Palignon had moved deeper into Special Operations. Around the time Bryne had taken the place of the late Sir Allemon as commander, Palignon had disappeared. Kieve had later learned that the man had been given command of the Northern Division, and he hadn't been seen in Capital City since...until now.

Palignon was acting amiable enough with his longtime colleague, but Kieve was good at reading body language. The twitch of one side of his lips, the glances toward the door, and the forced laughter were all signs that Palignon had somewhere he'd rather be and that he was quickly losing patience. Kieve stepped outside and made his way to the yellow tree, which wasn't that color at all. The tree had been given that name because it was where the men flocked when the tavern's bathroom became too filthy to stand. He whistled a tune, undid his britches, and let loose, something he'd done hundreds of times before. Sure enough, Palignon soon exited the tavern and walked with determination into the night. Kieve cut off both his tune and his stream, returned everything to his pants, and went after the older man.

Palignon kept his head down and his shoulders slightly hunched, but his speed made it difficult for Kieve to follow him quietly. He must have been deep in contemplation, though, because he didn't seem aware that he was being tailed. Kieve thought it unlikely that Palignon hadn't caught wind of him, given his Special Ops background. He probably just didn't perceive any threat from Kieve.

The building they ended up at had once been an oversize townhouse, as if any one person truly needed such luxury for themself and their family and servants. It had since been converted into sensible apartments, though the rent for each was probably comparable to the mortgage a family would have paid for the full house before Davin sat on the throne. The windows that faced the street on all three floors were dark. It was the middle of the night, after all, nearer to dawn than sunset. Still, Palignon apparently felt the need to pay someone a visit. He reached into his coat, brought out a ring of keys, and without the aid of a light, ran his fingers along them until he found the correct one. He unlocked the front door on the first try, went in, and closed it behind him. Kieve knew better than to follow him inside, so he backed between two tall shrubs across the street and faded into the shadows.

After a minute, a window on the third floor illuminated. Kieve caught a glimpse of a woman in a robe carrying a candle, presumably on the way to her front door. She disappeared, and then the silhouettes of both Palignon and the woman appeared. Tension was evident even between their dancing shadows. Arms flailed, and Kieve could hear the faintest reverberation of their yelling three stories down and across the street. Another candle lit in a different window, and a teenage girl appeared, gazed out at the street below. Sadness or shame was painted on her face as she looked to the outside world for escape.

A wind picked up completely out of nowhere. It was late autumn, but Capital City had remained moderately warm with calm skies. The bushes rattled. Tree branches shook violently, sending their remaining leaves spiraling to the ground. Kieve stepped out of the shrubbery to investigate the freak storm when he felt eyes on him. He looked back up at the window, and the girl's glare dug into him. He'd been marked. Pulled out of hiding. Revealed. Perhaps that was as good a reason as any why he'd not been asked by Special Operations to go on a secret mission alongside Gemma. The girl's expression softened, and she waved to Kieve. He didn't know what else to do but return the gesture. Moments later, a crack from the tree that loomed above him sent him running; a massive branch tore off and plummeted to the ground. The earth rumbled around him from the impact.

If there was ever a sign that he was in the wrong place, that was surely it. He turned and ran out of that neighborhood, finding himself in calm weather and under clear skies once again.

Kieve couldn't sleep that night. Suspicions about Cragen Palignon and what had happened at that apartment ate away at him as he failed to slumber. From the tension he had witnessed, he had no doubt that the woman was Palignon's ex-partner. The girl was surely their daughter. Things had obviously gone badly for Palignon, so Kieve doubted the man was planning to stick around. Either he would return to Fort Braxen in the morning, or he'd take the train back north to Pinedrop, where he was stationed. Kieve bet on the second option and made his way to the railway station with a knapsack of spare clothes. His intuition was correct, and he boarded the train one car behind Palignon.

Gemma had suggested Kieve take the train south and enjoy his time off work, but fate seemed to have another plan for him.

He traveled north instead.

CHAPTER 5

GEMMA

Plentimore Valley was only part of a day's ride from Capital City, but the two cities couldn't have been more different. Buildings taller than two stories were rare in the Valley. Streets were as likely to be dirt as paved. Outside of the main business district, houses and shops shared no walls. And then there were the people of Plentimore Valley. Whereas in the big city, one would likely be sneered at for saying good morning to a stranger or receive an obscene gesture in exchange for a wave, it was out of the ordinary *not* to say hello or wave when passing someone in Plentimore Valley.

Despite the inherent kindness in the air, Gemma felt a pang of sadness as she looked around the block outside the train station. The short and stout figures so common in the region reminded her over and over of the late Arnem Wynstone. There was a certain way the locals laughed, and an upward slant to their sentences that shone with optimism, followed by phrases of self-deprecation, a humorous humility. Gemma hadn't spent more than a few minutes with Arnem's onetime close friend Maachel when he'd arrived in Emyhrsen, but the way Arnem and Maachel had interacted so intimately was mirrored by the friendships she witnessed here.

Gemma shook off her thoughts as she walked toward the inn. She was on assignment and needed a clear head. She glanced to the side out of habit, ready for a random factoid or sarcastic observation from her partner—those always pulled her out of her worries. Kieve wasn't there, though. They'd worked nearly every case together during her time in the Committee. She'd spent more hours of her life with him than anyone but her parents and brother. Even her longest relationship, with Walker, had only been off-and-on for a couple of years before he'd been killed during an ill-fated stroll into the town of Ferathan. Kieve often gave Gemma the credit for the outcomes of their cases, but she relied on him to poke holes in her theories, to break the tension during heated interrogations, to keep her focused on their missions. His companionship was a fairly good replacement for that of her family or a lover.

And yet she had kept him more at arm's length than normal in recent months. Something had changed in him. He held eye contact during their conversations slightly longer than before. He seemed to look deeper into her eyes, searching for extra meaning in her words, exploring her thoughts. He invited her to pricier restaurants than their per diems would cover and made more of an effort to dress up. She never acknowledged it; she didn't want their partnership to change, didn't want to let anyone in emotionally. She didn't like entertaining these thoughts even when she was alone.

"Room for one," Gemma told the woman behind the desk at the Village Vine Inn. She'd chosen the place because it wasn't the typical roadside inn with a noisy tavern downstairs that served ales all through the night, the ceaseless noise keeping her awake.

The short but solid innkeeper pulled her nose out of her book, annoyed at the interruption. "Why, yes, missy, we've room for one. More than that, if you can fathom it." Her attention returned to the book.

"Great, um...may I please have a room, then?" Gemma asked.

The woman's hand shot out, her pointer finger aimed at the window behind Gemma. "Sign," she said.

Gemma turned and read it out loud. "Check-in late afternoon." She looked at the innkeeper again. "I suppose I'm early. Do you have any rooms ready yet? I can pay a few coins extra."

At the mention of money, the woman closed her book and faced her customer with a smile. "Now that you mention it, I do have a clean room available for our early check-in fee of five coppers, collected in advance. Room rate is posted on the sign."

Gemma forked over the money to cover one night plus the extra fee the lady had invented on the spot. As long as the bed was soft, Gemma didn't mind. She'd stay within her budget, since Kieve wasn't there to demand fancy meals and accommodations.

The woman led Gemma up the creaky staircase and opened the second door on the right. Gemma stepped in to a room comparable to her studio apartment. She dropped her bag onto the bed, then glanced at a shelf of books next to the fireplace.

"You have Jestan the Just's book," she commented, pulling *Journey of Perils* off the shelf. Reminders of Arnem would never cease here, it seemed. "Have you ever met Arnem or Maachel?"

"Met them? Ha! Used to change Maachel's diapers. Lived in the same neighborhood in the west end when I was younger. My mum and his were close friends. I was his nanny for a couple of years and made a nice chunk of change. Arnem lived on the other side of my folks' house, and those two were inseparable little devils. But the less said about Arnem, the better."

"Why is that?" Gemma asked. She wasn't sure what the locals knew about Arnem's fate.

"Left his family behind, he did. Made them go to work. My own husband did the same, left me to run this place on my own."

Heat rose to Gemma's cheeks, but she took a deep breath to calm herself. "I'm sure he left to do something heroic, just like before. I think his wife and daughters probably understand that."

"Ha! It's not something any woman would take lightly, my dear. Off with another woman, I'm certain, while she's still here, growing her business better than he ever could. Anyway, I've got to be getting back to the counter downstairs. Enjoy your stay."

Once she was alone, Gemma opened her bag and pulled out her machete. She began to fasten its sheathe to her belt, then thought better of it and tucked it back inside the bag. She shuffled through her clothes and pulled out a black outfit. She changed, then descended the stairs and slipped past the innkeeper, who never lifted her eyes from her book.

Gemma wasn't sure she was in the right place. The address was 805-A, which was a bakery. The smells of freshly baked pastries were inviting, but she persisted in her search.

The next door was 806, a barber shop. The address she was given was 805-B, which didn't appear to exist. Gemma turned and made her way into the bakery.

Two pairs of patrons sat at the only tables in the front of the bakery, one duo drinking tea while the other had coffee. Long loaves of bread wrapped in thin cloths jutted out of wooden half barrels in front of a counter that ran the width of the interior. Trays of cakes and cookies and puff pastries covered the countertop. Nobody looked up at her, and Gemma couldn't see anyone working.

"Hello?" she called. She heard the shuffling of baking sheets in what she assumed was the kitchen just beyond an open doorway behind the counter. She found the gap in the counter and slipped through it. "Excuse me, is anyone back there?"

Just then, a woman walked through the doorway and started when she saw Gemma in her space. She dropped the tray she was carrying, sending a dozen small cakes to the floor, a cloud of powdered sugar wafting up behind them. "Lords of the Stony Crag, you frightened me!"

"I'm so sorry," Gemma offered. "I called back but didn't think you'd heard me."

As Gemma approached the woman to help clean up the mess she'd caused, she took in the baker's features. She was unusually compact, even for Plentimore Valley. She was shorter and sturdier than most and muscular in a way that spoke of decades of hard physical labor. Her skin was so pale that it almost gave off a sheen, a glow, but the woman didn't appear sickly in any way. Her hair was black and silver in equal amounts, and her eyes had a look of distrust in them, though her cheeks looked creased from constant smiles. Her nose was wide and flared with frustration at the loss of the cakes. A couple of whisker hairs protruded from her chin, twirling halfway down the length of her neck, and even more stemmed from her ears and a mole on her left cheek. When she turned to Gemma, she gave a smile that revealed teeth that seemed off somehow. They were wider and thicker than usual and lacked the normal shine, almost like pale white stones.

"It's quite all right, dear," the woman said in a husky voice. Gemma detected a hint of an accent but couldn't place it. "I can whip up another batch easily." The now-misshapen cakes rolled around the tray as she returned to the rear of the bakery and dumped them into a rubbish bin. "What can I do for you?"

Gemma stood awkwardly behind the counter, unsure if she should return to the other side, but the baker made no indication that she minded. "I'm looking for an address, 805-B, but I can't find it. Do you happen to know where it is?"

The baker raised her eyebrows. "You're in it now. Well, it's back here." She reached under the counter, retrieved a sign that said TEMPORARILY CLOSED, WILL RETURN SOON, and set it up. Then she motioned for Gemma to follow as she walked back through the kitchen, past a staircase that presumably led to an apartment upstairs, and into a room farther back. She pushed open the door, and a wave of heat wafted out.

A circular table took up the center of the room with six chairs evenly spaced around it. While five of them were typical wooden dining chairs, the sixth stood taller, with a plush maroon cushion that sat just below the table. Gemma didn't need to be told that this seat was meant for the baker, who pointed at the chair directly across from the cushioned one. Gemma sat. The woman walked to a cookstove at the back of the room. From a shelf next to it, she pulled a stoneware jar. Gemma thought the woman was about to offer her tea, but instead she pulled the lid off the jar, took out a handful of something, and tossed it into the cookstove. For a second, the fire glimmered emerald green. Then the woman closed the stove door, hiding the flames within, opened a vent on the side of the fireplace, and took her cushioned chair.

"Now we may begin. I am Madame Hvalsi. What you are about to experience may change you profoundly. It may change what you know about the world, about life and death. You may hear details about a loved one that are so intimate that it will change your perception of them. Ultimately, though, you shall emerge from this room with the wisdom you seek, even if it takes you some time to truly decipher what you learn. The departed do not always communicate in a straightforward manner, but that does not mean that what they say is any less valuable. Are you ready to begin?"

Gemma stared at her in confusion. An earthy smell coming from the fireplace filled the room. The heat was overwhelming, and already Gemma could feel sweat forming on her forehead and under her arms. "Wait, what is this all about? Someone gave me this address and told me I'd find answers here, but I'm not sure I understand."

"It's okay, my dear. You are exactly where you are meant to be. If someone told you about my services, they know you are seeking answers that cannot be found in this plane of existence."

"Plane of existence?" Gemma wiped her forehead. She looked toward the stove, where a faint green cloud of smoke escaped the vent.

"The realm of the living," Madame Hvalsi said. "There is more to the world than what your conscious mind and body can see and hear and feel. There is another realm beyond what our senses show us. It is the place where those we love go when they pass on from this one, where they await what comes next. There are only a few in our realm who can communicate with them when they move to the Realm Beyond. I am one of the chosen few."

The cloud of smoke seemed to invade Gemma's insides as she breathed in its earthy mineral odor. Her mind fogged. Her limbs tingled.

"This doesn't feel right. What is happening?" Gemma asked.

"Be calm, my dear." Madame Hvalsi's voice softened and slowed to a dreamy cadence. "Relax. We are entering a state that will allow us to communicate with the other side. You will not be harmed, but you must be calm if we are to speak to those who long to reconnect with you from the Beyond."

Madame Hvalsi breathed in deeply through her mouth, loudly sucking in a lungful of the green-tinged air. She held it in for a few seconds before slowly exhaling, making *pa-pa-pa* sounds as she opened and closed her lips. "Try it with me," she urged Gemma.

It took all of Gemma's willpower not to roll her eyes and walk out of the room. Yet she didn't think this assignment was a prank. There had to be something behind this little charade that held meaning.

Gemma imitated the woman, breathing in deeply. The airborne particles tickled her throat, and she fell into a coughing fit. "Sorry," she managed when she regained her composure. She tried the breathing exercise again, this time finding it easier. She felt as if there was a green fog inside her head, filling her mind, even overtaking her eyesight. She released the breath, copying the sounds Madame Hvalsi made with her lips.

Madame Hvalsi whispered in between rounds of the breaths and *pa-pa-pa*s. Gemma couldn't quite make out the words, so she leaned in over the table. They were in another language, one that Gemma couldn't place. There were clicks of the tongue, some from the front of the mouth, others from the back, and noises that reminded Gemma of clearing phlegm from one's throat. Madame Hvalsi began rolling her tongue as she held a nasally, high-pitched note. Then the rolling stopped and her pitch lowered sharply as she hummed a tune. It was mostly one note, though it occasionally trilled half a step higher or lower.

Gemma realized her eyes had closed at some point. She tried to open them but found the lids were heavy, as if she were deeply asleep. Her chin touched the top of her chest, her head bowing down toward the table.

The humming stopped. "Spirits of the passing place, hear me from the world you once roamed. Hear the voice of one who wishes to learn from you. See us now as we seek to look upon your faces. Bring to us those who long to reconnect with us, those who have unfinished business with us, who were never given the chance to make amends or provide comfort, to ask for forgiveness or provide it to us. We come to you with our hearts and souls open."

She resumed her breathing exercise. Gemma followed suit, unable to do anything else. With her eyes closed, her mind's eye was filled with a backdrop of blackness, and in the foreground was a green haze. It mesmerized her, reminded her of the times in her childhood where she had lain on the lawn of a park and looked up at the clouds as they passed overhead.

The temperature in the room dropped rapidly, chilling the sweat that covered Gemma's body. She shuddered.

"Welcome, spirit. Thank you for gracing us with your presence," Madame Hvalsi said. "We are seekers, here to learn from your wisdom. Please, show yourself to us."

Something isn't right, Gemma thought. *If this is a spirit, it's not one we want to meet. No, no, no.* She wanted to speak her dissent, to scream it out, but she couldn't. It was then that she noticed her lips were moving rapidly. Her tongue, too. She was whispering the same foreign words Madame Hvalsi had used even though she didn't know what they meant.

The green fog shifted, forming strands that danced through the air, intertwining and taking shape like pieces of a puzzle coming together.

Legs, like those of a person.

A torso, slightly hunched.

The legs bent like a man falling to his knees.

The hands reached up to the face, a featureless cloudy emerald green.

A mouth of blackness opened, a gaping hole in the fog.

Something snakelike slithered out of the maw.

A sound accompanied it, yet it seemed so far away: a pained groan, which morphed into a scream of terror, then a sickly wet sound.

The serpentine creature continued to emerge from the smoke-man's mouth. It flapped around in the air aimlessly at first, then halted, facing Gemma. It had seen her, recognized her.

The screaming stopped long enough for the man to speak around the object protruding from his throat. The words were gibberish, but she knew what they had been: *Run, Gemma.*

Walker's last words.

The serpent arched backward, then pounced toward Gemma.

Another scream, this one from Gemma. She flinched hard, causing her chair to tilt backward and fall to the ground. As the back of her head hit the floor of Madame Hvalsi's parlor, Gemma's vision returned to her. She was aware of the room around her again. Walker and the monster that had killed him were gone.

She rose to her feet and looked across the table at Madame Hvalsi. The woman's eyes were wide open but rolled back into her head, revealing whites and bloodred veins. Her mouth was agape, her lips twitching as if trying to speak. Then a pained crying sound came from her throat; it sounded as if she was choking on her tongue. Gemma ran around the table and shook the little woman's shoulders. The cry grew wetter, and then the woman's torso shot forward, snapping her chin hard against her chest. Hvalsi unleashed a stream of vomit onto her lap. Gemma moaned in terror as she backed against the wall.

The vomiting stopped. Gemma watched from behind as Madame Hvalsi convulsed for three seconds, then stilled. Her head lifted to its regular position. Her shoulders twitched in a shrugging motion, and then she returned to full consciousness. She looked at the overturned chair across the table, then spun around to find Gemma behind her.

"Well, dear," she said, her voice freakishly normal again, "it doesn't always go as planned. Perhaps we can try again tomorrow?"

"What..." Gemma's voice was shaky. She struggled to take in a deep breath and release it. "What just happened?"

Madame Hvalsi stood, the vomit sloshing down to her feet. "Not everything in the Realm Beyond can be explained in terms we understand. It's usually a bit more straightforward than that, but when someone dies a painful death, they may get stuck in a loop of their final moments. Looks like this friend of yours couldn't escape what happened to him when he passed on."

Gemma stared at her in shock, unable to understand how she could sound so casual about everything, apparently not even disturbed by the vomit that covered her lower half and pooled around her.

"Well, I must be getting back to the kitchen. Cakes to bake, coffee to make. Can I expect you again tomorrow for another try?"

"I...I..."

"It's okay, dear. Take your time to recover." And with that, Madame Hvalsi left Gemma alone in the room.

Gemma looked around, noticing that the smoke coming from the stove now lacked the emerald tint. The earthen scent had dissipated as well, leaving only the smell of burning wood. Her eyes burned from the fumes, and she knew she had to get out into the fresh air before her stomach turned the way Madame Hvalsi's had. She made for the door, stopped, turned around, spotted the stoneware jar on the shelf behind the stove, and grabbed it.

"Hey!" she shouted as she stormed through the doorway.

Clomping footsteps echoed in the stairwell. Gemma followed. The single door on the landing was open, so she stepped inside the apartment. The front room was curiously devoid of furniture, even more sparse and undecorated than Gemma's dump of an apartment. A little round table that matched those in the front of the bakery had one chair in front of it and a mug that held what looked like coffee, the cream drying into a chunky layer on the top. No stuffed chairs to relax on, no shelves of books, nothing on the walls to add character. On the far side of the room was another doorway, this one with a curtain pulled across it in lieu of a door. Through the ten-inch gap between the curtain and the floor, she made out Madame Hvalsi's bare feet and legs. The little woman's soiled dress dropped to the floor, and she kicked it out of the room under the curtain. Gemma shoved her nose into the crook of her left arm to avoid gagging.

A few moments later, Madame Hvalsi pulled the curtain back. She was wearing a clean dress identical to the one she'd changed out of. The smile she'd used downstairs was nowhere to be found when she saw an intruder in her private space.

"What do you think you're doing with that?" Madame Hvalsi's eyes dropped to Gemma's right arm, which held the jar against her torso. "That's not a toy, young lady."

"You are correct. It's not a toy. It's dangerous and powerful contraband that you are not registered for," Gemma said with authority.

"Registered? What are you on about?"

Gemma set the jar gently on the table, then reached into the pouch on her belt. She pulled out a piece of folded leather and opened it, revealing her silver-plated brass badge. "I'm Agent Gemma Calvertson of the Royal Mystic Committee. You're running an unlicensed commercial enterprise using magical elements that are highly regulated in the Kingdom of Aepistelle. Under the law of King Davin, mystic code five-five-nine, section four, operation of such an unregistered enterprise is forbidden, and its operators can be sentenced to as many as forty years in prison."

The woman's jaw dropped. "I've done nothing but help people connect with those they've lost! You've come in here under false pretenses and set me up. I didn't even charge you. I don't charge *anyone* for this gift, so you can take your 'commercial enterprise' rules and shove them up your arse! And another thing: what you saw was real. You knew that man and the freakish thing that emerged from him, didn't you?"

"I..." Gemma put her badge away and crossed her arms. "Yes. You're right, I did know him. Walker was a former partner of mine. He died a very gruesome death caused by dark, unregulated sorcery. That's exactly why the Royal Mystic Committee must make sure that those with special abilities have them under control and that government officials know who can do what."

"The Royal Mystic Committee is nothing but a pack of murderers and lackeys of that monster of a king," Madame Hvalsi said.

Gemma reeled back a step, but she knew what the woman meant. "I'd be lying if I said I've never felt the same. I joined up three years ago on the condition that the Committee would change the way it operated and stop imprisoning people. I had an audience with King Davin, who agreed that a change was necessary. I'm trying my best to see that change through. I am sorry I threatened you with arrest, but what I saw upset me." Gemma gestured toward the jar on the table. "I believe I was chosen to come here and investigate how you can reach those who have departed this world. Please, can you tell me what is in this jar?"

The woman studied Gemma with a hard face for a long minute. Then she softened and sat down at the table. She reached for the jar and pulled off the lid.

"I brought a sack of this with me when I left home. It was all I took," Madame Hvalsi began.

"And where was home?"

"Bahrun Ik-Chalak Ghulem," she said. Gemma had heard of the place in her studies of Aepistelle history, but the pronunciation had been flattened to match the blandness of the common Aepistelle language. Madame Hvalsi spoke the words with their intended guttural sounds.

"The Cavern Citadel?" Gemma asked in wonder, using the name more common in Aepistelle. "I have heard stories of it, but it was always treated like a myth! Where is it located?"

"Myth? No, dear. Legend, perhaps. It's more majestic than any tales you flatlanders tell about it. I could sing you ten dozen songs about its beauty and still not capture even one iota of it. Our lands are located deep within what you so blandly call the Esteron Mountain Range. My people have names for every peak and valley, each low hillock and rocky tower and plummeting cavern."

"And your people found this green mineral there?"

"My people are miners first and foremost—that's one of the few bits others know about us. While your people grow sick from spending too much time in their mines, ours thrive off the minerals in the dust. We rely on it like any other nutrient. The substance in this jar is but one of thousands of minerals and metals we coax from the earth and use in the ways the gods of the deep intended. It may be the most powerful."

"Because it allows you to hallucinate?" Gemma asked.

"Was that a hallucination? Did we both share the same hallucination of your friend Walker meeting his freakish end? No, Miss Calvertson, it does not cause you to hallucinate. You witnessed a brief tear in the veil between our world and that of the deceased—a window crafted by the gods and opened by my people under divine direction. There are secrets we can learn from the Beyond. Truths about our world. Revelations sent to us by those who walk among the deities. It is up to us to interpret what they mean, a responsibility I and a few others have been given. What is in this jar is a holy gift."

Gemma thought back to when she had decided to abandon her rebellion—on the surface, at least—and join King Davin in overhauling the Royal Mystic Committee. She had been surrounded by Davin and his army, then forced to connect with a young seer through some freakish monster that linked their minds together. Through the boy's abilities, she had witnessed the death of Arnem and the obstacles faced by Denny and Marzele. The boy had told her that he believed there was a way to reach Arnem even in death, to bring him back into this world. In every case Gemma had worked during her time with the Committee, she had tried to find ways to reach the dead by bending the powers of those she helped.

This was the closest she had come.

"Madame Hvalsi, have you or your people ever been able to physically reach the dead?"

"You mean like reach out and touch them? Hold their hands and such?"

"Yes. Can the minerals assist with that?"

The little woman laughed like Gemma had asked her if she'd ever seen an Ogressi dance. "You experienced the power of the mineral yourself, dear. It provides a window, not a door. Although..."

Gemma leaned forward as the woman considered her next words carefully. Madame Hvalsi noticed and shook her head. "Never mind."

"What?" Gemma demanded. "You were going to say something. There is a way, isn't there?"

"No. The mineral dust in my jar will not allow you to do whatever it is you want."

"What aren't you telling me?"

"The ways of my people are our own. They are *not* for an agent of the Royal Mystic Committee." Madame Hvalsi pushed her chair back and rose to her feet. She grabbed the jar and hugged it against herself like a baby. "Now, if you'll excuse me, I must get back to my bakery. You're no longer welcome to return tomorrow for another try at reaching those beyond. Good day to you."

With that, she brushed past Gemma and clomped down the stairs. Gemma stood in disappointment for a moment, then followed her down. She took the back door, keen to avoid the little woman.

BACK AT THE INN, GEMMA PACED AROUND HER ROOM, thinking about her time with Madame Hvalsi and all the times during their conversation that she'd said the wrong thing. It was too late, though. Madame Hvalsi had made it clear that she didn't wish to speak to Gemma again. Whatever the point of this mission was, she had squandered it. The only interruptions she had from her fretting were thoughts of Arnem's family. If she wandered around Plentimore Valley long enough, she'd run into them sooner or later. It was a small town, and fate had a cruel sense of humor. If she had to see Selah and her daughters, she was sure her feelings of failure and guilt would be the end of her. She decided to stay in her room the rest of the night instead and take the first train out in the morning.

Gemma sat and scribbled musings in her notebook, then threw it aside. She looked around, her eyes falling on the bookshelf. *Journey of Perils* sat there as if waiting for her. It was the story of that fabled journey just before her birth, when Jestan and Arnem and Maachel and Richard had saved the world against all odds.

She grabbed the book and lay on her bed, flipping through the story she'd read a hundred times before. She avoided the pages she knew contained portraits of Arnem. Instead, she focused on a section where Jestan and Richard became separated from the others. Maachel and Arnem had wandered off on their own after some petty argument among the party and stumbled into Teyla-te-Anya and her warrior tribe. Meanwhile, Richard and Jestan had journeyed to the easternmost section of the foothills known as the Fingers, where they'd camped just inside the mouth of a cave.

There was one brief mention of something Gemma had

only the vaguest memory of reading before; it wasn't in the current edition, since the Royal Mystic Committee and the Minister of Propaganda had forced Jestan to heavily edit the book and retract many of the more mystical elements of the Great Journey. Fortunately for Gemma, the copy of the book she now held was a first edition. She found what she was looking for.

Jestan stated that in the middle of the night, while Richard snored so loudly that Jestan feared the sound would attract predators, a noise from deeper in the cave had stirred him. He'd followed the sound, unsure from the echoes how far away it was, until he'd spotted the silhouette of a very little man. At first he had thought it was Arnem or Maachel, but he'd quickly realized this man was much too small to be them. This was something else entirely. Realizing he'd left his sword back with his blankets, he had turned, run back, and woken Richard, and the two of them had left the cave and wandered through the night.

Gemma had visited that very section of the Fingers, a few days' hike east of Ferathan, during her journey through the Forest of Despair. It was at the base of the Esteron Mountains. The cave in the story could have been an entrance to the Cavern Citadel.

To Bahrun Ik-Chalak Ghulem.

To the secrets of the Realm Beyond.

CHAPTER 6
KOSAR

"**D**id you send Gemma away?" Kosar demanded as he stormed through the double doors of his father's office.

Davin glared at the guards who rushed in behind him, then waved to dismiss them. "How dare you show me such a lack of respect in my own palace?" he growled once the doors closed and they were alone. The old man swiped a crystal decanter off a side table so quickly, Kosar expected the lid to pop off and the amber liquid to spray out. That didn't happen, however, and Davin poured out a small amount into two glasses and handed one to Kosar. "Now, what is this about your little girlfriend?"

"She's off on some kind of mission, one her own partner wasn't invited on. I went to Fort Braxen and asked Commander Bryne about her assignment, and he said that he'd been given orders but was not cleared to know the details. It sounds like a setup to me, and who else is above Bryne besides you?"

Davin downed the contents of his glass, grimacing as he

swallowed, then poured another drink. "I assure you that I know nothing about this. I admit I haven't been watching the girl closely in recent months. She's been a perfect agent since her recruitment to the Royal Mystic Committee. I should have known she was up to something."

Relieved that his father had nothing to do with whatever peril Gemma might be in, Kosar sank into a chair and tasted the liquor. It burned in his throat, a feeling he'd grown used to. "I'm sorry for the accusation, then, Father. Please forgive me. I've just been on edge lately, if I may speak freely."

Davin rolled his eyes. "I have given you everything an aimless young man could dream of, Kosar."

That hurt, a stab through the heart. Kosar finished the contents of his glass and slammed it on the redwood top of Davin's desk. "I am not aimless, Father!"

"Stop calling me that. There are ears everywhere, even in here."

"But why? Why must we continue to hide my parentage? The time has come. You are not getting any younger. You must announce me as your son and heir so the people know, so they'll respect me."

"How dare you question me or give me demands?" Davin growled as he kicked the chair next to Kosar. It flipped, clattered to the floor, and slid back three feet on the slick tile. As if he needed to show off his anger even more, he threw his empty glass down with full force into the spot where the chair had been. "I have had men hanged for far less than this!"

"But were those men your own flesh and blood?"

"Of course not. You're my only bastard, as far as I am aware. A sorry one at that, but the only one I have. If I hadn't seen so much of your mother in you, I'd have had you smothered in your crib decades ago." Davin kicked at the shards of glass, then leaned against his desk. His bottom nudged

Kosar's glass, which he picked up and smashed on top of the remnants of his own.

"Please understand, sir. I gave up my place in the Southern Reaches, gave up my half brother's life, damned the man I grew up believing was my father, all because you promised me a path to the throne."

"And you shall have it in time."

"But *when?* All I do is stalk around this castle like a ghost. Even the servants look at me in confusion, wondering what I'm doing here, why King Davin would take in such a ward at my age."

"They're probably wondering why you're unmarried at your age as well," Davin said, clearly knowing the remark would sting.

"Yes. About that—I think I would be more respected by the fairer sex if my true position were made public."

Davin scoffed. He pushed off the desk, then walked around to his own chair on the other side. "If you think the Calvertson woman will ever truly fall for you again, royalty or not, you're more pathetic than I thought."

"But—" Kosar began, only to be cut off by Davin kicking the desk between them in frustration.

"But that doesn't mean she won't marry you if I order it. She won't be able to deny her king."

Kosar didn't need to think about this. "I appreciate your offer, Father, but I have to decline. I do not want to force her hand in marriage, but *perhaps* her view of me would change if I were officially crowned as your heir."

"I don't plan to give up my seat or my final breath anytime soon, Kosar. I am in no hurry to abandon Aepistelle. I want to see much more growth in you. More cunning. More tact. I need to see that you can handle all aspects of this role, and then, when the time is right, I'll do what I have promised you."

Kosar rose to his feet and bowed his head. "Thank you. I promise to make you proud."

"You can start by finding out what that girlfriend of yours is up to."

"I sent one of my men out to tail her, sir. He should report back soon."

Davin laughed at this, but Kosar couldn't tell if it was mockery, pride, or surprise. "Well, it seems you're learning already."

With that, Davin unrolled a scroll and dipped the tip of a quill into his inkwell. He began to write before tilting his head up and flashing a confused look at Kosar. "That's it, boy. We're done here. Off with you."

Had he a tail, Kosar would have tucked it between his legs as he departed his father's study. Still, he knew his time would come for the glory of the throne, for the fitting of his crown, and for the hand of Gemma Calvertson.

CHAPTER 7
GEMMA

Gemma rounded the bend in the road and caught her first glimpse of the gates. The sign above them reassured her that she was in the correct place. WYNSTONE AND FAMILY FARMING SUPPLY COMPANY, it read. She wasn't sure if Arnem had changed it from WYNSTONE AND SONS before he and Denny had sought out Gemma to rescue Marzele or if Selah had renamed the business after her husband's death.

A wagon came toward her on its way out of the complex, its flat rear bed piled high with hay bales, shovels and forks, and bundles of goods she couldn't identify. The driver looked to be a contemporary of Selah's, while her companion was a younger man. Gemma recognized neither, but they noticed that she was out of place.

"Here for a pickup?" the woman asked as she pulled the mules to a stop. "Follow this road past the house to the warehouse beyond. Signs will guide you." With that, she snapped the reins, and the mules resumed their journey.

"Thank you," Gemma said as they passed her and headed out to make their deliveries.

Ahead of her was a farmhouse. The wooden siding showed its age, but it appeared to be quite large and comfortable. She climbed the first two steps to the porch, then stopped, one foot raised. Her hands shook.

What if Selah doesn't want to see me? she thought. *What if the girls blame me for their father's death?*

A woman called out orders to someone in a firm voice of authority. It wasn't coming from the house, but rather from the building several hundred feet to the side. Gemma had met Selah only once, but she was sure she recognized her voice. She made her way toward what had surely once been a large barn and stable. The building had since been converted, different wings jutting off on either side to accommodate a warehouse and offices.

"Add another three sacks of feed to the Macaffery Ranch order, Lucius," Selah commanded as Gemma walked up to the largest set of doors, which hung open to let the breeze pass through the warm interior. "And don't forget to—" She turned when she caught sight of the visitor. Her eyes widened. "Gemma Calvertson?"

Gemma locked eyes with her. Both women stood frozen, waves of emotions crashing over them. Gemma couldn't be sure, but she thought her cheeks were the first to moisten with tears. Selah, however, was the first to move. She wrapped her arms around Gemma and pulled her in tight.

"I'm sorry," Gemma cried. "I'm so sorry for what happened."

"Oh, Gemma, nonsense. You have nothing to be sorry about."

"I couldn't even face you all this time. Couldn't visit you

or even write. If Arnem had never met me, he'd still be here with you and your daughters. If—"

Selah pulled back so she could look Gemma in the eye but kept hold of the younger woman's shoulders. "You listen to me, Gemma. My husband fancied himself a hero, even if he was a reluctant one, a clumsy one. For years, his doubts and fears hid a longing to find adventure again. If it hadn't been the adventure of helping the people of Emyhrsen, rescuing that priest, and reuniting young Denny with his parents, it would have been something else. I believe the fates planned that one way or another, he would go out as a hero. You mustn't place any blame on yourself or anyone else."

"Thank you, Selah. I needed to hear that."

"Come on," Selah said, taking Gemma's hand and leading her toward one of the side wings of the building. "The girls will want to see you."

A section of the structure had been converted from horse stalls into an office. Parchment was stacked in neat piles on the desks and tables. A woman sat at a desk in front of an open book, doing calculations in black ink while her companion read off figures from a piece of parchment.

"Lyria Marinah, Rosaline Maachela, take a break, my dears. We have a guest." They stopped their task and looked up, then stood in unison at the sight of their visitor.

"You aren't just girls anymore," Gemma observed. "You're proper young women! How did you grow up so fast?" She felt foolish for even asking, realizing they'd *had* to grow out of childish things and step up in order for their mother to run the business in Arnem's absence.

The older of the two ran over and threw her arms around Gemma. "It's amazing to see you, Gemma!" Lyria said. Rosaline stood her ground behind the table, her arms crossed.

"Rosaline, it's Gemma Calvertson," Selah said, but Gemma knew the young woman recognized her.

"It's okay, Selah," Gemma said. "Girls, I'm sorry it took me so long to come here and see you. You all could have used my support when your father died, and I wasn't here for you then. I hope you'll forgive me."

Rosaline slammed her book shut and banged it against the table. The sound made Gemma jump. "You should have been there for *him*! You were supposed to be some big hero, but you couldn't even save him. You should have been there to pull him out of the fire!"

"Oh, Rosie, you mustn't blame her," Selah said, but her daughter ignored her.

"And what about Denny? Why didn't he come back? Dad left everything behind to take care of that stupid little vagrant, and look what it got him! A terrible, brutal end!"

Rosaline turned and threw open the back door. The other three stood and watched as she ran off and disappeared in a maze of farming products in the warehouse.

Lyria went in for another hug. "Don't worry about her. I'll go calm her down." She walked off to find her sister.

Gemma wanted to apologize again for Arnem's death, for her own failures, even for what Denny had done. It was then that she realized Rosaline didn't seem to *know* what had happened with Denny in the forest of Xaeltúve. It had been his inability to control his emerging powers that had caused the fire that had burned Arnem to death. Gemma knew only because she'd been shown a vision of it by a young seer under King Davin's control. Whatever Selah and the girls knew about Arnem's death had come from the Royal Mystic Committee agents who had tracked down Arnem and Denny. Gemma hadn't read the report, as it was part of a classified Special Operations mission she had no clearance for. Of course they wouldn't have included details of magic usage if they hadn't apprehended the person responsible.

"Let's get some tea," Selah said. She led Gemma across the yard to the house. The silence pained Gemma as Selah prepared the tea. She approached the table with a tray containing two teacups, the kettle, and some small cakes. She poured the tea and nodded to Gemma to drink up.

"I shouldn't have come here unannounced," Gemma said after taking a sip.

"Shouldn't have done this, shouldn't have done that...we all do as we need to, and there's no going back to undo it. I don't live in regret. I don't teach my girls to either, though Rosaline still struggles, as you witnessed. And you mustn't." She patted Gemma's hand on the table.

"A part of me has been so determined to undo the past, I haven't really unpacked my emotions. I haven't talked to anyone about it."

"Your parents included," Selah said. "They're worried sick about you."

"They must be. I haven't even written them a letter in at least a year. I've been too ashamed to visit them after everything that happened."

"You mean joining the Royal Mystic Committee?"

"Especially that. I don't think they understand why I did it."

"That makes several of us," Selah admitted. "But they trust, as I do, that you must have your reasons for what you've done."

"I haven't moved past what happened. I don't have the strength you do. I mean, look at this place. You're thriving!"

Selah smiled at this. "I'm quite proud of it. And of the girls. We've all stepped up. Before Arnem first went off to reunite with Richard, where he met Denny and then you, he refused to let our daughters be part of the business. That man was stubborn as a boulder. Where Rosaline gets it from, I suspect. But when he and Denny came home from Emyhrsen, he was a changed man. He'd witnessed what you could do and realized he'd underestimated the women in his own family. He started showing us the ropes, resolved to change the name of the business. Those weeks were short, but they were some of the best times we ever had. That's what pushed us forward after he left. This business has been in his family for generations, and we weren't about to let that end. We'd hoped Denny would return and join us, but I suppose he felt as much shame and guilt as you do."

Gemma was careful not to mention Denny's role in Arnem's death. She didn't feel it was necessary, lest the knowledge bring pain and confusion back into their lives.

"Now that you've taken this step," Selah said, "please tell me you'll go see your mother and father. They would love to see you, even just for a brief visit. Your mother and I write to each other all the time. I've even gone a couple of times to stay with them on the coast. But it's you they need, Gemma. You're their baby, and they won't hold your choices against you."

"You're right," Gemma said. She finished her tea and set the cup back on the tray in the middle of the table, then stood. "Tell the girls goodbye for me. I have a few days before I'm expected to report back to my superiors. It's enough time to travel to the coast and see them."

Selah leapt to her feet and gave Gemma another motherly hug, then led her to the door.

"We're okay here, Gemma. Thriving, as you said. Now, go be a hero to someone who needs it. Go make things right with your parents."

CHAPTER 8
GEMMA

"**O**h, my baby!"

Serena Calvertson leapt from the porch, skipping the step. In her quickness to embrace her daughter, her head knocked into Gemma's, and they both laughed despite the pain. A deeper laugh came from the doorway, but it wasn't her father's. Geoffrey Calvertson hadn't come to greet Gemma.

"Wonderful to see you again, Quincy," Gemma said when her mother loosened her grip enough that she could breathe. Quincy Harpon stepped down from the porch and hugged Gemma with one arm, as Serena still clung to the other half of her.

"Look at you, girl! You have a proper warrior physique about you now. When I saw you last, you were just starting to get that rustic look from your time up north, but now you look like a soldier!" Quincy approved, having been a soldier himself nearly thirty years ago. The man had been in the same unit of the West Aepistelle Army as her father, and they were among the only survivors of the war. Even though they hadn't reconnected in years because of Geoffrey's mental health, Quincy had welcomed the family with open arms when they'd arrived on his doorstep as fugitives after their rebellion against King Davin.

"Where's Dad?" Gemma asked, unable to hide the fear in her voice. "Is he—"

"He's regressing," Serena said. "We knew it was only a matter of time. He held out for so long. His mind was clear for more than a year after you left, but the last couple have been difficult for us. Come."

Serena took Gemma by the hand and led her up to the porch and through the front door. Quincy remained outside to give the family space. On the other side of the house, the wide, hunched figure of Gemma's father loomed in front of a window overlooking the crashing waves of the sea. He did not acknowledge their approach.

"Daddy? It's me. Gemma." She stopped a few feet from him. Her heart dropped.

"It's your daughter, Geoffrey. She's come home." Serena patted Gemma's shoulder, then joined her husband. "You haven't seen her in so long, but she's here to visit you now. Gemma is here."

"Here...see...home..." His gaze remained fixed on the shoreline even as his head bobbed and swayed like a seagull floating on the waves. Gemma noticed his hands were on his belly, the interlocked fingers wriggling rhythmically. His chin dropped to his chest, his eyes closed tight, and his breathing turned to snores.

"Oh, he does this sometimes, but not to worry," Serena said, the concern hidden in the singsong quality of her voice. "It's just like before. I'm only happy we had some good times together after Emyhrsen. I'm just—"

Gemma knew from the rapidly rising pitch of her mother's voice what was coming. Serena buried her face in Gemma's shoulder and wailed like a baby. Gemma held her mother, using every ounce of willpower to swallow down her own emotions, keeping it all inside. She remembered why she'd put everything else in her life below her work and sunk all her energy the last few years into being the best at what she did. When she was vulnerable like this, all she felt was pain and sorrow and regret.

AFTER GEOFFREY WOKE FROM HIS NAP, SERENA NOTICED that he'd soiled himself. She led him back to their room to clean him up. Gemma used the opportunity to step outside and follow the seaside path down to the docks. At the nearby port, Quincy and his crew had a warehouse where they stored their boats and fishing gear along with their weaponry. They were the top commercial fishermen in the region most days, but they also moonlighted as mercenaries, traveling the kingdom when the right jobs came along. They had assisted Gemma, Arnem, and Denny in breaking Marzele out of Terminus Rock, the island prison, three years ago.

Gemma was relieved to find the door unlocked. She stepped in to see Quincy repairing his nets and traps. He looked up and flashed his warm smile. "I'm sorry you had to see your father like that."

"If I had been a good daughter and written them letters or come to visit sooner, it wouldn't have been such a shock," Gemma said.

"Three years is a long time, but I know you realize that now. I also know that look in your eyes—you didn't come out this way just to check in on them, and you aren't planning on staying long. What is it, Gemma?"

"I don't have the money to pay you and your crew yet, Quincy, but there's something I need. I must travel north."

He looked at her with disbelief. "We're already as far north as you can get in the kingdom of Aepistelle. Unless you're talking about Emyhrsen."

"Exactly. I must go back, but I don't want to travel through the Forest of Despair. I don't know what condition those lands are in these days, but I don't think I'd survive the journey on my own. Traveling to Emyhrsen by sea would be much simpler. Quicker, too."

Quincy set the net down. "My vessel and crew are at your command if that is what you want. I just don't know if your parents can take another heartbreak."

"I wish George were here. I can't be everything my parents expect me to be, and I wish I could share that burden with my brother. In any case, I can't let that stop me from living my life and doing the things I know must be done."

"And what are those things?" Quincy's kind face turned inquisitive—probing, even. "What have you been chasing this whole time you've been working with the enemy of our people, all that you once fought against?"

Gemma reeled from the stinging truths. If there was anyone she could trust right now, however, it was Quincy. She *had* to trust him, to let him in on what she planned to do, because he was risking his own well-being and that of his crew to assist her. Traveling beyond the northern border of Aepistelle was expressly forbidden under King Davin's law.

"I have a lead on something. A way to interact with the dead."

"The dead? Gemma, listen to you."

"I know how it sounds," she said. "I get it. I was a skeptic once, too—the biggest. But I've seen so many things, not just in the last three years but in the last couple of days. I've seen that the dead can be reached, and there's someone I must rescue."

"Rescue from death? That just isn't possible. Gemma, I'm sorry about your friends and whatever happened to them down in Xaeltúve. Arnem was a good man."

"A good man whose wife and daughters still need him."

"And what of your parents? They still need you."

"I know, and after this is done, I'll resign from the Royal Mystic Committee, bring them back home, and take care of them. I just need to do this first."

"I'm in, whatever the mission is, Captain."

Gemma turned to identify the speaker. She recognized Selinda's limp as the woman walked toward her and knew it was a result of her fall on the stairwell of Terminus Rock during the mission to rescue Marzele. Yet another person who'd been hurt by Gemma's quest. But Selinda didn't appear to harbor any ill will toward her. She punched Gemma playfully on the shoulder. "I've seen this gal fight. I'd go to war at her side."

They set sail in secret that night. Gemma couldn't bear to look into her mother's eyes, and she didn't think the woman could bear to say goodbye to one of her children yet again.

CHAPTER 9

GEMMA

"We have a problem, Gemma," Selinda said.

Gemma sat up in a rush, not realizing she'd fallen asleep, let alone for most of the night. She followed Selinda out of the small cabin and onto the deck of the ship. She could see the first rays of the sun just beginning to break over the distant coast on the starboard side, but the ship's crew was looking in the other direction. Gemma turned to see the blue-and-yellow sails of the Royal Aepistelle Navy stemming from a large vessel closing in on Quincy's ship.

"Can we outrun them?" Gemma asked. "Isn't this ship fairly nimble?"

"Nimble, absolutely." Quincy looked up and down the deck with a pride that quickly faded. "I've modified her for speed and maneuverability, but look at the size of their hull. They have the westerly wind, too, and they're angling to cut us off in minutes."

"Nets are good and full, Captain," said one of the crew members from the stern.

"And the weapons?" Quincy asked.

"Dragging below us, sir," said a sailor who looked like she could be Selinda's younger sister. She had the same muscular build and height that made even Gemma look petite but no gray hairs streaking her Ferromini black locks. Quincy had collected Gemma's machete at the start of the trip and added it to the crew's weapons cache. In the event of a naval inspection, they would have to wrap the weapons in several layers of a watertight fabric and drop the bundle into the sea, where it would drag along like the many nets and traps the fishing vessel employed.

Gemma felt uneasy without her trusty machete, as if she'd lost a part of her body. "How will we fight them with no weapons?"

Quincy raised one eyebrow at her. "You underestimate my ability to smooth talk my way out of situations. This is what we do for a living. Just remain calm, and we'll take care of this. Besides, you'll still have a blade." He pointed toward an over-turned barrel flanked by two buckets. A fillet knife sat in one of them, soiled with guts and scales. "To your station, Calvertson."

Gemma groaned. During her downtime at Quincy's house three years back, he'd taught her how to fillet a fish so that she could prepare meals for her parents. The process had made her sick to her stomach, reminding her of the young soldiers she'd maimed during the battle at Harold's Keep in Emyhrsen. But as Quincy had explained when they'd set sail last night, everyone onboard had a role to play, including Gemma.

She set to work preparing breakfast for the crew, though she didn't think her stomach would permit her to eat any herself. As Quincy had predicted, the larger ship was on them within minutes.

"Greetings!" Quincy called to the naval crew as the ship loomed over the smaller fishing vessel. "Lovely morning so far, and the fish are plentiful."

The soldiers made no reply, nor did they smile at Quincy. The frigid ocean breeze washed over Gemma; coupled with the ominous feeling she had, it made her shiver.

"Back up!" one of the soldiers growled. The larger vessel was now roughly parallel to their port side. The soldier signaled to someone else onboard. Ropes shifted as a long piece of wood Gemma had assumed was part of a mast began to lower toward the smaller boat—a bridge to board them. Quincy waved his crew back to make room. The boat leaned as the weight of the bridge bore down on its side.

"Make way for the captain!" the soldier called, and the men on the larger ship shifted to create a corridor on either side of the boarding bridge. Their captain clambered up onto the bridge and unsteadily made his way across. Gemma was afraid—or perhaps hopeful—that the man would slip and fall into the ocean.

"Welcome aboard the Ferromini Flyer, Captain," Quincy said.

"Whadda we 'ave 'ere?" the captain slurred. He swayed in front of Quincy like a loose sail in the wind. "Buncha for'ners, looks like." He quickly pivoted toward the space between the two ships, and up came his breakfast and the liters of liquor he'd apparently already chugged already that morning. Only some of the chunky liquid made it over the edge. Then the man turned back to Quincy as if nothing had happened. "Yer in Aepistelle waters here. Got papers?"

"Sir, we're not foreigners. We are longtime citizens of this fine kingdom. Most of us were born here."

The captain looked at Quincy with suspicion. "Most? Whaddabout you?"

"I came over from the Ferromin Islands as a child. My father joined up with the Western Aepistelle Army during the battle on Thule Isle during the Oceanic Campaigns and was given citizenship after that. As soon as I was old enough, I signed up and served until retirement age."

"They lettin' yer kind into our ranks, eh?" The captain spat on the deck, then turned to his crew across the bridge. "Hear that, boys? They think they're just like us."

The men on the larger ship hooted with laughter.

"Let's see if they float like our kind, too!" one of the soldiers shouted.

"Looks like they're heading into northern waters, Cap! What are we going to do about that?" another yelled.

The captain turned back to Quincy with distrust. "Jus' what're ya doin' so far north, anyway?"

"We make our best hauls up here this time of year. Migration sends the northern species down to these parts before they turn west to seek warmer waters. Every year we come up here without issue."

"Well, this jus' ain't yer year, then. These waters is my domain, an' I say who gets ta taste the fishes out here." He signaled to his crew to come onboard. "I share my sailor's curiosity 'bout how well ya float. Boys? Send 'em overboard."

The sailors roared as they pulled their swords and ran across the bridge. Quincy snapped his fingers toward Selinda; she had a hand on a rope and pulled at his signal. A splash over the starboard side caused Gemma to turn and watch as the sack containing their weapons rose out of the water. Two more of Quincy's crew pulled the sack onboard and tore it open as soon as it hit the deck.

The soldiers were quick to board. Quincy blocked a clumsy blow from the drunken captain. He twisted the man around and put him in a hold, but the first soldier over the bridge lunged at Quincy, forcing him to let go of the captain.

The mercenaries distributed weapons to the crew. Gemma waited for her machete, but a soldier approached her before she got her hands on it. Her attacker had a patchy blond beard and chunks of hair missing from malnutrition or perhaps ringworm. The sight would have made her wince at any other time. Without thinking, she flung the partially filleted fish at the man. He batted it away with his sword and lifted the weapon, ready to slash down at her. Gemma threw the knife at him. The handle bounced off his chest, and it fell to the ground. Gemma took a step backward, tumbled over the bucket she'd been sitting on, and landed on her back.

The soldier loomed over her, sword held high. "What a shame that Captain won't let us keep more prisoners. Not enough food on board," he said.

"Gemma!" A mercenary kicked Gemma's machete toward her, and she reached for it. She brought it up just as the soldier swung his sword down toward her. She slowed its arc, but the wind was knocked out of her when the blow forced the flat side of the machete's blade to slam into her chest.

The mercenary had finished distributing weapons and leaped to Gemma's defense. Gemma rolled away and struggled to her feet. With all the soldiers pouring onto the smaller boat, the deck felt unsteady. A trio of soldiers rushed at her. She used her free hand to brace herself against a mast, then lunged at the nearest attacker. The man didn't expect Gemma's ferocity or skill with the blade, but she had gained more than enough fighting experience during her time with the Royal Mystic Committee and her various adventures before that. The other two soldiers had held back to watch their friend slaughter the young woman, but one realized victory for his comrade wasn't as certain as expected and rushed to join the fight. Gemma had defeated much more intimidating opponents than these. She screamed out a battle cry and darted at her first attacker as he briefly shifted his gaze to the newcomer. Her blade took off his sword hand, and she rammed her shoulder into his torso, knocking him off his feet.

The second attacker watched in shock. Gemma swung at him, but her blow was parried by the third man. "Try again, girl," he said.

"That's not a fair fight," boomed a woman behind them.

The third man turned and craned his neck back to face Selinda.

"Nobody told us we'd be slaughtering ladies," he said, feigning confidence. "Not that I mind."

"And I wasn't expecting to crush bugs—I would have brought my other boots," Selinda quipped.

The man grunted as he lunged at the taller woman. Selinda stepped aside, and the man stumbled. He landed on one knee, jumped back up, and met Selinda's blade through his neck.

Gemma swung her blade at her opponent. He deflected it, then rushed at her, backing her up against the railing. His blows rained down at a rapid clip against her machete, but she managed to block each strike. The man quickly became winded—perhaps a product of too much drink this morning. Gemma swept a leg out, attempting to trip the man, but he held his ground. He swung once more, and Gemma lost her grip. The machete clattered to the deck. The man lifted his sword, ready for the killing blow.

"Aaah!" Selinda yelled out as she charged him from behind. He turned to face her, and Gemma used the opportunity to crouch, wrap her arms around him just below his waist, and lift him. She pivoted her body, attempting to throw him overboard. He punched her in the temple, and lights popped in her vision. Her grip loosened, and the man got one foot back on the deck. But Selinda's momentum caused him to lose his balance as she slammed into him. He tumbled over the railing and splashed into the ocean below.

"Are you okay?" Selinda asked, but Gemma had already reclaimed her machete and figured out her next move.

"Cover me!" She ran up the deck, slid on her knees, and retrieved the short bow that lay on the open sack of weapons. After fishing through the bundle for an arrow, Gemma tore off a sizable strip of the dry inner sack. She rushed to an oil canister meant for filling the lamps, popped the top, and drenched the cloth. She wrapped it around the tip of the arrow, dangled it into the lit cookstove, and nocked the flaming arrow. Selinda and the other mercenaries fended off the soldiers, allowing Gemma to take aim. She fired the arrow, which struck its mark: one of the massive sails of the naval vessel. The flames spread rapidly. She repeated the process until all three of the primary sails were burning.

A round of cheers rose from the mercenaries while the soldiers cried out angrily. The latter group fought harder out of distress. A particularly massive brute swinging twin war hammers that Gemma thought her blacksmith brother would appreciate backed Gemma and Selinda into a corner. With every missed swing, the ogrish fellow chipped away parts of the boat. One blow crushed Selinda's dominant left shoulder. She screamed and dropped her sword as her arm went limp. The man laughed, which infuriated Gemma, who slashed her weapon across his bare chest. He shook it off like it was merely a paper cut, then swung at Gemma. She moved toward him, taking a blow to the head from his fist and the hammer's handle instead of its business end. She fell to the ground.

Selinda was using her right arm to punch at the man,

distracting him from finishing off Gemma, when a shadow fell over them. Gemma watched both Selinda and the ogre glance at the source of the shadow, and their eyes widened in unison. One of the fiery towering masts of the larger vessel had cracked off its base and was falling toward them.

Selinda jumped to her right. Gemma rolled to her left, her head pounding from the blows she had taken. The brute just stood there, watching in shock, until the burning mast flattened him.

Quincy's boat split in half.

CHAPTER 10
KIEVE

At a glance, Pinedrop seemed to be a pleasant little town. Kieve had passed through it several times on his way to and from Esteron by train, but he'd never had reason to disembark at the town's station. It looked like the kind of place he and Gemma could have found any number of quaint bistros to dine in after a hard day's work, perhaps some alehouses to wind down in. He wished she were there now, but her assignment was the reason he had come this far from Capital City to begin with.

Kieve kept half of a block between himself and Lieutenant Cragen Palignon, pedestrians strolling up and down the sidewalk in between them. Once or twice, Palignon glanced back over his shoulder and Kieve thought his superior officer had spotted him, but his genuine interest in his surroundings and his civilian attire made him look like a legitimate window shopper and tourist. Or so he hoped. Still, Palignon was a career spy and took many seemingly unnecessary steps to lose a potential tail—stepping into shops and exiting through back doors, circling back through a neighborhood twice. These actions would have been unnecessary had he just been returning to the Committee's outpost at an army base on the west end of town. If Palignon was involved in clandestine activities outside of his job, however, his behavior made more sense. That was what piqued Kieve's interest most.

After zigzagging through the town's trendy dining and nightlife district, Kieve dropped back farther as Palignon led him through the more sparsely populated streets of an industrial district full of warehouses in the northeast quadrant. Kieve peeked around a corner where he'd seen Palignon turn. His mark stood just two buildings down and across the street, chatting with another man and two women. One of the women gestured repeatedly toward a wagon visible beyond the open stall doors of a warehouse. In the dimness beyond, Kieve could just make out two small masses of cargo covered by canvas tarpaulins in the wagon. The other woman walked into the darkness of the warehouse and emerged a minute later, leading a pair of mules. She and the man secured the animals to the wagon's yoke. Palignon produced a money sack from within his cloak and handed it over, shook hands with the other woman, and climbed up on the driver's box. He took the reins and urged the animals into motion.

What could any of this have to do with Gemma? Kieve wondered. *Whatever it is, it seems like trouble for her.*

Kieve rushed back to the nearest alley, where he faded into the shadows until the wagon passed him. When the clopping of hooves faded just enough to indicate a safe distance, he resumed tailing Lieutenant Palignon. The cart made another turn and closed in on the northern edge of town. At the outskirts, it crossed a bridge spanning the River of Giants and headed toward the farmlands beyond. Kieve knew he'd lose his cover trying to follow Palignon over the bridge, so he turned and walked back into town.

The laughter of rowdy patrons led Kieve to the nearest tavern. He peered through the windows at the crowd that drank and sang and chatted at a volume only a pack of drunks could achieve. A pair in uniform was the perfect target for the next step of his plan.

"Good evening, my good men," Kieve said a couple of minutes later as he set two mugs of ale in front of the soldiers.

"These for us?" a soldier with unkempt muttonchops asked, eyeing Kieve with suspicion. His bearded friend didn't wait for an answer, seeing as his own glass was empty. He grabbed a mug and downed half its contents in one gulp.

"For your service and your bravery," Kieve said.

Beardo polished off his remaining ale, emitted a belch that Kieve felt in his bones, and patted his patron roughly on the shoulder. The first soldier nodded and reached for the other mug.

"Thank you, good man," Sideburns said after a sip. "Nothing like a few rounds after a long day."

"I can imagine," Kieve said. "After all, men of your position must be ready to defend our good king's lands at any moment. Never know when an enemy of His Lordship might present themselves and threaten the peace of this kingdom."

"Aye," the second soldier said. "The stress of it can weigh us down." He looked pleadingly at Kieve, hoping to get another free drink out of him. Kieve locked eyes with the bartender and put up two fingers, signaling another round.

"Perhaps just one more, and then we need to talk business," Kieve said.

Sideburns slammed his mug down on the table. "I knew there was something up with you. A salesman bothering us at the end of our day? No thank you." He pushed the mug toward Kieve.

"I think you misunderstand. Let me start over. I am Private Kieve Fallbrook of the Royal Mystic Committee." He flashed his identification and badge at the incredulous soldiers. "I arrived in Pinedrop this afternoon on a mission of utmost importance to the Crown. It is likely that a service member high in our ranks is a spy for a cell of resistance fighters against our mighty King Davin. He poses an immense security threat if we fail to neutralize him. I don't have time to rush back to the base and call for help, but fortunately for His Majesty, I ran into you two here. Will you help me? Nay, will you assist your mighty king?"

Of course, Kieve had no such mission, nor any evidence that Palignon was a traitor, but he had a feeling deep in his bones that the lieutenant was up to something wholly nefarious. Something that would put Gemma in harm's way as she completed the mysterious assignment Palignon had sent her on. The two soldiers leaned in, intrigued. Kieve had them where he wanted them.

"What would you have us do?" Sideburns asked. He reached for the mug he'd pushed away, no longer suspicious.

The bearded soldier looked around. "Is the spy here in this tavern, then?"

"No, gentlemen. He has a wagon full of supplies that he drove north over the bridge."

"Across the river?" the second soldier asked, rubbing his chin. "Only things out there are a few farms and hundreds of miles of wastelands. The Forest of Despair, if you've heard of it."

"Must be a farm he's headed to, then," Kieve said.

The first soldier gulped loudly. "Your lot confiscated one of them a few years back. Farthest one north."

"Confiscated? What for?" Kieve hadn't heard of this, though there was much in the Committee's history that he was unaware of.

"Oh yes, I remember," the second soldier said. "Belonged to Richard the Elusive."

"Wait, *that's* where Richard the Elusive smuggled his paraphernalia?" Kieve slapped his own forehead.

Of course there was history in Pinedrop that he should have known about. It had been just less than four years since one of the kingdom's most celebrated heroes had fallen from grace. Kieve had signed up as a recruit around that time, and he'd heard rumblings among his instructors and commanding officers about Richard. Word had spread all throughout the kingdom that Richard the Elusive, Jestan the Just, and Arnem the Loyal—all three remaining heroes of the Great Journey— had participated in illegal acts of sorcery. Richard's den of depravity had been discovered here in Pinedrop.

If Palignon was secretly spending time there, he must be studying the books of sorcery. He must be preparing for something big. And for reasons Kieve couldn't fathom, he had tricked Gemma into playing a part.

"Return to your base, gather a garrison of soldiers, and meet me at Richard the Elusive's farmstead. I'm going to sneak out there first to monitor the spy. The place may be crawling with rebels against our good king."

The men stared at him a moment longer, hoping for one last round for the road. Kieve slammed a fist onto the table, rattling the mugs. "Now!" he ordered. He thrust a stack of cash at the bartender, then rushed out of the establishment and toward the bridge on the north end of town.

WERE IT NOT FOR THE FRESH TRACKS ON THE DILAPIDATED road, Kieve would have thought he'd passed the farm a mile or two back. There had been a field belonging to one farmstead and an orchard of fruit trees at another, but beyond that there were only unkempt fields, long since abandoned.

Kieve crested a hill and spotted smoke rising from the chimney of a single-story dwelling. Behind it was a barn. Kieve realized he'd be easy to spot where he was standing, so he stepped off the road and maneuvered his way into an outcropping of shrubbery. The angle prevented him from seeing through the open barn doors, but the wagon had stopped just outside the barn, the mules still hitched and waiting patiently. Palignon stepped outside and pulled back the tarpaulin, but Kieve couldn't make out what the piles of goods were. The lieutenant unloaded the items and hauled them into the barn.

No assistance from others, Kieve thought. *If not for the smoke from the house, I'd say he must be here alone.*

Once the wagon was empty, Palignon unhitched the mules and led them around the back of the barn, where Kieve presumed there were stalls for the animals. A couple of minutes later, he reemerged and trekked across the yard and through the front door of the house.

Kieve made his way down the hill toward the property. He avoided the main road, sticking instead to the brush and weeds that grew untamed around the farm. A low, decrepit fence did nothing to keep him off the property that had once belonged to one of the kingdom's most celebrated heroes-turned-traitors. Now it seemed the place held another such traitor.

Kieve crouched low as he passed the house. Most of the

windows had been boarded up. The remains of bookshelves, desks, and other furniture littered the yard, apparently thrown outside during the raid of the house by the Committee nearly four years earlier. Kieve saw none of the old books about magic and religion that Richard the Elusive was rumored to have amassed in the house, but the plethora of mismatched shelves hinted at such a collection. Kieve assumed the Committee had burned the books or taken them to a secure location as evidence of Richard's crimes.

A noise came from within the house—the scraping of a chair, perhaps. Kieve dropped flat in the tall weeds poking between the debris. The back door of the house stood only twenty feet away, but it remained closed. Kieve got back to his feet and rushed toward the barn. As he approached, he caught sight of a stream that ran down a mound behind it. Perhaps the water had been diverted to the property for farming, but the route it took toward the barn looked too new and well maintained to have been from Richard's time. The water appeared to terminate at the back of the barn. Also curious was a pair of metal pipes jutting out of holes cut in the side of the barn. Steam billowed from each.

Kieve made his way to the door Palignon had gone through to unload his wares. He listened for any signs of life from inside but could hear only the mules braying just around the corner. Kieve placed his hand on the handle and took a deep breath. *What could be inside?* he wondered. *Weapons? Is Palignon amassing an army to fight King Davin?* It didn't make sense to him, though both the remote location of this potential makeshift armory and its history seemed fitting. Kieve exhaled and pulled the door open.

During one of his earliest assignments, just weeks before he'd been paired up with Gemma, Kieve had been part of a raid on an unsanctioned printing facility. The warehouse he and his compatriots had entered had contained two massive steam-powered printing presses in the process of pumping out hundreds of pamphlets full of anti-Crown filth. The machines had been nearly identical to the hulking one that loomed over him in the middle of Richard the Elusive's former barn. The machine's valves still leaked steam, but the drum had ceased spinning. Several mismatched tables lined one wall, covered in what Kieve recognized as bookbinding tools and stacks of manuscript pages ready to be sorted and bound together.

So Palignon was not amassing an army at all, but rather something else equally dangerous. Something with the power to derogate the mighty King Davin and corrupt the minds of the citizens of Aepistelle.

Kieve shuffled across the barn floor toward a stack of wooden crates. One was partially filled with finished volumes. He reached in and picked up a book.

He gasped.

The cover read GEMMA CALVERTSON.

"I saw you following me through town. Back on the train as well."

Kieve turned to face Lieutenant Palignon, who lurked in the doorway.

"It's no accident that I allowed you to find this place. We've been watching you for some time, Mr. Fallbrook. We know you are quite fond of your partner and suspected you would try to protect her."

Kieve shook the book in his hand. "Why would you slander Gemma this way? Why frame her for whatever you're doing here, Lieutenant?"

"Frame her?" Palignon took two steps toward Kieve. "I

think you misunderstand what you're holding. And there's no need to call me Lieutenant here. On this farm, I'm not acting under the authority of the Royal Mystic Committee."

"But I am." Kieve slammed the book onto the counter. The sound caused birds to flee from the rafters above. They dove out through the opening behind Palignon. "Lieutenant Palignon, under the authority granted to me by King Davin and the Royal Mystic Committee, I am placing you under arrest for your crimes against the Crown." Kieve pulled one of his two daggers from its scabbard and pointed it toward his traitorous superior.

The zing of steel behind him made him turn his head. A woman lurked there, holding out a sword. She smiled. "Nice blade you have there, soldier. Mine's bigger."

Kieve pivoted from the waist and threw his dagger. He was an expert with small blades and had silenced all those who had mocked him in the Academy when he'd insisted on fighting with throwing weapons rather than the larger swords his peers had chosen to wield.

Still, the dagger missed its mark. The woman was quick with her weapon and batted the dagger away. It flew off course and sank into the spine of one of the leather-bound tomes on a shelf. Instead of reaching for his second dagger, Kieve grabbed a wooden chair and lunged toward his opponent. Her lips were twisted with enjoyment, and he thought he heard her laugh as he swung the chair at her. She stopped its trajectory with her sword, but the attack sent her staggering back a couple of steps. Her back hit the hulking printing press behind her, which let out a reverberating *clang*.

With his opponent momentarily stunned, Kieve let out a guttural scream, dropped the chair, and ran at her. One hand reached for her sword arm, stopping her blow mid-arc, while his other shoulder rammed her between the breasts, knocking the wind from her and pinning her against the machinery.

"Stop!" Palignon yelled. "She's a friend of Gemma's."

Kieve tightened his grip on the woman's wrist and slammed it against the press, causing her to drop the sword. He turned to see Palignon approaching with another copy of the book. "What is this trickery?" Kieve asked.

"Just look at it for a moment. Flip through these pages. You're a bright man, Mr. Fallbrook. There's a reason you were assigned to work with Gemma."

"You had something to do with our partnership?" Kieve asked as he slammed once more into the woman's torso, causing her to grunt in pain, then stepped away from her to grab the book from Palignon.

"I've been behind much of your short career. Gemma's, too. Your achievements are your own, but some of your assignments have been guided. Commander Bryne is an old and trusted friend. While Gemma was placed on the Royal Mystic Committee because of King Davin's orders, Bryne and I have pulled strings to protect her place there, and yours, too, by extension. And now it's time to bring you in on this." He gestured at the book in Kieve's hand. "Open it. We won't hurt you."

Kieve stared at the volume, ran his fingers over the gold letters that spelled out his partner's name. He knew Gemma had trained as a historian at Capital City University and had worked briefly for University Press. He had always assumed the injustices she'd studied from throughout the kingdom's history had inspired her to take a more active role in enforcing King Davin's laws. Perhaps the book he held was something Gemma had written about an obscure part of Aepistelle's past. But when he opened the book and flipped through it, the frequent mentions of Davin's name implied otherwise.

"But why?" Kieve asked. "Surely Gemma doesn't know you're doing this."

"Gemma fought for truth and justice," the woman said. She moved around Kieve to stand at Palignon's side. "She had her reasons for setting aside her rebellion and joining King Davin. She's protecting those she loves."

"What Syntha says is correct," Palignon said, gesturing at the woman. "Gemma has a story to tell, but her earlier attempts to tell it to the world were foiled by Davin and his son. Look around you—we have enough books here to distribute to the northern half of the kingdom. More crates have already been distributed through our network to Centeron, the Southern Reaches, and Southplains. A train car full of books sits in one of the cargo depots in Capital City, ready to discredit the old man on the throne there. Gemma's power isn't in her work for the Royal Mystic Committee. That's all a front. What you're holding is her true weapon against the evil that is King Davin."

Kieve thought about it. Gemma had never outright stated her opposition to Davin, but her disdain for the king was quite thinly veiled. She was the most gung-ho out of everyone they worked with to enforce the rather sudden changes to the Royal Mystic Committee, a course correction that was almost unbelievably extreme. Could she really have been working in secret to bring down Davin and his regime?

Kieve's thoughts shifted to himself. His association with Gemma, their close partnership, would paint a target on his back if word got out about her true intentions. Those books would destroy not just Gemma's reputation but his own. The woman he'd fallen so madly in love with over the course of their partnership would be his downfall if these books were released to the people of Aepistelle, or even if they were confiscated by—

"Oh no." Kieve's confused expression turned to one of alarm. "Oh gods, no. I am so sorry. Please forgive me."

"What is it?" Syntha asked.

"I've made a mistake. Davin's soldiers are on their way here this very moment. We must gather what we can and flee."

CHAPTER 11
KIEVE

The wagon burst from the barn, shedding a crate of books as the horses veered left to the pathway. Palignon had opened the stall doors and let the mules go free, opting for the speed of his and Syntha's horses.

"Is there no other road out of here?" Kieve called from the back of the wagon, where he attempted to hang on to the cargo during their bumpy escape. He dove to his side, barely hooking his fingers through the bars of a birdcage teetering off one edge of the cart.

"As long as we get to the bridge before the soldiers, we should be fine," Syntha said. "We can lose them once we're in town." Kieve felt less confident when he noticed the tight grip Palignon had on the sword that lay across his lap at the front of the wagon.

"And what of the birds? Special pets of yours?"

"Insurance," Palignon called back, not offering more of an explanation.

Kieve didn't require elaboration once he inspected the six

birds. Each had a tiny scroll attached to its leg. They were carrier pigeons. "One for each region?"

"Aye," Palignon said. "We have warehouses in all six parts of Aepistelle, fully stocked and ready to distribute copies of the book to the masses."

Kieve's stomach dropped as the wagon hit a bump at the crest of a hill. They descended at what felt like double the speed the horses should be able to pull their load.

"Stoking rebellion among the people." Kieve rubbed his temples. "If your crew is successful, this kingdom will fall into chaos. Civil war, even."

"*My* crew?" Palignon bellowed laughter. "You're a part of this now, too, Private Fallbrook. There's no going back."

"What makes you think I won't arrest you? I haven't agreed to any terms yet. I'm not a part of anything."

Syntha handed the reigns to Palignon and rose to her feet, balanced at the head of the wagon as if the bumps and speed didn't faze her. She unsheathed her sword. "You're either a part of this, or you're a rotten feast for the crows on the side of this road. Up to you."

Palignon patted Syntha's arm. She glared at Kieve, then returned her sword to its place, turned, and resumed guiding the horses. "For Gemma and for truth," Palignon assured both of them. "Whether that means discomfort or war, I cannot say, but I guarantee it will mean change in this kingdom. People will die. The Royal Mystic Committee will likely be a casualty of what is to come. The truth is bigger than all of that, however, and it's what the people of this kingdom deserve. Are you with us or not, Private Fallbrook?"

Kieve sighed. "Please, just call me Kieve."

They rode on in silence. The wagon climbed one final hill, and the trio took in the town of Pinedrop on the other side of the river and the bridge that linked them to it.

The bridge was lined with soldiers.

Syntha pulled the horses to a stop. "What now, boss?"

"I'm so sorry," Kieve said. "I've brought this upon us."

"And you're going to help us get out of it," Palignon said as a lone rider broke from the garrison on the bridge and guided his steed up the hill.

"Lieutenant Palignon?" the man asked in confusion. "Sir, we were told there was subversive activity occurring out this way. We didn't expect to see you here."

"Good evening, Lieutenant Nisson," Palignon said. "I am off duty at the moment, but I have not witnessed any such activity. Haven't crossed paths with any nefarious or wayward souls, either."

The army officer coaxed his horse forward and approached the wagon. He eyed the crates. "And what are you carrying on this cart?"

"Ah, those are books."

"From that traitor Richard the Elusive's home? I've heard there were many, though I thought they'd already been seized as evidence and taken to Capital City."

"We uncovered several more crates in a hidden chamber in the basement," Palignon lied smoothly. "We're taking them to the Royal Mystic Committee office now so we can get them processed and sent out on the first train tomorrow morning."

"You said you were off duty."

"Did I?"

"Yes. And who are your friends?"

"Private Kieve Fallbrook, here to escort these books back to Fort Braxen, sir."

"And the lady?"

"I'm their bloody chauffeur, what does it look like?"

Syntha said. Kieve shook his head. Apparently improvising a lie was not one of the woman's strengths.

A pair of soldiers made their way through the crowd on the bridge. "Sir!" one called up to Lieutenant Nisson. Kieve recognized the man's unruly sideburns even at a distance. "That's the man who warned me about the traitorous activities, sir!"

Palignon and Syntha looked back and shook their heads at Kieve in unison.

"Yah!" Syntha shouted as she shook the reins, spurring the horses into action. With the momentum of the downhill trajectory, they picked up speed quickly. Nisson's horse reared, sending the lieutenant sprawling on the road. The crunch of the back of his skull against the rocky ground made Kieve wince as the wagon sped past.

"Sorry," Kieve called down to the man. He was only doing his duty, after all. Kieve turned his attention forward. "There's no room for us on the bridge! What are we going to do?"

"Act first, think later," Syntha called back. She maintained her grip on the reins with one hand and unsheathed her sword with the other. Palignon followed suit. Kieve pulled out his throwing daggers.

"I feel woefully unprepared for this skirmish," he said. Palignon turned back to see the tiny blades and laughed.

"The bundle just behind my seat has what you need," he said. Kieve pulled open the cloth sack to reveal a battle-axe. "A bit heavy for you, to be sure, but the steel handle will deflect the blows from their swords. Found it in Richard's collection. The man had a small armory down in his cellar."

Kieve lifted the axe and nearly toppled over. While not out of shape by any means, he was also not made of muscle. The knives suited him just fine. A short sword would have been preferable to the axe.

"Can we trade?" he asked. Palignon chuckled but obliged.

As they approached the bottom of the hill, the soldiers on the bridge readied their own weapons. Syntha rose to her feet and let out a fierce battle cry.

"Come and get it!" she yelled. She tossed the reins to Palignon, then leaped from the driver's box to the horse directly in front of her, then onto the ground ahead of the wagon's trajectory, knocking into the frontmost soldier.

In confusion or fear, the horses veered to the right, causing the wagon to swerve and smash a soldier against the railing of the bridge. A crate teetered at the edge of the wagon. Kieve pivoted to catch it, but the sword in his hand clanged against the birdcage. He let the books tumble off, choosing to save the tipping aviary instead. Up ahead, Palignon dropped the reins and took the axe in both hands. He swung hard at a soldier speeding by on a horse, connecting with the young man's chest. The blow knocked the soldier off his mount and over the railing into the river below.

"Open the cage and let those pigeons fly!" Palignon ordered just as the wagon's horses swerved in the other direction, sending the vehicle onto two wheels.

Kieve released his grip on the birdcage in an attempt to steady himself, but a shifting crate knocked him off his feet. The cage went flying off the side. "No!" he shouted, but all he could do was watch it plummet off the bridge toward the rapids below.

He looked around to find Syntha surrounded by soldiers but holding her own for the time being. The Aepistelle Army was untested, as there had been peace in the kingdom for as long as most of its soldiers had been alive. What training they had paled in comparison to Syntha's skill, though their sheer numbers would soon make up for it. Palignon apparently thought the same, so he jumped into the crowd to assist her.

If their time was nearing its end and this operation was truly Gemma's desire, Kieve had to see to its success. He hopped from the cart to the railing of the bridge. The cage bobbed up and down as it moved downstream. The pigeons flapped their wings frantically within it. Kieve flung his sword toward the bank on his right. As it spun through the air, he dove into the water twenty feet below.

Water filled his nostrils. He sank with the momentum of his fall, stunned by his frigid surroundings. He tumbled around in the depths until his left hand brushed something. He righted himself, then kicked off the river bottom. His boots sank into the mud as if he were being sucked into it. He struggled to pull them out without losing them, lest he return to the battle in naught but his socks. The motion of the river helped loosen him, and he found a rock to kick off of instead.

The air felt miraculous as he gasped to refill his lungs. He looked around, reorienting himself, as he let the flow take him. Up ahead, the cage had nestled against a clump of branches jutting out of the water. The birds were shaken, the little scrolls affixed to their legs soaked through, but Kieve knew their recipients would understand where the birds had been sent from and what their arrival meant. He also knew what it would mean for him to be the one to release the creatures into the wild. What it would do to the peace and order of the kingdom. How it would end his career and Gemma's, destroy his professional partnership with the woman he admired and whose success he longed to emulate. The shame he'd bring on his parents should he join the resistance against King Davin.

Kieve yanked the cage from the tangle of branches and pushed it away from him toward the steady flow of the river. It bobbed, overturned, and dipped below the surface. Little bubbles rose up as the cage sank lower and was pulled downstream. He stood there, watching as it faded from view. "I'm sorry," he whispered.

A scream sounded from the bridge. Kieve snapped out of his introspection and turned back toward the melee. A soldier plummeted off the bridge, blood spraying from his severed wrist. Syntha and Palignon still held their own against the garrison. They were putting their lives on the line to fight for that manuscript apparently written by Gemma. For whatever truths it held, whatever secrets she aimed to expose.

For Gemma herself.

He splashed toward the center of the river, swam with the flow, took a breath, and dove down. Kieve returned to the surface with the cage, the birds shaken and chirping fiercely but alive.

He unlatched the door of the cage and set them free.

Then Kieve made his way to the riverbank, retrieved his sword, and joined the fight.

In minutes, the trio had taken out or scared off the remaining soldiers.

"We actually did it," Kieve said. "I thought that was the end for us."

Syntha was bent over, her hands on her knees as she breathed heavily. Blood dripped from her arms and stained her clothes, though Kieve couldn't tell if any of it was her own.

"Wait a minute," Palignon said as he set the head of the hefty battle-axe down on the wooden bridge, its weight making a *clunk* that Kieve felt through his boots. "The cart is gone."

They all looked at each other for a moment, then turned and ran in the direction of the town. A gathering of citizens had cautiously watched the fight from a distance; Kieve was sure he'd seen them during the chaos, but they'd apparently all fled the scene. The street nearest the bridge was empty.

The trio jogged up one more block and found dozens of residents of Pinedrop crowded around the overturned wagon —the horses had apparently made a turn too fast in their panic. The crates had spilled open, their contents scattered all over the street.

Gemma Calvertson's book was now in the hands of the people.

CHAPTER 12
JESTAN

"Make way! Under orders from the governor regent, please make way!"

Jestan winced at the title George had used, but it was the title Richard had insisted on adopting. The late King Harold of Emyhrsen had no children and no surviving relatives after the decades of enslavement by the foreign Tzakabyan invaders. Richard was the son of Harold's closest friend and advisor, whom many elderly survivors remembered quite fondly. When Emyhrsen had been liberated, Richard had decided to stay in his ancestral lands and help the people rebuild. In turn, they had asked him to take the late King Harold's place on the throne. Richard had refused, saying he'd help them establish a new way of governing. Thus, *governor regent* had been coined.

"Move it, please," George commanded as he led his horse through the crowd and up to the porch of the farmhouse. Jestan followed his lead. They dismounted their steeds and tied the reins to the porch railing.

"Now, will someone tell us what is going on here?" Jestan

asked, and the men and women around them all shouted at once. Jestan lifted a hand, and they quieted. He pointed to an octogenarian to his left. "Sir, could you please explain the situation to me?"

The old man beamed at the request. He reached out and clasped his gnarled hands around Jestan's own. "Thank you, Liberator." The nickname was one both Jestan and George had earned when they'd helped to slaughter the oppressors at a farm three years prior and free an army of enslaved people. He despised the name but motioned for the man to continue. "A pack of Tzakabyan scum are hiding out here. We've sent requests to the king—"

"Governor regent," George corrected.

"—to help us get rid of them. We're grateful Sir Richard has obliged. We've plenty of rope to hang them all," the man said, pointing to a middle-aged man who might have been his son. The other man held a bundle of fraying cord. It was battered and decaying, like everything in this country.

"We've plenty of fire, too!" a woman shouted from the crowd. A chorus of cheers rose up as the congregants waved their torches. "Let's just smoke them out!"

Jestan patted the older man on the shoulder, then ascended the steps to the porch. He raised both arms and again quieted the crowd. "Friends, I can't claim to understand even one iota of the pain and suffering you all have endured under the despicable rule of the Tzakabyans and their dark sorcery. I can only tell you that you are free of them now. Free to rebuild. To take ownership of the lands they stole from you and forced you to work under threat of beatings or execution. To establish a future for your families. To start fresh. You have many opportunities, and the governor regent and his appointed council are dedicated to ensuring that you receive all the assistance you need. We're here for you. However, we must put our violence and rage behind us. We must forge ahead together in peace, show our children what a good place this world can be."

"But these are the ones who destroyed our lives!" another man shouted. "Why should we let them live among us freely?"

"Yeah!" several in the crowd cried out.

"We hear your frustrations and concerns, my friends," Jestan reassured them. "Still, I don't believe that any Tzakabyans who remain in Emyhrsen will ever feel like they are living freely. They know what they've done. Many have tried to atone for their misdeeds. Let me speak to them in peace. Please disperse and trust that my friend George and I will ensure that these folks mean you no further harm. Will you do that for us?"

Some in the crowd looked at him with distrust or dismay. They had come here thirsty for blood, and their thirst would remain unquenched. Still, they murmured their agreement and turned away. When all but a few had gone, George followed Jestan up to the front door, which opened at their approach. They couldn't see into the dark room beyond, but trusted they were safe and stepped inside.

The door closed as Jestan's vision adjusted to the dim surroundings. Someone kindled a fire in the hearth while others lit lanterns and sconces around the room.

"Tzakay," Jestan greeted them in their tongue. He and George had picked up quite a few words during their travels overseas to escort the majority of the Tzakabyans back to their lands.

"Tzakay," a couple replied.

"We mean them no harm," a Tzakabyan man said behind him. Jestan turned to face the man who had let him in. "We are not like the others."

"I am Jestan, and this is George. We aren't here to arrest you or hurt you. We're just here to help find a solution."

"I am Kahle," the man said. He had the thick gray flesh and pointed teeth that made the Tzakabyans stand out among the people of Emyhrsen. Others around the room, however, looked different. Some were clearly Emyhrseni men and women, while others were harder to place. Children sat among them. They all looked fearful, some watching out the window as if expecting torches to come crashing through at any moment. All of them appeared thin and frail. "As you can see, we are not some fearsome band of warriors here to continue the misdeeds of our kinsmen. We just want to live. To eat. To work these lands."

"You want acceptance," George said. "We understand that, but I'm sure you also understand why the Emyhrseni do not trust you."

"Of course." Kahle looked down in shame. "I can never take back what was done. My kin did horrible things here for decades and deserved far worse in return. That they were allowed to leave without punishment was a mercy most here do not agree with. But I was born here, part of a younger generation. I know nothing else, no other lands besides these. Many of us did not agree with the misdeeds of our fathers. Some were punished for speaking out, imprisoned, put to work with the Emyhrseni. Others were killed, my own brothers among them. I was part of the former group. In my time among the people of these lands, I have found friendship. Love. Family." Kahle walked across the room and sat with one of the Emyhrseni women. He put one arm around her and another around a child. "Perhaps I do not deserve a place among the people here, but what about my children? Must they suffer? Must they always be seen as monsters?"

Kahle's wife stood and stepped into the center of the

room. "We could have gone with the Tzakabyan people, but I would have been the monster among them. My children would have been outcasts. Emyhrsen is our home, even if our children will never blend in. There are others like them living in fear, hiding in the dark. Is that the kind of world Governor Richard would be proud to rule?"

Jestan turned and glanced out a window. Though the crowd had dispersed, he could make out several people still watching the house from a distance, hopeful that they'd see an execution or at least an arrest.

"You're right," Jestan said. "It's not a safe world for you folks. There is so much pain here, so much healing that needs to take place. Acceptance isn't something we can force. It will take time. But just as the governor regent has promised to help provide for the natives of Emyhrsen, so too will he provide for everyone else who calls these lands home."

George grabbed Jestan's arm and leaned in. "What are you suggesting?" he whispered. "Richard didn't tell us to help the Tzakabyans."

Jestan patted his friend's shoulder reassuringly, then continued to address those in the room. "I have an idea that I must run by our good leader. Until then, please lie low. We'll leave behind a few people to stand watch and ensure you have peace for the time being."

"THEIR OWN *CASTLE*?" RICHARD ASKED. "AND HOW WILL that make the people of Emyhrsen feel any better about all of this?"

"It's for the children, Richard." Jestan paced around the dining room at King Harold's Keep while George and Richard picked at their meals. "They never enslaved anyone here. They had no choice but to be born with a foot in each world. These children deserve to start fresh. They deserve the same opportunities as any others. Now, I understand that they won't be accepted in schools here just yet as the people of Emyhrsen continue to heal and adjust to all the changes. So what else can we do but allow these children to thrive in a place that is just removed enough for everyone? We can open admission to anyone who wishes to send their children to school there. I think there must be some in the kingdom willing to accept them and make amends."

"Is the castle of the Vheisenia even in any condition to house these children?" George asked.

Richard set his fork down on his plate and nodded. "The Tzakabyan leadership lived there when they ruled over Emyhrsen because it was a much grander palace than this one, where they left Harold as a figurehead. They kept it up just fine. It's been abandoned ever since you two guided them back to their ancestral lands, but I don't think it would have fallen into disrepair in only three years. It's as fine a place as any."

"So you agree?" Jestan asked.

Richard stood and paced the room. He stopped at a window and stared out, contemplating. After a prolonged silence, he turned and eyed his old friend. "When did you become so wise? You were the member of our group who jumped into every situation without forethought. Like that time in Ravager Valley when you took on the pack of Grenwulves yourself as the rest of us looked on, eating our hard-earned meals. It wasn't until you were surrounded by the creatures that you realized you'd left your sword next to the campfire."

Jestan bellowed his trademark boisterous laughter. "I

somehow came out of that one with all my fingers intact! We've had some good times, haven't we?"

"We have. And you are right—this may be the best path forward. I can't force healing and acceptance among our people, and I also won't force the remaining Tzakabyans to leave. They have no other home, and they are not threats to our people. We must forge a new path forward and rebuild together. I'll work with our new secretary of education to ensure that we have the resources to create a residential school. We'll start with these children but open it up to all the people of Emyhrsen."

A door opened on the far side of the room and a castle guard rushed in. "Sir," he called to Richard. The look of fear on his face made Jestan's heart drop. "We have a problem. A ship bearing the seal of the Aepistelle Navy approaches."

Richard dropped back down into his chair. "Not again," he muttered before raising his voice. "Prepare for defensive measures," he commanded the soldier. Then he turned to George and Jestan. "I hope you two are ready for another fight."

CHAPTER 13
JESTAN

Sure enough, a red flag with a gold emblem of a seven-tentacled kraken—one holding a trident—flew high over the ship's deck. Jestan actually loved the Aepistelle Navy's sigil, even if he didn't welcome its presence just then. It could mean only trouble for what had become his new home since he and George had returned from their overseas quest four months earlier.

A door opened on the tower behind him and Richard came out onto the wall, flanked by two guards. A pair of guards was also positioned at each of the two cannons that had been installed when the walls had been rebuilt following the battle against the Tzakabyans and Davin's soldiers three years earlier. The cannons had been recovered from the Tzakabyan ships; such weaponry had been unheard of in Emyhrsen and even Aepistelle before the battle. As far as Jestan knew, the only ones in existence were this pair, two others that had sunk into the riverbed, and three that Captain Le'Nelle Nightstar had installed on her ship, the *Ales and Sails*.

"Hold your fire. Wait for my command," General

Cormoran, Richard's head of the castle guard, told the cannon operators as well as three archers.

The ship was coming upriver against the current, propelled by an army of rowers belowdecks. Richard took his place beside George and Jestan, dressed in a fine suit made for him by the castle's longtime seamstress, Addie.

"You look quite kingly, Richard. Or should I call you *my lord?*" Jestan quipped.

Richard gave a guttural grunt of disgust. The man truly despised the idea of being the king of this land despite the unanimous support of his people.

"You've turned out to be quite a leader yourself, Jestan," George noted. "Shall we call you *prince?*"

Jestan gave a hearty laugh and slapped George on the back. "Has a nice ring to it, I must admit!"

"Stern faces, you two," Richard said.

"Almost sounds like an order. From a king."

Richard glared at the man, though one corner of his lips quivered as he fought back a grin.

The swishing of oars grew louder as the boat came nearer. Jestan could just make out the crew on deck. "Something's not right," he said.

"What do you mean?" George asked.

Richard nodded. "You're right, Jestan. No naval uniforms. Clearly skilled at sailing, though. Pirates, perhaps?"

"That might be it," Jestan said. "Except that woman reminds me of—"

"Gemma!" George called out. He turned and made for the stairs down to ground level. "Open the gates!" he called to the guards below as he ran under the parapet and out of Jestan's view. As the gate's hinges groaned open, Jestan watched the younger man run out of the castle walls and toward the rebuilt docks. George stopped and called toward Jestan, "Come on, guys! It's just my sister!"

Jestan glanced over at Richard, surprised to see that he still had a look of concern on his face. "What's wrong, old friend?"

Richard shook his head. "I'm not sure. Seeing her under the banner of King Davin, I suppose. It doesn't seem right."

"We won't know what's going on until we talk to her. Let's go!" Jestan followed George's path. He turned back to find Richard trailing cautiously.

The ship docked a few minutes later. The gangway was lowered, and Gemma Calvertson descended. She ran first to her brother.

"I didn't expect you to be here," Gemma said as she hugged George. "You've been away for so long, we had no idea if you had survived the journey overseas. I thought the Tzakabyans might have turned against you all once they realized they outnumbered you."

"Not at all. We spent more time away from these parts than we thought we would, but we made some priceless memories along the way." George pulled one arm free of Gemma's embrace and beckoned Jestan over.

Gemma wiped her tears, then released her grip on George. She turned to Jestan and flashed a warm smile. "Thank you for taking such good care of my brother all this time." She went in for a hug, and Jestan returned it. He hadn't spent more than a couple of days in the company of the young woman. Their paths had crossed only at the end of the journey into Emyhrsen and during the fight against the Tzakabyan invaders, yet she had been the catalyst for most of the changes in his life over the last few years.

"George took care of me," Jestan said. "We taught each

other a lot, discovered much about ourselves once we were free from the confines of Aepistelle."

Gemma turned to face Richard, who hesitated for a moment before stepping forward and embracing her. "I'm so glad to see you again, Gemma."

"We went through everything together, and now you're here. You're home." She pulled back and observed the rebuilt castle walls. "You've made Emyhrsen new again. It's beautiful."

The wariness left Richard's face at that. Pride washed over him, though Jestan knew the man was humble beyond reason and correctly predicted his response. "I'm just here to support them," Richard said of his people. "They've done it them-selves. They're really healing, Gemma. Rebuilding this country into what the stories say it was like before I was born. Before Harold's downfall."

Jestan noticed commotion on the deck of the ship. "Hate to break up the reunion, guys, but what's happening over there?" He pointed at a ragtag crew directing a motley bunch in ill-fitting Aepistelle naval uniforms toward the gangplank.

"Ah, yes," Gemma said. "That needs some explanation. But first, are the dungeons available for a dozen prisoners?"

THE PRISONERS WERE LED AWAY TO CELLS BELOW THE castle courtyard. Richard directed Gemma and her friends to follow him, Jestan, and George into the dining hall, where the staff brought them tea and fresh fruits. The scents of baking breads and smoked pig wafted in from the kitchen while the group settled into seats at the long table.

"Allow me to introduce everyone," Gemma said. She pointed first to a man close to Jestan's age. Based on the man's features, Jestan wouldn't have been surprised if Gemma had introduced him as an uncle. His skin was darker and rougher than Gemma's and George's lighter brown tone from years spent at sea, but his hair, the shape of his nose and ears, and the slight roundness of his cheeks all reminded Jestan of the Calvertson family and their Ferromin Islands heritage. Gemma went on. "This is—"

"Quincy?" George asked, finally recognizing the man.

"I wondered if you'd remember me, Georgie. I haven't seen you since you were maybe five years old."

"Our parents always talked about you," George said. "I couldn't forget my father's best friend. You look just as I remember you. Do you ever age?"

"Well, it's all that sun and salt in the air," Quincy joked. "I hear you've spent some time at sea these last few years as well."

"Indeed! We've been back only a few months now, and it took some time to shed my sea legs."

Gemma let their conversation run its course before introducing the rest of the crew—two women named Selinda and Verena, as well as four men whose names Jestan quickly forgot. The food was served shortly after, and then Quincy and his crew returned to the docks to meet the local shipmaster Richard had summoned to repair the captured naval vessel. Richard led the rest of them into his sitting room.

"So, you two are, what, sheriffs of Emyhrsen now?" Gemma asked George and Jestan.

"Keepers of the peace, I guess?" George said.

"Peacekeepers. I like that," Jestan said. "Richard here has done a fine job of getting the people of this country back on their feet, helping them build up their lives from nothing, but there are still skirmishes and misunderstandings."

"It hasn't been easy," Richard admitted. "The Tzakabyans

took everything from the people of Emyhrsen, and the handful who were alive in the days before the enslavement are in their golden years now. Most of the Emyhrseni people were born into captivity and have never known a life of freedom."

"People are constantly looking over their shoulders, fearful of repercussions from slavers who are no longer here," George added.

Richard nodded. "We're doing what we can to help them feel ownership of this kingdom. I'm more of a guide than a king. I don't want them to feel like I'm yet another foreign usurper, coming in and taking control of them."

"Richard, my boy, nobody feels that way about you," Jestan said. "They look up to you. Admire you. You are a hero, a local boy returned home to lead them. You must stop shying away from that." Jestan turned to Gemma. "Richard is too humble for his own good. Always has been."

"Mom and Dad are so concerned about you," Gemma said to her brother. "Did you ever try to reach them?"

George looked ashamed, but Jestan knew he had no reason to be. "About a year ago, Jestan and our crew and I were docked for a couple weeks in Taelwynd Isle, not far from the Ferromin Islands. A fleet of ships with the Aepistelle Navy emblem sailed in and filled the port one day. Aepistelle sailors and soldiers were everywhere. We wanted to hear the latest news from Aepistelle, so we bought them some rounds in a tavern. Didn't take much for those boys to start gossiping. We heard all about how Davin was back in command after a brief disappearance, how he'd crushed some attempts at rebellion and reestablished order in the kingdom."

Jestan took over the story. "We knew we couldn't go home after that—we were surely wanted men after fighting off Davin and his soldiers here in Emyhrsen. So we returned to the safety of the north with Richard and his people."

"I can't speak for Jestan," George said, "but I want nothing more than to go home to Aepistelle, embrace Mom, take care of Dad. I don't know if we'll ever be able to return, though."

"I want to go home as well," Jestan agreed. "Don't get me wrong, Richard, we love being here and helping you rebuild, but I have a life back in Aepistelle." A smile overtook his face. "And a fan base, too. They must be so hungry for my return to the stage! Imagine the crowds that'll come to witness my triumphant return. The applause... Sorry, it's just been so long."

"No need to apologize," George said. "I was at your final performance in Capital City. You were certainly in your element, though I think you have another trait that has become just as important to who you are."

"What do you mean?"

"Helping people, Jestan. Leading. You are a natural at it. Your charisma, your way with words—you can use those for more than just entertainment. People listen to you. Look at what you've done here. You are a leader, truly."

Jestan hadn't thought of it that way. But between returning the Tzakabyans to their homeland and leading ships' crews over the last couple of years, he really had found a knack for compassionate leadership. It all came in handy here in Emyhrsen, where he'd helped Richard's rebuilding campaign and the people showed him a respect he'd never known before. It was different from the adoration or lust he'd received from fans of his stage shows and his books and his songs back in Aepistelle. Maybe that was all behind him.

Maybe Jestan had a new calling altogether.

CHAPTER 14
GEMMA

"So, tell me about the captives," Richard said as he led Gemma through the courtyard. Despite the years she and her brother had been separated, George had apologetically cut their reunion short. He and Jestan had a previous engagement—breaking up a skirmish in a village a few miles northeast of the castle. Gemma had promised she wouldn't leave without catching up with him and exchanging tales about their wildly different experiences these last three years.

"Quincy and his crew were escorting me here when we were chased down by the naval vessel," Gemma explained. "Something seemed off about their commander. He and his crew attacked us, and Quincy's ship was destroyed. We held our own, though, and overpowered them. Once we got onboard their ship, we found the actual crew in chains belowdecks. They had been raided and imprisoned by pirates. We made to free them, but they threatened to either arrest us or throw us overboard. Even showing them my identification didn't help. So we left them locked up and repaired their ship enough to get us the rest of the way here."

"Wouldn't proving your identity have made things worse?" Richard asked. They'd climbed the stairs up to the top of the rampart, and Gemma headed to the spot where she'd been positioned with the other archers during the battle here. She looked across the river at where the enchanted trees had come to life and begun to attack them. Gemma sat on the parapet and faced her old friend. She took a deep breath and let it out.

"I need to tell you something else, Richard. For the past three years, I have been working with the Royal Mystic Committee."

Richard's expression warped into a grimace. He staggered back a step. "You've *what*?"

Gemma watched the heat rise in him and held up her hands to soothe him. "Please let me explain." She told him about her last stand at the edge of the cliff in the Southern Reaches, how she either had to jump to her death or accept King Davin's offer and try to change things from the inside. She explained how the enslaved boy had shared his visions of where Marzele and Denny and Arnem had gone, of Arnem's death due to Denny's inability to control his budding abilities. She recounted how Davin's seer had told her there was a way to reach Arnem in the Realm Beyond and possibly rescue him from the clutches of death.

At the mention of Arnem's death, Richard's knees buckled. He sank to the floor and sat with his head in his hands. "He's been dead this whole time?"

"I'm sorry I didn't tell you sooner. There was no way I could have traveled here—Davin's men watched me constantly for the first couple of years, testing my loyalty at every turn. I've only been free of the king's suspicion for a short time. And it's not like Aepistelle's postal service comes up north to Emyhrsen."

Richard smiled briefly through his tears, but then his face quickly fell again. "Arnem was always there for anyone who needed help, as selfless as a man could ever be. And then there is Selah. And their daughters." Richard slammed his fist against the stone walkway. "I should have been there."

"No, Richard. You're right where you are meant to be. Look at this place! You rebuilt a broken nation. You reinvigorated a people who once knew nothing but pain and oppression. You found your place in this world. Arnem knew that. We all know it."

"But he's gone."

"He doesn't have to be."

Richard furrowed his brows in confusion. "What are you saying?"

"I didn't come here for a reunion, Richard, as ecstatic as I am to see you and George and Jestan again. The reason I've spent these three years with the Committee wasn't just for my own survival. I've been searching for clues about how to reach the Realm Beyond, like Davin's young seer said. I think I've figured it out, Richard. I think I know how to bring Arnem home."

Richard rose to his feet, towering over Gemma. "Whatever you're thinking, I'm sure it's dangerous. I'm coming with you. I'll help you rescue my old friend."

Gemma stood so she was eye to eye with Richard. She threw her arms around him in a tight embrace. "I can't let you do that." She released him and gestured to the rebuilt castle, the newly constructed village that sprawled just outside the walls. "Look at all this. These people need you here. This is your home now. This is where you belong. You're a king now, fair to his people."

"Governor regent, actually," Richard barked. She thought he was serious until his lips twitched into a playful grin. "Point taken, though. Will you invite your brother along?"

"I need to do this alone. I'll leave tomorrow after I say goodbye to George. Thank you for taking care of Quincy and his crew. As soon as the ship is repaired, they'll take the Aepistelle soldiers back home and release them. He'll find a way out of this mess. He always does."

"Some sailor," Richard said.

"Mercenary, actually," Gemma said with a grin, giving Richard a taste of his own humor.

———

GEMMA SPENT THE REST OF THE EVENING CATCHING UP with Richard, admiring the relationships he had built with his staff, meeting the team of advisors he'd brought on, even having tea with Addie, the castle's seamstress. The elderly woman was one of only a small handful of people who had survived all the years of enslavement by the Tzakabyans. In her youth, she'd served King Harold along with the rest of her family. She'd grown up alongside Richard's father and had been present at Richard's birth. She had shown hospitality to Gemma three years ago and had even assisted in the fight against the Aepistelle soldiers who'd sought to keep the people of Emyhrsen in bondage.

The next morning, Gemma breakfasted with Addie, Richard, Quincy and his crew, Jestan, and George. To her surprise, George made no attempt to tag along with Gemma on her journey.

"I've learned to let you go," George said when she joked that he didn't seem to care that she was heading off into potential danger. "If there's anyone who can achieve whatever crazy thing you have in mind, well, it's you, Gemma."

"Your brother acts like he's incompetent, but I can assure you that he shares your bravery," Jestan said, one arm around George's shoulders, the other ruffling the younger man's hair. "Plus, we've had enough adventures of our own to last three lifetimes."

"Richard can use you both around here much more than I can wherever I'm going," Gemma said.

"I must insist you take us with you," Quincy said, motioning to Selinda and the rest of their team. "I can't go back and look your parents in the eyes knowing I left you alone to face danger. Not again."

"No, Quincy. When King Davin hears that I've abandoned my post, he may come looking for me. He surely knows where my parents are. He'll use them as leverage."

"Understood, but I don't like it. Can we at least transport you to wherever you need to go?"

Gemma pushed her chair back, setting her napkin atop the crumbs that remained on her breakfast plate. She rose to her feet. "I'm just crossing the river and heading southeast. I've been that way before—nothing but an empty town once I get south of Amassa Lake."

"An empty town?" Addie asked. She swatted Richard's shoulder with her napkin playfully. "You mean you didn't tell her?"

Richard flashed a look like an ashamed child being scolded by his mother. "I was going to." He turned to Gemma. "Ferathan isn't abandoned. Many of the buildings fell into ruin after Naliah lifted the curse and left the place, but some are still livable."

"Who's there, then?" Gemma asked.

"The gifted. Folks with abilities. Refugees fleeing"—

Richard's eyes flicked away from Gemma's—"the Royal Mystic Committee. Fleeing oppression."

Heat rose in Gemma's cheeks. "But things have been better in Aepistelle. We've turned the Committee around. We help their kind now."

"You tag them like specimens." This from Selinda, sitting at Quincy's side. "You catalog their abilities, send the information back to King Davin and his ilk to do with as they please. Sure, he's let you think you're making big changes, but all he's doing is delaying the inevitable, working toward his end game."

"What are you talking about?" Gemma asked. "Why didn't you tell me you felt this way?"

"Because," Selinda answered, wrapping her fingers around her glass of water, "more of us than you know have secrets of our own."

Gemma's eyes fell to the water in the glass. Bubbles rose up from the bottom. At first she thought the woman was shaking with anger, but as the bubbles grew more rapid, Gemma realized the water was boiling. Selinda's hand grew red like an iron in the fire. The glass shattered between her fingers.

"You have powers?" Gemma asked. "I never knew!"

"And I would never have entrusted that information to a member of the Royal Mystic Committee," Selinda said. "Even you."

Quincy rested a hand on Selinda's forearm to calm her. "Now, now. Gemma is our friend. She has no ill intentions toward anyone with abilities. You know that, Selinda."

"I do know it, but that doesn't mean others with access to the information won't use it against us. Gemma, your intentions may be pure, but you must understand the new risks your work has created. The people hiding out in Ferathan clearly feel the same."

"I am sorry," Gemma said. "When I'm back, I will make sure those records are destroyed. If you would be willing to help me, I'd gladly have you, Selinda."

"We must do more than just destroy some records, Gemma. We must take down King Davin once and for all. We must finish what was started right here in Emyhrsen."

"His rule has gone on too long," Quincy agreed. "Our people should be serving as good neighbors, helping Richard rebuild Emyhrsen. Instead, Aepistelle keeps its vast resources to itself. Your brother and Jestan cannot go home as long as Davin remains in power. I don't even know what kind of mess our crew will be in when we return with a bunch of Davin's soldiers as prisoners."

"Even Arnem will be a wanted man if you succeed in reviving him," Jestan said. "He won't be able to go home to his wife and kids."

"I'd love to see Mom and Dad again," George said. "They can't spend the rest of their days in hiding. It's not right."

Richard raised a hand to get a word in. "You're all welcome to live here in Emyhrsen. There is more than enough room for your families. We could use some good folks here to help us rebuild."

"It's only a matter of time before Davin comes for Emyhrsen, Richard," Quincy said. "As soon as word gets out that your people are thriving, he'll try to crush you."

"Quincy isn't wrong," Gemma admitted.

"Then I will join this fight," Richard said. "The people of Emyhrsen know that Davin was responsible for the arrival of the Tzakabyans and the downfall of Harold. There will be many willing to join my army and fight."

"Respectfully, Richard," Addie said, "you are staying put

right here in this castle. The people here depend on you now."

"Aye," Jestan said, pounding his fist on the table. "You may gather the troops, Richard, but *I* will lead them."

"Don't try to leave me out," George said. "I'm in as well."

"Gemma, we'll give you five weeks to return with Arnem," Jestan said. "In the meantime, we'll gather forces, train them as best we can, and arm them. If you aren't back by then, we'll strike without you."

Quincy rose. "My crew and I will return to Aepistelle. The prisoners will have to stay here longer than we intended. I know many hopeful revolutionaries back home who are itching to see Davin's rule come to an end."

And so the revolution against King Davin and his regime began.

CHAPTER 15

GEMMA

S moke from chimneys rose up through the crisp morning air, the first sign that life indeed existed in Ferathan. Gemma skirted the borders of the town, shame keeping her from wanting to be seen. Instead, she walked along the bank of Amassa Lake as she made her way toward the rolling foothills known as the Fingers.

Just to the northeast of the town's limits, a large estate loomed on a mound. She hoped the refugees had avoided this place. As the sun crested behind Ferathan Manor, it cast a shadow over her path. The place was as eerie as it had been during the reign of the Witch of Ferathan.

The neglected iron gate squealed on rusted hinges as Gemma pushed it open and stepped onto the estate grounds. She was greeted by a menagerie of grotesque statues: animal-human hybrids and unimaginable beasts, some engaged in violent acts against their prey. These lined the pathway leading to the manor, perhaps to scare off unwanted visitors or perhaps to assert some twisted dominance over the village below.

Gemma had parted from her brother and friends the previous morning stocked with food, a full skin of water, and supplies, but she'd forgotten to bring a lantern. The caverns she hoped to find would certainly be dark, and her last chance to obtain a light source was Ferathan Manor. A wave of unease flowed through her as she sped between the statues. She thought she caught a fleeting movement of one of the wings on a particularly gruesome beast. She stopped in her tracks and turned her head up to face it. The creature's eyes appeared as cold and dead as they should have. She shrugged and moved on toward the mansion.

The cavernous porch had frightened Denny when she'd arrived here with the boy, Arnem, and a severely injured Richard during their journey. In his visions, he'd sensed true danger at the end of this corridor, thinking it was a cave rather than the lead-up to a brooding mansion. In reality, while the witch, Naliah, had certainly been a threat, they had forged a partnership of sorts with her. What danger lurked here now, however, Gemma could not say.

The towering front doors were locked, and there was no sense in ringing the bell. Instead, Gemma walked around to the side of the mansion. As she approached the door nearest the kitchen, another movement caught her eye. She looked up just in time to see a curtain fluttering behind a closed window. The manor was not empty after all. She ascended the three steps to the side door.

Perhaps some of the refugees had taken up residence in this place after all. It was spacious enough to house several families quite comfortably. Perhaps Naliah and the children had returned from their journey overseas, though her plan had been to remain in those distant lands for the remainder of her days. Perhaps some wayward souls from Emyhrsen had left the land they'd been enslaved in, fleeing the dark memories of their past and finding solace in this remote locale.

Gemma didn't need to wait to find out. Footsteps approached from within. She took a step back on the small porch landing and nearly teetered down the steps. The door flew open with force. Gemma gasped as she took in the sight of the man behind it.

His hair had grown out, full and wavy, flowing down to his shoulders. Instead of the curled mustache he'd had when they'd first met, he now had a long beard covering his cheeks, upper lip, chin, and throat. He'd been full of doubts and internal struggles over his faith when Gemma had last seen him, but he now had the look of a confident man, one who had conquered his fears and knew his place in the world.

Gemma stepped forward and threw her arms around him.

"Marzele," she said. "Have you been here all this time?"

When her hold on him loosened, he leaned back to take in his unexpected visitor. "I needed to get away from Aepistelle and reflect on the things I'd done after we parted ways in Capital City. We both did."

"We both?" Gemma asked. "You mean—"

"It's really you, Gemma." The voice came from the kitchen behind Marzele. The boy stood in a beam of sunlight shining through the dirty windowpane, a half-eaten apple in his hand. He dropped the fruit onto the countertop and walked over.

No, not a boy. "You're a young man now, Denny," Gemma tried to say, but the words caught in her throat. He pulled her into a tight hug, and Gemma didn't want to let go. "I can't believe it's really you! I didn't know if I'd ever see you again."

She pulled back and observed Denny's face. He'd grown into his skin over the years, as Gemma's mom would say. He'd put on weight in a healthy way now that he was several years removed from his life on the streets of Esteron. Yet his eyes remained the same as they'd always been, full of an ancient and knowing quality that seemed to stem from his ability to see potential versions of the future.

"You saw me coming?" she asked.

"He saw more than that," Marzele answered for the boy. "He watched some of your journey here."

Gemma looked back at Denny, who blushed like he had frequently done all those years ago. "Nothing creepy," he insisted. "Just some visions of you at sea with Quincy and Selinda. A skirmish, but also how bravely you fought and got out of the situation."

"Is that the only time you've seen me in your visions these last few years?"

"Well, I've seen a little of what you do to help people like me. I know you're part of the Royal Mystic Committee now, and I can feel this growing bravery in you, much stronger than ever before. And a benevolence, but that was always there. Your compassion defines you."

"Denny's powers have increased," Marzele explained. "His control over them, too, and over his own emotions. He can do much more than see what someone is potentially going to do. He can weed out false paths. He can feel what his subjects feel. He can even target specific people when he's in the right frame of mind."

"Still having difficulties doing that under pressure, though," Denny admitted. "The worst of it was when I found out where my parents were."

"I've seen it," Gemma said. "Davin had a seer who showed me what happened in that forest."

"So you know about Arnem?" Denny asked. Tears welled in his eyes. He turned away to hide them, walking back to where he'd dropped his apple. He reached for it, but his hand trembled, and he knocked it onto the floor.

"Easy, Denny," Marzele said.

"It's okay," Gemma reassured the boy. "I don't blame you for what happened. You were pushed to the extreme. You lost control, but it sounds like you've overcome that now. You can't blame yourself."

"I killed him. It will never be okay. His girls will never have their father in their lives again. I know what that's like, and now I've put others in the same situation."

A crack sounded from the hearth as a fire erupted. It didn't start small and build but rather emerged fully formed. Gemma exhaled loudly in surprise.

"He has it under control," Marzele assured her. "Even two years ago, that would have been the roof of this kitchen going up in flames. We didn't start here in the big house, but after nearly burning the down village a handful of times, he finally learned to control it."

"I don't think Arnem is fully gone," Gemma offered.

Denny looked from her to the fire and back. "He burned up just like the kindling in that hearth," he said. "I watched the life escape him with my own eyes. There's no coming back from that."

"What if I told you we may have a second chance?"

Denny and Marzele gaped at her, incredulous. It was the older man who spoke. "Is this a cruel joke, Gemma? Not what I would expect from you of all people."

"Please, let me explain," Gemma pleaded.

"Very well. Let us move to the parlor so you can get off your feet."

Marzele led Gemma and Denny out of the kitchen and down the hall to what had once been an elaborate sitting room. Gemma sat and explained everything to them, from her mysterious assignment that had led her to Madame Hvalsi to what the little woman had told her about the people under the mountains that guarded the secret to entering the Realm Beyond. Marzele nodded along, clearly believing everything Gemma said, but Denny looked doubtful. After she finished her story, they sat in silence. Denny finally broke it.

"If anyone should risk their life to retrieve Arnem from the Realm Beyond, it's me, not you. I killed him, after all."

"I drove you over the edge," Marzele said. "This is on me. I'll do it."

"I got all of you involved in the first place," Gemma said. "If I hadn't gone to see Richard, that journey through the Forest of Despair may never have happened. I'm responsible for shaking up all our lives."

"Perhaps it was predestined," Marzele said. "Perhaps even without any of us, it all would have happened anyway."

"You still believe in that stuff?" Gemma asked. She looked at Marzele's hair and beard, a stark departure from the Solendaron tradition of priests shaving all the hair on their heads and faces except for their finely groomed mustaches. "Do you even still follow your god Solendaron after all that has happened?"

"I..." Marzele trailed off. The battle between his heart and mind was evident on his face. "I'm not entirely sure what I believe. These years have been especially trying for me."

"Well, whatever you pray to now, I suggest you double up on it. We may need it where we're going."

With that, they gathered supplies and set out together to locate the entrance to the Realm Beyond.

CHAPTER 16

DENNY

"**D**enny?"

He stopped in his tracks at the side gate of the estate that had once belonged to Naliah, the Witch of Ferathan. He knew the voice without turning. He took a deep breath, readying himself to reply. The girl's voice went on instead.

"Were you not going to say goodbye, then?"

As he turned toward her, his eyes met Gemma's. He quickly looked away in embarrassment.

"Sorry, Iyola," Denny muttered. *Pathetic*, he scolded himself. *Speak up!* "Um, well, we weren't expecting company, but my friend—"

"Not expecting company? You, the wonder boy who can see the future, couldn't see that this beautiful woman was going to come and pull you away from the safety of Ferathan? Or is it just that you weren't enough of a man to tell me you were leaving?"

"It's not what you think, Iyola." Denny flushed with shyness. He hated doing this in front of Marzele and especially Gemma, so he dropped his pack and led his girlfriend away from his companions. They sat together on two large rocks in the overgrown grass. In his peripheral vision, he watched as Gemma followed Marzele through the gate and up the path toward the foothills.

"Is that Gemma, then?" Iyola asked. She wiped a tear from the corner of one eye. "I see why you like her."

"It's not like that at all. We went through a lot together. Looked into the face of death several times. Fought giants and witches and tree monsters."

"Broke Mr. Marzele out of prison. Yes, you've told me the stories."

"She's like a sister to me," Denny said. "A much older sister, at that. There's nothing between her and me, not like what you and I have. Promise."

"Oh, Denny," Iyola said. She flung herself at him, wrapped her arms tight around him. As she did so, a wind picked up. Humidity swirled around them like a wet funnel cloud.

"You're doing it again," Denny said.

Iyola loosened her grip and looked at the spectacle around them. "Sorry," she said, and the small tornado dissipated. "I can't help but lose control around you sometimes."

"I know exactly how it is."

"That's why I love you." She leaned in and planted a kiss on his lips. "Don't be gone for long."

"I can't promise that. We must help a friend. It could be dangerous, but I think we stand a chance." Denny returned the kiss, then rose to his feet. "Please tell the others in town that we're leaving and don't know when we'll be back. You'll all be just fine without us."

"Could she have led others to us? Those who aren't friends?"

"Gemma wouldn't do that. She wouldn't put you in danger.

If anyone comes looking for her, it will be friends from Emyhrsen. You must treat them well."

Denny planted one last kiss on her forehead and jogged off toward his companions without looking back at Iyola. He grabbed his pack and passed through the gate. As he crested the first hill, he caught sight of Marzele and Gemma waiting for him.

"Sorry," he offered. "Just a little goodbye."

Gemma turned to him with a proud smile. "The boy is becoming a man," she joked. "I love seeing you grow up, Denny."

Denny returned the smile but felt a slight blow inside. He'd always known Gemma was older than him, that he had no chance with her, but she had been his first real crush, and that would never change. When he had first seen her in his visions, he had immediately taken to her. First it was because of her beauty, since all he knew of her was her looks: flowing brown hair and a darker complexion than was usual for Aepistelle; an air of inquisitiveness; an assuredness that was not quite overconfidence. He could *feel* these things about her through those visions, just as he could feel the fear in Richard.

When he had met her in person, she'd been everything he had dreamed, yet there was also a severe sadness about her due to the events that had transpired just before he and Arnem had arrived: the freakish death of her partner, Walker, and the severe injuries suffered by Richard. These hills they now trekked through were the very same ones he'd traveled with her the day after they'd first met, when he'd gotten to see her bravery and intuition and compassion in action. His boyish crush on her had grown throughout that first journey, but deep inside he'd known she would never return his feelings. She was nearly ten years his senior, after all, and she saw him as a little brother and a friend. That was okay. He knew he could love her the same way, could pick back up where they'd left off three years ago. He would follow Gemma into whatever depths of darkness she expected to face on the road ahead.

"I suppose we could have sent word to the village that we were leaving," Marzele said. "It's been a long time since I've led a flock—more than twenty years since I was allowed a congregation of believers in the Solendaron temple before the fall. Leadership no longer comes naturally to me."

"You never asked for it here," Denny reminded him. "But they were led to Ferathan anyway."

"They found their way, yes. Led? I'm not so sure."

"You don't think your Lord Solendaron led them to Ferathan?" Gemma asked. Denny wanted to interrupt, change the subject. He knew how Marzele got when asked about his faith these days.

Marzele stumbled over a loose patch of gravel as the trio descended a hill but managed to recover his footing. "A lot of things have changed over the years, Gemma. My relationship with the Lord Solendaron is among them."

"I know a little about the cult from what Davin's young seer showed me," Gemma explained. "I was able to feel some of your emotions, if that makes sense. Your doubts. It was all fleeting, yet I felt as if I were living out those moments with you."

"Then perhaps you know that I was conflicted. Never about Solendaron's existence as a deity, mind you, but about the fact that walking in the light was the only choice. But in the shadow, I was capable of such despicable and damaging acts. I could lose control and cause harm. And the things I witnessed members of that cult doing...those powers certainly did not come from Solendaron. It all felt so corrupt.

"After what happened to Denny's parents in Xaeltúve, and after what my actions led Denny to do there, I knew my path through the darkness was wrong. I vowed to myself and to Solendaron that I would turn back from where I was heading. That I would once again seek the Lord's favor."

Denny's own shame washed over him as he listened to Marzele recount that dark day in the forest when he'd watched his parents die at the hands of Marzele's companions. He'd come so close to rescuing them from the prison camp in which they and other gifted folks had been hidden away from society by King Davin. The Cult of Arun had beaten Denny to the camp by mere hours and slaughtered every last person as Denny had watched through a vision he could not escape. Distraught, Denny had set the entire forest ablaze. Fire had consumed not only the corpses of the prisoners, their guards, and the cultists but also Denny's father figure and hero, Arnem Wynstone.

"And did you not find His favor?" Gemma asked.

Marzele thought for a moment and shook his head. "I outright rejected Him and all He has done for me throughout my life. I spat on His Holiness and killed in the name of His enemies. There is no atoning for that. There is no forgetting what I've done or forgiving myself. I know it goes against the teachings of Solendaron, but I feel that all I can do at this point is help others, do good works to make up for my dark deeds."

"Someone led the refugees to Ferathan, though," Gemma said. "Could that not have been Solendaron?"

"Now you sound like a believer," Marzele said. Gemma had always been skeptical of the supernatural, and though she'd never outright said it to Denny, he was quite sure she had never believed in Solendaron or any of the other gods once worshipped in Aepistelle.

"I just feel like there's something at play here," Gemma said. "I may have been part of the reason these people—the gifted—were driven out of their homes. I fought for changes within the Committee, but I never thought my work would harm them: documenting their powers, adding their names and abilities to the archives. I thought that if they were no longer being imprisoned or executed for their abilities, they were safe. So many of them obviously felt differently."

Denny spoke up. "However they found their way to Ferathan, Marzele welcomed them. He helped them feel at home."

"They helped me as well," Marzele admitted. "Even though I felt lost, and still do, caring for others has given me the purpose I lacked. I coached them just as I did with Denny, helping them to better control their powers."

"To feel normal," the boy added. "I feel like I actually belong here now that they've arrived. Like I'm not just a freak."

"As do I, my young friend," Marzele said, and left the conversation at that.

CHAPTER 17
MARZELE

Marzele's footing was clumsy as they moved through the foothills, resulting in sore ankles that he nursed during their rests. Even Gemma, who was half Marzele's age, and Denny, ten years her junior, had far more experience crossing uneven terrain. One long hike through what was left of the Forest of Despair and a bloody rampage across Aepistelle on horseback with the Cult of Arun paled in comparison to the experience of his companions. Even when he'd first traveled to Emyhrsen nearly three and a half years ago, he'd been a prisoner on King Davin's boat, and his ride to Xaeltúve was via railroad on a private line operated by the Royal Mystic Committee.

They had camped for three nights already along their easterly path, and now the peak Gemma called Hightower loomed over them, its shadow consuming them and blocking out the early morning sunlight. Marzele sat up under the canopy they'd hung between trees the night before and massaged his ankles and feet. He didn't let the pain get to him, however.

The morning breeze brought with it the scent of the forest that surrounded the campsite, the sound of a nearby creek trickling between stones. It was nothing like the claustrophobic Capital City or Centralia, where he'd been stationed for the bulk of his priesthood. Instead, it brought back thoughts of his old mentor, Bertram, and the man's stories about his days in exile. Bertram had lived and worked on a farm with a family who had done everything the clergymen had passed up in their younger years. Bertram and Marzele had both been so dedicated to serving Lord Solendaron and getting others to walk in the Way of the Light. In doing so, they had forsaken love and romance and procreation until their lives crumbled around them.

And where has that gotten me? a part of Marzele wondered, but he pushed the thought deep in the recesses of his mind, where the Shadow still lay in waiting.

"Tonight we enter the darkness," Denny said from a few feet away. The boy kicked off his blanket and sat up. Three years together, and still Denny's eyes struck Marzele. The wise-beyond-his-years depth. The apparent ability to peer into Marzele's deepest secrets. The loss and the damage and the hurt the boy had experienced—far too much, given how young he was.

"What do you mean?"

"The caverns are near."

"Did you have visions of them?" Gemma asked as she pushed back her own blanket to let the morning coolness wash over her and banish any remnants of slumber.

"No, I just remember from when we were here before with Arnem and the Nazseke warriors."

Denny had told Marzele about that trek through these hills. During that time, the group had had to deal with the threat of two giant beasts called Ogressi. Gemma had also undergone an accelerated training regimen with the warriors, which had slowed down their progress toward the very caves they now sought to find.

"At least we don't have to worry about slaying a giant at the end of our journey," Marzele said.

"I bet Denny could take one down himself this time, if need be," Gemma said. She smiled at the boy. "With all the training you've done to control your powers, you could probably just set one on fire."

Denny's face remained serious and stern. "I don't use my powers to harm others. I've done enough of that in the past." He got up from his warm spot and hastily rolled his blankets up.

"Denny, I'm sorry. I didn't mean anything by it. That was insensitive of me after what happened with Arnem."

Marzele made a calming gesture toward Gemma. He knew that Denny would quickly forgive and forget, but talking about Arnem would prolong the wave of guilt that had washed over the boy. Another downside of never having children of his own was that it had taken Marzele quite some time to learn to communicate with Denny effectively, something a parent learns as they grow with their kids. As a priest of Solendaron, many of his duties had revolved around teaching and performing ritualistic acts and caring for the temple to which he had been assigned. There were others on his pastoral team who had been given the more nurturing assignments of caring for their congregation and those in need.

The trio cleaned up their camp, snacked on some of the rations they'd brought with them, and started on their way. Just as Denny had said, they reached the base of Hightower by midday, just as the sun escaped the mountain's imposing form and began to heat up the valley in front of it. As they approached the mountain, Marzele noticed the holes that dotted not just the bottom but the faces of the cliffs. Each one swallowed the light. Each was full of shadows.

Gemma stopped a few feet ahead, and Denny followed suit. They turned and looked at Marzele. He knew they would see reluctance on his face.

"Are you sure you're up for this?" Gemma asked.

Marzele knew his actions had led to Arnem's death at Denny's hand. His own failures had led him to this place. He swallowed his fear.

"Let us proceed."

They walked on. The mountain had appeared close enough to touch several minutes before, but Marzele realized he'd underestimated its sheer magnitude. It wasn't until they heard the sounds that they were truly only minutes from stepping inside.

The noises emanated from the many nooks in the cliff face and the half dozen cave entrances around ground level. It sounded like a choir of children completely off their rockers, babbling incoherent phrases, calling over each other in a contest of who could be the loudest and most nonsensical.

"What is that?" Denny asked.

"I don't remember anything like this when we came here before," Gemma said. They both looked to Marzele for answers. He found a fallen tree branch that was sturdy but small enough to lift, then gestured for the others to follow as he trotted across the clearing at the foot of the cliffs. At the entrance to one of the caves, he lifted the oversize stick, gripped it with both hands, twisted to his right, and then swung it as hard as he could into the stone rim of the opening. It clacked loudly, and the sound echoed through the depths.

Some of the noise stopped. A faint flutter replaced it, then immediately morphed into a loud *swoosh*. "Step away from the entrance," he instructed his companions. They stepped to the other side of the mouth of the cavern as the noise rushed at them. Crows blasted out, cawing as they reached the sunlight. Marzele tilted his head up to see many more crows pouring out of all the caves above them.

"There must be hundreds," Gemma called over the noises. Marzele could barely make out individual shapes in the seemingly endless flow of birds.

"Thousands, easily," he yelled across the opening.

Three minutes passed before the last few crows exited. The sky was dark with birds, making it appear like late evening. Marzele wanted to whisper the words of the Solendaron tongue, incantations he'd perfected during his priesthood to give him some control over the crows. Pigeons had been his specialty, though he'd made do with other birds before, even vultures. He knew better, however. His connection with Solendaron had long been severed. So too had his power to communicate with the creatures.

Gemma and Denny stepped inside the cave before him. Denny turned and signaled for him to follow. He took one last breath of fresh air and entered the tunnel behind his friends.

"This way," Gemma said, her voice echoing off the rounded stone walls. "I'll show you the lair of the Ogressi." She turned a corner to the left, where the cavernous entrance split in three directions. "I expected it to smell worse, but I suppose the body has decomposed by now." She stopped at what appeared to be an oversize entryway to a room and took a startled step backward. "There he is."

Denny and Marzele peered into the room. The skeletal remains of the giant male Ogressi lay prone on the floor. The rib cage alone was large enough that Marzele could imagine laying a canvas tarp across the bones and crawling inside to make a fair-size tent. He shuddered at the thought of running into one of these in the wild, let alone fighting one like Gemma had. She had been the one to slay this beast, or what had been left of him in his old age. He'd slunk back to this hole to bleed out and breathe his last after she'd severely injured him with her machete.

"I'm so sorry," she whispered to the remains. Marzele thought she hadn't meant for everyone to hear it, but the echo chamber in which they stood had other plans. She wasn't alone in her feelings. All three of them had deaths they felt responsible for. Guilt plagued each of them.

Gemma turned away from the eerie scene and headed back toward the main cavern. Marzele stood for another few moments while Denny waited patiently at his side. He thought about how the creature's female partner had joined Gemma and her crew in the battle for Emyhrsen's freedom and risked her safety to rescue Marzele and the elder Calvertsons from drowning in the Amassa River. That act had led to the Ogressi being caught off guard, attacked by monstrous trees, and ultimately killed.

Sacrifice for the unworthy, Marzele thought. *No. Stop that. Get away from me!*

"Tell me what's happening in your head," Denny demanded. Marzele met his eyes and knew he could not hide from them.

"The dark thoughts are stronger than they've been for some time now."

"Is it this place?"

"I only know that no light reaches us here, and we are not even in the caves' depths yet. However shallow, the shadow has already swallowed us. I fear for you as well, Denny. Your visions may be shaded by this darkness. Be mindful."

"On the contrary," Denny said, motioning for Marzele to follow him in the direction Gemma had gone, "I feel no fear here. I feel opportunity. I feel hope."

"Let us hope you are right, then," Marzele said, unconvinced. *Let us hope you will maintain your composure when we're unable to bring Arnem back from the dead* is what he really meant.

CHAPTER 18
KOSAR

The summons to his father's office was quite unusual, Kosar had to admit, but perhaps it was a sign that things were on the up for him. Perhaps this would be the day his father announced Kosar's parentage to the world, his place in the line of succession.

He smiled at the thought as he careened past what felt like armies of filthy servants and babbling advisors. And then the smile faltered as another thought crossed his mind.

Gemma.

Somehow, he suddenly knew this summons had something to do with that fierce, stubborn, idealistic, beautiful thorn with whom he was so hopelessly in love. Gemma, who could not understand the blessing of the position Kosar and his father had put her in despite all her acts of rebellion, who could never just accept the favors handed to her by her king and would-be prince. But by gods, Kosar was mad about her despite it all.

He turned the corner, pushed past the guards who had been leading him, stepped between the two who flanked the doorway, and threw open both doors. They swung faster than expected on their well-oiled hinges and slammed into the walls on either side. Kosar yelped in surprise, then reprimanded himself for breaking his stoic demeanor.

I deserve to be here, damn it. It's time they all see it.

His father obviously didn't feel the same way. King Davin jumped to his feet and scowled.

"Do you think this is your own personal playhouse, boy?" the king growled.

"I apologize, Your Majesty. I did not want to keep you waiting." Kosar winced at the way his voice cracked. He sounded like a child. He *felt* like a child in his father's presence, no matter how much he hyped himself up beforehand.

Davin waved off all four guards, who were watching the younger man's insolence with dumbfounded expressions. They didn't need to be told twice. The two escorts exited first, and then the others pulled the doors shut with the appropriate amount of force. Kosar walked over to the chair in front of Davin's massive redwood desk and plopped into it, but his father remained standing, glaring down at him.

"What's wrong, Father?"

"Your damn manners. You don't sit in the presence of your king until he sits first. Didn't Governor Herron teach you anything back home in the Southern Reaches?"

"Is that a joke? The man is missing a leg. He is always sitting. How was I supposed to learn when the right time was?"

Davin sighed, and Kosar followed suit—yet another meeting had started about as badly as it could have. At this rate, Kosar feared his station might never change.

"I was told you wanted to see me," he said.

Davin arched an eyebrow. "Obviously. Why else do you think the guards let you through those doors? They have orders to keep you from bursting in during one of your childish tantrums."

They fell into silence. Davin's eyes bored into Kosar, and the younger man knew he was being tested. His father expected him to have another outburst, prove that he was not ready to be a public member of the royal family. Kosar wouldn't give him the pleasure. Finally, Davin went on.

"We have reports of dissent among the people, starting in the north and spreading rapidly."

Kosar swallowed louder than he intended. *Don't say Plentimore Valley...don't say Gemma...*

"A couple of our Committee agents are involved, one of them a commanding officer—Palignon. Seems he's gone rogue."

"And the other?" Kosar asked, then regretted it as soon as the slightest hint of a smile formed on his father's face.

"A young man by the name of Kieve Fallbrook. I presume you're aware of the man."

"Gemma Calvertson's partner, yes. I've heard of him. His reputation has been made by Gemma's own strengths as an agent. I assume he's pretty useless without her to lift him up." Hatred ignited in Kosar. *If Fallbrook has tarnished Gemma's reputation, I'll skin him alive.*

"There's one more with them, my men say. You'll like this."

Kosar was sure he wouldn't like it at all, judging by the mocking look on Davin's face. "Who?"

"That no-good cousin of yours, Syntha, has somehow found her way into all this. I never should have let her walk away alive when I had to go clean up your mess down in the Southern Reaches three years ago."

"That's not possible," Kosar said. "She's a dolt. She's

muscle, servant class at best. Does what she's told. There is no way she is masterminding a rebellion against us."

"Underestimating others is a weakness of yours, my boy. It seems your cousin learned from you during the time you spent in that barn with your little pirate newspaper operation."

"So these three are out there distributing anti-Crown leaflets? That doesn't sound so unmanageable. We can easily deal with it."

Davin opened a drawer in the desk. He retrieved something and slammed it down on the desktop.

"What is that?" Kosar asked.

Davin flashed him a scathing look. "A book, you dolt."

"No, I mean..." Kosar trailed off as he reached for it. The golden letters embossed on the cover answered all his questions.

The title THE AEPISTELLE CHRONICLES spread along the top of the cover, while the name GEMMA CALVERTSON adorned he lower third of the book.

"She really did it," he whispered, but not quietly enough to avoid his father hearing.

"She damn well did. So you knew about this? Knew this was coming?"

Kosar shook his head frantically, though he knew it only made him look more guilty. "No, I swear it. I promised to publish her manuscript to keep her working with me back in the Southern Reaches, but that was before you revealed the truth of my parentage to me. After the barn was destroyed and the group was disbanded, I thought she had abandoned this. I thought the idea had burned with the printing press."

"Yet here we are." Davin rose to his feet and paced. "We gave her opportunity. Gave her a new life. Took the pressure off her parents in their little hiding place up on the north shore. Placed her on the Committee and softened our methods to appease her. Yet that insolent brat still betrayed us."

"No, Father, I don't believe she had anything to do with this." Kosar shook the leather-bound volume in his hand. "Syntha must have rescued the manuscript from the barn and set up a new facility. Perhaps she wanted to bring me down after I betrayed everyone back home. I'm sorry I did not see this coming. How bad is the damage?"

"It appears they formed a network to distribute the book. We've confiscated a few hundred copies throughout Pine-drop, Esteron City, and even here in town. But there must be thousands more, as well as more printing presses we don't know about."

"I told you about all the facilities I knew of. I have no idea how she pulled this off."

"Palignon is my guess," Davin said. "We confiscated printing presses throughout the kingdom and arranged for them to be shipped off to holding facilities. It seems many never made it. Paperwork was forged. Witnesses likely lied because they'd been paid off or threatened. They've been planning this for three years, likely printing copies of this book that whole time. The damage is done, Kosar."

"I can make this right. Please, let me bring Gemma back here. I can get her to retract what she's written. I'll make her tell the people that these are all lies, all fiction. She's a nobody, Father." That pained him to say, even if he didn't believe the words. "She has no credibility."

"Nor do you, boy!" Davin screamed. Kosar dropped the book in fright as the words reverberated around the office; doubtless the guards were sniggering at the door.

"Then let's change that. Announce me as your heir, as prince of Aepistelle. Let the people know who I truly am. It is beyond time that I begin serving this kingdom as a member of your royal family with the power I wield in my bloodline. I will bring Gemma here as my bride, and then no one will doubt my word and hers that this book is nothing more than fictionalized rubbish."

"You are as idiotic as your mother was, Kosar." The venom in his father's voice stung. "Perhaps I should just use my powers, though it weakens me to use them at such a scale."

At this, Kosar's face dropped in confusion. "Powers?"

"*Visuexienes*—the power of persuasion." Davin dropped back into his chair. "The freaks I've had the Committee go after all these years aren't the only ones with abilities, you know. I have secrets of my own."

"You mean you—"

"I've used them when I needed to. As a child, when I wanted to humiliate my parents or get my brother out of the way. To undermine challenges to my authority in my younger years. To unite the kingdoms of Aepistelle into one. To—"

"My mother?" Kosar interrupted. "Did you trick her into loving you and leaving my fa—leaving Joseph Herron?"

Davin let out a mocking laugh at this. "Don't fool yourself, boy. That was all her own free will. The woman was drawn to my political power and my wealth. No magic necessary."

Kosar didn't know how to feel about that answer. He moved on from it. "And why do you not use this power to rid yourself of all opposition?"

"These days I don't need to. I got the ball rolling in the right direction years ago and have since relied on my cunning and intelligence. Life would be quite boring otherwise, don't you think?"

"So you didn't use it on me to make me betray my brother and fa—Governor Herron?"

"That was all you and your reckless ambition, Kosar. Your

own thirst for power drives you to do things people don't expect. My own kin, no doubt."

"Yes," Kosar said. "There is no doubt. So please, Father, make it official and let me end all this, bring Gemma in, and set Aepistelle on the right course."

Davin studied his face for what felt like five silent minutes, plotting, scheming. Then he stood and waved toward the door.

"Prove yourself to me first," the king ordered. "Bring her in and show me you can fix this. Show me you're not the fool you make yourself out to be at every turn. Only then will we talk about the future."

It wasn't the commitment he'd hoped for, but Kosar knew not to push the man another inch. He ignored the verbal slap in the face, bowed to his father, and departed.

CHAPTER 19
DENNY

"I should have warned you," Denny shouted to Gemma between panting breaths, his voice shaking with each heavy footstep. "Though I'm able to contain and control some of my abilities now, the accuracy of my visions has been a bit hit or miss."

"You can say that again," Gemma called back.

Denny was impressed by her agility. In the time they'd been running—at least an hour now, he assumed, though time in the caverns could be deceptive—Gemma had dashed, slid, leaped, and climbed with far more prowess than he had. Marzele trailed behind them, and they often had to stop and wait impatiently for the older man to catch up. Yet the creature continued to pursue them.

"Just go on without me," Marzele yelled to them. "I know I'm holding you two back."

Denny had no intention of leaving Marzele behind. They'd come so far together, had spent more time in each other's company than Denny had spent with Arnem or anyone else since his early childhood, before his parents' arrest. Their time together after Arnem's death had started off contentiously, the hatred and blame Denny held for Marzele burning hot for months. But at the same time, he'd allowed Marzele to lead him out of the burning forest, through the desert, north into Aepistelle, and on a cross-country journey in the shadows, avoiding arrest, until they'd found their way to the abandoned town of Ferathan.

"I would never," Denny said as he stopped to allow Marzele to catch up again.

Behind them was the tacky sloshing noise that indicated their pursuer hadn't lost steam. Even if it was growing slower, its apparently endless stamina meant they could not rest for long or pause to calculate their position under the Esteron Mountains at each fork they came across. A few times, they'd chosen the wrong tunnels and gone in circles, only to end up back in familiar chambers. And yet the creature continued to follow.

Three years ago, Denny would have hated himself for his lack of vision. However, Marzele had worked with him unceasingly to boost his confidence, to teach him how to forgive himself. He'd learned to appreciate the times he correctly interpreted positive visions and to deftly avoid the visions that were potentially harmful. But he hadn't had even an inkling of this pursuer in his dreams. He had been confident that this journey would be painless.

And yet the thing had found them and decided to make them its next meal.

They were on their third night underground, disoriented and uncertain whether they were heading southward as intended. With no sunlight entering the depths, they'd had no idea when it was nighttime but had opted to settle in for a sleep when they'd found a wide cavern with a few flat niches in the walls that looked near enough like beds. They had laid out their bedrolls, swallowed down some nuts and what remained of their softening collection of berries, and shut their eyes. Within minutes, Denny had heard a strange sound —moist and sticky, accompanied by the gravely scraping of stone against stone—that made him involuntarily shrink down into himself. Marzele had been the first to light his lantern and search for the source of the unpleasantness.

He had walked a little ways back down the tunnel they had come from but returned a minute later and shrugged at his companions. It was then that pebbles had rained down on his head from above. He'd looked up, and Denny had followed his gaze. The light of Marzele's lantern had barely penetrated the darkness, but it had been enough for the trio to notice for the first time that there was an opening to a higher level above their ceiling. Or there had *once* been an opening. At that moment, it was stuffed to the brim with what Denny could only describe as an oversize slug squeezing itself through. It was bigger than any cow Denny could remember seeing, huge enough to consume all three of them whole.

The metallic zing of Gemma's machete being pulled from its sheathe had yanked Denny's attention away from the monstrosity.

"Marzele," she'd whispered, "run."

"No," Marzele had said. "No no no!" Fear had gripped him as he'd continued to stare straight up at it. It had been Denny who'd leaped forward and grabbed his hand, breaking Marzele out of his spell. Denny had snatched up his pack and small sword, leaving his blankets behind. Gemma had done the same with her pack, but there'd been no time to worry about the blankets. Marzele's belongings had been a lost cause, as his pack was directly below the opening in the ceiling.

Even after an hour in motion, the thing continued to

pursue them. The tunnels twisted, with very few stretches straight enough for them to turn back and see the predator, but those sickly noises told them it was still behind them.

Gemma pushed on ahead. "There must be a way to lose that thing," she shouted. "Can you use your fire abilities, Denny?"

"Nothing in here will ignite," he replied. "I doubt that overgrown slug is combustible."

"Then I guess we'll have to fight it up close, unless—Wait!"

Denny made his way around the corner she'd just turned and slammed right into her. They both teetered at the edge of a drop where the floor bottomed out. About thirty feet away, the path continued, but the gap was impossible to jump across.

"There used to be a bridge here," she said. Denny followed her gaze. Sure enough, tattered ropes hung from the cave walls on either side of them, dangling down into the abyss. A few damp, swollen wooden boards remained affixed to the ropes, the last remnants of a way across.

"The people you're seeking must have used these tunnels," Denny pointed out. "They—"

He broke off at the sound of rushing footsteps and wheezing, the telltale signs of Marzele rushing toward them. He had clearly picked up his pace. "Marzele, slow down!"

It was too late. Marzele came flying around the corner with wind in his sails. He slammed into Denny, who hadn't braced himself for the impact. Denny fell into Gemma, and all three toppled over the edge. Gemma was the first to grab hold of a piece of jagged wood affixed to the old rope. Denny released the lantern he was carrying to free up his hands. His fingers grasped Gemma's hair and the back of her cloak. She screamed at the pain of a handful of her hair being ripped out as Denny managed to use his other hand to grab another board. Marzele's body whooshed past both of them on his way down, narrowly avoiding a collision.

"No!" Denny called, unable to help the man.

Marzele yelled in terror as he plummeted. His cry of shock and terror echoed through the vertical shaft. Against his better judgment, Denny looked down, following Marzele's path into the darkness below.

Except it wasn't pure darkness.

The lantern he'd dropped was down there. Not freely descending but stationary.

There was a thud. Not of a heavy body crashing into stone, as he'd expected—the sound reminded him of throwing large rocks into a thick, muddy bog. Sticky. Wet. Squishy, even.

"Oof." Marzele was alive.

"I think I can pull myself up," Gemma said as her movements rocked the dangling rope bridge. "I just—"

Snap!

The ancient threads gave way. Denny and Gemma felt a rush of cold air as they plummeted toward whatever Marzele had landed in.

Denny hit it and sank several feet into a gelatinous blob, its edges enveloping him, keeping him from falling farther. Then it expanded as if to push him back upward. He flew up a few feet before landing on it again. He caught sight of Marzele a few feet away from him and Gemma just another couple of feet beyond that.

"We..." Gemma started. "I think we're safe!"

"But can you move?" Marzele asked. His voice was weak, winded, but otherwise it sounded like he was okay. "Because I am utterly stuck here."

Denny rolled from his back to his side, though it was no

easy feat. Tendrils of sticky sludge pulled at his clothing and exposed skin, holding him against the blob on which they'd landed. "I think I'm stuck as well," he reported.

"My machete," Gemma grunted as she attempted to reach her blade, but Denny saw that she'd landed on her side, pinning the weapon against the blob. His own curved sword was similarly stuck.

"It's no use, is it?" he asked. He looked up as much as he was able to without lifting his upper body. "That creature will pop out at any moment and drop down on us."

"We may be in its nest," Gemma said. "That'll make it even angrier."

"Solendaron save us," Marzele muttered. His fear discouraged Denny. As an adult and a former clergyman, Marzele was best positioned of the three of them to keep his composure, but the days in this world of darkness had weighed him down. It was as if the immeasurable mass of rock over their heads had crushed the man.

"Wait," Denny said. "Maybe there's hope." He glanced a few feet to the side, opposite where his companions had landed. A jagged board from the collapsed bridge jutted out of the blubbery mass. "Kindling," he said.

Denny took a deep breath, let it out. Nothing. He closed his eyes to concentrate and tried another breath. Another.

Crack.

A spark. The faint scent of smoke reached his nostrils. Illumination, not just at his side but above them—another rope on the other end of the gap was studded with more pieces of the bridge. One board lit up, and the flames quickly spread. A flickering light filled the cavern.

A sicklier scent emanated from next to Denny. He turned his head toward the burning board at his side, where the fire-light glinted off a newly forming puddle of moisture.

"It's melting," he said. "The heat is affecting it!"

"The rope above Gemma is turning to cinders," Marzele called out.

Denny looked up just as what was left of one of the two ropes detached from its anchor. The remnants of the bridge fell several more feet, now held only by one last decaying rope. The flames lapped at the anchor point as if working hard to bring the rest of the bridge down.

"Uh, Denny, what were you hoping to accomplish?" Gemma asked as she stared helplessly at the burning mess threatening to crash down on her.

"I'm sorry," Denny said. "I just thought..."

His voice trailed off as the mass below him rumbled. He shifted his weight, and warm liquid pooled around him and soaked into his clothing. As his cloak lapped it up, he found that he could tear himself away from the ground. "It's like it's lubricating itself as it melts," he said. It shook again and made a sickly sound like congealed fat sloshing around in a saucer.

"Can you bring the burning wood closer to us?" Marzele asked as he watched Denny fight his way free of the tacky trap on which they lay. Denny looked at the board, searching for a few inches that weren't on fire so he could grasp it and jab it into the blob's flesh between Marzele and Gemma.

As the blob softened under the flaming wood, a glow spread inside it. The mass was pink and fleshy and translucent and slimy and gooey all at once, but something inside looked like a mutated oversize shrimp.

"Something is alive in there," Denny told his friends.

"And something is alive up *there*!" Gemma shouted as the squishing sound of their pursuer echoed from the tunnel above them. The light of the burning bridge illuminated the opening as the creature reached the ledge above them.

Without concern for his own safety, Denny reached over

and grabbed the burning wood. He ignored the pain as he swung it in an arc over his body and jabbed it into the blubber between himself and Marzele. The creature above screeched as if it felt the penetration of the fiery board. A smaller muffled screech came from below as the freakish shrimp critter navigated its way upward through the gelatinous goo toward Denny.

Snap!

"The bridge!" Gemma screamed. The ropes supporting the bridge tore away one strand at a time. Marzele freed his arms and torso and reached for her, yanked her arm, but the tacky surface kept its hold on her.

Marzele cried out in pain as he ripped the rest of his body from the blob and jumped over Gemma, straddling her, bent over at the waist to shield her from any debris. The last strand of rope gave way, and the fiery remnants of the bridge plummeted, crashing down inches from the pair. He rolled off her in apparent relief. Denny peered down, reached for his sword, and yanked it from its sheathe. A mucus-like string stretched from the handle to the sheathe, but his speed caused it to snap off. He plunged the blade down into the blob just as the shrimp came within a few inches of the surface. The screech it made as it moved cut off abruptly as the blade pierced through its face.

Skrawwllll!

From above, the sounds of the larger slug grew angrier. Kneeling, Denny pivoted his upper body to look up at it, careful not to slip as more liquid pooled around him. Pebbles rained down as the massive beast threw itself off the edge toward Denny and his friends.

Schlop!

There was another wet sound, this one coming from all around him at once. Enough of the blob had melted that its hold on the rock walls had weakened. Denny felt his stomach rise to his throat as he and the blob and Gemma and Marzele began to free-fall. Making it worse, the enormous slug monster was also falling, albeit about twenty feet above them, threatening to crush them even if they survived the eventual landing.

Denny realized he still held his sword. He thrust it upward, hoping the larger creature would be impaled on the blade should it come crashing down on him.

Splash!

Frigid water consumed Denny. Darkness overtook his vision as he sank down into what must have been an underground lake. Pressure weighed him down. His last thought was that the slug must be crushing him as they all submerged to the bottom of this body of water. And then he thought no more.

CHAPTER 20
DENNY

Denny's slumber held no visions of what was to come. No memories of what had been. No visits from his mother from beyond the grave. Just darkness.

This is what death feels like, isn't it? he asked himself. *This is... Wait. No. If I'm thinking this, I'm still alive. I'm—*

Laughter pulled him out of the darkness. Denny's eyes snapped open, yet his vision was blurry, as if he were staring through a window smeared with grease. Even so, he could see the whale-size slug levitating six feet above him.

Liquid dripped off the creature, splashing down onto Denny's face. It was thicker than water, snot-like. A putrid odor came off of it, stinging Denny's nostrils as the stringy stuff stretched down his cheeks.

Is it dead? he wondered, but the answer came to him immediately, as if the thing had heard him think it. The monstrosity squirmed, sending it swinging erratically and causing more slime to rain down on Denny. It let out a wheezing squeal, high pitched like the ringing Denny sometimes got in his ears, yet at the same time low and deep, rumbling within Denny's bones. Beneath it all was a sickly rattle like lungs full of water. As the slug swung in the air, Denny's eyes focused in on the ropes that held it. He followed them up to a pair of pulleys protruding from the cavern's ceiling, then down to a group of children struggling to hold up the creature's enormous weight.

No, not children. Many had beards, Denny realized as his eyes adjusted, and they were far too muscular. Squat little men and women. They laughed again, and this time it sounded more nervous than the laughter that had pulled him from unconsciousness moments ago. A couple more ran over to help with the ropes. Denny glanced back up at the slug as it stabilized above him. A cheer rose up among the group.

Motion to Denny's right pulled his attention from the strangers and the beast. He turned to see both Gemma and Marzele stirring from their stupor. He tried to sit up, but he was held down by the slime that had drenched him. He pushed with all his strength and forced the sticky strands to stretch. He watched Gemma's eyes widen with fear as she took in the same sight he had—the overgrown slug hanging above them—then saw relief pour over her when she realized it was being held captive. On the other side of her, Marzele looked up with barely any emotion, as if he'd learned to just accept the strange and terrible things that were happening in his life.

"Our new friends are awake," one of the women at the ropes said. Her accent was as thick as her voice was deep. Denny hadn't heard such an accent before. Next to him, Gemma and Marzele forced their way into sitting positions as well.

"What is the meaning of this?" Marzele asked, gesturing

to the beast dangling above them. "You rescued us from drowning only to taunt us?"

At the sound of Marzele's voice, the creature above them grew agitated. It writhed and wriggled, swinging wildly through the air. Cries of *whoa* came from both groups at the ropes as the little people tried to maintain their hold. Some laughed maniacally.

"Dinner, my new friend!" one of them called out.

"You mean to feed us to this thing?" Marzele asked.

Raucous laughter filled the air. "If that's what you wish, we can make it so!" another said.

"Lower the haruhl!" someone ordered.

Their grips on the rope loosened. The creature came down toward Denny and his friends.

"Stop!" Gemma yelled as she tried to push herself to her feet. The slime held her legs down like glue. Denny tried to do the same but could not free himself from the muck's hold.

It was too late.

The sluglike creature squealed and wriggled as it was lowered. The mouth at its tip opened and closed, raining strings of mucus on the trio. Denny and Gemma shied away from it, lying back down on the ground in hopes of keeping out of reach of its mouth, but Marzele managed to break out of the tacky slime and launched to his feet. His sudden movements alarmed the slug, who twisted and lunged at him.

Its mouth enveloped him whole.

"Marzele!" Denny screamed, though he could barely hear himself over the laughter of his tormenters.

"Hope your friend can hold his breath," a woman called out.

"Hope he can swim," said another.

"You killed him!" Denny yelled. In his rage, he struggled

out of the slime and shot to his feet. He darted toward the nearest group at one of the ropes.

"Denny, wait," Gemma said. He stopped and turned around, and Gemma pointed up at the creature.

It was translucent, its inner workings on display—distorted somewhat by the thick sludge that filled it, but visible nonetheless. Within the monstrosity, Marzele was in one piece, flailing and kicking. The creature wriggled in discomfort, having taken in more than it could process. It cried out, its wheezing worse than before. Muscles and organs flexed and relaxed, flexed and relaxed, sending Marzele toward the creature's backside.

Up and up Marzele went, squeezing through the narrowest portion where the ropes tightened around the creature's torso, just avoiding the barbs that had been stabbed through its flesh to maintain the ropes' hold.

And then the thing erupted with flatulence.

Sprayed its pinkish-clear slime like a geyser.

Clogged at the topmost tip.

Contracted. Pushed.

With a sickly sound, Marzele was excreted in a blob of gelatinous sludge. He fell past the ropes from the highest point of the creature and landed on the ground two feet away from Gemma with a plop.

Ignoring the mocking laughter of their captors, Denny ran over to Marzele and dug his fingers through the clear, slimy sac to release his friend. Once Marzele's head was free, the man gasped in a deep breath. The stench was horrific, but he was alive and well.

"You see, my friends," one of the onlookers said, "not much danger from this thing, only the smell. You ran and hid for no reason."

With that, a few broke off from the groups and jogged

over to help free Gemma from the sticky trap that kept her down. They pulled Marzele from what was left of the sac of fluids. They grabbed Denny's arms, but he swatted their hands away and moved on his own. Once they were at a distance from the still-dangling creature, they watched as the groups pulled the slug up as far as it could go, then released it. The creature plummeted to the cavern floor. Like a glass of water dropped onto stone, the creature shattered open, sending its liquid contents everywhere.

"Come, friends," a man with wild red hair said as he beckoned the stunned trio toward him, "let us leave this place and wash the stench off of you."

Denny looked to Marzele and Gemma. Marzele's expression was shocked, but there was something else on Gemma's face. Accomplishment, perhaps. Victory. These cruel little folks were exactly who she had set out to find. These were the people who would lead them to the Realm Beyond somehow, who would lead them to Arnem.

CHAPTER 21
GEMMA

Their surroundings changed as they followed the odd crew of short, muscular folks through an arch carved into the cavern wall. Once the last of them were through, two of the women at the rear of the procession pulled heavy steel gates closed behind them. The clicking of heavy bolts indicated that the gates were locked to keep something out—or perhaps to make sure nobody could leave. This seemed to disturb Marzele, who jolted at the sound. Gemma reached over and patted his slime-covered back.

"Sorry," she whispered, to which he nodded and resumed walking.

Up ahead, the leaders of the procession snuffed out their torches. Everyone else followed suit. Gemma was confused at first, but she quickly realized the carved tunnel walls were glowing. They didn't need to burn lanterns or torches down here. The light was green, a specific shade that Gemma had seen once before: that of the powder Madame Hvalsi had tossed into the stove, sending an unsettling green cloud through her parlor.

Gemma was certain she had come to the right place.

"Bahrun Ik-Chalak Ghulem," she said, knowing she had butchered the pronunciation but still proud that she had remembered the complicated name. The men and women around her all stopped, recognizing the words despite her poor attempt at saying the name of their homeland. Denny and Marzele looked at her with confusion. "Is that where you're taking us?"

The man with the red hair left his position at the front of the line and pushed past the others. He stopped in front of Gemma and stared deep into her eyes. She returned the stare, noticing that the man's eyes were brown with flecks of green that matched the hue of the mineral glowing all around the tunnel.

"We need to go there, unless you are willing to help us here," Gemma said.

The others around her grumbled in their own tongue. "Just like a flatlander to make demands of their captors," said the red-haired man.

"So you are our captor, then?" Gemma asked. "We are your prisoners? Tell me, please, what we have done to deserve such treatment from you. What was that little display out there—hanging the creature over us, feeding our friend to it, no matter the outcome?"

The man's expression shifted from a glare to a thoughtful stare. A smile crept across his lips. "Not afraid of us, are you? Not like the old man who travels with you." He gestured at Marzele, then put his hand over his chest, pounding a fist twice against his rib cage. "I am Muulik. We are, of course, the Bahruni people, made up of many groups that primarily reside in the caverns under the mountains. We also have some smaller citadels up on the mountaintops, scattered from here to the border of what your people call Aepistelle. South of that until the mountains trickle out, our people remain below to avoid the rule of your cruel kings.

"We are not accustomed to visitors, as you can tell. Please accept my apology for our initial treatment. We just had to get it out of our system, I suppose." The others around him laughed at this. "Still, you're fortunate that we found you first. There are other groups of Bahruni who would not be so welcoming. Now, tell me about yourselves."

"I am Gemma, and these are my friends Marzele and Denny," she replied, gesturing to her companions. "I met one of your people recently. She lives in a town in Aepistelle called Plentimore Valley."

"A Bahruni among your kind?" one of Muulik's peers said. The woman pushed her way from the rear of the procession and stopped a few feet from Gemma, hands on her hips, sizing up the young woman. "Maybe you're telling the truth. You didn't seem shocked at the sight of us. But I can tell you one thing, girly. Any Bahruni disgracing themself by living in your lands must have first disgraced themself quite badly here. Banished, more likely than not."

"Perhaps," Gemma said. "She didn't mention why she'd left your people. She goes by the name Madame Hvalsi."

At that, the woman and Muulik exchanged a glance. Others around them shifted uneasily.

"You know her, then?" Gemma asked.

The woman started to reply, but Muulik held up a hand to stop her and spoke instead. "As Maevin said, it is neither common nor accepted for our kind to mingle with yours, let alone live among them."

"What's so special about this place, then?" Marzele asked, his voice full of disbelief. "Why would anyone prefer cramped quarters, no sunlight, and attacks from oversize insects over living out in the open world?"

Silence washed over the group for a moment, and then, as if on cue, all their new companions broke into fits of laughter. Gemma and Marzele eyed each other in confusion.

When she'd regained enough composure to speak again, Maevin answered, "You really think what you have is so special? My new friend, you've seen absolutely nothing of our world yet. Come, let us guide you to our city."

"You mean there's more to it than these tunnels?" Marzele asked.

"Oh yes. Prepare to be amazed." Maevin turned to her peers. "Let's get a move on. Show these sun-lovers what we're about!"

With that, the procession continued. They weaved their way through several more tunnels, past large chambers where dozens of Bahruni labored, using various tools to mine the glowing green minerals in the cavern walls. They loaded their haul into carts on a sophisticated network of tracks not unlike the one that made up Aepistelle's railroad system. Some carts were harnessed to creatures that resembled the enormous slug that had pursued Gemma and her friends just hours earlier, only smaller and less translucent—these had spotted brown skin. Most of the miners' attention was focused on their work, though those who chanced looks at the passersby did double takes at the sight of the taller trio from the world outside of the mountains and glared with distrust or disgust.

"Almost there," Muulik assured them after about an hour. "Come around this bend, and your eyes will be opened."

Gemma turned to her friends and took in the smile on Denny's face. The boy had claimed he hadn't had visions of what was to come, but he had not expressed any of his characteristic worry. From the time Gemma had first met him, Denny had never been a happy-go-lucky boy. The hardships he'd endured—losing his parents at a young age, living on the streets of Esteron, having powers that fed him dark images as he slept—meant he carried the weight of the world on his shoulders. In the last three years, though, despite the tragedies that had befallen him, his growing control of his abilities seemed to have taken the edge off. That, plus the prospect of reconnecting with Arnem, seemed to make him eager to follow the Bahruni wherever they led.

"Prepare to be amazed," Maevin said, repeating her earlier statement. "Nothing better than a city in Bahrun. Surely not those sorry towns you have in your land, no offense."

They followed their companions around a bend, and the air changed. The mustiness was replaced by a fresh breeze, reminding Gemma of standing on a mountaintop. The Bahruni folks ahead of her stepped to either side and let her and her friends pass to a ledge.

They were in a space bigger than the largest arenas she'd seen in her travels around Aepistelle. The roof of the cavern towered so high above Gemma, she could not see it. Instead, the mineral glow created what looked to be an illuminated emerald-green sky, the brightness similar to that of a dusky-pink summer evening in those last few moments before the sun disappeared completely. Below, stretching out over an area that appeared to be as big as a town like Pinedrop, buildings overlooked cobblestone streets. Most were one to three stories tall, but every few blocks there were taller towers, standing what Gemma thought must be eight to ten stories high. They were all made of brick or stone, though she thought she also saw beams of thick wood here and there that must have come from the forests on top of the Esteron Mountains. The city's residents were everywhere, going about their business: shopping at the open-air market, running errands, taking leisurely walks, everything Gemma would expect to see city people doing.

"This is not the capital city?" she asked Maevin.

Maevin scoffed. "That would be an insult to the people of Bahrun-Ahk. No, girly, this is but a fraction of the size of Bahrun-Ahk. Its walls are speckled with gold and silver, its wealth beyond comprehension to those of us here. No, this is a working town full of regular people. We are the lifeblood of the Bahruni people. Those in the capital are elitist soul-suckers. The best part of our country is right here."

"Don't go poisoning her already, Maevin," Muulik ordered. He gestured for Gemma, Denny, and Marzele to follow him. "Come, my new friends. It is here that we shall part from this company. Maevin and I will guide you down and get you settled in, and then I'll fetch Kuhlae Jakil. He'll know how to help you do whatever it is you came here for."

Gemma and her friends turned, unsure if they should say goodbye to the rest of their captors-turned-traveling companions, but the others had already left them and were headed back toward the mines, seemingly eager to complete their workday.

"Right this way," Muulik called as he descended an elaborate staircase carved into the rock, the edge of each step lined with a strip of glowing green mineral. Gemma took one last look at the grand city from their high perch and soaked in the wonder of the place before she found out what lay within it.

CHAPTER 22

MARZELE

The accommodations turned out to be far more comfortable than Marzele had expected. Despite the city being built primarily of stone, the bedding and overstuffed chairs and couches in his suite were lush and cushy. Where the air in the caverns had been frigid and damp and dusty, the atmosphere inside the suite was warm and relaxing. Marzele didn't recall seeing smoke rising from the buildings, so he assumed the exhaust from the hearth was piped out some other way. The furnishings hinted at more contact with the outside world than Marzele expected, as he'd gone most his life without seeing more than a handful of Bahruni folk around Aepistelle.

Even the *outside*, as it were, of the inn wasn't all that dark or dour. He and his friends had arrived in the late evening, but even then, the green glow of the minerals within the mountain surrounding them had provided a fair amount of light. During the daytime hours, he learned the next morning, the entire city was lit up nearly as bright and warm as if they were above ground.

"Mirrors," Maevin told the trio as she walked them to a nearby café for breakfast. "An elaborate system of mirrors brings the sunlight down from small openings at the surface and passes the shine on to us."

The complicated engineering and the ingenuity of the Bahruni people quickly endeared Marzele to the folks who were the crew's only hope of undoing the tragedy that had befallen Arnem. He grew particularly fond of Maevin between their march to the city the previous day and the time they spent talking over breakfast. Maevin had collected them from their inn, informing them that Muulik was the foreman of a new mining project and couldn't assist them that day. She had also relayed that Jakil was on his way back from a visit to the capital and would arrive by lunchtime. Muulik had already sent a messenger ahead to ensure that Jakil did not dawdle.

The trio found out that the Bahruni ate long, drawn-out meals when they weren't due at their jobs. One hour into breakfast, Maevin had already ordered a third course for herself. Gemma and Denny politely declined anything after their first course, which Marzele had likened to a sweet potato casserole, though the aftertaste of the mashed tuber differed from what he was used to. Maevin had called it by another name entirely that he could neither pronounce nor remember. For her second course, she'd ordered large chewy sausages of some sort. When she noticed Marzele eyeing them, she'd sliced each sausage in half lengthwise and shared them with him. The spices had cleared out his sinuses, causing Maevin to order a third course consisting of a yogurt-like substance. He feared asking what it was made of, as he didn't think the Bahruni had access to cows, but it cooled the burning sensation in his mouth as she'd promised it would, and the blackberries mixed in were the finest he could remember tasting.

"How long is the journey to your capital?" Gemma asked during a lull in Maevin's stories about her culinary adventures across the Bahruni territories.

As much as Maevin loved indulging them with stories of her own, she seemed put off by any questions about the geography of Bahrun. It was as if she feared them knowing too much about the land under the mountains, lest they report the information back to an enemy for a future invasion. Marzele realized they hadn't given her reason to trust them; they hadn't even fully revealed their purpose for venturing into the strange place to begin with.

"I'm sure Jakil will arrive shortly, Gemma," Marzele said. "I, for one, am enjoying this lovely meal and our gracious host." He took another spoonful of the yogurt, though swallowing it was tough, as he was extremely full. Maevin beamed at him and continued in her deep, cheerful voice.

"Jakil may be old—at least one hundred and twenty, though he likes to say he's not a day older than one hundred —but he's a swift one. He makes the journey every couple of months to visit our leaders. He is what you'd call a priest in Aepistelle, I think. Here he is called the kuhlae. Even though he doesn't hold political power, he is as respected as our board of governors in the capital."

"Marzele is a priest," Gemma said. Marzele turned to her, and she shied away. He wasn't sure what his expression looked like, but it was obvious it stung her, which wasn't his intention. "I mean, *was* a priest."

He didn't want Gemma to feel guilty, so he spoke up. "That's right. For most of my life, I was a priest of the Solendaron faith, one of the more prevalent religions in Aepistelle until King Davin declared organized faiths illegal. I spent years in hiding, and ultimately my personal faith did not survive the trials I faced."

"We all must believe in something," Maevin declared. She put her hand on Marzele's to console him, clearly realizing how painful such an experience must have been for him. His first instinct was to flinch away—he'd never sought out physical touch from others—but he found the warmth of her rough hand to be a comfort.

"I know of the Solendaron," she continued, "though you don't need to guess why that faith never caught fire in a place like this. The sun is a resource known mostly to the more advanced cities, and most of our population lives in darker, deeper parts of the caves that aren't lit up with fancy mirrors. You aren't even the first Solendaron clergyman to walk our caverns. We've had some come and live among us for a time, trying to convert us before giving up in frustration. One caused quite a stir. It was before my time, but Jakil can tell you all about it. The sun priest was abrasive, almost violent with our people, from what I've heard. As if he had a shadow over him rather than the light of Solendaron that he liked to preach about."

Marzele nodded. "There are indeed some in every faith who are overzealous and misguided in their ways. Unfortunately, they're often the loudest, and so people think they represent us all. They do far more damage than good." Marzele had known a few of these priests in his time, but it still pained him to discuss anything related to the faith he'd once held and still sought to regain.

"What is it your people believe in?" asked Denny. The boy looked drained after his meal and had sat half asleep at the table without a word for quite some time.

"There isn't enough time in the day for that, little lad," Maevin said. "I'll just tell you that we believe life sprang from the fiery core of this world. It's why the Bahruni remain as close to it as we can, under the mountains and the dirt. We also believe there is a fire inside each of our own cores, and we can let those fires guide us if we're mindful enough."

"That's quite similar to the Solendaron," Marzele said, "only we believe the same of the sun in the sky rather than in the center of the planet. Perhaps we're not so different after all."

"Aye, I don't believe we are," she said. Marzele blushed as she squeezed his hand with her callused fingers. He met her eyes and froze. They held a power over him, it seemed. After a few seconds, he shook it off and pulled away, reaching for his empty water glass just to do something with his hands. He felt Gemma and Denny watching him closely, clearly having caught the awkward exchange.

The ambiance in the café changed suddenly. Forks were set down on plates, voices dropped to whispers or cut off entirely. A reverent smile spread across Maevin's face. She pushed her chair back and got to her feet, which reminded Marzele of how short the woman was, her shoulders barely the height of the table. He turned around in his chair and spotted the new arrival.

"Kuhlae Jakil," Maevin said as the ancient man and his attendants approached. "You've had a smooth journey home, I hope?"

She held out a hand to him, which he took into both of his own and held for a few seconds, returning the greeting. He was even shorter than the other Bahruni adults they'd met so far, hunched with age, yet he moved just as swiftly as the most agile of them. He wore a beige shirt and matching slacks. His top had a ruffled pattern around the V-shaped neck and a green rectangle stretching most of the way down with a pattern of zigzagging stitching. His feet, visible in the sandals he wore, were perhaps twice as wide and double the thickness of Marzele's own. Marzele didn't think those shoes could possibly be comfortable for long journeys.

"A fine walk, my dear, and a nice sleep in Bahrun-Son-Silak," he replied. His voice was softer and higher pitched than Maevin's, like the roughness had been smoothed out by the decades he'd lived. It was melodic and relaxing. "And these are the friends I've been told about, I presume."

Marzele realized that Gemma and Denny had risen from their seats. Afraid he had already disrespected the kuhlae, he shot to his feet, slamming his hip into the table, which was lower than he was accustomed to. The dishes clanked, and Marzele winced.

"I am Gemma Calvertson from Capital City in Aepistelle." Gemma offered her hand. When the kuhlae released it after a few moments, Denny offered his own.

"Denny of Esteron. Also in Aepistelle."

"I know Esteron well," the kuhlae said. "It's not too far from our capital city." Marzele glanced at Maevin, who looked displeased, as if she still didn't want to divulge any geographic details about their nation to the flatlanders.

Jakil grasped and released Denny's hand, then turned to Marzele and met his eyes. There was something recognizable about them, the look of a man who had studied books for much of his life. A man with unspeakable depths of knowledge and wisdom, a man who notices everything happening around him, meticulously analyzing even the slightest of movements. He was clearly reading Marzele even now.

"Hello, my friend," Jakil said. "It seems we have much to discuss."

With that, he motioned for Marzele and his companions to follow him. The kuhlae and his attendants guided them across the courtyard, down the street, and into the most elaborate building they'd seen yet. It was clear that it was a place of worship with space for hundreds to congregate and a dais at the front for Kuhlae Jakil. Beyond that space was a room full of comfortable couches. Maevin sat on one and nodded for the others to follow suit. The attendants brought glasses of cool water and then left, closing the doors behind them.

"Now, it's not often that we have visitors from Aepistelle, let alone those so clearly on a mission. There is a look I see in all three of you, one of great loss. You seek something here in Bahrun even though you couldn't have lost it here to begin with." He gestured to Gemma. "You are the leader among your companions, are you not?"

"I don't know about that," Gemma said, "but it was my idea to come here. I met someone in a town in Aepistelle. She was from here originally."

"Yes, so I've been told—Hvalsi. I knew her once," Jakil said. Marzele tried to read the expression on the kuhlae's face. He wasn't as perceptive as the older man, but he thought there was regret in it, and a tinge of frustration. "And I can guess what she told you. You don't even need to ask—the answer is no."

Gemma shot to her feet. "If you knew why we were here, why did you greet us so respectfully? Why bring us here just to turn us down?" Denny reached out and grabbed her hand to calm her. She sat back on her couch but did not apologize.

"Please, Miss Calvertson, let me explain." Jakil took a sip of water, then cleared his throat. "You seek to enter the Realm Beyond, is that right?"

"Yes, sir," Denny replied. "You are right that we lost someone, a great man named Arnem Wynstone. A hero, really. He did not deserve to die the way he did. It was my fault."

"I am sorry, young man. The guilt that comes with knowing you've caused someone pain can be catastrophic. I can see that you never intended to harm him."

"I was so angry and hurt, and I have these abilities that I didn't know how to control at the time. I've changed, though. I've learned to activate them only when I need them. I just wish I could have a second chance, a way to undo the damage I've caused."

Marzele spoke up. "The boy is a different person from who he was when this happened three years ago. Nobody holds it against him. It was my fault he became as enraged as he did."

"No," Gemma said. "Everyone was in that position because of my actions. Arnem's death is on me."

"Now, now," Jakil said in a loving and calming voice, "we are not to blame for these things. We all play our roles, but when this world is ready to return a soul to its core, it will happen no matter what."

"I don't believe that," Gemma said. "I *can't* believe that. I cannot fathom sitting around and letting someone die if I can stop it, nor letting someone remain dead if there is a way to retrieve them."

"Retrieve them?" Jakil asked. "Do you think it's as easy as that?"

"Madame Hvalsi showed me a glimpse of the Realm Beyond. She showed me another friend who had died. It was so real—I felt like I could've reached out and touched him if I hadn't been so terrified. She said there was a way to reach their realm. If that's possible, then why couldn't we bring them back with us?"

"And break the very laws of life and death?" the kuhlae asked. He shook his head and turned to Marzele. "Surely you must know better. I can see you are one of great faith."

"I was once," Marzele said. Part of him wanted to avoid answering, but the old man's stare was so knowing, so piercing, that he knew he could hide nothing. "I turned against my god when I was tested. I actively rebelled against my faith in dark ways. Rebelling against death? That's nothing. I don't know if I even believe there is a plan for each of us—when we're born, what we do while we're here, when we're taken from this realm and sent to the next. I thought I knew. For so long, I was so certain of it. And then I lost it all. But I do have faith in something." Marzele gestured toward Denny and Gemma. "These two. I have faith in what they can accomplish. They can stop people from suffering. Bring peace to our land. Inspire others. That's where I've placed my faith in recent years. If they enter this Realm Beyond that Gemma speaks of—if it really does exist—then isn't that the plan of your god, or of the god I once followed?"

"If the Realm is reachable," Denny said, "then it must be for a reason."

The room fell silent other than the whistling of Jakil's breathing. He studied each of them without a word, his eyes drilling into theirs, reading each of them—their deepest thoughts, their hearts, their souls. They remained still as statues, as if under a spell.

"It is true that people have visited the Realm before," the kuhlae said, finally breaking the silence. He got up and began to pace around the room slowly. "It was done on rare occasion, mostly before my time. Many of us have heard the stories, read accounts in our holy texts. Hvalsi was part of a group that petitioned for access, which my fellow clergy and I fought against. We took it to the governors. Eight of our leaders rejected the idea, but the ninth went against her peers and supported it. That one dissenter was enough to inspire thousands of Bahruni to rebel and call for access to the portal to the Realm Beyond, which had always been closely guarded.

"The protests were loud and disruptive, yet the eight governors stuck to their decisions. As unrest grew, so too did the number of guards required to ensure no one entered the portal without permission. Violence erupted there, and many died. Hvalsi and her sister Evana used the chaos as a diversion and slipped past the guards. Hvalsi watched as her sister disappeared into the portal. She waited as long as she could, but Evana did not come back through. Hvalsi made to go in after her but was caught and imprisoned just as she was about to cross over into the Realm Beyond. The guards and protestors stopped quarreling at that moment. They waited and waited outside, but Evana never returned.

"Days passed. Weeks. Months. After a year, Hvalsi was released from prison and immediately resumed petitioning for access, but again she was denied. The best she could do was to learn to communicate with those in the Realm. One of my colleagues taught her in secret, as it is a sacred art in our religion. She conjured a plethora of other souls with ease but was never able to reach her sister. In her frustration, she left our lands and ventured out to Aepistelle. That was many years ago..."

Jakil's voice faded. Sadness tinged his story, and it spread among them all until they sat in melancholy silence.

Denny sniffled, cleared his throat, and then spoke. "Why do your people own the portal? Why do you get to make the decisions? We're all in this world together. Can't we have a say as well?"

"I..." Jakil seemed at a loss for words. Perhaps the kuhlae was not used to being questioned, or maybe this particular question had never occurred to him.

"Do you believe your god made only the Bahruni people?" Denny asked. "Or did He make every living being in this world? Did He make the portal to the Realm Beyond only for the Bahruni?"

"I cannot say," Jakil admitted. "That is beyond my humble knowledge, but it is a very striking question indeed."

"Your world is quite small," Gemma said. "How many Bahruni are there? A few thousand? Aepistelle has more in its capital city alone, not to mention the hundreds of thousands more who live in the surrounding lands. Beyond our borders, there are more nations than we know. There are millions of people out there. We may not be allowed access to the portal to the Realm right now, but one day others may hear about it. They may force their way in here. You may find you are not as safe and isolated as you think you are."

Marzele realized he was shaking with rage, not at the stubborn kuhlae but at his own companions. "Gemma, Denny, that is enough! Jakil does not deserve threats. Please, let us all calm down."

"I'm not making threats, Marzele," Gemma retorted. "The truth is, Aepistelle is led by a power-hungry despot. King Davin has already prolonged his life by years with dark sorcery—I'm certain of it. He's done so much to grow his power and to stay in command. He's destroyed so many lives and cultures and religions with his insatiable hunger for control. Sooner or later, he will come for Bahrun, and when he does, he'll find the portal and use it for his own purposes."

"It's better that we know how it works so we can make sure he never does," Denny said.

"Listen to you two," Marzele said. "You act as if you have more of a right to the portal than everyone else. Perhaps no one was ever meant to enter, not us or the Bahruni. This is all just madness. I think we made the wrong choice by coming here. Arnem is gone. We must accept it and stop trying to position ourselves as gods who can change fate. Maybe we should accept that there is no god controlling our destiny, only good and evil, and it is the decisions we make that determine which prevails. Nobody is coming to save us, and we cannot save anyone else from death. Please, let us go back home."

Jakil said nothing, and Marzele looked at the man with confusion. "What are you thinking, Kuhlae? I don't know how to interpret your silence. I'm sorry for my friends and for my own outburst. I—"

"Hush, good man," Jakil said at last. "You are wrong. I cannot tell you which of our gods is the right one—or which of our interpretations is the right one—but I know with all my heart and my soul and my one hundred years on this planet that there is more to life than what we mortals can control. The very existence of the Realm Beyond is proof of it. Yet how can I say that if nobody can experience it for themself? I believe there is power in you, even if it hides along with the once-unshakable faith you still hold deep down. Perhaps our young friends here are right that the Bahruni should not be the sole gatekeepers of such powerful proof of something greater than ourselves."

"So you'll let us enter?" Denny asked.

"What about the governors?" Gemma asked. "If they didn't want Hvalsi and her peers to enter the Realm, why would they allow us to go?"

"I was originally responsible for the decision, but I did not want to make it, so I deferred to them. Had I said yes, that would have been all the permission they needed." Jakil gave each of them another hard stare. "Should I allow you to do this, I cannot guarantee your safety. In stories of old, some visitors were able to come back, but Hvalsi's sister did not return. I can't say what happened to Evana, but there is a chance your fate will be the same as hers and you will not leave the Realm Beyond."

"We've faced impossible tasks before," Gemma said. "I

may not believe in any specific god, like you or Marzele"—Marzele frowned at her, though what she said was true—"but I've seen so much in the last few years that leads me to believe there's more to the world than we can ever hope to understand. I do feel that I was led here for a reason. I'm willing to take the chance."

"As am I," Denny said. "If there is even a remote possibility that I can undo the damage I've caused, I'll take it."

Marzele sighed. "I would be a fool to underestimate these two. If they go, then I will follow."

"Perhaps you'll find something you lost along the way, too," Jakil said.

Marzele nodded. "I truly hope so."

CHAPTER 23
GEMMA

For a man a century old who had legs half the length of those of his companions, Jakil was tireless and quite nimble. They'd left the city that afternoon after a lunch that had thankfully taken less time than their breakfast. After what she presumed had been around eight hours of hiking through the tunnels, Gemma finally asked if they could rest. Jakil frowned but relented, to the relief of not just Gemma and her friends but also Maevin and the three other Bahruni who traveled with them.

"There are faster ways to get around our lands," the kuhlae said. "At least, when traveling between the bigger cities. We have tunnels dug at angles, half filled with water from the natural reservoirs. Our narrow boats just fit, though I imagine your kind would have to lean back to avoid a haircut."

"It's not for the faint of heart," Maevin joked. "Those boats move fast. You can feel your stomach being left behind."

Gemma took a sip from her waterskin. "Why didn't we take one of those?"

"The portal is not anywhere near a city," Jakil explained. "There are boats leaving that area, but none that approach it from this direction. We're at the mercy of the water flow. This tunnel system we're in isn't traveled often except by the teams of guards that rotate once every cycle. They have an outpost near the portal where they reside when on duty—quite self-sufficient, if a bit lonely."

"I've never seen the place myself," Maevin added. "Never had a reason, since we aren't allowed in. Even the guards who protect the portal always remain outside the chamber."

"I have been inside many times," Jakil said. "I visit a couple of times each year to bless the guards, and then I enter the chamber privately. There is no place where I feel as close to our revered deities and to those we've lost than at the gates of the Beyond. You will feel it soon, my new friends."

Gemma noticed that Jakil's gaze bore sharply into Marzele as he spoke. The kuhlae seemed to revere him, once a holy man himself. Perhaps Marzele returned the respect, but the man had seemed conflicted all day. Gemma could only imagine how torn the former priest was, how his agnosticism tore at the very fabric of his being after decades in the Solendaron faith. He had risked everything to ensure the success of a prophecy, seen his fellow clergymen slaughtered by Davin's soldiers, lost his prisoner and found himself in chains. Even after he was freed, life hadn't gotten easier for Marzele; his faith had been shaken to its very core, and he had been manipulated into believing in the teachings and methods of a murderous cult and had participated in despicable acts before coming to his senses. He had attempted to redeem himself these last few years, but he would not let himself be forgiven by his god or anyone else. It was clear that Jakil sensed the storm inside of him.

Gemma wondered how their destination would affect Marzele. The Bahruni worshipped a vastly different god from Marzele's Lord Solendaron. Which of those gods, if either, was lord of the Realm Beyond? How would Marzele respond to the ultimate truths he would certainly find in the Realm? Gemma feared it would break him.

"I think I should go in on my own," she blurted out as the others got to their feet to resume the journey.

"Absolutely not," Denny said. "We've been over this. Arnem is dead because of me. I'm the one who should go in after him."

"And I will not let the boy go without me," Marzele added. "He's become my ward after everything that happened with his parents and Arnem. All of which is my own fault, I must add. I must atone for that."

"I don't think it's that simple, though. As you said, Marzele, Denny needs you. And Denny, we don't know if we'll come out of this alive. You have a long life ahead of you, so much to accomplish, a lovely girl waiting for you in Ferathan."

"You're not much older than me, Gemma." Denny crossed his arms. "Besides, your entire family is still alive and well. This is my last chance to see my parents again. You can't stop me from going."

Marzele nodded. "This may be your plan, Gemma, but it's not up to you who is allowed to go and who isn't."

"What if you find truths you aren't ready for?" Gemma asked the older man. "What if you find that Solendaron is a fabrication? I've seen you struggle with your faith and expectations. I fear you will leave that place more broken than ever before."

This seemed to hit Marzele with a physical force. He

plopped back down hard on the rock he had been resting on moments earlier. Then he shook his head and answered, though he pointedly avoided eye contact with Gemma. "That is of no concern. I've been hardened by the trials I've faced. It will not be a problem. In fact, no matter what, this visit to the Realm Beyond will bring me clarity I've never truly had, only thought I did."

Denny reached out a hand and pulled him to his feet. The pair turned away and followed their Bahruni companions, leaving Gemma on her own, reeling at her failure to convince them to stay behind in safety.

THE SOLDIERS AT THE ENCAMPMENT NEAR THE PORTAL chamber were shocked to see the three tall flatlanders, but they did not question the kuhlae. It was clear how much they revered him—several bowed before the old man. They brought refreshments to Jakil and his followers, which Gemma and the others accepted with gratitude. If the journey into the Beyond didn't work out as Gemma hoped, this would be her final meal. As she chewed the seasoned root vegetables, she considered sneaking away from the group and entering the portal alone, but she knew her friends would only follow her. There was no avoiding it; they would all enter the Realm together.

After the meal, Jakil guided them along a winding corridor. They'd traveled for at least twelve hours, and Gemma was certain that if she'd had view of the sky, she would've seen that it was the middle of the night. As physically exhausted as she was, though, she knew she wouldn't be able to sleep so close to the portal. Jakil seemed to realize this, as he did not even provide the option. And so they approached the gates of the chamber that would lead them to an entirely different world.

Gemma felt the gates before she saw them. There was a sizzle in the air. An energy. The faint chime of bells that were inaudible yet deafeningly loud at the same time, resonating through her bones. Senses she didn't know she had fired off within her very soul in a way she could not describe. Looking at her companions, she knew they felt the same unexplainable awe.

Around one more bend, they saw the massive gates. They glimmered gold around the frames, yet there were also emerald greens, royal reds, deep blues, and many other colors, none of which looked painted on or tinted. The gates were a mosaic of materials, not just metals and minerals but faded white bones, lush furs, rippling water that did not fall, brown and orange leaves, dirt and grass and rock, all blended together as one.

"When you walk through these gates, you will find your-self at the precipice of another dimension," the kuhlae declared. "All reality as you know it exists on this side of the gates before you, and on the other side is an entrance to a whole new reality you could never dream of, one that our souls will ascend to when they leave our bodies."

He turned and looked at Marzele, Denny, and Gemma, studying each of them in turn as if searching for something within them. Were they worthy? Were they strong enough to survive the journey?

"Very few have entered the portal in our distant past, and even fewer have returned. Whether that was by choice or by force, I know not. All of you seek a person you lost. One of you seeks a faith he lost. One of you seeks knowledge. One of you seeks forgiveness. I guarantee you each will find some-thing, whether it is what you are looking for or not. I do not know if you will be able to leave the Realm with your newfound bounties, however, or if you'll even wish to."

Jakil took a few steps toward the towering gates, then placed his hands on them. The spots he touched rippled as if a stone had been tossed into water. The ripples moved away from him, shooting outward in all directions. The gigantic doors shimmered as if they were thin as blankets blowing in an unfelt wind.

As the gates opened on silent hinges, the ringing bell sounds grew louder within Gemma, the sensations more intense. She stepped through them ahead of the others, feeling called, pulled forward by an unseen force. The others followed behind her.

The chamber beyond the gates looked unremarkable in almost every sense: another massive cavern with stone walls. In the center, however, was a pool. No sunlight made its way in from a fancy series of mirrors like those in the town they'd visited the previous day. There were no torches, no sconces hanging from the walls. Yet there was a brightness in the room that was almost blinding. Green light, the same color as the minerals that spider-webbed through all the Bahruni tunnels, shone from the pool. The liquid itself was the same glowing green, as was the steam that rose off the surface.

Gemma stepped to the edge of the pool and gazed into its depths. She found herself wanting to speak, to sing, to cry. Yet she had no words to say, no song to sing, no emotions to let out. At the same time, she had every word, every song, and every feeling all at once. It overwhelmed her, but it relaxed her. It drained her, but it energized her.

Denny came up alongside her. He dropped to his knees and reached out, not plunging his hands into the glowing green water but letting the steam swirl around his fingers. On the other side of him, Marzele bent over, the tears running down his cheeks reflecting the color of the pool.

"You are certain this is what you want?" Jakil asked.

Gemma snapped out of the daze the chamber had put her in and turned back toward the holy man. She tried to speak but found herself unable. She wondered why the magic of the place had no hold on the kuhlae, as it did over her and her friends. She could only nod, so that's what she did.

"Then this is where we must part. I do not wish to follow you through. I have been stationed in our realm to guide the Bahruni people through their own journeys that will lead them to the Realm Beyond in the ways intended by our creators, much as Marzele has been.

"You must enter the pool. Submerge yourselves. From there, I cannot say what will happen. Those who have returned have been unable to describe what it was like. And now I will take my leave. When—if—you return, the guards will guide you back up to the surface so you may return home to your own people. May you find all that you seek."

With that, the kuhlae turned and walked out through the gates. Gemma noticed that Maevin and the others who had traveled with them had remained outside the chamber, as if afraid to enter. She watched as the guards pulled the gates closed, leaving Gemma, Denny, and Marzele inside.

They all stared at each other without speaking for several moments, then pivoted back toward the pool. They dropped their weapons and belongings on the dry ground. Denny dove in first, fully clothed. Marzele followed suit.

Gemma bent and ran her fingers through the water. It was neither hot nor cold. She plunged into the unseen depths.

CHAPTER 24
DENNY

Denny wasn't sure if the others heard the tinkling of the bells. He'd first caught their tune as they'd walked up the final corridor toward the gates. Once Jakil had pushed them open, the sound had hit him with force. Even that description didn't quite capture the sensation, though. A force would have repelled him, pushed him away, caused him to run. Instead he felt drawn in, compelled to step forward. His full and undivided attention was wholly devoted to the source. He needed it with all that was in him. He walked up to what seemed to be the center of the sound, the lush pool in the middle of the chamber, and dove in without a care for his clothing. Nothing else mattered.

Once he splashed through its surface, it was as if he were inside a living organism rather than a little underground pool. The water was exactly the temperature of his own body. He felt neither weightless nor heavy, but as if he was in his natural state of being, like a fetus in its mother's womb. He was right where he was meant to be. The splashes and ripples of his two companions registered somewhere in the far corner of his consciousness, but he paid them no mind. Instead he let himself go entirely, let the water become a part of him.

It was his lungs that pulled him out of the daze.

Panic set in.

Denny was drowning.

The moment the feeling of bliss lifted, as he struggled to lift his head and swim toward the surface so he could take a breath of fresh air, something pulled at him. It wrapped around one ankle. He kicked at it with his other foot, but a second tentacle grasped that. He managed to get his nose out of the water for just a fleeting second. He greedily breathed in the earthy stale air, but he snorted some water up his nostrils as well. Without meaning to, he gasped through his submerged mouth and swallowed a mouthful. The back of his throat stung all up through his sinus cavities. Lights flashed behind his eyes as shock hit him.

This was the end for Denny of Esteron.

CHAPTER 25
MARZELE

Marzele's last thought before entering the chamber of the portal to the Realm Beyond was that he'd quite like to get to know Maevin better once his business in the Realm was complete. Perhaps she'd be willing to accompany the trio as they ventured back north—assuming Gemma returned to Ferathan with them rather than finding another way out closer to the civilized parts of Aepistelle.

He had not had feelings for a woman in many years. During his two decades in exile from the priesthood, he had gone on a few dates that his acquaintances had set up for him, but he hadn't connected with any of those women. He couldn't be open and honest with them about who he truly was, what he had done for a living, the faith that defined him. Maevin, however, would not judge him for the way he had once lived in service to Solendaron. He was certain of it. And he was sure she was as fascinated by him as he was by her. Sure, they had quite a size difference. She lived under a mountain and he in a manor in what was practically a ghost town.

But what did it matter? Love was love, and he was ready to experience it.

Of course, he didn't tell her any of this before the chiming reached his ears, before he dove into the pool, before he sank down deep.

And now he'd never be able to tell her anything at all.

Marzele of Southplains was dead.

CHAPTER 26
GEMMA

Gemma didn't have to save anyone this time. She had done her part time and time again. She couldn't have saved her friends in that moment even if she wanted to. She couldn't even save herself. The portal was ready for them. Waiting. Expecting.

It was hungry. Greedy. It swallowed her whole.

She breathed her last before stepping into the water.

Gemma Calvertson sank without a struggle and drowned.

CHAPTER 27
GEMMA

The water had seemed so clear and calm and peaceful when they'd stepped into the portal chamber, yet within its impossible depths, it was murky and violent, filled with carnivorous beasts that slammed into Gemma's sinking corpse.

Corpse? No, that couldn't be. She was aware. She was thinking. She was alive.

But was she? She could not move her arms or legs. She had long since breathed her last and had taken in a lungful of water she could not expel. She must have been sinking into the depths for several minutes. Gemma had never been able to hold her breath that long, even in her younger years swimming on the coast with Walker.

Walker...her last vision of him in Madame Hvalsi's bakery came back to her, that ghastly green version of him being consumed from the inside by the creature that had killed him back in Ferathan years ago.

Walker, who must have gone to the Realm Beyond

through the intended entrance, through death itself. Just where she would soon be.

What would Walker be like, should she find him there? Would his body be restored? Would his jaw be torn off, a serpentine creature protruding from what was left of the mouth she had once loved to kiss? Or would his cocky but handsome face greet her, restored and perfect? She would know soon. Surely she'd be dead soon.

She couldn't move of her own accord, but something came into her field of vision in the murky water. Hair, waving in the flow of the current: Denny's hair. Denny's corpse, bloating with the water flowing into his gaping mouth. Beyond him was Marzele. She thought about what it would have looked like if the man had still had that curly-tipped mustache he'd once worn as a priest of Solendaron. How it would have flopped around in the water like the tails of two fish.

A sick, twisted thought for a dying woman.

Again, she thought—if she really could think—that perhaps she was not dead. Or perhaps this *was* death: eternity trapped inside one's own decaying body, with no agency to move the muscles or limbs. No control whatsoever.

And then something else came into view. As big as the slug that had chased them through the caverns a couple of days ago, something careened through the depths toward Gemma and her friends. An enormous fish, perhaps, or maybe an eel the size of a whale. Impossible, perhaps, but what in Gemma's life over the past three and a half years hadn't seemed impossible, only to surprise her and redefine what she knew about her world?

The beast opened its mouth. In one gulp, it took in Marzele, Denny, and Gemma. She wanted to fight it, to kick her legs, to flail her arms around and force her way out, but alas, she could not.

Complete darkness overtook her as it closed its mouth. Its muscles contracted, forcing its meal toward its stomach. An oily substance flowed over Gemma. It reeked. In a different scenario, she'd have gagged, maybe thrown up from the stench. All she could do now was take it. The pressure of the enormous fish-eel-whale's body was too much for her, and somehow, as if she were still alive, she blacked out.

CHAPTER 28
DENNY

Denny had been helpless to swim. Helpless to fend off the massive serpent that had come at him and his friends. Helpless to fight his way out of its mouth and avoid being swallowed whole. Yet he had not been too helpless to stop the creature's digestive process. He'd clogged its throat, along with his friends.

It was in pain now. He could tell because he could feel it in his own throat. Denny knew he shouldn't be feeling anything at all, and yet he could sense the water on his scales. The particles floating into his eyes as he navigated the submerged tunnels that led from this world to the next.

He *was* the creature.

Where am I? What's happening? he asked it.

Calm, young one. Be calm.

I've never had this power before, Denny thought or said or transmitted in a way he didn't even comprehend. *I've never been able to connect with animals, yet this feels just like the few times I was able to commune with my mother from across an entire country.*

You've also never been dead before, young one.

So it's true? I am dead? My friends...they're dead, too?

Silly boy. How else did you think you could enter the Realm Beyond?

Through the thing's eyes, which felt like his own, he could see the end of the tunnel. Blinding light pierced through the water. They were almost there. They were almost gone from his world and into a new one.

The creature swam faster. Faster. The sight of the end had excited it. Motivated it to finish the journey. Like the chiming of the unseen bells in the chamber, the Realm called to this sea serpent, and it answered with haste.

The head of the serpent breached the open sky, and the rest of its body followed, then flipped. Still watching through its eyes, Denny realized it was tumbling through the air. He took in quick glimpses of an impossibly tall waterfall the height of a mountain. Round and round. Down and down. He also saw the sky, a green glow like that of the minerals mined by the Bahruni under the mountains. The ground was somewhere far, far below, unseen through clouds that the serpent —Denny—was quickly plummeting toward.

As if one death hadn't been enough, Denny was certain he was about to experience another.

And then the bird came—a falcon. It called out, a majestic sound, yet terrifying all the same. Threatening. Signaling to the serpent that it was hers, she was its. They would soon become one when it was in her stomach.

But how big could a falcon be? Was this an illusion? The serpent was massive enough to swallow Denny, Marzele, and Gemma whole, so the falcon had to be even larger.

It swooped at the serpent. Denny readied himself for the bird's beak to open, to be consumed in mid-air, but instead the falcon grabbed the serpent in its talons and flew off, away from the waterfall.

There was no fighting the bird's grasp on the serpent Denny shared his consciousness with. The talons' hold was firm. It was, Denny had to admit to himself, quite comforting to be in such safe hands. The breeze felt good on his skin, or the serpent's scales, or whatever. Soon Denny found himself drifting off to sleep, a part of him wishing this was merely a fever dream.

CHAPTER 29
MARZELE

Marzele's eyes opened.

He took in the sky above him first thing. It was tinged with the same green as the Bahruni caves. As the speckles in Maevin's eyes. Clouds formed odd patterns he'd never seen in his more than fifty years. The sun was not yet visible, but deep within him, Marzele knew it would have a completely different quality than the sun he'd lived under his entire life. Perhaps it was green, the source of the sky's odd hue.

An itchiness overtook him, making him aware of the rest of his surroundings. He was soaked. He moved an arm, his hand scraping against rough straw or twigs. A smell, primal and fishy, washed over him, and he remembered that he'd been swallowed by some kind of whale or equally massive sea creature.

A squishing sound. A wet chewing.

Marzele pivoted his head, looked behind him. A falcon the size of a hillock loomed large, its beak and talons making surgical incisions in the creature that had swallowed them in the pool back in the caves. It pulled at some kind of tendon or muscle that stretched and snapped, sending a rain of fishy guts down on Marzele and his companions.

His companions! He looked around and caught sight of Gemma lying next to him and Denny on the other side of her. The boy was rolling over, dangerously close to the edge of what Marzele assumed was the falcon's nest. And if it was indeed a nest, that meant—

"Denny!" he shouted. He pushed to his feet and lunged past Gemma just as the sleeping boy's body rolled over the edge. Marzele caught hold of Denny's waterlogged slacks, but he was weak from his slumber and what had come before it, and he was pulled down by Denny's weight. Down, out of the nest, and through the air toward the unseen ground below.

The falcon cried out as it leaped from the nest. Its talons wrapped around the free-falling pair, and with the flap of its wings, the bird returned to the nest and deposited them safely next to the torn-open fish carcass.

Denny blinked awake.

"Are you okay?" Marzele asked, though he wasn't even sure *he* was okay. The boy's eyes met his, and not a word needed to be spoken. *We'll be fine. Stay calm*, those eyes seemed to say, and Marzele nodded his understanding.

Denny's eyes shifted to the falcon. Marzele followed his gaze. The bird hunched just behind him, ignoring its prey for the moment. Its eyes were locked with Denny's. Its head twitched ever so slightly. Marzele looked back to Denny and saw the boy's brow almost ripple from temple to temple. Marzele didn't need to ask. The boy was communicating with the creature. Of course he was. He kept discovering new abilities, and Marzele could not be prouder.

"Where are we?" This came from Gemma, who seemed groggy and confused as she sat up and took in the view.

"A bird's nest. Miles in the air, from the looks of it," Marzele explained. "Denny and I would have plunged to our deaths had it not been for that creature."

"Can we die a second time?" Gemma asked. "Because I'm pretty sure we already did that once today."

"Today?" Marzele thought about the word. "Somehow that doesn't feel like it happened today. It feels like an eternity ago and also like one hour ago."

"If we're truly in the Realm Beyond, perhaps time doesn't work the same way here," Gemma replied.

Marzele pondered that but could not wrap his mind around the concept of time being anything other than predictable and linear. And yet, *The Illuminarion* did say that in the afterlife, time would not be the same. That eternity would negate measured intervals of seconds and minutes and hours and years. He hadn't understood it when he'd read it, nor did he now.

Marzele walked carefully toward the perimeter of the nest, looking for the horizon, but all he could see were impossibly tall trees scattered about, stretching up, piercing through the clouds. Birds soared through the sky, all seemingly as large as the one that had now saved Marzele and his friends twice. Wherever they were, it was not the streets of sun-tinted gold the holy book had promised. It did not seem to be the land of the Lord Solendaron at all.

Marzele's heart sank at that realization, and he wept.

"Marzele," Denny called, making the man look up, "Tchat-Challai will take us down to where she says our kind roams. Perhaps we'll find Arnem there among the wandering souls."

Marzele wiped his wet cheeks with the back of his hand

and followed Denny. Together, they climbed up an outstretched wing and onto the falcon's back. Gemma situated herself behind them, all three straddling the enormous bird's curved spine, holding on to its feathers as tight as they could, praying their grip was strong enough for a safe descent to the surface of the Realm Beyond.

<h1 style="text-align:center">CHAPTER 30</h1>
<h2 style="text-align:center">DENNY</h2>

"Tchat-Challai, huh?" Gemma called to Denny. She was just behind him, one arm around his torso, the other holding on to the falcon's feathers for balance as the creature soared through the air. He was glad Iyola wasn't there to witness this. It wasn't that there was anything romantic or scandalous about Gemma's arm around him. She was merely holding on out of necessity. Besides, she was much more of an older sister figure to him now. He wasn't so sure Iyola would see it that way, though.

When he didn't answer Gemma for a few seconds, she tugged on his shirt. "You awake?"

"Sorry," he said. "Yes, she told me her name. Or, you know, sent it into my mind."

"You talk to animals now? I knew you had developed a way to speak to your..." Gemma trailed off, and Denny knew she regretted bringing up his deceased parents. "Sorry. But you communicated with your mom that way in her final days. Is this like that?"

"Very much so," Denny said. "There's a first time for everything, I guess."

"And where is your new friend taking us?"

The falcon had swooped down below the clouds, giving the trio a better look at the world around them. There were trees like the one they'd awoken in standing few and far between, stretching to unknown heights, reaching for the sky. Below, the fields of grass and weeds, forests of smaller trees, hills and valleys, and lakes and rivers reminded Denny of Aepistelle. He also saw small, rounded structures that he thought might be huts. He assumed they were inhabited by people—deceased folks from his own realm living out their afterlives without modern conveniences. Perhaps Arnem was down there among them.

Would he remember Denny?

Would he *forgive* Denny?

The boy wasn't sure about the former. He was entirely doubtful about the latter. Denny had gotten Arnem arrested. Had killed him, burned his body to cinders and ash. Had taken the man away from his wife and daughters and destroyed the Wynstone family.

The strong wind buffeting his face wasn't enough to distract Denny from his thoughts and regrets. It was Gemma, her warm body pressed against his, her face so close to his ear, who shook him from his daze.

"How far are we going?" she asked. "I'm pretty sure we're flying in circles. Is Tchat-Challai waiting for your instructions?"

"Sorry," Denny said. "Let me try to ask her."

Denny tightened his grip on the bird's feathers as if that would open the line of communication. He hadn't tried to speak to the creature before; it had just come naturally.

Denny wasn't certain how to begin a conversation, to reach the falcon with his brainwaves.

Tchat-Challai, he thought as the bird swooped through a canyon. *Can you hear me?*

Instead of sending a message back, the bird called out. The majestic screech echoed off the canyon walls, sending smaller birds into a panic. They flew away, hoping to avoid becoming the bird of prey's next snack.

We're looking for someone, Denny though in hopes that Tchat-Challai would understand. He conjured up an image of Arnem in his mind: a stocky man around fifty years old, shorter and wider than Denny, though not to the extent of the Bahruni people. Kindness oozed off the fatherly figure even in Denny's vision. He kept the image in his mind as long as he could, feeling a change in the rhythm of the bird's wings as if she too was focusing on the picture. Perhaps she was digging into her own memory wells to recall any run-ins she'd had with the man.

And then, as inevitably happened whenever Denny tried to remember the brave fatherly figure, his picture of Arnem shifted. The smile on his face turned into a frown, then into a fearful, screaming mouth. Flames erupted from the man's clothing. Death overtook him.

In response, Tchat-Challai let out a cry full of the very misery that Denny felt. She changed course, ascending out of the canyon and rising high into the frigid air.

"What is that?" Marzele called from behind Gemma.

Denny turned his head back and peered over Gemma's shoulder to see Marzele pointing off to one side. Denny looked in that direction.

Darkness, rising up from a far-off forest like a funnel cloud.

It was no cloud, though. Even at a distance, it looked

nothing like any cloud he'd ever seen. It appeared to be made of shadow, though there was nothing in the vicinity that could have cast it—no mountains, no sky-piercing trees, no visible structures whatsoever. He squinted, taking in more details. The land looked less fertile than the rest of the Realm he'd seen so far, as if it were dying, the rot spreading outward in all directions. Corrupted.

What's happening over there? Denny asked his animal companion. *Please tell me that's not where we are going.*

Not with me, you aren't, Tchat-Challai assured him. She went on to explain. Denny relayed the words to his companions:

"Some time ago—when exactly by your measurement of time, I cannot say—a new breed of darkness was birthed in these lands. The Realm has always hosted the good, the bad, and the neutral. All come here as part of their eternal journeys. The durations of their stays are extremely varied. Some are guided elsewhere and then return after an indeterminate amount of time. Such patterns are beyond my understanding.

"Despite the makeup of the population, the souls here respect one another. Many leave their old selves behind when they come here, though whether it's by choice or not, I cannot say."

The falcon continued flying, bringing them closer to the darkness, but they weren't moving directly toward it. Denny noted Gemma's grip tightening around his torso.

"That all changed with the arrival of one man. He brought the darkness with him from his former life. It started small. Internal. So strong within him that he could not be separated from it even by death. Naturally, or perhaps unnaturally, that evil expanded outward to those he interacted with. Like a parasite, he infected his newfound companions, some of whom were intrigued by his words, his teachings about a god of the shadows. More and more, people here went to hear him speak. His followers multiplied in numbers, congregated around him. They built a massive camp around him. When some were taken to the next realm, they were quickly replaced by newcomers.

"A society that large needs resources: food and potable water, shelter and clothing, goods and services. They began organizing raids on others who were not part of their group. They employed merciless, brutal violence, the likes of which had never been seen before in this peaceful land. And humans weren't the only targets—they also attacked the animals, my own brethren. My companion. My offspring, who hatched in the very nest I brought you to. All gone at the hands of this nefarious band.

"Their leader has conjured an evil that should not exist here. He has reached through to other realms I'd rather not have known about. The veil between this realm and others is getting thinner all the time. We are powerless to stop him. His name is—"

"Arun Daamgard," Marzele interrupted.

Denny turned and locked eyes with him. The fear he saw on the man's face matched what he felt from Tchat-Challai.

When the bird heard Marzele, she stopped talking to Denny through the mind link, listening instead.

"What do you know about him?" Denny asked the man. His stomach dropped as Tchat-Challai shifted course away from the shadow cloud and descended to a hill clear enough to land on. Once the bird settled, Marzele spoke.

"I know of Arun. He was once a priest of Solendaron. That was a few decades before my time, though some of my earliest mentors had met him before he'd fully lost his way. He was quite charismatic, always with several lackeys who ate up his every word. He was a hard-liner, dedicated to studying and following the earliest versions of our holy scriptures. Hundreds of years ago, prophets of the Order of Solendaron received divine inspiration directly from the Lord Solendaron to reinterpret and rewrite many of our texts. These changes softened the order's teachings, removed problematic violent rhetoric, transformed the religion into a peaceful and loving one rather than the almost militaristic organization it had been for centuries. That helped the faith grow in the centuries before Davin's rule of Aepistelle, as followers began to find it more inviting.

"When Arun came to the priesthood as a young man, he was granted access to the historical archive. There, he studied the ancient texts and compared them with the modern versions. He apparently concluded that the prophets had entirely fabricated their revisions and lied about receiving divine inspiration. Arun told everyone he could about his conclusions and begged them to return to the old ways. This caused chaos among the clergy, though thankfully not much among their congregants.

"Arun was swiftly admonished by his superiors and sent away with a team of traveling missionaries. They were dispatched to the lands far north of Aepistelle, even beyond Emyhrsen. At that time, communication and roads between the Aepistelle territories were still open, and Arun's fellow travelers regularly sent reports back to Solendaron leadership. Until they didn't. At some point in their journey, they went silent. Years passed with only whispers of dark deeds done in northern countries in the name of Solendaron. In the name of Arun, most likely. The whispers didn't spread far, but there were some folks in the order who began to question their own faith—not in the Lord Solendaron, but in the Order's history and leadership. They eventually broke off and became known as the Cult of Arun. They experimented with dark arts they believed came from the true Solendaron, something they called the Tihn."

"Was that the group you joined up with three years ago?" Gemma asked.

"That was a group following in their footsteps. The things they did—the things I did with them—were not of Solendaron at all. They were despicable, harmful, murderous. If that truly is Arun out there, the Realm Beyond and any other realms he may be able to reach are in danger of destruction."

"Hold on," Denny said. Tchat-Challai had started to speak to him again through their mind link. He translated for his friends. "There's a group mostly made up of survivors of various raids Arun's people conducted. Those who want to restore peace in the Realm and resist corruption."

"That's where Arnem is," Gemma said. "If he's here still, if he hasn't moved on to another realm, that is where we'll find him. Can Tchat-Challai bring us to these people?"

Denny closed his eyes for a moment, then reopened them. "Better hold on tight," he said, and the bird took flight away from the darkness behind them.

CHAPTER 31
MARZELE

The falcon soared over rivers and valleys. The wind rippled through Marzele's hair, something he'd gone most of his adult life without feeling. As a priest of Solendaron, he'd had to expose his pate, allowing the rays of the sun to penetrate the pores on his head—a direct way for the light of Solendaron, the wisdom of God, to reach his brain. Now, in his uncertain state, he no longer conformed to those ancient standards. He had watched the last handful of his fellow priests and priestesses, the final holdouts in Aepistelle after Davin's purge, suffer brutal deaths at the hands of the king's guards. A traitor among them had sold them out and walked away unharmed while Marzele's own survival had led to the degradation of his once-unshakable faith.

As he sailed through the air on the back of an enormous bird in a dimension of the afterlife, he found himself reevaluating his beliefs. If this place existed, surely someone or something was in charge of creation and life and death. There was some sort of order, an entity making decisions about who got to move on and when. But it seemed that deity had gone missing, allowing the Cult of Arun to take over and threaten the well-being of all the souls there.

"Solendaron save us," he said, not meaning to utter the words out loud. He hoped the wind would drown out the words, but Gemma's ears were inches from his face.

She turned her head to the side. "There must be enough other people in this Realm to outnumber the members of that cult," she said.

"They're like mold, spreading and corrupting, making those around them sick. I agree that there are likely many more good folks here, but it's not just about good versus evil. It's about the light of Solendaron piercing through that dark shadow."

He fell silent again, and Gemma turned away from him.

"Look!" Denny shouted. He pointed ahead, where Marzele's aging eyes could just make out what appeared to be a large camp. A makeshift town, he realized as they neared it, with several cabins made of logs from the surrounding forest interspersed with tents. Scores of people congregated in a central market, and others toiled in the fields that stretched between the town and the forest.

"The sun shines brightly on them," Gemma called back to Marzele. He smiled at that, knowing what she was implying. There was hope in this place. There was light.

Tchat-Challai circled the town three times, calling out, making sure her presence was felt by all. Announcing, perhaps, that she came bearing the gift of newcomers, of additional souls who would resist the shadow dwellers. In response, the people of the town all stopped what they were doing and looked up in unison. Marzele scanned their faces, hoping to spot Arnem. While he did not see the man they had traveled across the borders of reality to locate, his eyes caught something else: about a dozen folks in matching once-white robes stood in a cluster, as if they were outcasts. Marzele recognized the embroidered golden logo of the Ever-Giving Sun. How could he not? He'd worn such a robe for most of his adult life.

"Have her bring us down there," Marzele ordered Denny while pointing toward the cluster of priests and priestesses. The boy nodded and silently communicated with their host in his incredible and mysterious way.

Thousands of recently deceased men, women, and children filled the place, and likely hundreds of thousands more were spread throughout the Realm Beyond, yet Marzele had already found his former compatriots. "Solendaron guides me here, even after everything," he whispered. His stomach seemed to leave him as Denny got through to the bird, who dropped into what felt like a free fall. Tchat-Challai's enormous wings caught the wind beneath her and slowed their descent just feet from the ground. They landed with the smoothness of plopping down on a plush mattress.

Just as instructed, the majestic creature had landed feet away from the Solendaron clergy. They stood there in their exclusive group, a dozen in all. Even without Horace, whom Marzele had no doubt was scheming in the shadow that loomed several miles away, fifteen souls had perished at the gates of King Davin's castle in Capital City three and a half years prior. Perhaps the rest had ended up in another part of the Realm. Marzele hoped they hadn't turned to the darkness and joined the Cult of Arun.

The eldest man in the group scanned the riders of the giant bird, not recognizing Marzele at a glance. Marzele couldn't blame him; Bertram had never seen him with a full head of hair and without his curly mustache. It was Marzele's leap from the back of Tchat-Challai that caused the octogenarian to give him a second look, and confusion took shape on his face.

"It can't be," Bertram said, his voice a higher-pitched croak than Marzele remembered. "Your work in Aepistelle isn't finished. You are not supposed to be here yet."

With open arms, Marzele approached his former mentor. He ignored the bib-shaped stain of blood that adorned the front of the man's robe and pulled him into a warm embrace.

"My old friend," Marzele said, "I've missed you so. Things never should have ended as they did."

"Damn right, they shouldn't have," a younger man said. Gregory was the youngest among the group of mostly elderly priests and priestesses who had participated in the failed attack on the castle. A couple of years Marzele's junior, he had been the most vocal about his uncertainty that the plan would work. If only they'd all listened to him then. "If it wasn't for your stupid mistakes, like tipping off that woman who worked in the castle, we'd still be in the land of the living."

"Oh, hush now, Gregory," Bertram snapped, his voice tinged with annoyance. "Solendaron forced us to serve in eternity together, but that doesn't mean I want to hear your unceasing negativity."

"It's okay," Marzele assured his old friend, then turned to Gregory. "I would have agreed with you in the first several months after the tragedy. Davin spared me to show me the error of my ways, to make me live in guilt while every part of our plan failed. I..." His voice faded as his companions descend from the bird.

"Is everything okay?" Gemma asked as she came up alongside him. Denny followed.

"Please let me introduce you all to the Inquisitive One

and the Dreamer." He gestured at Gemma and Denny respectively. "I've seen them succeed in everything the prophecy said they would. Everything our people died for."

"So Davin has been defeated?" Gregory demanded.

"Not quite," Gemma responded.

Marzele nodded. "Not yet, anyway. You see, Gemma has found her way into an arrangement that keeps her close to King Davin and his regime. She has a more advantageous position than we ever had. Once we achieve what we came here to do, Gemma's quest to remove Davin from power will resume. His poisonous rule will be terminated in due time."

"How will you all do that if you are dead, my boy?" Bertram asked. He had taken one of Marzele's hands into both of his in an affectionate grasp.

"We didn't die," Denny said. "Not really, anyway. We entered a portal that allowed us to come here and bring someone back." Impatience grew in the boy's voice as he looked around, scanning the crowds beyond the old priests and priestesses. "If you all are the resistance against the evil forces, then he must be here, too. His name is Arnem Wynstone." Denny's eyes flashed back to Bertram. "Do you know him?"

"The Loyal One," Marzele added, giving the title from the prophecies that had led the clergy to act when it had. "He suffered an untimely death due to actions of the Cult of Arun."

"You know of the cult?" asked a priestess named Ganessa. "They've been dormant for years. Since before your time, I thought."

Grief and guilt overtook Marzele. His head drooped. He closed his eyes in shame. "I know of them all too well, and I do so wish they had remained dormant. To my dismay, they became quite active around Aepistelle not long after your deaths. They were led by someone we trusted, someone who is not among us now."

Bertram grasped the implication immediately. "No! Not Horace. He was the reason we were unsuccessful, then?"

"I'm sorry to say that Horace had worked out some kind of deal with Davin. They knew we were coming. He was allowed to live. Once he was free, he faked his own death, then took control of the Cult of Arun. He even set a trail for me to follow. To my shame, I became ensnared in their trap." Marzele paused, breathed in, and released a deep sigh. "I joined them. Bastardized Solendaron's holy name. Did horrendous things to so many people around Aepistelle."

"But Marzele has redeemed himself," Denny chimed in. "He saved me when I was at my lowest. He has helped dozens of people like me—people with abilities—to find themselves and rebuild their lives in a new place away from Davin's reach."

"Now, *that* I can believe," Bertram said. "I always knew that Marzele of Southplains was Lord Solendaron's greatest weapon and torchbearer in Aepistelle. The light in the darkness."

"Which is why I must stay here among you," Marzele said.

"What?" Gemma and Denny cried in unison.

"You can't stay here," Denny said. "We need you back home. *I* need you."

"You will have Arnem once again, my young friend. He will take care of you, and once Davin is defeated, the others in Ferathan can return to their old lives as well." Marzele put a hand on the boy's shoulder and pulled him into an embrace. "I've seen so much growth in you these last three years. You don't need me anymore. There is nothing more I can possibly teach you."

"But Solendaron has a purpose for you, Marzele," Bertram insisted.

"His mission for me has always been, as you say, to bring light to the darkness. That is a battle that has apparently reached beyond the realm of the living. We have seen the rising shadow. It's close. The cult can be here in no time and snuff out what little flame burns here. You must fight back, and you'll need help."

"Then you'll need *our* assistance, too," Gemma said. "We'll stay with you."

Marzele released Denny and looked at Gemma. "No, this is not your fight. You must fight for the living in Aepistelle. You must fight to restore a different kind of light, that of the truth, to the people of the kingdom. And Denny, all your training, all your trials, have prepared you for whatever you may face in that battle. Neither of you belongs here. I should have died with my fellow followers of Solendaron. When that failed to kill me, I should have perished with the cult members I so stupidly joined. And now that I'm here, I won't pass up Solendaron's calling a third time."

"But..." Denny began, though he apparently couldn't find the words. Marzele was right, and they all seemed to know it.

"*But* nothing. I will help the two of you locate Arnem and ensure that you return to the portal unharmed. The realm of the living needs you. Your time in the Realm Beyond has not yet come. It will not for a very, very long time, I reckon."

Speechless, Gemma and Denny left it at that, and Marzele was grateful. He had a talent for asserting what sounded like full faith and assurance, a complete lack of doubt. Before Davin had outlawed religion, when Marzele had had a flock of believers of his own to teach in his temple of Solendaron, there had been many times when he hadn't had the answers his congregants were seeking, but he'd still responded with complete confidence every time. In the years since, especially after the deaths of his peers, he'd lost that ability entirely. But now it had returned. That was how he knew this was right. That was how he knew that his life in Aepistelle was done and his new life had begun.

CHAPTER 32

DENNY

The chance happenings ended there, to Denny's dismay. He and Gemma circled the camp with the elderly priestess Ganessa as their guide, asking everyone who gave them the time of day if they knew a man called Arnem Wynstone. Those who had come from Aepistelle knew of him from the tales of Jestan, and one stout man who had lived and died in Plentimore Valley claimed to have been a neighbor of the Wynstone family. But nobody had seen Arnem in the Realm Beyond.

By the time the sun set—Denny couldn't say how many hours it had been, as time seemed to move differently in the Realm—they'd all but given up. They were invited by a group of kind strangers to share their fire and their meal of roasted mushrooms. These folks did not speak the Aepistelle tongue, for which Denny was glad. He wasn't up for conversation or feigning cheerfulness. Sitting in silence sounded like the best way to pass the remainder of the evening.

But Gemma had other ideas. "I think Tchat-Challai is waiting for us," she said, pointing up into the sky. Denny gazed up and caught the bird's dark silhouette circling the camp in twilight.

"Maybe it's a sign."

"What do you mean?" Gemma asked.

Denny let out a sigh. "Maybe we should call her down here and let her guide us back to the portal. Maybe we won't find Arnem here after all. Maybe all we did was lose another friend to this place."

"*Maybe, maybe, maybe,*" Gemma said. "That's not the self-assured boy I know, the one full of wisdom and premonitions, who interrupted his own life to cross a deadly forest in an attempt to rescue two strangers all because of a dream he had. You and I both know Arnem is here, and we won't give up. We won't go back home until we find him."

"And how are we supposed to do that?"

Gemma looked at him, seemingly searching for the wisdom she claimed he had inside, the wisdom that escaped him along with his courage and hope. Then she turned away, reached for a large stick, and jabbed it into the fire. She held it there until the tip went up in flames, and then she stepped away from the pyre, waving the stick around to signal for the bird's attention.

On cue, Tchat-Challai swooped down and landed twenty feet away, the wind from her wings putting out the flame on Gemma's stick and fanning the larger fire their hosts gathered around. Denny hoped nobody was singed.

As if awaiting instructions, Tchat-Challai's ancient eyes locked with Denny's. The boy felt intimidation wash over him and turned to Gemma.

"What do you expect me to do?" he asked. He winced at his tone, which was full of ice. He hadn't meant for it to come out that way.

Gemma seemed to understand his frustration and brushed

it off. "However you're communicating to her, show her an image of Arnem. Show her who we're here for. Let her take care of the rest."

"I already tried that, but I..."

Denny's voice faded away. Conjuring up a picture of Arnem was simple enough, but the first time he had tried, his mind had been filled with the image of Arnem in pain while flames consumed his body. The same thing happened this time—the last moments of the man's life had filled Denny's nightmares almost nightly since the horrible event in Xaeltúve. In response, Tchat-Challai jumped back away from the fire and cawed.

Sorry, Denny told the bird. *That's not what I meant.*

"Focus, Denny," Gemma said softly.

He nodded, then closed his eyes and thought back to that fateful day in Esteron more than three years ago when he had first spotted the man at the train station. Throughout his life, Denny had idolized the heroes of the Great Journey in the tales Jestan had written. He'd always had a special affinity for Arnem in particular; the man was described as unceasingly loyal to his friends and his homeland. He hadn't saved the world because of personal stakes or monetary rewards, merely out of love for his friends and countrymen. That same man, just grayer and plumper, had stumbled into Denny's life and taken him in, become the father Denny hadn't had in years. He had served in that role until the end. This time, *that* image was what came to Denny's mind, not that of a body in flames.

Please find him.

In understanding, Tchat-Challai let out another call, then leaped into the air. This time, her wings fully extinguished the campfire, causing the group to mutter and complain.

"Sorry," they both called back in unison, along with good-natured laughter. They thanked their hosts for the meal, then set off across the camp until they located Marzele and the clergy of Solendaron. They settled into the tents they were offered and slept soundly that night, Denny full of hope that in the morning, Tchat-Challai would return with Arnem in tow.

DENNY JOLTED AWAKE AS THE ANIMAL SKIN TENT COLLAPSED on him. Even through the material, he felt the gust of air that had caused the destruction of his makeshift dwelling. He rolled out, untangling himself from the skin, and took in his surroundings. The sun hadn't yet risen over the eastern mountains, but the glow of the sky announced that it would soon arrive. He peered over to where Gemma had settled down late last night. One flap of her tent had blown inward and caught on the rope that held it up between two trees, revealing the young woman still sleeping soundly despite the breeze. Her long dark hair covered her face, her chest rising and falling in the rhythm that comes with deep slumber.

Hovering low above him was Tchat-Challai, circling like a scavenger ready to swoop down on its prey. The bird wasn't alone, however—two other nearly identical behemoths trailed her around the camp.

Do you come bearing news of my friend? Denny asked her.

Quickly, young one, Tchat-Challai sent back. *The one you seek is in trouble.*

"Gemma," called Denny, but the girl turned onto her side, away from the opening of her tent. He looked around for Marzele, but the priest was nowhere to be seen.

Come down here, Denny ordered the bird. Instead of

landing and allowing him to mount, Tchat-Challai used her talons to scoop the boy up. Denny barely had time for a second glance at his sleeping companion before the camp shrank far below him.

The dawn air was frigid and thick with moisture. Smaller birds seeking their morning meals scattered at the approach of the massive creature from which Denny hung and the two that followed them. Below, he could make out men and women starting their day in the fields, perhaps out of habit from their previous lives as farmers or perhaps out of necessity to feed the growing population of the nearby camp. Some looked up at the huge birds. Then, as Denny watched, the people faded into darkness as the burgeoning sun quickly disappeared behind ominous storm clouds.

Where did those clouds come from so suddenly? Denny asked.

Evil approaches from all sides. With it comes darkness. The daylight cannot stop the corruption.

The clouds closed in, swirling, accompanied by a frigid wind. Below, dust was sucked into the funnel cloud along with rocks and debris. Plants were yanked from the soil, roots and all. Tchat-Challai buckled from the force of the wind against her wings; even her massive feathers were no match for its power. Denny covered his eyes to keep out any shrapnel and peered through the cracks between his fingers. On either side of Tchat-Challai, the other two birds struggled to maintain their flight path.

"Look out!" Denny screamed, unable to keep his communication contained to the mind link as a splintered tree trunk shot upward, straight into the path of the birds. Tchat-Challai swerved left, smashing into her companion as the jagged tree speared through the breast of the bird on the right. It let out an agonized cry, flapped its enormous wings a few more times, and plummeted downward. Denny didn't see it hit the ground; its limp body immediately became part of the spinning mass of cloud and debris.

Tchat-Challai and her surviving companion regained their composure, increased the pace of their flapping, and broke through the funnel cloud's rotating wall. Once out of the freak storm's hold, the birds sped away, calling back and forth to each other but not letting Denny in on the meaning of their communications.

I'm so sorry, Denny sent Tchat-Challai, but he received no reply. Instead, he could feel the sorrow in his host and her companion emanating like heat from a stone under a summer sun.

They continued west for what felt like hours, but it was hard to tell with the morning sun behind them blocked by fathomless walls of black clouds that stretched from the ground to the ether above. Denny didn't feel like there was enough distance between themselves and the storm. It kept on them, following, expanding, swallowing everything in its merciless path.

Denny's stomach left him behind as Tchat-Challai made a sudden descent. His eyes narrowed when he noticed something moving below, running.

Is that a horse? he asked. He received no reply, but he didn't need one. As the birds closed in, he got a better look at the galloping four-legged creature and its rider.

A man.

Relatively short and plump.

Arnem.

"Arnem!" Denny screamed.

His animal companions called out in their own ways, causing Arnem's mount to swerve off the path and buck at the realization that two massive birds of prey were swooping toward it. Arnem lost his grip and flew off the terrified animal. Inches from the ground, the second bird scooped Arnem up in the talons of one foot and landed on the other in an impressive balancing act. It set the man down gently and watched as Arnem's steed darted away from the scene. Tchat-Challai lowered Denny to the ground and flew off, her companion in tow.

Water, she told the boy as they faded from view.

Denny stood there, his friend's back to him as the man watched the birds leave, perhaps worried they'd hunt down and consume the horselike creature he'd been riding. Then Arnem turned slowly, and realization dawned on his face.

"It's..." the man choked out. "It's..."

Denny took off at a sprint, closing the distance between them. He jumped with his arms wide open, and the man caught him and embraced him in the tightest hold Denny could ever remember. They remained that way for minutes on end, crying into each other's shoulders.

"It's really you," Arnem finally said as he pulled back and took in the boy's appearance. "Look at you, grown into a man." He smiled for a second before his lip quivered and tears flooded his eyes again. "And if you're here, that means you're—"

"Dead," Denny finished. "Sort of, I guess. But I have a way out. A portal that brought us here."

"Us?" Arnem asked in confusion. "You mean..."

"Gemma and Marzele. But Marzele is staying behind. We came for you, Arnem. We came to bring you home to Aepistelle. To Selah and the girls. And...and to me."

Denny studied the man. His skin looked different—scarred from the burns Denny had given him, though not as bad as it should have been. The Realm Beyond had apparently softened his injuries much in the same way that the Priests of Solendaron still had their throats intact after the brutal deaths they'd faced in Capital City.

But if Arnem goes back through the portal, will he still look like this? Or will he be as disfigured as he was in his final moments?

Denny shook off the fear and doubts. He'd come all this way for Arnem, and he wasn't about to back down.

"I can't believe you found your way here to me," Arnem said. "I feel like I've been here such a long time. A lifetime. Looking at you, it must have been only a few years."

"Three years."

"Three? That means my daughters are..." Arnem's voice faded as he did the math.

"They're doing great," Denny said. "Gemma visited them before she found me. Selah is running the business with them, and they're really holding it down. They miss you dearly, of course, but they're making it work."

Denny felt his heart skip a beat. Something was wrong with what he had said. The ponderous look on Arnem's face confirmed it.

"I mean," he sputtered, "they do need you back. In their lives. Their father. I need you too, Arnem. That's why I came for you."

"I know," Arnem said, his voice dreamlike. "I know they're succeeding and moving on as well as they can. I know they've been torn apart and put back together. Somehow, I've been able to feel the weight of their emotions. I haven't seen them, per se, but deep in my soul, I've felt everything they've gone through. And you as well, Denny. The changes in you. The growth. The man you've become."

"But I'm lonely, Arnem. I'm so lonely since you and my parents died."

"Your parents—I saw them. They were here for a time,

and then they were gone. Brought to another realm, I believe. They are at peace where they are, I'm sure of it."

Denny's knees gave out. He let himself fall to the ground, landing hard on his bottom in the weeds.

"You know, just like you said you've been able to feel how Selah and the girls have been," Denny admitted, "I've felt the same about my parents. I didn't come here looking for them at all, Arnem, only you. Is that terrible of me?"

Arnem crouched down and patted the boy's left knee. "Not at all, Denny. You can feel their lack of suffering wherever they are. They've had closure in their lives; perhaps their purposes have been served. But as for me, and for many stuck in this place..."

Silence fell between them. Denny's breath stuttered, his chest rattled, his hands shook. He sniffled, hoping it would preempt a full-on crying fit. "You have unfinished business here? Some reason for staying? But I... I..."

The two birds appeared on the horizon behind Arnem, returning from their venture. Denny watched as they approached, then flew past him as if they sensed he was not ready, giving him more time with Arnem.

"I really need you back home, Arnem."

The man wiped the tears from Denny's cheeks with his fingers, a fatherly gesture from the man who had been most like a parent to Denny as the boy had pulled himself out of a low place and begun to discover who he really was.

"But they need you here, too, don't they?" Denny asked, regretting the words and their implication as soon as he said them.

"Yes, but not just for the Realm Beyond, Denny. What happens here will influence your realm, too, and everyone there who will someday come here."

"I don't understand any of this," Denny admitted.

"Nor do I. But just as I knew deep in my core that I had to take that journey with Maachel and Richard and Jestan, and just as I knew when I met you that we had to find Richard and Gemma together, I know this is my purpose here. There is an evil force taking over and many good souls willing to fight. Many don't have the experience I've had, though. They need my help."

"They need you to lead them," Denny said as realization dawned.

"I've never been a leader." Doubt crept into the man's voice. "I've always had Richard for that, or Jestan, or Maachel. Or more recently, Gemma."

"It was all to prepare you, though. For this. For these people. For this realm. You're ready, Arnem. I know you have it in you after all the trials you've faced, all the obstacles you've overcome in Aepistelle. It all led you here." Even as Denny said the words and knew them to be true, he despised the realization. "You're right, then. It seems you must stay."

Arnem pulled the boy in for another hug. "Denny, I'm so sorry."

"I know. I only wish I could stay and help you, but Gemma and I must go back home. The fight against King Davin is not finished. We must make Aepistelle a safe place once again. They need Gemma there, and I know I'm meant to help her in that fight in whatever ways I can."

"I know it as well." Arnem looked around. "My ride is nowhere to be seen."

"Good thing we have mine," Denny said as he used his mind to call for Tchat-Challai.

The bird and her companion circled back around and landed a few feet away. They both crouched low. Denny walked toward Tchat-Challai while pointing Arnem toward the other bird. "It may be a bumpy ride through that storm, but they'll get us where we need to go. There are hundreds of good men and women ready to join you in your fight against the darkness."

With that, they were off on the backs of the magnificent birds, ready to take on the challenges ahead.

CHAPTER 33
MARZELE

"Incoming!" called a woman watching from the western edge of camp.

"What do we have?" Gregory asked. The man had always seemed to have a chip on his shoulder about anything and everything, but Marzele had to admit that Gregory had secured a fine spot as a leader of their camp. Two of the Solendaron priests had defected and joined the Cult of Arun, Bertram had explained the previous night, but the rest had built up a strong reputation in the area, drawing in dozens of smaller groups and lone travelers. Though Gregory lacked tact with his fellow clergymen, he had charisma in spades with the people, allowing him to develop a rapport that made them feel as if they belonged and even converted some of them to the faith. He was building up an army for the Lord Solendaron, Marzele observed.

And now Marzele was one of them. He was back in it. For the first time in years, he felt the Lord's light shining down on him. He was one with the Ever-Giving Sun.

"Two more of those giant birds," Gemma answered as she

ran past Marzele and squinted into the rays of sun that escaped the storm clouds. She turned to Marzele with a smile. "Arnem is with Denny! I'd recognize his shape anywhere."

"Well done, my boy. Well done." Marzele whispered this to himself but knew Gemma would hear it. Perhaps she'd pick up on the slight tinge of jealousy that surprised even him. He didn't mean to feel that way, nor did he want to. Arnem had been a father figure to the gifted youngster long before Marzele, and Marzele still considered himself responsible for Arnem's death—his own actions had caused Denny to lose control of his burgeoning powers. Yet in the years since, Marzele felt like he had not only redeemed himself but also formed a fatherly relationship of his own with Denny. There was a deep trust and bond between them. He'd seen Denny's first romantic relationship blossom; caught the boy in his first kiss on the crest overlooking Ferathan; taught Denny how to understand and tame his various abilities; helped him mourn the loss of his parents for a second time and the death of Arnem.

And in turn, Denny had given him what he'd never truly had before: family.

The birds landed, and the moment Arnem's boots touched the dirt, Gemma had her arms wrapped around him. Marzele walked toward the pair, not wanting to interrupt their reunion, when Denny's eyes met his. Marzele had become familiar with the emotions in the boy's impossibly expressive eyes, their unique language of wisdom and worry, and he read Denny's feelings clearly. Joy tinged with heartache. Elation at being reunited with Arnem and devastation that it would be for only a brief time. Marzele knew without a doubt that Arnem was staying in the Realm Beyond.

Marzele switched course and greeted Denny as the boy

dismounted from Tchat-Challai. "You did good, Denny. There is nothing you cannot achieve, it seems."

"Except for bringing him home." Denny's eyes flooded with tears. "Or you. Keeping my family safe and actually with me. I can't do any of that."

"You have Gemma now. I know she'll take care of you." Though he really had no clue what Gemma would do once she achieved her goals of exposing King Davin's atrocities and ending his reign. No idea where she would go from there.

His words weren't comforting, it seemed, because Denny turned and walked away, collapsing on a tree stump with his face buried in his hands.

"Back on the side of the light, I see!" Arnem's voice cut through Marzele's contemplation, and he turned to face the man he had last seen as a charred corpse in the forest of Xaeltúve. Arnem pulled Marzele into a warm hug, and the priest understood just then why Denny felt so intimately connected to him. Arnem the Loyal was just that: a man who exemplified loyalty and love and friendship and fatherhood. He was jolly and uplifting and selfless. He would be a powerful force for the Solendaron army, and if Marzele had read Denny's emotions correctly, it seemed he'd be joining the Lord's team imminently.

"So glad to see you, old friend," Marzele managed through the embrace. He pulled back and motioned toward Denny. "There is nothing this boy wouldn't have done to reach you again. He has spent every minute since your passing working to control his powers, always hoping he'd make you proud. It's been an honor to work with him and watch him grow."

"I couldn't have asked for a better mentor for him," Arnem said with the pride of a father.

"What's wrong with Denny?" Gemma asked. "The emotions are too much for him?"

Marzele looked to Arnem, who nodded and answered, "I let him know that I cannot leave this place. We decided together, really. This place is mine to take care of now."

Gemma gasped. "Do you know what we've gone through to get here? You can't just *stay*. I saw your wife and daughters, and they—"

"They're getting by," Arnem said. "They're healing and thriving. I cannot change what happened to me, can't take back my death or the trauma it inflicted on them or on Denny. I've never been one for gods or fate, but being here and seeing what I have seen, I know I'm meant to stay and fight with these folks. Denny has matured greatly in my absence, and he understands."

He gave Gemma another hug, then patted Marzele's shoulder and walked over to Denny, who appeared to be communicating with Tchat-Challai through their mind connection. Denny turned toward Arnem, his cheeks streaked with tears. They embraced with what seemed like finality.

And then the sky went dark.

CHAPTER 34
GEMMA

Gemma sensed the panic of the onlookers before she realized the dimness was more than the moving shadow of the gigantic bird Arnem had ridden in on. A low murmur shifted to cries of panic as people fled to the safety of their tents and cabins.

"The time has come!" the priest Gregory called out. "We must fight back. Stand with me, good people. Stand up to the darkness and banish evil from this realm."

The bird stood tall, leaving space for Gemma to run slightly hunched under its breast toward Arnem, Marzele, and Denny, who were standing next to Tchat-Challai.

"Can someone even be killed in this place?" Denny asked the older men as Gemma approached.

Marzele appeared dumbfounded, but Arnem answered as best he could. "I've seen it happen. These shadow worshippers have attacked other groups I've been part of. Killed them all over again."

Clouds as black as night moved unnaturally fast over the village, yet curiosity kept the four in place between the birds.

"But if people have to be dead to come here in the first place —present company excluded—how does that work?"

"There are other realms besides this one, Denny," Marzele answered. "In some disputed ancient scrolls, so-called prophets of Solendaron wrote about a hierarchy of afterlives while others spoke of an unending pattern of death and ascension. Those teachings were never fully accepted in the Order. Death has remained a mystery to us."

"And yet here we are," Arnem added. "We— Look!"

Gemma followed his panicked gaze to the sky, where five figures emerged from the clouds. They were hard to make out, as their darkness blended in with the black clouds, but she could see massive wings flapping. "More birds?" Gemma asked. She glanced at their two avian companions and realized their shapes were completely different from whatever was approaching.

"Something else," Denny said. Panic shook his voice. "They have riders."

As the creatures descended, Gemma spotted their tails, adorned with what looked like spikes or triangular fins. Their heads had snouts rather than beaks. The wings and bodies were scaly and reptilian.

Gemma reached for the machete at her waist, only to remember it hadn't made the journey with her into the Realm Beyond. Denny saw her gesture and met her eyes.

"At least I can do this," he said, closing his eyes. His head and shoulders trembled as if he was freezing.

"Denny, wait," Marzele said with little conviction.

"Is he..." Arnem trailed off.

A fireball cut through the inky clouds and shot down at an angle toward one of the incoming creatures. It struck its mark, and a man fell from the creature's back, fire engulfing his body.

"But how did you...?" Arnem looked terrified, and Gemma felt the same way.

"I've been working with him not just to contain his abilities but to direct them." Marzele looked proud as he said this.

"I've never been able to make something so big, though," Denny said. His voice was weak with exertion, but his face was full of pride and awe. "I've certainly never been able to conjure them out of nothing. It just felt right, and it worked."

Marzele nodded but motioned for the others to follow him as he took off at a jog away from the clearing. "It doesn't surprise me that your powers are heightened here. The logic of our world doesn't apply."

Behind them, the riderless creature shifted course. It was headed straight toward where the group had been standing.

"The birds!" Gemma yelled just as Tchat-Challai and her companion leaped into the air, their wings flapping. They flew off in opposite directions, and the creature chose Tchat-Challai's companion as its first target. It veered sharply to give chase. While the birds had a graceful way of flying, a natural motion Gemma had seen all her life—albeit in much smaller form—the thing chasing it moved through the sky with violence. It was as if its wings reached out, grabbed the air, and pulled itself forward, its entire body wriggling and gnashing behind them.

And it was fast.

The creature opened its mouth and let out a terrible roar as it gained on its prey, its yellowed teeth just visible from where Gemma stood. Its mouth opened wider than Gemma thought possible, as if it had unhinged its jaw, and it lunged at the bird. It clamped its razor teeth down on the bird's left wing and jerked its head to the side. The wing tore clean off, and the bird spun and plummeted toward the ground. It crashed through the roof of a cabin with a sickening thud. The creature followed the bird down.

Gemma and her companions dove under the canopy of a cluster of trees and looked on as the door of the cabin opened. Two men and a woman fled, but they were no match for the creature's speed. It lunged through the wall, sending splintered logs in every direction, and pounced on one of the men, crushing him, while its neck snapped forward and its jaws shut around the woman. The other man tripped, and rather than scrambling away, he turned onto his back to watch the woman being consumed.

Gemma looked around, finding nothing to use as a weapon. Rocks wouldn't hurt the creature, nor would the small twigs or branches that littered the ground.

"What do we do?" she asked, disappointed by the tinge of panic in her voice.

"You run," Arnem said. He met Gemma's eyes, his warmth radiating toward her, calming her. He shifted his gaze to Denny. "However you plan to leave this place, now is the time to do it."

"But we can't leave you here with all this!" Denny cried.

"You can, and you must," Marzele said. "This is not your battle to fight. You must return to Aepistelle at once and finish your mission. Expose Davin for the evil despot he is. Bring peace back to the people."

Gemma saw motion in her periphery. She turned and couldn't believe her eyes.

The priests and priestesses of Solendaron had formed a circle around the evil creature as it consumed the woman. Their bloodstained white robes fluttered in the breeze. The creature dropped the remnants of its meal and spun slowly to look at those who stood around it. They were chanting words

Gemma didn't understand but knew to be of the ancient Solendaron tongue.

Smoke rose from the creature. It began to shake. It cried out in anguish but did not pounce on any of the clergy.

There was a wet gurgling splash as the creature exploded and rained guts down, drenching the robes of the Order of Solendaron and spraying Gemma and her companions. A smattering of grayish-brown sludge splattered onto Arnem's right cheek. They stood there in stunned silence until the cry of Tchat-Challai broke their trance.

"The bird is calling for you," Arnem told Denny and Gemma.

"We have this covered," Marzele reassured them. "As you can see, this realm is in good hands. My brothers and sisters and I will stand with Arnem and the others here and fight to bring light back to the Realm Beyond."

Tchat-Challai landed a few feet away, the wind from her wings blowing the blob of guts off Arnem's cheek. He wiped off the remnants with his sleeve.

"But how will we know you've succeeded? How will we know you are safe?" Denny asked.

Marzele put one arm around the boy's shoulders, the other around Gemma's, and directed them toward Tchat-Challai. "I will send you a sign. I will find a way. I promise."

He pulled Denny and Gemma into an embrace. When he stepped back, Arnem took his place.

"Tell my girls how proud of them I am. Tell my wife how much I love her and that I miss them so. Tell them I am doing this for them and that they must carry on." He locked eyes with Denny. "Let them take care of you, too, my boy. You'll be in good hands, I promise."

"I know," Denny sobbed into his shoulder. "I love you."

"I love you, too. Just as your parents did. I'm honored to have been there for you, Denny."

"As am I," Marzele added, and shifted his eyes. "And thank you for everything, Gemma Calvertson. For what you've done, and for what you are about to do."

Denny settled in on Tchat-Challai's back. Gemma followed and gave a final wave to two heroes, and then the bird took off into the gloomy sky, sneaking past the remaining airborne beasts engaged in brutal combat.

Tchat-Challai soared higher, and they broke through the pitch-dark clouds and were nearly blinded by the magnificent brilliance of the sun on the other side.

CHAPTER 35
DENNY

With a splash of lukewarm water, Denny's head emerged from the pool in the cavern under the Esteron Mountains. He flailed as a different kind of consciousness came back to him. It felt as if the couple of days they had spent in the Realm Beyond had been just a dream.

He knew dreams, though, better than most. Knew the normal kinds, and the premonitory ones, and the ones where his consciousness shifted to other places in real time. His journey to the Realm Beyond felt like none of those, but now he had returned to the reality he knew best.

Water sprayed him as Gemma flailed to the surface. She gasped for oxygen and greedily drew in her first breaths. Denny reached out and held her arm, guiding her toward the pool's edge. They both pulled themselves out and panted as they lay on the ground next to the water, not saying anything. Denny wasn't even sure he *could* find words that would fully explain what they had experienced on their journey, only to arrive back in this cavern like babies in the womb.

They remained sprawled out for some time, and then a change in Gemma's breathing pattern made him look over at her. "Everything okay?" he asked, but his voice came out groggy. He cleared his throat and spat out mucus to one side.

Gemma sat up and looked around. "Something is different here." She gestured around the cavernous room. There were torches burning in sconces on the wall, providing the only light. Someone had been there, awaiting their return, but they weren't there now.

"Maybe it's nighttime and they're sleeping," Denny proposed.

"Not just that. The walls are different. The green glow is gone."

"Do you think we did that?" Denny asked. "Do you think using the portal diminished the mineral's properties? Depleted whatever power it contained?"

He watched Gemma's face contort as she processed the implications of his questions, but before she could answer, the massive doors opened. The light was brighter on the other side, casting shadows toward them of Maevin and the two guards who flanked her. The stout woman eyed them with a mixture of wonder and disappointment.

"There are only two of you," she stated. Denny had observed her easy rapport with Marzele, the looks and slight smiles that had passed between the unlikely pair during their journey through the tunnels and caverns.

"Marzele decided to stay," Gemma said. Denny was glad she did, as he didn't know if he could get the words out without crying. He nodded instead. "Things weren't as peaceful there as we anticipated. He wanted to stay and help make things right."

Maevin looked down at her feet for a moment, then back

up. The look of concern on her face alarmed Denny. "Well, things aren't peaceful here either, I'm afraid."

"What's happened?" Denny asked. He pointed at the dull walls. "Is it something to do with the mineral?"

"The lifeblood of our mountain, of the Bahruni, has been depleted by your king and his troops." Denny winced at the look of blame the guards directed at him and Gemma, though Maevin's words hadn't sounded accusatory.

"Then that means…" Denny's voice faded out, but Gemma picked up his train of thought.

"Maybe we were followed here." Gemma kicked at a pile of pebbles in frustration. "I am so sorry. We'll do what we can to make it right."

"No, we would have known if anyone was on your trail when you arrived," Maevin said. "You flatlanders are not as slick as you think. Regardless, there is no fixing this. They cut out the heart of Bahrun. There is no coming back from that. This is the end for us."

"There must be something we can do to help you fight back," Gemma said.

"The only thing for you to do is leave this place. I have a cooler head about this than the others because I've met you and know your intentions. Others won't be as generous. Kuhlae Jakil went to smooth things over with the governors while a few of us kept watch for you. We thought you'd be back weeks ago."

"Weeks?" Denny asked. "What do you mean? We were gone only two days."

The guards behind Maevin turned to look at each other in confusion.

"Time passes differently in the Realm Beyond, it seems," Maevin said, then turned away from the cavern and motioned for them to follow. "Come. We have a river craft prepared for you, along with your weapons and other belongings. You must leave now."

They trailed her through the tunnels, Denny feeling stiff and clumsy, as if he had forgotten how to walk. Perhaps it really had been weeks, he realized.

After several twists and turns through caverns that had once been filled with brilliant green light but now required the use of torches, the sound of rushing water met Denny's ears.

"Here we are," Maevin said, coming to a halt. The two guards each took a side of the narrow wooden boat and lowered it into the river, maintaining their grip to keep it from rushing away without its intended occupants. Maevin gestured for them to climb in. "This river lets out into daylight. It'll be a bit of a dizzying ride if you're prone to motion sickness, but it's quite a thrilling rush."

Gemma climbed into the front position. Denny made sure they had her machete, his sword, and all three packs, then climbed in behind her. "Thank you, Maevin."

"We'll do what we can to make this right," Gemma said again. "At the very least, we'll make Davin pay for what he's done. I promise you that."

Without a word, Maevin motioned for the guards to release the boat and turned away.

THROUGH DARKNESS THEY SPED.

Denny imagined it would have been a beautiful ride with the green mineral illuminating the tunnel walls. Instead, they were pulled along through pitch blackness around dizzying turns, down unseen drops. Frigid water sprayed them at times and occasionally fully drenched them. The thought of eventually reaching the warm sunlight excited Denny, and it came sooner than he anticipated.

The light momentarily blinded him. Gemma let out a wordless sound of shock.

They moved down an open-air river, soaking in the beautiful sun that they had not seen in days, or apparently weeks. The river moved them straight along, lacking the twists and turns of the caverns, and for that Denny was grateful. They both relaxed, enjoying the sounds and feel of nature they hadn't realized they'd lost for so much time.

And then Gemma gasped. "Denny, we need to get to shore!"

"Why?" he asked in confusion.

"Waterfall!" Gemma frantically searched, but there were no paddles in the boat. "Throw everything to shore and let's jump," she ordered.

They were in the middle of the river, about ten feet from dry ground on either side. Ahead, Denny registered the sudden plunge. He and Gemma each threw their weapons off to their right, just making it to the muddy bank. Leaving their packs behind, they jumped off in unison and swam for shore. Before they even made it, the boat had gone over the edge of the waterfall. Gemma reached out and pulled Denny up, their boots sinking into the mud on the bank. They reclaimed her machete and the curved sword that Quincy had made for Denny years earlier, then went to peer over the edge of the monumental drop.

"Those rocks would have crushed us," Denny said as the water crashed into massive boulders at the foot of the falls. The boat lay in scattered pieces.

"You should've seen that coming, Premonition Boy."

They looked at each other for a moment and then

laughed. It felt good to lighten the mood after everything that had happened and before what was surely to come.

Once they'd squeezed out their soaked clothing and emptied the water and pebbles from their boots, they set out down the side of the mountain, trying to figure out where they were. When night fell, they built a fire and cuddled close together; neither of them was completely dry, which increased the chill of the mountain air.

After a night of what barely passed for sleep on the rough ground, Denny and Gemma continued their decent. A few hours later, the sounds and smells ahead told them that they'd arrived back in civilization. As they approached a road leading down from the mountains, Gemma pulled Denny into the brush.

"Let's wait and see who passes. We should know if we're near a military base or if these are just farmers or travelers," Gemma said.

As it turned out, dozens of horse-drawn carts made their way down the road toward the town, soldiers on horses flanking what must be precious cargo. The glow emanating from the open flap at the back of one wagon provided clarity.

"The mineral," Denny whispered.

After the wagon train passed, the pair followed the road to a line of stationary train cars, each being loaded to the brim with the green mineral stolen from the Bahruni people.

"Gemma, we have to do something."

Before she could respond, a twig snapped behind them. Denny turned to find three soldiers of the Aepistelle Army, two with their swords drawn, the other unrolling a scroll.

No, not a scroll.

A poster.

He turned it around so Denny and Gemma could see it.

"Does she look familiar to you two? Uncanny. Someone

should give the artist a raise. It seems we have a wanted woman in our midst. To be brought in alive, by order of King Davin himself."

And with that, Gemma and Denny began an uncomfortable train ride into the putrid bowels of Capital City in chains.

CHAPTER 36

KOSAR, THREE WEEKS EARLIER

The castle in Capital City did not hold a candle to the beauty of the governor's palace in the Southern Reaches.

Whereas Kosar's childhood home had been bright and airy and welcoming to guests and visiting royals from other territories, Aepistelle's seat of power was meant to intimidate anyone who set foot inside its walls. Crowded on all sides by the sprawling city, it didn't have the advantages of sitting high on a hill. As if the king felt the need to defend himself from the very people he served, the castle walls prevented commoners from getting close. Hard-faced guards patrolled the perimeter, more likely to spit on passersby than to smile at them. Perhaps Kosar could change that when he came into power, emulating Governor Herron, the man he'd thought was his father until three years earlier. Governor Herron had the love of his people, something that could hardly be said for Kosar's actual father, King Davin.

The inside of the castle wasn't any prettier: cold stone walls; narrow windows that scarcely let in the minimal sunlight that managed to filter through the polluted sky of Capital City; furniture that had once been grand but was now dated, magnets for dust despite the best efforts of the army of servants King Davin employed for minuscule wages. Kosar's own chambers were far from the wing his father resided in. The young man's rooms were surrounded by those of his father's stuffy old advisors, mostly ancient men whose coughs and wheezes echoed through the halls. The common spaces and reception rooms were equally unpleasant, large and drafty and overly resonant, making conversation difficult over the roar of the guests King Davin hosted in thinly veiled power plays.

The first subterranean level of the castle was used only by the servants, from the vast kitchens and food stores to the laundry and mending wing, the dim servants' quarters, and the broom closets and supply stores. Below that, two floors of storage rooms were stuffed with the relics of bygone kings and their families. These rooms seemed to number in the hundreds, and in his boredom, Kosar had explored many. While some were filled with what were sure to be valuables he could sell off one day, others held shelves of junk, from ancient moldy books—he was sure Gemma would love these, so he took note of where they were—to a room crammed from floor to ceiling with moth-eaten cloth napkins featuring the sigils of West Aepistelle kings so ancient that Kosar had never even heard of some.

Down another level, things got really grim: the dungeons. The stench of sewage from the castle's multitude of leaky pipes was intense, though the only folks with a right to complain were the guards who were paid to be there. These men were almost as unscrupulous as those they kept locked away—some were even more deranged, in fact—so they kept their mouths shut about the conditions, lest they find themselves locked up, too. Kosar had asked one of the guards a few months back about how many prisoners there were.

"On which floor?" the near-toothless man had mumbled.

"You mean this goes deeper?" Kosar had asked, and he'd learned that there were four more floors below them. The stench of death and decay had sickened him, so he hadn't explored further lest he run into cell after cell of dead forgotten convicts left to rot.

He had a purpose for being here on this particular morning, however. Today there was a special guest he had come to see. After descending the winding stairs, he ran into the same man he'd spoken with previously. The man flashed a smile, revealing dark gray gums, the couple of visible teeth on the sides protruding at odd angles and glistening a sickly yellowish brown.

"It ain't often we get repeat visitors. Must be my lucky day," the man said, and Kosar was taken aback by his good humor in such a disgusting place.

"I'm here to see one of your new arrivals," he said in the stiff manner of royalty. It wasn't a tone he'd learned from his upbringing; Governor Herron had been a man of the people and had not used such mannerisms to separate himself from those he served. It was something Kosar had picked up in the last couple years as he'd spent more and more time with King Davin, observing the man whose position he yearned to inherit, replicating all his techniques and habits as best he could to prepare for the throne.

"Ahh, the wee little one? What's your business with her?" the man asked, or at least that was how Kosar translated the sounds he made. It was hard to tell—with no front teeth, his *t*'s and *s*'s became airy, meaningless noises.

"She was brought in under my orders. Now, gather her up and bring her to the interrogation room. I'll be waiting."

"Will you be needing the tools?" the guard asked.

"Tools for what?" Kosar asked, then flinched at the realization. "Gods, no, there will be no torture. At least not yet."

"Never a bad option, being prepared and all." Disappointment tinged the guard's voice. "But all right, I'll bring her in, and you can let me know if you change your mind."

With that, Kosar stalked down the hallway to the interrogation room. There were several, but he chose the one that held the least *persuasive equipment* and had the fewest bloodstains on the floor. And walls. And ceiling, really.

Kosar paced around the room. There were chairs, but he didn't dare touch them. He hadn't a clue what kinds of bodily fluids had been spilled on them, which severed body parts may have landed on them. He was just thinking about how he'd burn his boots upon his return to the upper levels when the door opened and the guard shoved a woman inside.

"Knock when you're ready for me to collect her," the guard said, "or if you need any special tools." With that, he shut the door and locked it from the outside.

Kosar looked the woman over. Just as the spy he'd sent after Gemma to Plentimore Valley had described, this lady stood just taller than his waist, though she could not be mistaken for a child. Her hair was streaked with gray and white, and her skin was creased with age and appeared rough from years of labor and hard living. Her limbs and body were thick, as if she had larger bones than average, more muscle. And then there were her eyes, which looked different from those of any person Kosar had ever met. He could read the hatred in them.

"What do you want from me? I've done nothing wrong." She walked across the room and plopped down on one of the chairs. Climbed onto it, more like.

"Tell me who you are," Kosar demanded.

"My name is Hvalsi. I'm a baker from Plentimore Valley. Did your hounds not tell you this? They should know—they arrested me right in front of my patrons as I was serving cake and tea."

"Hvalsi. Madame Hvalsi—yes, I've heard of you. Best pastries in all of Western Aepistelle, some might say. Serving locals and tourists alike, fattening them up with your delectable goodies. And yet that isn't enough for you, is it? You have another business going on behind all that."

"A business collects money for profit. I know what you're getting at, but I don't charge for that."

"And what is 'that,' exactly? Telling fortunes?" Kosar's boot crunched over something. He looked down to see powdered remnants of what he thought were bones. He grimaced and kicked them away.

Hvalsi glared at him. "I'm not some lying fortune-teller. And I don't have gifts, either, so you can keep your Royal Mystic Committee dogs from sniffing at me."

"One of those dogs was a woman, was it not?"

She rolled her eyes. "I didn't invite her to snoop around. Someone told her about me, sent her to me. I had nothing to do with it."

"And yet you entertained her. Tell me, what service did you render her?"

Kosar saw a look of fear on the little woman's scrunched face. "She...she came to talk to the dead."

"Talk to the *dead*," Kosar said with a mocking tone. "So you are a medium, then? Is that the right term?"

"I have the ability to speak with souls in the Realm Beyond," Hvalsi admitted. "There's a connection my people have that—"

"People? Who are your people?"

"I came from the Mountain Citadel. The Bahruni people.

There is an ancient tradition, a practice only some of us are trained in. We can commune with those who have passed on from this life, can help others reach out to those they have lost."

Kosar scoffed. "Do I look like a fool to you?"

"Do you really want me to answer that?" Hvalsi shot back. Kosar felt his lips curl upward. Maybe he liked this woman after all, or would have in other circumstances. Hvalsi went on. "It's not just magic mumbo-jumbo. There is a mineral that my people mine from deep beneath the Esteron Mountains. It spreads like veins through the rock. It is sacred to us and has countless purposes. I smuggled some out when I left my people, and for that crime I am no longer allowed to return."

"And this mineral allows you to talk to the dead?"

"It's more than that. It connects our world to others, our reality to other realities. It connects the land of the living to the afterlife. There are some, like me, who have been trained in various arts that utilize the mineral. We all have our own specialties, and communing with those in the Realm Beyond is one of mine."

"So Gemma Calvertson, the agent of the Committee who visited you, sought to speak to the dead?"

"More than that, I think," Hvalsi said. "She seemed to want to visit them. To find someone among them."

Kosar thought about that for a while as he paced the room. Who could Gemma have lost for whom she'd risk her burgeoning career? Her parents were alive. According to reports from sources overseas, her brother had been traveling on ships with Jestan the Just for the last few years, playing savior to folks in need in the island nations. Richard the Elusive was alleged to be rebuilding Emyhrsen in the north. There was the late Arnem the Loyal, but what good would come of bringing back that charred wreck of a man? And there were her other companions, like the boy Denny and the Solendaron priest, but they hadn't been seen since Arnem's death.

"What else can this mineral do?" Kosar asked. "What kinds of powers does it grant?"

"Why, it is without limits if one knows the right ways to manipulate it. We use it for everything from lighting and heating our cavernous cities to making medicines."

"Medicines?" Kosar reached into his pocket and retrieved a sack that his spy had brought back from Hvalsi's bakery. He loosened the string and peered inside. The glow of the contents cast his face in a warm green light. "This rock can do all that?"

"How do you think we live so long?"

"What do you mean?" Without thinking, he plopped down in one of the chairs at last and stared hard into the woman's strange eyes.

"The Bahruni are not plagued by serious injury or illness. We live much longer than your kind."

"By consuming the rock?"

"We're surrounded by it in the caverns. Its powder fills the air we breathe."

Kosar forgot all about Gemma's use of the mineral. There was someone who would not be able to ignore him after this discovery. He rose to his feet, walked behind Madame Hvalsi's chair, and rested a hand on the woman's shoulder. "I think you and I are going to be good friends, my dear."

"You mean you'll let me go?"

"Not quite yet, but obviously this has all been a misunderstanding. I'll be sure my father compensates you fairly."

"Your father? Who is he?"

"Oh, you'll know soon enough. Everyone will know soon enough. Come with me, and I'll find you some more comfortable accommodations, even for someone who grew up in a hole in the ground."

With that, he led her out of the dungeons, ignoring the angry cries of the toothless guard who now had one fewer prisoner to torment.

One week later, Kosar rode with a train full of soldiers and miners to Esteron, journeyed on a wagon through the hills, and began plundering Bahrun Ik-Chalak Ghulem.

CHAPTER 37
JESTAN

The tension grew thick like the humidity in the air of Emyhrsen's castle. In his time on the seas, Jestan had longed for stable ground, and he'd relished his first few months in Emyhrsen. Since Gemma's brief visit, however, both Richard and George had been entirely on edge. Richard often paced the audience chamber in the middle of the night, fretting. George escaped to the castle's workshop and rekindled his old love for blacksmithing, whacking his worries out with a massive hammer.

Jestan, meanwhile, kept himself occupied with the work he'd committed to doing: helping the people of Emyhrsen rebuild their lives and their society following decades of enslavement by the Tzakabyan invaders. His biggest headache was figuring out what to do with the few Tzakabyans left behind—those who had formed bonds with people in Emyhrsen—the partners who loved them, and their mixed children. While these individuals had severed ties with their slaver kin, they were still seen as monsters by most people in Emyhrsen. Their homes were frequently vandalized or destroyed. Many had been subject to violence while dozens stood by and watched. Jestan understood the frustration and trauma of the Emyhrseni, but he couldn't let them commit murder against individuals who wanted only peace.

And so he'd worked up a plan: he would move them into the abandoned castle across the river that had once belonged to the Ancient Ones. This would remove the individuals who so reminded the Emyhrseni people of their prior captors, giving them time to cool down and heal and move on. It would also give their children an opportunity for an education and a peaceful life for the time being. Jestan had even found a few folks willing to work as teachers for the kids. There was enough land around the castle for farming and hunting, so they'd practically be self-sustaining. Not everyone in Emyhrsen was happy about these outliers being awarded a castle of their own, but it was the best solution anyone had come up with, and Richard fully supported it.

For the last three weeks, Jestan had been traveling back and forth between the two castles, securing resources and personnel, commissioning repairs to make the abandoned castle habitable, and convincing the mixed families that moving there was their best option for the time being. He was quite proud of himself, even if Richard and George had been too preoccupied to appreciate his achievements. It was a far cry from the applause he had received nightly for his theatrical performances in Aepistelle, the adoration of fans, the rush of adrenaline from the curtains pulling back and the orchestra striking up a tune. This life was nothing like the one he'd spent more than twenty years relishing, and yet he was beginning to realize he had never been more satisfied.

If only Roddy could see me now, he thought.

Rodnego Deveron had been his manager and partner in his former life. The man had traveled with him across Aepistelle and the neighboring island nations, securing the most impressive stages and booking peerless musicians to bring his shows to life. Outside of their business, Roddy had been a friend. A housemate. A protector. Their last conversation had involved Jestan screaming at Roddy for intercepting a series of letters Richard had sent him over the course of several years, pleading for him to join the battle against a coming evil. Jestan had been furious when he'd found out but later realized that Roddy had only been trying to protect him from the prying eyes of the Royal Mystic Committee, saving him from certain incarceration.

What would Roddy make of this new life I've built?

It was early morning. Jestan had crossed the Amassa River on a recently conscripted ferry after breaking fast at the Ancient Ones' castle. He'd done all he could there for now—getting suites set up for the incoming families, ensuring that the supplies for farming and cooking and setting up classrooms had all been delivered—and he needed to return to Richard at King Harold's Keep to request more money and resources. The castle's new residents would need more food in the early months of the program before the newly sown farmlands had time to produce. He was on horseback now, speeding up the road that ran alongside the north shore of the river, when a vessel came up next to him, its rowers outpacing the opposing flow of the Amassa. Ships were rare in Emyhrsen. Trade had not yet resumed with other nations after the overthrow of the Tzakabya, and the Aepistelle Navy hadn't come this far north since the battle at the Keep three years earlier. Some old ships had been repaired and were used for fishing, but this was not one of them.

It was, however, a ship he'd seen before.

A ship he'd spent considerable time on.

"Well, what do you know?" he asked himself. Louder, he shouted out the name of the ship. "The *Ales and Sails!*"

On cue, cheers and whoops and rowdy cries rang out from the deck. Jestan pulled on the reins to halt his horse. At the next dock large enough for the ship to land, the crew extended the rampart, and Jestan and his horse joined them on board, greeted like a pesky brother by two dozen lady pirates and their captain.

"Captain Le'Nelle Nightstar," he said as he embraced the woman. "You can't tell me this meeting is a coincidence."

She signaled one of her crew members to pop open a cask and pour out ale for everyone in celebration. "Did Georgie-boy not tell you?" she asked, a foamy mustache on her upper lip. She thrust her mug at Jestan, who politely declined.

"I've been taking care of some business these last couple of weeks. I haven't seen much of him or Richard. He sent out a messenger?"

"Aye, that he did. I didn't know the people of Emyhrsen were the seafaring type, but they found us at Kullin Island, just where you pair last left us. Those lads were greener than the sea, worse than George when he first set foot on this ship. After a good bout of hurling off the docks, they told us what was happening."

"And what did they say is happening?" Jestan asked.

"That George's sister is in need. That our chance to reset things is coming."

"Reset things? That's one way to look at it, I suppose. Or to die a dishonorable death at the hands of the Aepistelle military in a failed coup attempt."

The rowdy chatter on the deck faded at Jestan's words. Le'Nelle glared at him. "Look around you, Jes. These ladies have been away for far too long, even for sailors. They all have people they love in Aepistelle. They want to go home. I owe it to them."

"I'm sorry. I got you into all of this when I chartered your ship to bring us north in the first place."

"And I took the job knowing the risks involved. Perhaps it's on both of us. So let's make it right."

With that, the rowers took their places belowdecks, and they made the rest of the journey upriver to Richard's castle.

———

"WE ARE A FAR CRY FROM HAVING AN ARMY," GEORGE SAID with a noticeable slur.

He pushed his glass across the table and nodded for one of Le'Nelle's crew to provide a refill. Ale was rare in Emyhrsen. Addie, the ancient seamstress who had lived in King Harold's castle for decades, had told stories of a brewery in neighboring Ferathan that used to deliver carts full of casks to the king in his youth. There had been many ale-smiths in Emyhrsen in those days, she'd explained, but none with ales as fine as those from Fielders' Fancies of Ferathan. In the three years since the liberation of Emyhrsen, there had been some movement among farmers to grow the necessary grains and hops again, but there were no large-scale brewers so far.

The lack of alcoholic beverages didn't matter much to Jestan. He'd given up the stuff back in Aepistelle after decades of overindulging, and he knew he was better for it. A clear mind, ambition, and the ability to make solid choices were all things he hadn't had when he was under the influence most hours of the day during his tours of Aepistelle. Still, he was happy to see Le'Nelle's cargo being put to good use by those assembled in Richard's audience chamber. The joking and laughter and singing and merriment brought new life to the place.

"Aye, we're small in number, but I would never bet against my ladies," Le'Nelle said to a round of cheers from her crew.

"Nor mine."

The voice came from the back of the room. Jestan and his companions turned in unison as an unusually tall woman entered the room, trailed by ten more of equal height.

"Teyla," Richard said, pushing himself to his feet. Normally the man stood a head taller than most in his presence, but these women towered over him. "I'm so glad you've joined us." He tasked one of the castle attendants with bringing out an additional pair of tables and a dozen chairs.

"Don't tell me George arranged this as well," Jestan said as he greeted the women.

"I believe that was his signature on the scroll the pigeon delivered," Teyla said, taking a seat at the main table while her warriors patiently waited. "It was a wise strategy, invoking the names of Gemma Calvertson and Arnem the Loyal. There is nothing I would not do for those two, who liberated my warriors and me from bondage and reunited us with our people."

"Well, I apologize for even proposing that you leave the rest of the Nazseke," George said, his speech clearer now. "I know you were separated from them for many years. The last thing I want is to take that away from you, but what we're up against is more than we can handle alone."

"And just what is it you're asking of us?" one of Teyla's warriors asked, settling into her new chair.

"Gemma was here a few weeks ago on a mission to find Arnem, and—"

"Arnem is missing?" Teyla asked.

"Try *dead*," Le'Nelle said. "Burned to a crisp, from what we've heard."

"Yes," Richard said. "His companion Denny lost control of a fledgling ability and accidentally set Arnem on fire." His voice buckled under the weight of his despair.

"That was three years ago," Jestan continued. "Arnem perished, and the boy has been in hiding ever since. A seer showed Gemma a vision of what had happened, and later she discovered some information that led her to believe she could reach Arnem's soul and bring him back."

"Is this some kind of sick joke?" Teyla asked. Jestan's heart broke at the sight of tears pouring down her cheeks. He knew Arnem and Teyla had had a close platonic bond decades earlier.

"I'm so sorry," he said, as if that could make any of this easier. "It's not a joke, though it sounds farfetched. That's not even why we called you here. While Gemma was here, we decided to assist her in overthrowing King Davin."

A chair scraped as one of Teyla's companions jumped to her feet. "But we already did that right outside these castle walls not four years ago!"

"We did," George said. "But Davin escaped on his way back to Aepistelle and returned to power."

"So Sybelle died for nothing?" the warrior said, and sat back down in disbelief.

"Not for nothing, Clauda," Teyla said. "We accomplished much with that battle. We freed the people here, for instance." She turned back to Jestan. "So, what is it you would have us do?"

Jestan looked around at the group, closed his eyes, took a deep breath, then opened them again. "We agreed that if Gemma didn't return in five weeks, we'd proceed with planning and carrying out an attack on Davin's castle in Capital

City. A companion of Gemma's and his team of mercenaries are assembling resistance forces down in Aepistelle. They've had a head start over the last few weeks, so we can only hope their numbers are larger than ours. George and I can't go home to Aepistelle safely, nor can Captain Nightstar and her crew, so we've had to remain here until it is time to strike."

"I have missed home these last few years, but I wouldn't take back what we did to that despot's ship during the battle here," Le'Nelle said, to a round of cheers from her crew. "It'll be good to slap the golden spoon out of his mouth a second time. We can pick up some more ships at the northern ports. Davin and his lackeys have crippled us silly with tariffs and regulations, so our kind has no love for him. We'll have the battle covered from the sea."

"So we'll fight on land?" Teyla said.

Jestan nodded. "Once we're through Capital Bay and into the port, we'll rush to the center of the city. Davin's palace is heavily guarded for blocks in all directions, so it won't be easy."

"If our timing is right," George said, "Quincy and his forces will be ready to sail into Capital Bay with us. Davin may have increased security around the castle in the last three years, but we'll have the element of surprise."

"And what will we do once we're inside?" Teyla asked. "Does anyone know what it's like in there? Do we know about the layout and internal defenses?"

Jestan turned to George. Richard did the same. He gave them an uncertain look. "Well, I've been there before for some receptions, but it's my mother who really knows her way around. She used to work there as a maid."

Le'Nelle made a show of looking around. "I don't see her. Is she here?"

"Well, I'm hoping Quincy will think of that. He's more

accustomed to this kind of operation. He's with my parents now, so I have faith that he'll ask my mother to draw him a map or at least tell him about the layout of the place and any defenses we should know about."

"*Hoping*," Le'Nelle repeated with an air of defeat. "Well, we beat Davin once with just hope and luck. Perhaps it'll happen again."

"We are far more prepared this time," Richard said with authority.

"He speaks," Teyla chimed in. "I was starting to think you weren't part of this plan."

"He isn't." All eyes shifted to Jestan. "Richard must remain in Emyhrsen. The people here cannot afford to lose his leadership just as they're starting to rebuild their society."

"And here I was thinking that three of the four heroes of the so-called Great Journey were partaking in this little adventure. And now one is staying here, and one *may* come back as—what is Arnem anyway, a ghost? This is going splendidly."

Silence fell over the room except for the sounds of people nervously shifting in their chairs and drinking from their glasses of ale. Jestan studied the faces of his peers, reading their fears and uncertainties. Some looked as if they knew this campaign meant certain death. And yet he did not see defeat. No one looked ready to quit.

"This is the right thing to do," Jestan said, rising to his feet. "I can see that you all know it in your bones and in your hearts. The odds will always be against us, and yet we will resist anyway, because we fight for what is right and good and true, and our enemy thrives on lies and chaos and death. We will prevail. We will beat those odds. We will inspire others, mere laymen, to pick up makeshift arms and join the fight. Our actions will serve as cinders that set the kingdom and reign of Davin alight and burn them to the ground. And then —only then—will we be able to bring peace and order to the people of Aepistelle *and* the Emyhrseni, the Nazseke, the seafarers, and beyond. We stand to lose everything, but we also stand to gain it all."

Without gauging their response to his words, Jestan turned and walked toward the double doors.

"Where are you going?" George asked from his seat at the table.

Not halting, Jestan called back, "I have a stop to make. Get all our ships ready and leave some extra room. If I play my cards right, we're going to need the space."

CHAPTER 38
JESTAN

Jestan had spent enough time with Naliah Lunarra during the journey to return the Tzakabyan captives to their ancestral lands to know that the town of Ferathan still stood. But she'd told him that when her enchantment over Ferathan ended, the buildings would likely age rapidly along with their inhabitants and that some structures would fall into immediate disrepair. She'd made the place sound borderline unlivable.

The town he saw in front of him, however, was anything but derelict.

Ferathan looked like a slightly impoverished village at worst, nicer than any other part of Emyhrsen after the decades of chaos they had suffered under Tzakabyan rule. Some fresh coats of paint, replacement windowpanes, and roof repairs would make it nearly as presentable as many adequately run towns Jestan had performed in throughout Aepistelle over the years.

As he rode through the streets, the silence unsettled him a bit, but he wasn't too surprised. From what he'd learned, around three hundred gifted folks had fled here from Aepis-telle over the last three years with their family members and friends, seeking to escape King Davin's discriminatory laws. Among them, Jestan assumed, there must be a few folks with powers of premonition much like Denny's, and they had likely warned the others about his approach.

"There are half a dozen arrows aimed at you right now," a woman called out. The voice echoed through the alleys. "Make one more movement, and our archers will let loose. They do not miss."

Jestan pulled his horse to a halt and raised his hands to show that he was not holding any of his weapons. He looked around but could not spot the speaker, nor any archers.

"I am not here to do you harm," Jestan assured the unseen onlookers. "I come from Emyhrsen in the north."

Silence fell over the town, making the seemingly deserted place feel even more eerie than it had just moments before. The voice broke it just as Jestan's nerves nearly drove him out of there. "We have met with representatives from Emyhrsen in the past. We went to them to propose trade, but the leader said they were unable to help."

"Yes, they were rebuilding. Still are, but—"

"*They?* You sound as if you are not one of them, yet you claim to come from their lands. Explain."

Jestan glanced at some of the nearby buildings. He expected to see curtains fluttering, eyes peeking through dusty windows, but there were no signs of life other than the voice. He would have preferred to treat with them face-to-face, but that did not appear to be an option just yet. "I only meant that I was not among them when you spoke to them last year. I arrived a few months ago. They've rebuilt quite a lot since then."

"Then what can you offer us?"

Jestan smiled at this. "The opportunity to return home." He left a dramatic pause, then continued, "To Aepistelle." The last sentence was meant to be enticing, even pleasantly surprising, but it came out more like a question as doubt crept into his mind. *What if they have no desire to return?* he thought. *What if they think I'm here to drive them out of safety?*

The creaking hinges of an opening door pulled him from his thoughts. A girl in her teens walked out of what appeared to have once been a bakery, judging from the peeling gold letters on the section of window that wasn't boarded up. She studied Jestan curiously.

"You're him," she said with wonder in her voice. It was a reaction he recognized but had forgotten in the three years he'd been away from Aepistelle. "The old hero."

Jestan bellowed his trademark laugh, a thing he'd seldom done recently. "Hero? Absolutely. Don't call me old, though, that's just mean!" he joked as he dismounted his horse.

"I agree—what would that make a man like me?"

Jestan turned at this ancient-sounding voice. A hunched white-haired man emerged from an alley, having come from a hiding place Jestan hadn't spotted. The man leaned heavily on a cane. He smiled, revealing gaps where several teeth had fallen out. Surrounding him were six snakes, slithering alongside him like trained pets. When he stopped ten feet from Jestan, the snakes stopped and reared up, their tongues darting in and out of their mouths. Jestan took a step back.

"Do not worry, new friend. I have them under my control." The man clicked his tongue, and the snakes simmered down. The girl came up alongside him, unfazed by the serpents. The older man went on. "Now, what is Jestan the Just, once a celebrity and now an infamous fugitive, doing here in this ghost town hundreds of miles from the home you claim you wish to return us to?"

"My companions are gathering forces. We have friends we believe to be in trouble, and—"

"The woman?" interrupted the teenager. "Gemma Calvertson?"

Jestan furrowed his brow. "Yes, but how did you know that?"

The girl's face dropped in dismay. "Then that means Denny is in danger." She turned to the old man. "And Marzele as well."

"How do you know them? They don't have anything to do with this."

"But they do," she said. "Denny told me all about her, and about what your group accomplished in Emyhrsen, and where you went after freeing the people. I was a bit jealous of the way he talked about *her*. I...I love him, after all."

"Oh, children," the old man said in a lovingly mocking tone.

"You mean Denny and Marzele were here among you?" Jestan asked.

"Aye, they were a vital part of this community." This came from a woman clearly much more mature in years than the teen. Jestan turned to see not just one person approaching but dozens, pouring out through doors and from behind buildings. For runaways and refugees, they looked to be well fed and adequately dressed. Ferathan had been good to them, it seemed.

"Marzele worked with many of us," the old man said, gesturing at the crowd. "Taught us to control our abilities. To home in on what makes them tick. To hide them properly, should we ever feel the pull to return to Aepistelle under fresh identities."

"And where are Denny and Marzele now?" Jestan inquired.

"Gone." Tears streamed down the girl's cheeks. "That

Gemma came here—it must have been a month ago—and convinced them to leave with her on some new adventure. She took Denny from me. Marzele, too." She turned and threw herself toward the old man, burying her head in his shoulder. She nearly trampled the snakes that stood around him, but with the flick of the wrist, he calmed them. If only he could do the same with the bawling girl.

"It was a noble quest they set off on," Jestan assured her and the others, "but I do fear something has happened. Before Gemma left, we agreed to give her five weeks before putting our plan into action without her. We're beyond that time now, so we must move."

"What is it you intend to do?" asked a man around Jestan's age.

"Not planning to bring trouble upon us, are you?" a younger man asked accusingly. "Seems you've seen enough of it in your lifetime."

"I assure you that I don't mean to cause you any harm. If you want to remain in Ferathan, that is your prerogative. However, if you're like me and you miss the people and places you love back in Aepistelle and long to return in peace, I have an offer for you."

"Peace?" someone asked. "How is that possible?"

"Admittedly, there will not be peace right away. We'll have to fight for it. My friends and I are putting together an army. We have others in Aepistelle gathering forces as well. Whether or not our group will be formidable enough, I cannot predict, but I do know that everyone involved will fight with everything they have. King Davin and his regime have taken too much from us. You know that too well—all of you."

The girl stepped toward Jestan and sized him up. She wiped the salty tracks from her face and cleared her throat.

"Denny believes in you and those you wrote about in your book. He idolizes you. There is a saying about never meeting your heroes because they'll only let you down, but Denny ignored that, and he was not disappointed by you and the others. If you say you will fight for us, I will join you."

Jestan looked around, a smile growing on his face but stopping halfway. Those assembled were whispering to one another. Quiet arguments broke out between husbands and wives, parents and children, friends and neighbors. Those whispers turned to chatter, which turned to shouting. Jestan picked up bits and pieces:

"We're not wanted in Aepistelle."

"They hate our kind."

"Only because Davin tells them to."

"They'll accept us if he's gone."

"I like it here. We have a place of our own."

"I miss home."

"I miss my parents."

"We have a chance to take it back for ourselves."

The confusion and anger shifted, and hope rose as the chatter took a positive turn. Jestan clapped loudly.

"My friends, if you will join me in this fight, I cannot guarantee success. I cannot guarantee your safety. The odds are almost entirely against us. The stakes are massive." He paced among them, looking each person in the eyes. "But in you I see desperation. Pain. Rejection. Longing. Anger. Spite. And there's even more down deeper than that—bravery, hope, faith. I see in each of you the power to bring freedom. To yourselves. To your families. To those still hiding their abilities, quietly praying to the gods that they're never discovered. We have an opportunity to change all that. To end thirty years of discrimination by Davin and his cronies. To free not only yourselves from King Davin's reign of terror but all the people of Aepistelle.

"Now, tell me, are you with me?"

A hush fell over those gathered around Jestan.

Perhaps I misjudged the situation, he thought. A bird cawed in the distance. The snakes around the old man hissed, and one made its way up his leg.

A younger man pushed through the crowd and studied Jestan as if to make sure he was serious. He smiled as if he saw just what he was looking for. "Aye, I will join you."

"And I, but you already knew that," the girl added.

And then the rest of the crowd cheered in agreement.

Jestan didn't know what kinds of abilities they all had nor what Marzele had done to train them. He could only pray that they were powerful enough to do their parts. They would, after all, be severely outnumbered.

CHAPTER 39
GEMMA

Even before the door opened in her room at the castle, she knew who it would be. She could almost smell the stench of him, the fear he had of his father, of rejection. It wafted off him in waves.

The knob turned, the door swung ajar, and Kosar stood there, waving off the guard at the door. He stepped in and closed the door gently, avoiding eye contact with Gemma, and set a wrapped bundle on the small table by the door. He walked across the room, picked up a chair—she suppressed a smile when it was heavier than he expected—and plunked it down in front of her bed.

"Sit," he ordered, motioning toward the bed while he plopped down on the chair. Still, his eyes had not met hers.

"What are you afraid of?" Gemma asked as she walked toward the window instead, defying her captor's orders. "Can't bear to face me?"

"It's not...I'm not..." he sputtered, but couldn't find the words.

Gemma laughed. Cruel, perhaps, but not undeserved.

Kosar flinched at the sound, which sent a twinge of guilt through her chest. She was not normally one for mocking people, even in situations like this. She sighed, walked to the bed, and sat.

"What happened to the man who rescued me from the soldiers who came to arrest me at the university? Where's the Kosar who fought on that rooftop for my safety, or who masterminded the heist of a printing press so he could bring truth to the masses?"

His breathing grew heavier with each sentence. "Enough!" he snapped. "I am right here, Gemma." He jumped to his feet with such force that the chair tipped backward and clattered to the tile floor. "I am right in front of you, making sure you have a nice room instead of a dank hole in the dungeons below the castle. I made certain the posters with your name and face on them said that you were to be brought in alive and unharmed. I have been on your side every step of the way!"

She leaned back to avoid his erratic windmilling arms. "On my side? By having me arrested? By having all your old friends murdered at the hand of the Royal Mystic Committee three years ago? Turning against your own brother and father?"

"Joseph Herron is not my father, as I've told you. He's a liar. And the rest of them...they weren't...it wasn't..." He tried to sit on his chair, forgetting it was no longer upright. His bottom-first tumble was disgraceful. Gemma turned away to hide her laughter; she didn't want to give him one more reason to lose his cool. She'd seen that happen too many times now, and it was clear that he was hanging by the last threads of his sanity and patience.

That was what really hurt her, deep in her heart. She had been in love with him for only a matter of weeks, but she had felt more strongly for Kosar than she ever had for Walker or any of the other boys she'd dated over the years. But Kosar had seemed like a completely different person then. Apparently that had been merely a mask, much like the one he'd been wearing when she'd first met him on that fateful night.

"You mentioned the truth," Kosar went on after recovering from his outburst and his fall. He brushed off his slacks and crossed his arms, standing over the fallen chair, refusing to clean up his mess like the stubborn child he had always been.

"What?"

"Bringing truth to the masses. How I gave that up to join my real father here. Well, have a look at that." He pointed to the bundle on the table. Gemma eyed it suspiciously, then crossed the room and unwrapped the cloth that was wrapped around it to conceal the contents like a gift. By the shape she knew it was a book. She flipped it over to read the words printed on the cover in gold.

"*The Aepistelle Chronicles* by..."

"Gemma Calvertson. Yes, that's you. You are bloody famous now, my love. You got what you've always wanted."

"But..." Gemma trailed off and flipped through the opening pages. She recognized the words, though she hadn't spent as much time with the manuscript as she'd wanted. "You did this?"

She turned to Kosar, studying the conflicted look on his face. If she could read him as accurately as she thought, he was trying to decide if he should lie and take credit for the publication of her manuscript.

"I... uh..." His teeth clacked together as he closed his mouth quickly.

"It was Syntha, wasn't it?" Gemma asked as realization dawned. "Your cousin made this happen. I left the manuscript behind, and she walked away with it. How did she manage this? How many copies are out there?"

"I'm having my people investigate, but from what we can ascertain, she had some help from rogues within the Royal Mystic Committee. They used stolen printing presses hidden throughout the kingdom, including one in the barn of your old friend Richard the Elusive."

Tears dripped onto the pages as Gemma stared at the text in disbelief. More than three years had passed since she'd last seen Syntha. If she was honest with herself, she'd barely even thought of the woman, who had been her friend for only a brief couple of weeks. They'd been through a lot together during that short and turbulent time, but she never would have guessed that Syntha would spend three years putting her own safety on the line for Gemma's sake.

But no—it wasn't for Gemma's sake, at least not exclusively.

"Syntha believed in the cause," Gemma said. She looked up at Kosar, who shook with anger at the thought of his cousin's rebellion. "The same cause we all fought for together. The cause you killed our friends over—Alyssa and Zinnie and the others. Before you sold out yourself and everyone who loved you. Of *course* Syntha did this."

Kosar stormed toward her and ripped the book from her hands. "You are going to help undo this mess!" he screamed in her face, spittle flying from his mouth. "I am trying to get things under control here, to secure my place on the throne, but every time you undermine me, my father pushes me farther away!"

"I'll never help you bury the truth, Kosar. That's everything I've worked for."

"No?" He grabbed her by the wrist and tugged her roughly toward the door. He threw it open and yanked her down the hallway as guards stepped aside and watched with irritation, as if they were seeing a spoiled child throw yet another tantrum. Not too far from the truth, Gemma knew. "I think you'll change your mind very quickly."

"Let go of me. This isn't who you are, Kosar." Gemma forced her hand back, causing him to lose his balance and stumble. He recovered his footing, then launched himself at her, pinning her against the wall.

She saw the murder in his eyes and gasped.

"You do that one more time," he growled in a low voice she'd never heard from him before, "and I will show no more mercy to anyone you care about. I will make you watch as the life escapes each and every one of them." He grabbed her arm and pulled her around a corner to another guarded door.

The man there did not need to be commanded to move. He pulled out a ring of keys, fumbled for the right one, and unlocked the door. Kosar barely waited for the man to step aside before he threw it open and thrust Gemma forward.

"Madame Hvalsi?" Gemma said.

The compact woman glared at her from a puffy chair under the window where she'd been reading. She looked neither surprised nor alarmed by Gemma's presence.

"Here comes trouble," Hvalsi said with a strong tinge of annoyance. She didn't bother getting off her chair. "Did you find what you were looking for? I sure hope it was worth all that." She gestured at the window.

Kosar shoved Gemma toward it. She looked out and took in the view of an interior courtyard three stories below. Carts were being pulled in by horses. Several crates that had already been unloaded were being pried open and inspected. The contents shone with a green glow.

Gemma let out a whimper. "I'm sorry," she said. "I'm certain I was not followed to Bahrun." She turned and stared at Hvalsi, wanting to beg for forgiveness yet also sure that she was not to blame.

"Oh, Gemma, always the humanitarian," Kosar said. "This little woman was the one who told me all about the mineral. I didn't need to have you followed on your cross-country journey. I just needed to have someone trail you to *her*. Once we brought her in, she gave up the secrets of her people after only a few measly nights in the dungeons. She's not honorable like you."

"So, you did make it there?" Hvalsi asked Gemma, ignoring Kosar. "Before all that was plundered, I mean?"

"I did," Gemma answered. "I was with your people for a short time and—"

"Not my people," Hvalsi interrupted. "Not for a while now."

"They knew you. Knew of you, at least. The kuhlae spoke as if you two were contemporaries."

"What in the world is a *kuhlae*?" Kosar asked.

"A holy man," Hvalsi said with scorn.

"Ah, by the way you say that, I can tell your feelings on the subject." Kosar gestured at Gemma. "She knows all about so-called holy men gone rogue, don't you, Gemma? Your mustachioed Solendaron priest who went on a murder spree, for instance."

"It's not like that," Gemma said. She met Hvalsi's eyes. "The kuhlae was good to me, Madame Hvalsi. He brought my companions and me to the portal. We visited the Realm. Thanks to you, we were reunited with our departed friend, and—"

Hvalsi's eyebrows shot up. "Evana! My sister. Did you see her? Was she there?"

"Enough!" Kosar said. "This woman is no longer useful

here. She told me enough about the mineral to allow me to impress my father. Gods know I need that right now."

"What is it you want with the mineral?" Gemma demanded.

"Everlasting life."

"That's not how it works," Hvalsi said. "I've tried to tell him, but nothing gets through to this moron."

"Listen, you little wench," Kosar growled, "you already told me it can regrow severed body parts, heal the nastiest of diseases, apparently even connect us to our dearly departed. My father is convinced this means he'll be able to rule for all eternity. Don't you dare spoil that right now."

"Like I said," Hvalsi quipped to Gemma, rolling her eyes, "complete and utter moron."

Kosar glared, though his eyes met neither woman. Before Gemma could speak and try to deescalate the situation, he reached for the hilt of his sword. It made a metallic *zing* as he yanked it from its sheathe. With one rapid arc, he sliced the blade through the smaller woman's face.

Gemma's screams and Madame Hvalsi's cries mingled with Kosar's shouts. "Look what you made me do! You asked for this!" He snapped the sword back and forth through the air just inches from the women, the blade making swooshing sounds. "I am your prince, gods damn it!"

"Kosar," Gemma tried, "put the sword down. Please."

"No, I..." He shook his head, wiped the blade on the fabric on the side of Hvalsi's chair, then slid the sword back into its scabbard. Madame Hvalsi whimpered in pain, her torn-up face buried in her arms.

"Why would you do such a thing, Kosar?" Gemma asked. "This is not who you are."

"It's... I... You're right. What my father is doing to me has changed me. But he has toyed with me long enough."

Gemma wanted to go to Madame Hvalsi and comfort her, figure out how to help her, but she was frightened that Kosar would snap again. "Why would you give your father the key to everlasting life, whether it works or not?"

His face fell. "I'm desperate, can't you see? I would do anything, give up anything, for him to name me his heir, but the only thing he seems to want is more power." He scrunched his brow in a way she had once thought was cute. Now she just wanted to punch that face, smash it under her fists. "And you, Gemma. He said that if I brought you here and had you set things right, made you denounce your book and tell the kingdom it was all lies written to defame him, then he would move things along for me."

Gemma took a step back, her heels bumping the wall under the open window.

"Please, Gemma." He held out a hand to her.

She looked back through the open window at the drop to the cobblestones of the bustling courtyard. Gemma had been in a similar position three years earlier, though Kosar's father had stood before her then. She had chosen to take King Davin's hand in that moment to protect her friends, to live on and fight another day. But now what incentive did she have? Going with Kosar meant giving up everything she'd worked for, everything her friends and family had sacrificed for, the things so many had given their lives to protect. Her book was out there in the world. Anyone who got their hands on it would learn the truth. If she were to give in, it would all be for nothing.

Kosar took a step toward her, his hand still outstretched. "Gemma, please—"

He didn't get to finish the sentence. Gemma lunged forward, slamming her shoulder into his chest, knocking the wind out of him. He crashed into the corner of the bed and fell backward. Gemma lost her balance and collapsed on top of him.

"Guards!" he managed to yell as he rolled over, pushing Gemma down. "Guards, come quick!" Gemma tried to push him off. He wasn't scrawny, but he wasn't a large buff man either. She thought that with all the training she'd done as an agent in the Royal Mystic Committee, she should at least be able to get free, but he pinned her arms against her chest and pushed them into her, moving them up toward her neck. Her legs flailed, but she couldn't slam her knees into him hard enough to faze him. The pressure on her neck increased, her own hands and his crushing her windpipe. She gasped, but it was useless—she couldn't get any air. She had seconds left at best.

And then came the sound of a sword being unsheathed.

CHAPTER 40
GEMMA

Kosar released the pressure on Gemma's throat, allowing her to breathe. Hvalsi had leaped off her chair remarkably fast, landed at Kosar's side, and slid the would-be prince's sword out of its sheathe. Kosar rolled off Gemma, landing on his back on the tile floor, and raised his arms and legs to absorb a blow from the blade. Had Gemma not been gasping for air, she'd have laughed at how much he looked like a dog in that moment, cowering as Hvalsi held the sword up.

"Stop!" Gemma wheezed.

"What?" Hvalsi asked weakly. Her left cheek dangled in two chunks that revealed the molars behind it, her shoulder drenched in crimson.

"If you kill him, you'll never leave here alive," Gemma managed.

"I'll be executed either way. May as well get revenge before they finish me off."

Kosar let out a growl of anger as he jumped to his feet. Gemma fought through the pain in her throat and launched herself up as well. She dove for him as he reached out for the sword in Hvalsi's hands. Hvalsi swung at the same moment Gemma slammed into Kosar, knocking him off balance. The blade missed him entirely, grazing Gemma's left shoulder instead.

"What have you done?" Kosar screamed as he spotted Gemma's wound.

"I...I..." Madame Hvalsi dropped the sword and backed away from the carnage.

"Now I really will kill you!" He pushed Gemma out of the way, stepped over the sword, and lunged at the smaller woman.

"Kosar, no!" Gemma called, but it was no use. His weight knocked Hvalsi backward into the same spot he'd backed Gemma into moments earlier. Her compact form fit perfectly through the open window, and she plummeted out of view.

Gemma didn't need to look out the window to know the woman didn't survive. The thud of her body against the cobblestones three stories below was telling enough.

Gemma wept.

"Oh, quit it, Gemma. She gave you up far too easily," Kosar said. He grabbed her right hand and pulled her toward him. In her daze of shock and grief and pain, she didn't fight back. "Now, let's get that wound cleaned up. My father has the finest doctors in his employ."

They walked through the maze of hallways and corridors on their way to the castle medic's suite. The staff and guards met them with shocked stares around every corner.

Gemma's mind drifted to her mother. Had Serena Calvertson worked behind any of these doors during her career as a maid in this castle? Had she known about the depravity of King Davin and his associates? She'd never talked about witnessing any cruelties, at least not to Gemma.

Perhaps her mother had saved that talk for her father, Geoffrey, who had spent years in such a poor state of mental health that he likely couldn't have answered back. Or maybe her mother had internalized it all, absorbed it as she had with other difficult aspects of her life. Gemma had never thought of her mother as a strong woman, but rather someone who went along with whatever hand she was dealt. Gemma, on the other hand, had dedicated herself to fighting the various injustices she'd witnessed, and look what messes that approach had gotten her into.

"Are you unwell?" Kosar asked. "You look like you're in shock."

Gemma glanced around to find she had been escorted to a chair by Kosar and an attending nurse while thinking about her mother. "I'm fine," she said, and allowed the nurse to clean and stitch her wound.

"Cut's not deep," the woman said as she worked. "It'll hurt, but you'll be fine."

Gemma groaned as the stitches pulled her flesh back together. Kosar reached for her hand and squeezed. In her shock and pain, she didn't pull away from his touch. Instead, she wrapped her fingers around his. They remained that way as the nurse continued her bloody needlework.

"Let's go see my father after this," Kosar said as the nurse traded needle and thread for a long strip of cloth to wrap around the wound. "We'll get everything sorted with that book, as well as with our future."

Gemma's senses returned in that moment. She slipped her fingers from Kosar's grasp and wiped the sweat from his palm onto her slacks.

"You still have the wrong idea, Kosar," she said, not caring what the nurse overheard. Let the woman whisper to her peers. Let the rumors spread as far as Gemma's manuscript apparently had. She was done with secrets and lies.

"But..." Kosar apparently could not find the words for what he wanted to say. He turned away from Gemma and glared at the nurse, who didn't need a verbal warning from the unstable man-child. She didn't know he was a prince, the son of King Davin, but she had seen enough spoiled, overly privileged boys to know to walk away before the tantrums began. She gave one last tug to secure the bandage and exited the room without another word to either of them. Gemma wanted to follow her, beg for the nurse not to leave her alone with this maniac, but she didn't.

Kosar took the opportunity to speak again. "Gemma, don't be ridiculous. All your friends will die. Your parents will die. Your—"

"We've been over this already," she interrupted. "If you're going to kill me for refusing you, just do it. If the book with my name on the cover is so dangerous, you'll just create a martyr." She studied his face and grinned. "And it seems to me that you agree."

Kosar rose to his feet and screamed in frustration. He kicked the small table next to the chair where Gemma was sitting. The nurse's medical tools flew up and crashed into the wall before clattering to the ground.

"You are too stubborn for your own good. If you don't cooperate, I will not be able to protect you or anyone you love!"

"A list on which you don't appear," she quipped, hoping it stung. His grimace confirmed that she had struck her mark.

"I... I... What is that commotion?" Kosar turned and stomped to the door. He pulled it open as a half dozen guards jogged down the hall. "Where are you all going in such a hurry?" he demanded.

One guard stopped, his hand on the hilt of his sword, and turned to face Kosar. "We have a situation, sir. Crowd forming outside the gates."

"A crowd? Are the men at the wall too incompetent to take care of a little gathering outside?"

The guard swallowed loudly. "Not just a few folks. It's practically an army."

Kosar turned back to Gemma. She read the worry on his face loud and clear. "Stay there and give it some more thought," he said. "I'll come back for you once this is resolved."

He exited the room and slammed the door behind him, leaving Gemma alone. She pushed herself off the chair, wincing at the stinging sensation under her fresh bandage. She ran to the window, pushed open the shutters, and looked out. This window faced a different courtyard from the one Madame Hvalsi had met her demise in, situated between this wing of the castle and the large walls that had been rebuilt in the three years since the failed attack by Marzele and the Solendaron clergy. Below, guards darted frantically back and forth, clearly spooked by whatever was happening on the other side of the wall.

Gemma took a deep breath. Part of her wanted to smile, and another part wanted to tremble with fear. The fight had come to the castle. The resistance was upon them. Many could die, but they might also claim a decisive victory.

Either way, the truth would be brought to light in Aepistelle. The shadows no longer held power.

The door burst open, and Kosar walked back in with more authority than he had displayed moments earlier.

"On second thought," he said as he grabbed her good arm and tugged her into the hall, "you're too sly to be left to your own devices. I'm bringing you with me."

CHAPTER 41
KIEVE

Kieve had seen the town house from the outside weeks earlier when he'd tailed Palignon there. At the time, he'd believed the lieutenant to be a traitor working against the Royal Mystic Committee and putting Gemma Calvertson in danger. His instincts had proven correct, indeed, but what he hadn't intuited was that Kieve would soon join Palignon in his endeavor.

Much had happened since the events in Pinedrop, when Kieve had released the birds and had fought his fellow Royal Mystic Committee agents and members of Aepistelle's military. Syntha and Palignon had carefully planned for all contingencies, including how they should escape the city should their conspiracy be unveiled too early. They'd made sure warehouses in all territories of Aepistelle were stocked and ready to distribute Gemma's manifesto when they were signaled by the arrival of the carrier pigeons.

What the conspirators hadn't known, however, was just how easily the truth would catch fire and spread through Aepistelle.

Within a week, protests sprang up everywhere from Esteron to the Southern Reaches. The trio traveled in disguise to check in on their network of associates around the kingdom, leaving this place for last.

Capital City.

The belly of the beast.

Word on the street was that King Davin had grown increasingly paranoid since the release of Gemma's book, and with good reason. The people he'd been fleecing and manipulating for decades had caught on. Gemma's words revealed quite a lot, but even her account was only a small piece of the picture. People who had firsthand experience with Davin, former cabinet members and advisors and associates, had all found their voices, speaking out about the injustices they'd witnessed in his employ. Many were quickly silenced by the Royal Mystic Committee, who either stuffed them into the darkest holes they could find or executed them behind closed doors.

The Royal Mystic Committee itself was not infallible, as its leadership soon learned. That Cragen Palignon, one of its highest-ranking members, had rebelled against the organization and the king after such a long, honorable career revealed cracks in the institution. Those loyal to King Davin began to question others in positions of power, particularly Commander Grushka Bryne, who was Palignon's close friend and confidante. Infighting abounded, with agents turning against each other and their leadership.

Despite Davin blocking the ports, railways, and roads into Capital City to keep out potential rebels and shipments of Gemma's book, Kieve and his companions managed to find their way into the heart of the kingdom. Palignon insisted that the first place they visit be the home of his ex-wife and daughter. They knew the place would probably be carefully monitored by Davin's agents, but neither Syntha nor Kieve dared to contradict their leader. He'd put his family in considerable danger, and he couldn't continue the fight without knowing they were all right. If Kieve had a family of his own, he knew he'd feel the same.

So there they were, looking up at the three-story town house that had been converted into apartments. They'd cased the neighborhood for thirty minutes—no guards outside, no passersby casting obvious keen glances around. Kieve knew the drill. The place looked safe. They'd even caught a glimpse of people moving about behind the third-floor apartment's windows, as was evidenced by the tears forming in Palignon's eyes.

"Well, I suppose it's time," the older man said. He took a step into the road, and Kieve made to follow, but Syntha reached out an arm to stop him.

"Wait, Cragen," she said. "We can stay out here and make sure you're not interrupted. We can give you privacy."

Palignon turned around. "That's kind of you, my friend, but you're not safe out here. Besides, we're in this together. My family may as well meet those I've risked everything with. Come," he said, gesturing for them to follow as he weaved between horse-drawn carriages moving along the road. Kieve nodded to Syntha, and both followed him into the building.

Palignon's key still worked in the front door. There was no sign that the door had been rammed in by the king's forces during a raid. No soldiers were stationed in the building's foyer, waiting to arrest them. Breathing easier, the trio climbed the two flights of stairs. When they neared the top floor, Kieve slowed down. Syntha did the same, letting Palignon have extra space as he approached the front door of the apartment he'd once shared with his family. They watched as Palignon reached the landing, hesitated, then took three cautious steps toward the door. He stood there as if unsure he'd be welcomed.

Syntha reached the top landing next and stepped to one side. Kieve scooted past her and pivoted to Palignon's left, stepping on a floorboard that creaked loudly. Both of Kieve's companions turned and stared at him as if he had done something wrong. He shrugged, not knowing how else to react.

They weren't the only ones to hear the creak, apparently, as footsteps approached from inside the apartment. Palignon sucked in a breath. Two bolts clicked on the other side of the door. The knob turned. The door swung open.

"Daddy?"

Kieve watched as Palignon's knees nearly buckled. The man stumbled before regaining his balance, then stepped forward and threw his arms around his daughter. The teenager returned the embrace, tucking her head into his shoulder and chest, and both of them wept.

Syntha was right, Kieve thought. *We should have waited outside.*

Palignon broke the embrace after half a minute, pulling back while keeping his hands on his daughter's shoulders as he took her in.

"Look at you, Jensa," he said. "Your mother hadn't let me see you when last I was here, and rightly so with the danger I put you two in. You've grown up in only a few years. How is that even possible?"

"She's had to face a lot," came a voice from inside the apartment, one filled with scorn. "We both have."

Jensa pivoted, and she and her father looked at the woman inside. Kieve was grateful in that moment to be out of view. Syntha was just a few feet behind Palignon, and Kieve could see the discomfort on her face as her eyes darted down to her feet.

"Llonda," Palignon said in a voice more unsteady than Kieve had ever heard him sound, "I'm so sorry if—"

"Come on, Cragen," she ordered. "You and your friends need to come inside before the neighbors hear us."

Palignon nodded and gestured for Kieve and Syntha to follow. Once inside, he closed the door gently and fastened the bolts.

Kieve looked around from where he stood just inside the entrance, instinctively searching for signs that this could be a trap, that a strike team of Committee agents could be waiting for them. The apartment wasn't large. The front door opened into a kitchen lined with counters on two walls, a small table pushed up against a third wall under a window. The fourth side opened into a sitting room with two open doors on the far wall that led into small bedrooms. There weren't many places for soldiers to hide. He breathed a sigh of relief.

"Llonda, I'm so sorry for the danger I've put you and Jensa in," Palignon said. "I didn't want to implicate you in any of this, which is why I didn't tell you what I've been doing."

"A rare smart decision on your part," Llonda said. Palignon flinched as if he'd been slapped across the face. "You know, they arrested us three weeks ago right outside on the sidewalk as we came home from the market with groceries. In front of all our neighbors. Girls from Jensa's class were across the street, and they saw the whole thing and told all their other classmates that she was some kind of criminal. She hasn't gone back since."

"It's okay, Mom. That wasn't his fault," the girl said, grabbing her father's hand.

"They brought us to the local precinct and interrogated us about you, but it became clear to them that you'd abandoned us long ago, that we had no idea what you were up to. They finally let us go, but they're out there watching."

"I didn't see anyone," Kieve said. "We scoped out the surroundings for a while before attempting to enter the building."

Llonda's glare shifted toward Kieve, and he immediately regretted speaking.

"They come and go," she answered. "They follow us around town, not even bothering to be secretive about it. How do you think that makes us feel, Cragen?"

"I never wanted this for you," Palignon replied. "I hoped our separation would be enough to protect you. I should have done more."

"Like what?" Llonda demanded. "Should you have brought us with you? We'd be further implicated. Should you have told us what you were doing? You know I would have told them everything if it meant protecting my daughter."

"I don't need protection, Mom," Jensa insisted. "I wish we *had* gone away with Dad and helped him. At least he's been doing something good for this world and not just hiding away like we are."

"We *have* to hide," Llonda said, slamming a fist down on the table next to her for emphasis. "We are exactly the kind of people your father and his comrades hunt down, and now there is an even bigger target on our backs."

Kieve and Syntha made eye contact, and he saw shock on her face that matched his own. "You have abilities?" he asked, immediately regretting that he'd opened his mouth. Again.

Llonda, Jensa, and Palignon all turned to look at him as if they'd forgotten he was there. Nobody answered his question.

"You can trust my friends, Llonda," Palignon said.

The woman sighed, then pulled a chair out from the table and sat down. "I'm sure we can," she said, her voice softening.

"We read the book, Dad. We know you've been out there

exposing that monster we call a king. That you've been fighting for us."

Palignon pulled his daughter in for another hug. "It's always been for you. For both of you. I only ever wanted this to be a safe world for you to grow up in, but for so long I didn't understand that I was only doing Davin's dirty work. I thought I was helping." He pulled back and met Jensa's eyes, then Llonda's. The woman's hard stare had turned to one of sympathy. "Once I learned the truth about you both three years ago, it opened my eyes. And then I met others like you, and for the first time in years, I didn't see danger in any of them. I didn't fear the abilities they had. I realized the biggest danger was King Davin himself.

"I helped a boy around your age, Jensa, as well as a man who treated him how every child with abilities deserves to be treated. *That's* when I decided to help take Davin down from the inside. It's why I've been away so long and been so distant from you both. I want to make things right, to set this world straight."

The room fell silent for a moment.

The creaking of the floorboards outside of the apartment's front door broke the silence.

"They're here," Syntha said, reaching for the sword under her cloak at the same time Kieve and Palignon reached for their weapons.

"Go into the bedroom and hide," Palignon ordered his family.

"We'll protect them," Kieve assured him.

"We'll protect ourselves," came a voice full of assurance that only a teen could muster up. They all turned to face Jensa, who displayed no fear.

The door buckled as a boot slammed into it from the other side. Everyone shifted into fighting stances, ready to defend the apartment. Another kick sent splinters of the frame flying as the door burst open.

"You're under arrest by the order of King Davin," a soldier called as six men wearing the uniforms of the Aepistelle Army rushed in with swords drawn. A wave of relief washed over Kieve as he realized these weren't agents of the Royal Mystic Committee whom he'd worked alongside during his short career. He didn't know if he'd have been able to fight them, to strike them down in defense.

He rushed at the soldiers and put his extensive combat training to use.

Two soldiers pushed back, forcing Kieve into the sitting room. He parried their attacks, batting away the slashing swords with his own, moving from side to side to ensure that neither man got behind him. He bumped into the rear of the sofa, which faced toward the two bedroom doors, and fell backward, tumbling over it. The soldiers rushed to either side of him as he lay supine on the floor between the couch and a low table. He blocked a blow from the soldier at his head and kicked out at the other, striking the man in the shin and sending him stumbling back two steps.

The man behind him kicked at Kieve, his boot slamming into the top of Kieve's head. Stars blossomed before Kieve's eyes, but he managed to stave off the blows from the soldier's sword. The other soldier lunged forward, his sword swinging down toward Kieve's groin, when the low table rose up off the ground. It spun through the air, knocking the sword out of the attacker's hands before he could prevent Kieve from ever having children. The soldier tumbled sideways onto the sofa. The levitating furniture also confused the soldier swinging at Kieve's face, and it was all Kieve needed to flip onto his stomach and push himself up. He stabbed his blade through the soldier's leather armor and into the soft pudge of his belly.

As the soldier fell to the floor, Kieve pulled the blade out, wincing as blood sprayed across the Palignon family apartment. He turned to see Jensa, who had one arm out as if directing the table. As she lowered her arm, the table crashed to the ground behind him.

Two soldiers were fighting Syntha, who was backed against one of the kitchen counters. Palignon had managed to force another soldier out into the stairwell, the clashing of their blades echoing through the doorway. The sixth soldier lay under the overturned kitchen table, which Llonda was sitting on, her weight keeping the man pinned down. Kieve watched as Jensa turned and reached a hand toward the kitchen counter. Three knives rose from the butcher block. They shifted in the air, taking aim.

"Duck!" Jensa shouted as she clenched her fist, then flicked her fingers outward. The knives flew through the air. Syntha dropped to the floor. Two knives stabbed into one soldier's back just below the shoulder, and the third blade dug into the exposed neck of the other soldier, who had just began to turn toward the shouting girl. He fell to the ground first, and Syntha popped back up and swung her sword at the other man's neck, nearly taking off his head.

The soldier on the couch regained his composure and leaped at Kieve, knocking him back toward the window overlooking the street. Kieve lost his sword in the surprise attack, so he used his fists and boots to fight off the man. He grabbed his opponent's shoulders, swung him around, and lobbed him at the window. The glass shattered, and the soldier plummeted three floors down to the sidewalk below.

Palignon was still combatting his opponent, who had backed him through the doorway and into the apartment again, as Syntha, Llonda, Jensa, and Kieve looked on. The soldier glanced around the room. Three of his comrades were dead on the floor, one more was alive but pinned under the table, and another was nowhere to be seen. Blood was everywhere. He knew defeat was imminent. He dropped his sword, turned, and ran for the stairs.

Syntha lunged for the doorway to give chase, but Palignon called out to her.

"Let him go. They know we're here. We're done hiding. There are no more secrets. The time has come to end this for good."

CHAPTER 42
JESTAN

"Look alive!" Quincy Harpon yelled to his crew on the deck of the Aepistelle Navy vessel he'd commandeered. Even from across the narrow stretch of water between that craft and the Emyhrseni cruiser, Jestan could hear the uncertainty in the mercenary's voice.

"He'll be okay," Selinda reassured Jestan. She had been at the helm, keeping the ship close on Quincy's tail, since they'd left the northern port the day before. Selinda addressed her own makeshift crew. "Attention! This is it, mates. Those in uniform, act like you have authority. The rest of you, get belowdecks or look subservient. The patrol is up ahead."

She gestured for Jestan to take the wheel while she jogged to the aft and repeated the order to the crew of the ship behind them, who would pass it along to their rear, and so on. Jestan stretched his arms, hoping to loosen the ill-fitting sailor uniform he wore. He was no stranger to costumes, having performed on stages across Aepistelle for twenty years, but it felt like quite some time since he'd last been in front of a crowd.

Perhaps that wasn't true, he thought. He'd played many new roles since leaving Aepistelle. That of a search party member when he and George had sought Gemma and Richard, who were journeying across the Forest of Despair. That of a liberator when he'd freed Emyhrseni men and women from bondage. He'd been a warrior during the battle at King Harold's castle and a sailor and guide afterward when he'd escorted the Tzakabyans to their ancestral lands. On the way back, he'd been an adventurer. And the last few months in Emyhrsen, he'd been a diplomat of sorts, attempting to reunite a broken society and assist in rebuilding a culture.

"Did you see George?" he asked as Selinda returned to take the helm.

"Aye, he received the message and passed it on. He's still upset, from the looks of it."

"That's to be expected. He's been separated from his parents for more than three years, so he was glad to reunite with them, but having his mother conscripted into this fight was not part of the plan."

"Serena is our best chance at getting into the castle. She said so herself. Nobody in our fleet knows the castle like a person who worked there behind the scenes for thirty years. I swear to you on my own life, as I did to George: we'll keep her safe."

Jestan stepped away, anxiety eating at him as if he could feel the pain of his dearest friend. George had a heart of gold, and the last thing Jestan wanted was for it to become tarnished. He turned and looked toward the ship on which George traveled, but before his eyes found the man, his own shipmates caught his attention. They were all looking straight ahead as the veil of fog lifted, revealing the inlet to Capital Bay.

The entire quarter-mile mouth was guarded by a blockade of dozens of warships.

"This is the moment of truth," Selinda called to him, though instead of sounding frightened, as Quincy had, she seemed to be enjoying this. Perhaps she should be leading their procession, Jestan thought.

He took a deep breath and held it for a moment. In his mind's eye, he saw a conductor in the pit below the stage lifting a baton, letting it hover while the orchestra readied their instruments, then flicking it rhythmically to count off the tempo. A dip of the baton signified the downbeat. The music blasted, cuing Jestan's entrance from stage right.

The show had begun.

Jestan let his breath out and smiled. This was all a performance. He was ready for it, had been training his entire life. All they had to do was convince the naval blockade that they were fellow soldiers bringing in a fleet of insurrectionists. They had the uniforms and the warship to prove it.

He only hoped that Quincy was as ready for the performance as he was.

A dozen ships from the blockade broke out of alignment and moved to intercept the oncoming vessels. One pulled up alongside Quincy and dropped its corvus, and twenty soldiers quickly spilled onto the deck. Another vessel pulled up to Selinda's starboard side, the captain awaiting orders from the first. The naval crew stared hard at Jestan as he greeted them from the railing. They took in his uniform, and he worried they might recognize how ill-fitting it was or that Jestan had clearly aged out of the role of second mate. If a man of his vintage was still working at all, he should be a senior officer behind a desk somewhere on dry land.

One of the soldiers broke off from the others and leaned dangerously far over the railing, studying Jestan as closely as he was able. The young man's head tilted to the side like that of a curious dog. Jestan's breath caught in his throat as the soldier spoke. "Hey, aren't you..." His voice trailed off as he apparently thought better of his comment. "Sorry, my mistake."

Jestan sighed in relief and turned away. Things were going equally well on the other ship—after talking to Quincy for a moment, the commander bellowed with laughter, patted him on the shoulder, and directed his crew back onto their own vessel. The corvus was lifted, separating the ships. They were free to proceed into Capital Bay.

One obstacle overcome, but there were surely countless more to come.

CHAPTER 43
JESTAN

An hour after landing in the eastern port, they'd finally regrouped without drawing too much attention from the port authorities.

"Everyone is distracted," George noted as he came up alongside Jestan. "Seems like something is going on here in town."

"Not the homecoming you deserve, my friend," Jestan said.

"Can't say I've missed this place, anyway." George reached over Jestan's shoulder and pulled up his hood. "Besides, no one would recognize me. You, on the other hand, better keep this on."

Jestan laughed and pulled the fabric farther over his forehead. George was right. Even three years out of the spotlight wouldn't be enough to make the people of Aepistelle forget who Jestan the Just was. He'd performed for tens of thousands of folks all around the country over the course of two decades. His books were among the most widely read in

Aepistelle despite Davin's regime's constant attempts to quell his popularity.

"At least we can get lost in this crowd." Jestan looked around at the eclectic groups congregating around the wharf. Some, like Jestan, wore the Aepistelle naval uniforms plundered from the ship that Quincy's crew had captured on their way into Emyhrsen a few weeks earlier. Most others wore plain garb so as not to stand out.

Among their ranks were Teyla and her warriors—those unusually tall and muscular women would stand out anywhere outside of the northern mountains no matter what disguises they wore. Jestan had recruited three dozen gifted refugees who'd been hiding out in Ferathan. Some Emyhrseni folks who had longed for a fight ever since their days in Tzakabyan captivity had volunteered to help overthrow the despot who'd teamed up with the foreign invaders decades earlier and again just three years prior.

Captain Le'Nelle Nightstar and her crew were in attendance, and they had picked up a few more ships full of pirates, smugglers, and merchants along the coast of Aepistelle, all ready to help topple Davin's regime. Likewise, Quincy's mercenary crew had a large network of acquaintances all around Aepistelle, many of whom were already planted around Capital City. Finally, Serena Calvertson wandered through the crowd, their unlikely guide into Davin's walled palace.

"Let's get started," Serena said as she came up behind her son.

George laughed, but his smile quickly faded. "Mom, I'd rather you just point the way and return to the ship. It'll be safer for you."

"Nonsense. I've been hiding for years now while you and Gemma have risked everything to help people. I'm through with that. We'll take this despot down, and we'll earn our safety. This has gone on long enough."

"Wow," Jestan chimed in, slapping George on the back. "And here I thought *I* was the one who was supposed to make the inspiring speeches. Now I see where Gemma gets her bravery from. You sure you aren't adopted, Georgie-boy?"

"Very funny. Let's get moving before we draw any unwanted attention. I'll see you when this is over, Jestan." George embraced his mother. "I love you, Mom."

"There's still time to switch groups," Jestan said. "You can keep your mother in sight the entire time, make sure she's safe."

"She'll be much safer with Teyla's warriors. They'll make a much stealthier strike crew than me." George hefted the battle hammer he'd forged at Richard's castle in Emyhrsen over the last few weeks.

"True," Teyla chimed in, "and with your heavy footsteps, you'd give us away from the start. I'll keep an eye on your mother at all times, George. You have my word."

THEY SET OFF IN THEIR PREDETERMINED GROUPS, LEAVING at staggered intervals and heading up different parallel streets as to not arouse suspicion. Jestan's group included Serena, Teyla, and the Nazseke warriors. They walked briskly, and Jestan wished they could flag down a fleet of taxi carriages, though he knew it would put the drivers in peril, branding them as accomplices should the plan fail.

They made good timing on foot through the seaside warehouse district and the neighborhood full of apartment buildings that housed many of that area's employees and their families. On the other side of an expansive park, they followed the sidewalk up an incline. The apartment buildings were replaced by single-family houses with space around them and blocks of retail establishments noticeably more upscale than those near the docks, the fishy stench of the wharf district replaced by the aromas of freshly baked bread and fine cuts of meat grilling to perfection. They managed to avoid attention in their plain robes, then made their way through the next few neighborhoods, which were less upscale.

"My family lived just two blocks north of here," Serena said. "I do wonder what's become of my old home."

"So many memories there, I'm sure," Jestan said. The Calvertson family had given up so much, just as he had. "Maybe after all of this is over, you can go back."

"I think not," she responded. He didn't hear any regret in her voice. "My husband has become so comfortable on the north shore. I think we'll stay there for Geoffrey's sake. We will need to find a place of our own, though. Quincy has been so generous, putting us up all this time, but it's time we gave him his space back."

"I'm sure he's been as blessed by you two as you have by him," Jestan reassured her.

"We've done our best to take care of him. He's a lifelong bachelor, much like you. Much like George as well, from the looks of it."

"Speaking of taking care of others, George has been a wonderful companion. You raised a special young man."

"He's got a soft heart, that one. He just—"

Serena stopped in her tracks. Jestan took another couple of steps before he noticed what she saw.

"Any idea what's happening here?" Teyla asked as she came up behind them.

Dozens of folks congregated in the streets, blocking the

paths of carriages, whose angry riders screamed for the crowds to move out of the way.

"Those are supply wagons heading to the castle," Serena observed. "Davin's sigil is stamped on every side."

"Looks like we're not the only ones who have come here to make Davin pay." As he spoke, Jestan spotted six local police officers moving around the corner. He pointed down an alley. "Let's go this way and avoid getting mixed up with that group."

"No, we're almost there," Serena insisted. "We need to go through them. Let's just make it quick."

Jestan relented, and they continued through the crowd. He caught bits of conversation between those congregated around them, though he didn't catch the context. He heard mentions of a book, of King Davin, and even of Emyhrsen, which took Jestan aback. The neighboring country had not been a common topic of conversation in the last several decades, since it had pretty much gone silent during the reign of the Tzakabyans. His eyes met Serena's. She looked equally intrigued.

"Excuse me," she said to a young woman who Jestan assumed was a local university student. "What's this about a book?"

The student shrugged her knapsack off her shoulders, reached in, and retrieved a leather-bound volume. The author's name caught Jestan's attention immediately. By her gasp, it seemed that Serena had noticed as well.

"Gemma!" she cried. She looked at the young woman. "Where did you get this? What is it?"

"It's the truth, exposing King Davin and his decades of deceit. Folks have been distributing copies around campus. Rumor has it that the author was arrested last week and that Davin is holding her in his dungeons. Everyone is up in arms.

The protest at the castle walls was getting too intense, so we came over here. This book has—"

"If you do not evacuate this area, you will be arrested and imprisoned!" an officer called out to the crowd, interrupting the student. "This is an unauthorized public gathering. Disperse immediately or face jail time."

The young woman snatched the book back from Serena. "Sorry, I must go. My parents will never forgive me if I end up behind bars." With that, she disappeared into the crowd.

Jestan had trouble reading Serena's expression, which hovered somewhere between pride and horror. Gemma's years of hard work had paid off, but she'd also painted a target on her own back, as well as on anyone else mentioned in that book—Jestan included. Worse, Gemma was allegedly in the belly of the beast at that very moment.

Jestan turned around, confirming that Teyla had heard what the student had said. "It looks like we have one more task when we get inside the castle."

Teyla looked deep in thought for a moment, then perked up. "If Gemma is there, then Arnem may be as well."

"Only one way to find out," Jestan said as the group continued on its way.

—

THE WAREHOUSE THEY ENTERED A FEW MINUTES LATER WAS a laundry and textile facility three blocks from King Davin's castle that handled the creation and maintenance of all linens, napkins, curtains, and banners. Serena Calvertson, who had done all sorts of tasks around the castle for more than thirty years, was well acquainted with its layout and its nooks and crannies. The tunnel they sought was one of several that connected the castle to various facilities that kept it running, like the food preparation kitchens and the blacksmith, allowing for easy transport of goods and personnel, bypassing the hustle and bustle of Capital City's main avenues. Serena had assured Jestan that the tunnels had always been minimally guarded by just two soldiers within each facility per shift.

The fact that the front door was locked in the middle of a shift on a busy weekday was the first sign that something was wrong. After smashing the lock and entering, they found all the workstations abandoned. On one lay a crisp cloth napkin with only half of Davin's sigil embroidered.

"They left in a hurry," Teyla observed. Her warriors dropped the sacks they'd been carrying through town. They pulled out the contents, which included pairs of shafts, connectors, and pointed tips. One of the women handed a freshly assembled spear to Teyla.

"This makes our job easier," Jestan said as Serena led them down a flight of stairs to the subterranean level. At the end of a corridor crowded with laundry carts, she pointed to a set of double doors.

"That's normally where one guard is stationed, with the other at the front door upstairs," she said.

"The guards must have sent everyone home for safety reasons when they were called to protect the castle from the protestors," Teyla guessed. She pressed forward, throwing open the doors as two of her warriors plunged forward with their spears in case any guards awaited them within. The tunnel was empty.

Jestan felt relief, but he saw the strife on Serena's face. "Gemma will be okay," he assured her. "Do you know the way to the dungeon? We'll stop there first. We could use her help."

Serena perked up, relieved to put her knowledge to use. "The tunnel lets out one level up from the topmost dungeon floor. In my earliest days working at the castle, I had to clean up the cells after prisoners were released or executed. The dungeons were usually minimally staffed, just the warden and two or three guards on each level. There were sometimes more if there was a particularly dangerous group of prisoners, but I doubt they see Gemma as a physical threat."

"Ha!" Teyla burst out. "They don't know that the girl trained with me. She's a physical threat all right."

Serena ignored her. "As long as nobody is waiting on the other side of this tunnel, we should be able to get down there without issue. The warden—or dungeon keeper, as he likes to refer to himself—is an odd little man. We can make him talk."

Serena pressed on ahead of everyone and led the way through the dark, cavernous tunnels below the streets of Capital City.

CHAPTER 44
DENNY

Denny lay in darkness. His cell lacked windows, and he couldn't even keep track of time by the meals the guards delivered, as they arrived as sporadically as the drops of pungent liquid that seeped through the cracks in the ceiling. He guessed he had been locked up for three or four days, but he couldn't tell the difference between day and night. There was nothing to do but sleep, and he was constantly awoken by the putrid water trickling from overhead no matter what part of the stone floor he sprawled on.

Anxiety crept into his heart. Someone he loved was in danger, yet all he could do was lie there, helpless. *This is how my parents must have felt*, he thought. *They spent years locked up, receiving nightly premonitions but with no ability to act on them.* And yet his mother hadn't been idle. Somehow she'd found a way to increase her abilities—to send out communications of her own instead of being merely a receptor. She had reached Denny in her darkest moments, including the minutes leading up to her death. As hard as Denny had worked under Marzele's tutelage since then, he still had not discovered the secret his mother had unearthed, at least not in this realm. Communicating with the bird in the Realm Beyond had been effortless.

Gemma, he thought. He pictured her in his mind's eye. *Are you out there?*

Nothing. His mind went to Arnem, then Marzele, but neither man was on his plane of existence any longer.

Richard? Still nothing, but that didn't surprise him, as the man was hundreds of miles north in Emyhrsen.

Denny's heart rate increased rapidly, thudding away in his chest like the flapping wings of a small bird evading a predator. The walls closed in around him, the ceiling coming down to crush him and the floor rising to meet it. He sucked in a deep breath, but the stench of sewage caused him to gag and fall into a coughing fit.

"Don't you die in there," someone called from the hallway. He recognized the voice of the hunched dungeon master who had led Denny and his captors to this cell days earlier. "Last thing I need is a high-profile prisoner croaking on my watch. His Majesty would have me locked away in there with your carcass."

Denny pictured the pale old man who had clearly spent far too much of his life in the subterranean prison with barely a glimpse of sunlight. *Open the door*, Denny commanded through his thoughts.

"Not going to happen, boy," the man yelled back as if Denny had spoken out loud.

"It worked," Denny whispered to himself as the footsteps retreated down the hall. *Come back and open this door*, he thought, but this time there was no response. It didn't feel the same, either—it lacked the feeling of personal connection he'd had just moments before. Denny closed his eyes, and this time he saw the hallway outside his cell. His view was shifting, moving, as if he were walking through the corridors of the dungeon.

He looked down and saw boots much larger than his own. Old cracked leather.

"What in hellfire is happening?" the old man said, or thought. Denny wasn't sure which, but he heard it clearly as if he were speaking. He was looking through the guard's eyes; he was in the man's head. The dungeon keeper looked around rapidly, seeking an explanation for the feeling of an intruder within his consciousness. "Hello?" he asked. "Is someone there?"

You've made a very big mistake, Denny thought to the man. *The kingdom will suffer for your actions.*

"Who is this?" the man asked, lurching around a corner as if he might find an intruder taunting him.

Open my cell, let me out, and I'll see you don't get hurt.

"Ha! A runt like you needs a good whipping, and I'm fully equipped to give you that."

Denny heard the man's footsteps approaching, and through the link he saw him retrieving a bullwhip hanging on the wall.

"Prepare to squeal, little one," the dungeon keeper called out. "If you think sitting on that stone floor is uncomfortable now, just wait until your bottom is torn clean open by me and —what?"

Through the man's eyes, Denny watched his attention shift behind him as a great many footsteps echoed through the cavernous halls.

"Who is that? I didn't approve any visitors. I—"

The corner he turned was dark, and all Denny saw through the man's eyes was a spear flying out of the blackness. Denny cut the link before he felt any pain, but before he had fully separated his consciousness from that of the dungeon keeper, he felt the essence of the man's life leaving his body.

"Help!" Denny screamed through the thick door, then second-guessed himself. *Could these be friends*, he wondered, *or am I in even more trouble?*

"Denny, is that you?"

A woman's voice. She had a strong accent that sounded unlike anybody he'd met in Aepistelle. He'd met only one group of women who'd sounded like that, but there was no reason any of them would be so far from their homeland, unless...

"Teyla?"

A chorus of laughter rang out behind the thick steel door, and Denny found himself smiling for the first time in days. If Teyla and her warriors had come all the way from the northern mountains, then perhaps Richard had assembled an army to rescue Gemma.

A key clanked into the lock. With a squeal of rusted hinges, the door swung open to reveal a crowd of twelve women and a man. It was not lost on Denny, even after having lived with Arnem the Loyal and adventured alongside Richard the Elusive, that one of the heroes he'd idolized his entire life had come to rescue *him* from peril.

"Jestan," he managed before lunging forward and throwing his arms around the living legend.

Jestan chuckled and patted his back. "In the flesh," he said. "Listen, kid. The last time we met was quite brief and chaotic, and then I sailed off to escort the Tzakabyans home. I promise to make more time to chat with you and get to know you, but right now we need to move. Do you know where Gemma is? Did she successfully retrieve Arnem?"

"Yes, where is my daughter?" said the only woman who

was clearly not a Nazseke warrior. As she stepped forward, Denny recognized her.

"Mrs. Calvertson, why are you here?" he asked, then felt ridiculous for questioning her presence. "You came for Gemma, of course."

The woman shook her head. "No, I came to help the team enter the castle undetected. I know the corridors of this place better than most. We're here to end Davin's rule."

"We only just learned that Gemma might be here," Teyla chimed in. "We didn't expect to find you, however."

"Clearly the boy has been locked up and doesn't know her whereabouts," Jestan said. "Let's check the cells for Gemma before any more guards come down and find that their friend has a new hole in his body." One of the Nazseke warriors smiled at this and thrust her spear into the air. A shower of blood flew off and splattered the floor beside the door to Denny's cell.

"I'm quite certain she's upstairs," he told his rescuers. "They separated us when we arrived. The guards brought me down here, but Gemma was escorted in another direction by some slimy-looking guy who seemed to know her. I've been stuck here ever since."

"And Arnem?" Jestan asked with a hope in his voice that hurt Denny.

"I'm so sorry, Jestan," he said. "He remained behind. He's in the Realm Beyond. It's a long story, but he was needed there more than here, so he chose to stay."

"No time for long stories," Serena chimed in. "I'm sorry, but we must go."

CHAPTER 45

GEMMA

Kosar had stopped dragging Gemma along at some point in their trek through the maze of hallways. By the time they exited the palace's interior and set out across the courtyard to the rampart stairs, Gemma had taken the lead.

Guards ran about frantically, taking their defensive positions, though most had never had to face any danger. Davin had increased their numbers after the failed attack by Marzele and his fellow Solendaron priests three years earlier, ending a long stretch of relative peace and safety.

Gemma looked to the left and right as she stepped onto the wall. She peeked through a notch in the parapet and saw a mass of people below. They were from all walks of life, from university-aged activists to middle-aged laborers to the elderly people and children. Was it a demonstration? A peaceful protest against King Davin? Had they come for blood, to overthrow Aepistelle's monarch? Their shouts were disorganized, chaotic, the words indecipherable. Some held torches, others weapons, both well crafted and makeshift, and still others carried books. She didn't need to be close enough to see her name to know what the books were. She didn't think *every* book being wielded in the crowd was hers, but Gemma had no doubt her words had been the catalyst for this.

"Look what you've done," Kosar said. She turned to see him scowling down at the assembly below. He shifted his gaze to her, his hateful expression softening as he took in her face. "As I said before, only you can undo this. We must convince my father to let you speak."

"No," Gemma said. "That is not going to happen, Kosar. None of this will just go away. I will not lie to the people about—"

"Hey!" someone shouted from down below. "That's her!"

Gemma scanned the crowd. A woman around her mother's age held up a large piece of paper for those near her to see. As the woman turned toward the castle wall, Gemma scanned it. Even from her high-up perch, she recognized the WANTED poster with a decent rendition of her face, along with those of her friends. The posters had been plastered all around Capital City after the events in Emyhrsen three years earlier.

"Gemma Calvertson!" someone else yelled. A murmur rumbled through the crowd, and within seconds, dozens, then hundreds of people began to chant her name. "Gemma Calvertson! Gemma Calvertson! Gemma Cal—"

There was growl from her right, drowning out the chanting. Kosar dug his fingers into her arm as he yanked her away from the notch in the parapet.

"This cannot be happening," he snarled. He guided Gemma back toward the stairs and pushed her forward. She nearly stumbled on the first stone step, which could have sent her to her death or at the least to the infirmary with a dozen broken bones, but she managed to catch herself. "My father will lay waste to every one of those mongrels when he—"

Thud.

Gemma turned back as something wet and warm spattered her cheek and Kosar stopped talking. Blood was smeared across the side of his head. A stone had struck him on the right temple. He looked at her in shock for a moment, and then his face filled with malice once more. He called to the nearest guards, "Don't just stand there, you incompetent morons! Unleash your arrows on those cretins. Kill them all!"

He tightened his grip on Gemma's good arm and forced her down the remaining stairs and into the castle as the crowd lobbed rocks and rotten produce over the wall. Gemma heard a commander instruct the guards to take aim and fire. And then the screams began as arrows rained down.

CHAPTER 46
KIEVE

Kieve had been away at the cadet training camp for the Royal Mystic Committee the last time the castle in Capital City had come under siege. He remembered how outraged his fellow new recruits had been; the destruction of the castle's outer walls and the threats to their kind had fueled them all to work harder at their drills and combat training. Some had even transferred to the military, not satisfied by the intelligence roles they'd signed up for. Kieve, on the other hand, knew the importance of the Royal Mystic Committee, of taking control over those with special powers who could quickly turn into dangerous weapons. If he'd been told back then how things would change in just a few years' time, he wouldn't have believed it.

Kieve led the way, navigating through the thousands of enraged citizens who surrounded the castle district for blocks. He pulled his hood over his face a couple of times when he spotted fellow Committee agents patrolling the crowd. By now, word of his traitorous actions would have spread through their ranks, and they were sure to arrest him on sight, or worse. Behind him was Syntha, followed by Palignon, Jensa, and Llonda. Kieve glanced back at Syntha, who looked uncomfortable in the crowd.

"Everything okay?" he asked her. "You don't strike me as someone who enjoys being in the middle of a swarm of people."

"I'm not, but that's not it. I'm a head taller than many in this crowd. Makes me easy to spot. If my cousin is lurking, he'll certainly pick me out. I'm probably endangering this mission."

"We won't let him lay a finger on you," the youngest member of their group called out. "Not if I can help it."

Kieve nodded. "Jensa's right. That coward won't have a chance to get near you."

"I fear for Gemma as well," Syntha said, not soothed by their support. "Kosar will sink to unfathomable depths to get what he wants, and the only thing he desires as much as power is her."

Kieve's heart sped up at the mention of her name. "He better not lay a finger on her either. I'll kill him myself. But she'll never give in to him, even if it's the only way to save Aepistelle."

"That's what I'm afraid of," Syntha said. "If she spurns him one too many times, especially in a powder keg like this, he may snap. We're talking about a man who had his own brother and closest friends executed just to impress King Davin. There is no end to his depravity."

Kieve didn't need to hear any more. He picked up his pace and only hoped the others would keep up. The walls came into view ahead as he continued down the street. Guards paced frantically, spooked that the rebuilt stone baileys might be knocked down again on their watch. Kieve didn't have the powers of the Solendaron priests who had attacked the palace before, but if those walls were all that separated him from Gemma, Kieve was ready to tear them down by any means necessary.

He was so focused on his mission that he wasn't paying attention to what was going on in the crowd. To his right, the masses parted in frustration as a girl pushed her way through at full speed and slammed into Kieve. He reached out to catch her, but he was too slow. She toppled onto the cobblestone road on her side.

"Are you okay?" he asked as he bent to help her up. Her eyes were a shade he'd never seen on a person. The greenish blue was the exact color of the ocean, as if water from the Western Sea had filled in the spaces behind her irises. He gasped as they rippled, like when a stone was dropped into a calm pond. She took his hand, and he pulled her to her feet.

"Out of the way! Release that girl!" These shouts came from two men panting their way through the crowd. As they came within twenty feet, Kieve recognized the pair.

"Fallbrook?" one of them said. They were wearing the tactical uniforms that some units of the Royal Mystic Committee used during particularly dangerous assignments.

"Both of you to catch one little girl?" Kieve asked in a mocking tone.

"It's not what you think," the other replied. "That one's dangerous. She's—"

His voice cut off as the girl began to whisper in a language Kieve did not recognize.

A splashing sound pulled his attention away from her. He looked back at the two agents, who were no longer standing on the ground. Both men were floating ten feet in the air, flailing their arms and legs frantically, sending them spinning in circles. They were submerged in water, a hovering pool with no solid sides, nothing to keep it contained. He watched in shock along with the rest of the crowd as the agents panicked, unable to breathe. One sucked in a mouthful of water, his face going blue. The other's eyes widened so much in fear that Kieve thought they'd pop out of his skull.

He squeezed the girl's hand. "Best release them now," he suggested. She flashed him a look of disappointment before relenting. She pulled her hand away from his and clapped twice. The blob of water burst and rained over the crowd, and the two men slammed down onto the ground. They coughed out the water they'd inhaled and greedily sucked air into their lungs.

"You're dead, little girl," one of them growled as he got to his feet.

Kieve pulled the girl behind him and reached under his robe for his pair of daggers. Before he could pull them out, a massive hammer swung out of the crowd and careened into one agent's stomach. The other agent lunged at the hammer's wielder with a truncheon he pulled from his belt. Syntha ran over and tackled him, knocking the metal club from his hand. It clattered as it hit the ground and rolled away.

Kieve turned to find that the girl had slipped off into the crowd. He shrugged before searching for the person with the battle hammer. He was a similar age to Kieve, if not a few years older, husky and muscular. His hair and skin had a darker tone that usually indicated Ferromini heritage. Kieve stepped forward and patted the man on the shoulder.

"Thanks for your help," Kieve said. The man looked stunned that he'd hurt a government agent. "Your first time using that thing?" Kieve asked, pointing to the hammer.

"Not at all. I just hope that wasn't a friend of my sister's."

"What do you mean?" Kieve asked.

"Never mind. Long story." The man turned away from Kieve to look for the girl, but it was a lost cause.

"Looked like she could take care of herself," Kieve said. "She—"

His voice faded as a murmur rippled through the crowd. Another group pushed through the mass of people to join the hammer-wielder. Some of them had similar skin tone but were a generation older.

"George," one of the men said, "are you okay?"

"I wish Jestan hadn't let the younger ones from Ferathan come along. Now I've lost one and—"

"Did you say Jestan?" Kieve interrupted. "And Ferathan? Are you Gemma's friends?"

The young man's eye's widened while the older man's narrowed in distrust. "I'm her brother," the younger one began before the older one grabbed him by the shoulder to stop him from revealing too much.

Kieve raised a hand in a placating gesture. "You don't have to worry," he said. He waved Syntha over. "We're friends of Gemma's. We're here to help her."

"That's her!" someone yelled from the crowd. In seconds, dozens began to chant her name. "Gemma Calvertson!"

They looked up at the wall. Gemma stood at the top, looking down at the crowd. Relief flooded Kieve as he noted that she looked healthy and unharmed with the exception of a bandage on one shoulder.

And then she was gone. A man had stepped forward and tugged her back. The crowd roared with anger. People began to toss stones and rotten vegetables up at the guards still visible at the top.

Syntha came up alongside Kieve. "That was my cousin with her," she said. "Just as I thought. I am going to kill him."

She turned away and disappeared into the crowd.

"Syntha, wait!" Jensa shouted, taking off in pursuit. Palignon's daughter had taken a liking to the woman in the couple of hours since they'd first met in the Palignon family's apartment. As the girl's parents chased after her, a scream of terror sounded out near the wall. The guards had nocked arrows onto the strings of their bows and were aiming down into the crowd.

"Scatter!" Kieve yelled. He ran after Syntha and the Palignon family as arrows rained down on the helpless citizens of Capital City.

CHAPTER 47
GEMMA

The thick doors were closed and bolted behind Gemma and Kosar as they returned to the castle's interior. She didn't want to be back inside with her enemies, but in her helpless state, it was all she could do to avoid the sounds of suffering and slaughter outside.

Where are George and Quincy and the others? she wondered as she blindly followed Kosar to his father's chambers. *Did they make it to Capital City, or was their mission thwarted before they even left Emyhrsen?* It would not have surprised her if Davin had sent spies to the country in the north. It was a place of chaos and rebuilding following the decades of enslavement by the Tzakabyans, with whom Davin had been in league. Would the recently freed folks really know if there were spies among them? Gemma didn't think so.

The halls of the palace were flooded with scrambling servants, guards, and guests, all trying to find safety or ways to defend their monarch. Everyone was so busy and flustered, in fact, that there were no guards or attendants outside the king's chambers.

"Nobody to stop you," Gemma said when they stepped into the vestibule outside Davin's door.

Kosar turned to look at her, dismay painting his face. "Whatever do you mean?"

"They wouldn't normally let a bastard like you visit the king in his private suite, would they? It's not as if you're officially his son or heir." She stuck the proverbial knife in and twisted. If she couldn't physically fight him at that moment, at least she could hurt Kosar in other ways. Gemma bit the inside of her cheek to contain her smile.

"Yes, well, you're about to change all that when you present your apology and say you'll retract everything in that damn book of yours." Kosar turned the knob and threw open the door.

The old man pacing in front of his desk seemed to have shrunk since Gemma had seen him last. He'd found unnatural ways to prolong his health and vigor, certainly, but now the years seemed to have caught up to him. He turned, flashing Kosar a look of such contempt that Gemma almost felt bad for the young man. Almost.

"Father, I—"

"I just sent my attendants up to gather that little cave woman so she could administer another dose of that green material. To their surprise, they couldn't find her, so they peeked out her open window. What do you suppose they found when they looked down?" Davin peeled his hateful eyes off Kosar and shifted his glare to Gemma. "Three servants scraping her guts off the cobblestones. Who knew such a small thing could cause such a large mess?"

"Father, I'm sorry I—"

"Yes, I'm sure you are. You always have been a sorry little weasel. Why I ever brought you into the fold, I have no idea. I suppose I thought you'd be of some use to me here, yet as more time passed, it looked like your earlier successes were just flukes. But then it seemed you had turned a new page, bringing in that woman and learning the secrets of the mineral. The mining operation went off without a hitch. It all looked so good until this latest disaster. Now I'm going to need more time to consider how to proceed with our succession plans."

Tears ran down Kosar's face. "I have a plan, Father. I will fix this." He pushed Gemma forward. "*She* will undo it all."

Davin rolled his eyes. "We're past that stage now, boy. I've tried to achieve most of my successes as king of this dreadful land without using the abilities I was blessed with when I came into the world. I cheated here and there, no doubt, but when it really mattered, I relied on my own cunning. Sure, most of my more nefarious misdeeds could be traced back to me if anyone really cared to investigate, but no one ever did." He glared hard at Gemma. "Until *Gemma Calvertson* came along. Too honest and noble for her own good. Even though I threw her a serious lifeline, she has fought to foil me at every turn for three years now. She inspires people with her unceasing idealism. The time has come now for me to combat that with my own unique skills."

"What do you mean?" Kosar asked, but Gemma didn't need to hear the answer.

"Wait," she pleaded.

Davin rolled his eyes. "Gemma, turn and kick Kosar as hard as you can between the legs," he ordered.

Gemma shook her head. "No," she said, but it came out with less force than she intended. Her mind frosted over, freezing her free will in place. She pivoted to her left and swung her leg out just as Kosar tried to back away from her. He was too slow, however, and Gemma's boot connected with his groin. He bent down and dropped to his knees in pain. "I'm sorry," she whispered.

"Kosar," Davin said, "while you're down there, please give the floor a good lick. It could use some spit shine."

Against his will, Kosar complied, leaving a long, slick line of saliva like the trail of a snail.

"You see?" Davin asked them. "It's just so pathetically easy that it feels like cheating. Not that I'm above cheating, but I do have a little more pride in myself than that most of the time. These, however, are extraordinary circumstances thanks to you two buffoons, so it seems I must use any means necessary to crush your little revolution. This is certain to be a bloody day. I do hope the servants scrubbing Madame Hvalsi's remains off the courtyard floor are taking notes, as they'll have many more messes to clean up by this time tomorrow."

CHAPTER 48
JESTAN

Jestan led the group, following the directions Serena called out. Due to her lack of fighting experience, they'd placed her in the center of their procession, and the Nazseke warriors were ready to defend her at all costs. Even though he knew Denny had been in a few tussles over the last few years, Jestan insisted the boy stick by Serena's side.

"Wait," Denny called out as they opened the door that led from the dungeon's front area to the stairwell. "They have my sword somewhere. I'm going to need it before we go upstairs." He broke off from the group, slipping between Teyla and one of her companions. He opened one of the doors meant for prison staff, then came out a moment later. He backtracked down the hall and checked a couple more doors while Jestan called impatiently for him to hurry. The last thing he wanted was to ruin their element of surprise by having the next shift of guards walk in as they stood waiting.

"Anything?" he called, his voice echoing off the stone and steel of the hallway and cell doors. Jestan's heart sped up as he awaited a response from the boy. He'd been in the last room a few seconds longer than Jestan was comfortable with. "Syntha, go check on him. I'll be ready at the door in case anyone—"

"Found it!" Denny called. He jogged back into the hallway carrying a machete and a curved sword the likes of which Jestan had never seen. Denny handed the former to Serena. "That belongs to Gemma. She's going to need it once we find her."

"Let's get a move on," Jestan ordered. He led them up the stairs toward the ground level of the castle.

CHAPTER 49
GEORGE

Some of the crowd outside the castle had dispersed when the arrows had begun raining down from the walls, finding shelter a block away. Many more had left altogether, realizing they were in over their heads, just mere citizens calling for the removal of a despot king with nothing but their voices and sheer numbers. In the face of danger, they had decided their lives were perhaps not so bad after all and had returned to the safety of their cozy homes.

George Calvertson had no such luxury. He was in deep, as were the people he loved most dearly. Not only was Jestan somewhere inside that castle, so was George's mother. And so was his sister, as he'd just seen with his own eyes. Gemma hadn't looked like a prisoner, peering over the parapet and taking in the crowd below for a few seconds before being pulled back. And then the attack on the mostly unarmed crowd had begun. George knew his sister wasn't on Davin's side, and by the chants of those congregated outside the castle, it seemed the people of Aepistelle knew that as well.

The attack from the walls had stopped, however

temporarily. Everyone alive who was still in the streets around the castle rose to their feet. George pushed aside the wooden board he'd hidden under, one on which a protestor had painted DOWN WITH DAVIN. He looked around, seeing some folks mourning fallen comrades and others screaming obscenities at the cruel guards for attacking helpless civilians. A burly man in stolen naval regalia rose up among them, a look of immense sadness on his face. George ran over to him.

"What's happened, Quincy?" George asked his father's longtime friend. "Is it..." His voice trailed off as he spotted the woman bleeding out on the cobblestones, an arrow in her left shoulder and another piercing her belly.

"Georgie-boy," she attempted before coughing up a mouthful of crimson.

"Le'Nelle, no," George wept. "Let's get you to safety. You can't go down here, Le'Nelle. It's not your time yet."

"That's *Captain* Le'Nelle, damn it." Her voice was weak. She groaned but still managed to continue. "You've become just like Jestan. Nothing like that shy boy he brought to us all those years ago. Make sure the ladies take care of my kitties for me, okay?"

"Nonsense. You're going to be okay. Let's get you to a pub nearby, get some drink in you. That always seems to bring you to life." Tears drenched his cheeks. A hand fell on his shoulder, and he looked up into Quincy's solemn face. The older man shook his head. George nodded. "I promise those little guys will be watched over—I'll do it myself. I..."

George didn't finish. Le'Nelle shuddered. The look in her eyes changed from one of pain and contemplation to one devoid of any thought or emotion.

"Help me move her," Quincy said, gripping Le'Nelle under her arms. George took his departed friend's feet and lifted.

They set her down on a nearby bench. "We'll come back for her after this is over. Bury her at sea where she belongs."

George looked around. The square had begun to fill up once again. Among those returning were some of Quincy's mercenaries, back from escorting vulnerable citizens away from the slaughter; Le'Nelle's crew, looking around for their leader; the people of Emyhrsen; and several refugees from Ferathan. Their numbers, along with all the enraged citizens of Capital City in attendance, far exceeded the number of people inside the castle walls. George was sure of it. Given the right opportunity, they could succeed. They only had to work together as a unit with one common goal.

Someone had to unite them.

"Where is Jestan when you need him?" George asked. Quincy looked at him with confusion. "To bring everyone together. Say something inspiring. It's a gift of his."

"I don't see why you can't do it, George. Your heart is as big as his."

"I'm no good at that sort of thing," George said.

Quincy pointed at a planter with thick stone sides. "Get up there. Extraordinary times call for extraordinary acts, my boy."

The thought terrified him. These people didn't know George, had not even the slightest inkling that the one-time blacksmith from the slums of this very city had gone on adventures most could only dream of before returning to fight for their freedom.

George nodded, took a deep breath, and stepped up onto the planter. "Um, excuse me," he started. His voice was uneven, his projection over the chatter of the growing crowd sorely lacking. "Excuse me!" he yelled again. A few nearby groups turned to look at him in confusion. "Listen, please. We need to—"

In unison, dozens of folks in the crowd gasped in surprise. George glanced from side to side, scanning the crowd. They weren't looking at him at all. Those whose attention he had caught turned away, following the gazes of their peers up to the top of the walls.

More arrows? George thought for a split second, ready to dive down into hiding once again. Before he could move, a chorus of trumpets sounded, signaling the arrival of King Davin.

The ruler appeared on high. Just behind him were two more figures. These people had been up on the wall only minutes before, but the way they carried themselves now was different.

A hush fell over the crowd. Everyone seemed uncertain whether they should hide before another attack began or bow in the presence of their king, no matter their feelings for him.

Davin raised his arms and addressed the crowd.

CHAPTER 50
KOSAR

Kosar had consumed his share of recreational mind-altering substances over the years, both natural and synthetic. In their teen years, Ysidro, Syntha, Kosar, and their circle of friends had spent many carefree summer nights in deserted corners of the castle in the Southern Reaches with various inebriating concoctions. They had numbed their minds, hallucinated, laughed hysterically, cried dramatically, all their inhibitions gone.

In the decade since, Kosar had sobered up and taken on responsibilities in his opposing roles as an insurgent leader with an underground publication and a scheming counterpart to King Davin.

Now, however, he felt very much like he had in his youth. Worse, really. He had little control of his body. He was aware of what was happening to him, what he was being made to do, but he lacked the ability to stop any of it. After his father had forced him to clean the floor of the king's chambers with his tongue like a dog, the man had forced Kosar and Gemma to escort him through the courtyard. Davin led them back up the steps to the landing atop the curtain wall overlooking a fraction of the would-be insurgents. The crying and shouting below faded as the king came into view and lifted his arms to command their attention. Despite Kosar's current state and his newfound hatred for his father, he wished in that moment that he could wield such power, that he could silence an angry mob just by raising his hands.

"Good people of Capital City, my wonderful citizens of Aepistelle: greetings. It appears there has been some sort of misunderstanding between us. Apparently, a certain book has been circulated around these great lands by rabble-rousers. The words staining the pages of this libelous filth aren't worth the ink they were printed with. Lies, all of it."

"It sounds real to me," someone shouted from below, and others called out in agreement.

"How can you prove it?" another voice yelled out.

From where Kosar stood, he could barely see some of the crowd through the crenels. To his shock, several folks appeared conflicted, as if they wanted to believe their king.

"You see," Davin continued, "I employed a brilliant young woman to ensure that my Royal Mystic Committee was serving as a benevolent force for the people of this kingdom. There were some people who did not appreciate the strides the Committee made, and they used this fine lady as a scape-goat. In their fictional account, which many of you appear to have read, they destroyed this poor girl's name and painted her as a repulsive character. I can assure you, Gemma Calvertson is the noblest of civil servants. She harbors no ill will against me or my reign. She was as shocked as I was to learn that her name had been abused in such a cruel and damaging fashion."

"Show us the girl!" someone demanded.

"Show us Gemma Calvertson!"

"Let's hear it from her!"

Kosar glanced at Gemma and caught the look of horror on her face. Davin turned around and gestured for her to step forward. He spoke to her just loud enough for Kosar to hear. "You will tell them the book is false. You will deny any involvement in its creation and distribution. You will place the blame on Richard the Elusive and the people of Emyhrsen."

"What?" Gemma cried. "I would never—"

"You will do so immediately, or I will decapitate that boy we're holding in the dungeon and force you to watch. Then my soldiers will travel up to the north coast, retrieve both of your parents, and bring them here for the same treatment. Now do it!" Davin grabbed her arm and thrust her toward the crenel. Kosar wanted to dash forward and make his father pay for mistreating her, but he could not budge. He forced his eyes downward to his boots.

With all his might, he attempted to wiggle his toes within them.

Nothing.

The crowd murmured at the sight of Gemma. Some cheered, others booed, but most seemed conflicted now that Davin had planted a seed of doubt in their minds. Kosar was not certain if his father had used his special abilities on them or if just his words had been enough.

"As you have surmised," Davin continued, his arm around Gemma's shoulders as if they were close friends, "this is the woman named on the cover of that book. This is Gemma Calvertson. I've brought her before you so that she can tell her truth and clear her name." Davin turned to her. "Go on," he said quietly.

Gemma stood there silently, scanning the crowd. Kosar was unable to see her face, but he knew the struggle that raged within her. He knew it was a bed of her own making, and he did not agree with her mission to destroy his father, but he also did not want to see her forced to retract her life's work in front of all these people. At one point, Kosar had encouraged her to spread the truth about Davin. He had promised he would help her print her manuscript and distribute copies. He'd been playing both sides, though, and only one could be victorious. As it turned out, Davin was the victor. This was the price that had to be paid.

"Tell them," Davin demanded, this time growling the words just loud enough to be heard by the crowd. Kosar could hear them whispering. They were starting to realize that Davin was lying about the book's authorship.

"I'm Gemma Calvertson," she said. "As His Majesty said, someone put my name on the books so many of you appear to be carrying. I never authorized the printing of those books. I was not aware of their existence. What King Davin said about the Royal Mystic Committee is true—I joined him to help revitalize it, change the way it operated. For too long, people who were born with abilities or learned to use them through the teachings of their religious factions were persecuted by the Committee. Most of them were good people, and they did not deserve such treatment. But others presented risks—those who were unable to control their abilities or intentionally used them for harm. We came to a compromise: the Committee would continue to regulate and document those with abilities while neutralizing any threats.

"The only problem was that the biggest threat of all was the man in charge."

"What do you think you're doing?" Davin asked in disbelief. He thrust Gemma against the merlon.

"King Davin is everything he claims to hate!" Gemma screamed. Davin slammed her head into the stone merlon, but she continued addressing the crowd. "He's able to force others to do his bidding. He—"

Davin yanked her up by the hair and slapped her across the face. She fell at his feet.

Afraid for Gemma's safety, Kosar tried again to move his toes, to take a step, to throw himself forward. Nothing. And then...

He felt his big toe brush against the leather of his boot. As if he were a gargoyle breaking loose from a building's stony exterior before leaping from its perch, Kosar's muscles felt like they cracked open as he flung himself at his father.

Davin saw him coming. The old man pivoted and punched Kosar in the throat. Kosar stumbled backward and collapsed, feeling as if his windpipe had been smashed closed.

CHAPTER 51
JESTAN

"If Gemma is here, she'll be in the north wing," Serena insisted as she led Jestan and the others up a narrow stairwell intended for servants. She had broken free of the protective bubble that Teyla and her warriors had formed around her, and now she wielded Gemma's machete as if she were a trained fighter herself. "She'll be right up..."

Serena's voice faded as footsteps came from one level above. She held up her right hand, signaling for the others to halt. Jestan stopped and repeated the gesture for Denny, Teyla, and the others. The steps coming toward them were light, not those of a guard.

"Lorinne?" Serena called out as a woman turned at the landing on the stairs. She wore the uniform of a housekeeper.

"Serena!" she exclaimed. "What are you doing here? It's been..." She stopped as she noticed the machete in her old friend's hand and the ensemble standing on the stairs. She studied Jestan with vague recognition. "Who are these people, Serena?"

"My friends. We're here to rescue Gemma."

"Oh, thank goodness." Lorinne took another step down and hugged Serena. "I recognized her as soon as I saw her, but I was powerless to stop them. I haven't been in her room, but my maids tell me His Majesty is treating her well...for a prisoner, anyway. At least she's not down in the wretched dungeons stewing in her own excrement."

"Please, Lorinne, take us to her."

"They'll execute me, but I will point the way: north wing, third floor, the mauve room. You remember it?"

Serena pulled her in for one more hug. "I do. Thank you. Now, you need to go down to the servants' hall with everyone you can gather and lock the doors. You don't want to get caught up in what is about to happen here."

The woman nodded and departed, squeezing past the Nazseke warriors on her way down to the lower levels of the castle.

"This way," Serena ordered, and darted up the stairs with renewed energy. She was going to need it, Jestan knew, if they were all going to fight off the guards that were sure to be outside Gemma's door.

They arrived at the third floor. They rushed through narrow corridors, some opening into linen rooms, tea stations, and other service areas. Serena had been through here a thousand times and was steady and sure as she led the way down endless hallways that looked identical to Jestan. The door they arrived at was a panel meant to look like part of the wall, hiding the service corridors from the castle's guests.

"This is it," Serena whispered. "As soon as we're through this door, go right. The mauve room is five doors down on your left."

"Let me lead," Teyla insisted. Jestan nodded, and Serena stepped away from the door to let her pass. Teyla gripped her spear, which was halved for close combat, the longer portion of the shaft strapped across her back. She pushed the door ajar just a crack and peered out. "Huh," she muttered, and pushed it the rest of the way open. She looked both ways, but as Jestan saw when he followed her out, the corridor was abandoned.

They checked Gemma's room, but there was no sign of the young woman.

"Listen," one of Teyla's warriors ordered.

Jestan stepped over to a window and pulled it open. It overlooked an inner courtyard that was equally vacant, but a reverberating voice echoed from the walls.

The voice of King Davin.

CHAPTER 52
KOSAR

"This dissension will end now," Davin called to all those in attendance, from the citizens below to Gemma and Kosar up on the wall with him. "If conflict is what you desire, it is what you will all receive."

Kosar writhed on the ground, choking as thick mucus filled his throat and blocked his airway. As his chest heaved, bile rose up his throat, and he vomited all over himself.

His father continued to address the onlookers beyond the castle wall. "Look to your left, to your right. These people around you, whether they are your kin or your neighbors or complete strangers, are now your enemies. They wish only to harm you. It is up to you to save yourselves. Fight them. Strike them down. Kill them if you must."

There was a chorus of confused whispers as Davin's persuasive magic flowed through the crowd's ears and into their minds. Kosar remained in a fetal position on the ground, but as he looked toward the stone railing, he realized a drainage opening at the bottom of one section gave him a sliver of a view. Everyone was doing as Davin had instructed, looking at those around them. One elderly woman bent down to pick up a loose cobblestone. She turned to the younger woman next to her and slammed it into the woman's skull. Kosar winced and turned away.

After a brief shocked silence, the sounds of carnage began.

CHAPTER 53
DENNY

Denny heard Davin's words: "They wish only to harm you. It is up to you to save yourselves. Fight them. Strike them down. Kill them if you must."

A fog like the one that had surrounded Terminus Rock in his premonitions three years earlier clouded his mind. He stood in a daze, his heart and body in conflict with what his mind instructed him to do.

My enemies...Jestan. Serena. Teyla. The Nazseke.

Kill them.

Kill them all.

He turned and lifted his curved sword. Jestan was the first person he saw.

"Denny, no!" He brought his own sword up to block Denny's first blow. "Don't listen to him. Don't do it," Jestan ordered, but after using his blade to push Denny's away, he swung it down at the boy. Denny rolled aside, tumbling onto Gemma's bed. Jestan's sword sliced into the mattress, sending stuffing flying through the air. Denny rolled off the other side and fell to the ground, narrowly missing his own blade.

"Aaaahhh!" a warrior named Korra screamed, lunging at him with her spear. Denny rolled under the bed, where he just barely fit. Splinters flew up as the spear jabbed into the floorboards, missing Denny by six inches. From where he lay, he could see the feet of his many companions, all positioned as if they were facing off against each other in deadly duels. Korra dropped to her knees and yanked her spear out of the floor.

"Get away from him," Jestan ordered. "He's mine!"

Denny heard a wet slicing sound, and blood rained down next to the bed, followed by a body. He met Korra's eyes and watched the life leave them.

"No," Jestan whimpered. "I'm so sorry."

"Korra!" the other warriors cried as they fought one another against their will.

"Stop it," Denny whispered and closed his eyes, hoping his companions would forget he was there. He breathed deeply, held in the air until he felt the tightening of his diaphragm, then released it. Keeping his eyes closed, he continued the breathing exercise Marzele had coached him through during their time together at Ferathan Manor.

Screams and grunts and slashes and the thuds of bodies hitting the floor rang out around the room, yet Denny breathed deeply, kept his eyes closed, and found his inner being.

CHAPTER 54
GEORGE

Chaos and suffering and hundreds of people completely devoid of free will surrounded George.

"Damn it, Jestan, where are you?" he said aloud as he used his hammer to fend off blows from the makeshift weapons of those around him. "Why did you abandon me out here? I hate you. I'll kill you."

No, a distant voice in his mind said. *This isn't you. This isn't right.*

George wasn't commanding his body to move, yet his arms swung in wide arcs anyway. His hammer had struck down several people—of that he was sure—but he didn't know how many and couldn't picture any of their faces. Bodies were everywhere.

Fight it, the inner voice pleaded. *You can stop this. You have the strength.*

"I don't have the strength!" he screamed, which only drew more mindless civilians toward him like moths to a lantern. He knocked away a piece of a broken lamppost that one assailant swung at him, but an old man snuck up behind him and jabbed a broken liquor bottle into the fleshy side of his torso.

It's not his fault, the voice assured him. *Just disarm, don't kill.*

"Like hell I will," George said. He turned to see the terrified look on the man's face, his lack of control as apparent as George's. "I'll pound your face to a pulp," George screamed. He lifted his hammer, then brought it down with full force.

This isn't you. Make it stop right now.

When the hammer was inches from the man's shoulder, George pivoted and grazed his arm instead. It was enough to make him lose his grip on the bottle but not crush his bones. The head of the hammer clunked into the cobblestones. The man stared in shock for a moment before turning tail and running away.

George carefully stepped up onto the bench that held Le'Nelle's lifeless body. He peered out into the warring crowd, trying to make sense of what was happening.

"Time to die!" a low voice rumbled.

From his vantage point on the bench, George spotted his father's best friend exchanging blows with his own second-in-command, Selinda. George hopped down and pushed his way through the carnage to reach the pair. They had lost their weapons and both looked to be fighting with nothing more than their fists and boots.

"Quincy, Selinda, stop fighting," George ordered, but they continued as if they hadn't heard him. Selinda pushed Quincy backward, and the man tripped over a fallen townsperson and slammed to the ground on his backside. George leaped toward the muscular woman and looped his arms under hers and up around her shoulders, putting her in a hold.

But he had misjudged her size. Selinda stood a head taller than George. He strained to keep a grip on her shoulders. She bent at the knees for a second, giving George a chance to tighten his grip. He realized his mistake immediately; that was exactly what she wanted. Selinda threw herself backward and landed on top of him, knocking the wind out of him and causing his head to slam into the cobblestone street.

Everything went dark for George Calvertson.

CHAPTER 55
GEMMA

Gemma Calvertson stood motionless, Davin's power keeping her feet glued to the ground. From her vantage point on the wall, several feet behind the merlons, she could see only the tops of heads, the swinging weapons. But she could hear the screams, the slams, the stabbings, the thuds of bodies being thrown to the ground.

They had all gathered outside the castle because of her.

They had all come to call for Davin's resignation because of her.

They were all dying because of her.

Davin stood a few feet away, his back to Gemma as he peered over the merlon and watched the carnage as if it were a stage play. She could imagine the twisted smile spreading across his wrinkled cheeks. The man had decades of depravity in him, had caused suffering to hundreds or thousands of people across Aepistelle and Emyhrsen and Xaeltúve and Bahrun Ik-Chalak Ghulem.

It's not my fault, her inner voice assured her. *He is a monster. He is the reason for every curse we've faced.* The thought made her feel better, but it wasn't enough. She remained on that wall, helpless and hopeless and unable to assist others.

Gemma shifted her eyes to her left as she sensed movement. She couldn't turn her head, but she could at least see things in her peripheral vision. Kosar picked himself off the ground and charged at his father. He slammed into the old man, pinning him against the stone banister just as Davin turned around. Davin didn't stay fazed for long. He tilted his head back, then whacked it into Kosar's face. Even from a few feet away and with all the chaos below, Gemma heard the crack of Kosar's nose breaking.

Kosar stumbled back with a cry. He reached up to feel the wound. Blood poured through his fingers. He turned to look at Gemma as if asking her for help. Davin used the opportunity to pull his sword from its sheathe. Gemma tried to scream, but the words stuck in her throat as Davin moved to slice the blade through his own son's body.

Shadows fell over them all, and Davin lowered his blade before it was soiled with the blood of his offspring.

CHAPTER 56
DENNY

The next thud was close, and a limp hand brushed Denny's elbow. It pulled him from his meditation. He opened his eyes to find himself still under the bed, still in the midst of a battle between his friends. He turned to see who had fallen.

Serena Calvertson.

Denny wanted to cry out, but he knew better. He'd lost the uncontrollable urge to commit acts of violence. The exercise had worked, but he still needed to help Jestan and Teyla and the others. Apparently it was too late for Gemma's mother.

But then her eyes opened, just inches from his. He saw no hatred or rage in them, no death, only pain and sadness. She was alive.

Denny rolled out from under the bed, not knowing what he was going to do but hoping he could appeal to the others.

"Stop it!" he pleaded. "Stop fighting. Jestan, Teyla, please stop." In addition to those two, five of the Nazseke warriors remained upright, many of them covered in the blood of their dearest friends. They all halted their melee and turned to face the boy. He scanned their faces and saw no free will among them.

Denny swallowed as he realized his misguided optimism would be the end of him. The seven adults stepped forward and arranged themselves side by side in a line. Denny had a wall behind him, a bed between him and the group that wanted to murder him, and a window to his left. Even if he could reach the open window and jump before they got to him, he'd fall three stories into the courtyard below. There would be no surviving that. But it *would* mean that when his friends who survived this madness woke up, they wouldn't have to deal with the guilt of having killed Denny—he'd have done it himself. His other option was to conjure up the power he'd learned to suppress and set his companions ablaze in self-defense, but he knew he couldn't live with himself if he did that. The last three years of coping with what he'd done to Arnem had been difficult enough.

"Don't blame yourselves," Denny said in a voice tinged with immense sorrow. Then he turned and ran toward the window. The others flinched and made to charge at him, but something stopped them. Just as Denny neared the window, the room darkened. He threw his arms out to either side, catching himself on the frame before he plummeted to his death. His head out the window, he looked to the sky.

Six massive falcons blocked out the sun with their wings as they soared overhead.

"They did it!" Denny yelled out the window in pure joy. "Arnem and Marzele saved the Realm Beyond!"

CHAPTER 57
KOSAR

Why is this happening to me? Kosar thought as he crossed his eyes to get a look at his nose. It was certainly broken; he could see that much. *This was supposed to be the day I took my rightful place with Gemma by my side.*

The sound of his father's sword being pulled from its sheathe was enough to pull him from his thoughts. The old man was not playing around. There was no love for Kosar in Davin's eyes, no fatherly pride. Just vengeance. Murder. The man was a lunatic. Kosar was helpless, weaponless. Gemma remained under Davin's spell, and she was just as likely to be struck down by the king's blade as he was.

A shadow fell over them as if the sun had suddenly been blocked by a massive dark cloud. It was enough to distract Davin from striking him down in that moment. Kosar looked around. Thirty feet away, further along the wall, two guards lay dying, having fought each other at Davin's provocation just like the mindless fools below. Beside each of them rested a sword. Kosar ignored whatever was happening in the sky and ran to the scene of carnage. His steps were clumsy, his head spinning from the blows to his nose and throat. One of the guards looked up at him with pleading eyes, as if begging for help, but he would get nothing from the would-be prince. Kosar stooped and grabbed the man's sword, covered in the blood of the other guard.

"Thank you, kind sir," Kosar said, with no pity for either dying man. He turned back toward his father, and that was when he finally took note of what was in the sky.

"Giant bloody birds?" he said aloud. They were the size of train cars with wings that spanned the width of houses on either side. "What madness is this?"

Davin turned at the sound of his voice as if suddenly remembering that he'd left his son alive, a loose thread still dangling. His face shifted from awe to anger as he noted that Kosar had a weapon. Kosar smiled. He hoped the blood glistening on his teeth looked intimidating.

"Stop these childish games, Kosar. Drop the sword."

"Whatever this spectacle is, Father, it's time for *you* to stop it. Are you making us see these giant birds? Another one of your little freak tricks?"

Davin tensed. "How dare you call me a freak?"

"If the glove fits..." Kosar sneered. He was poking at his father's nerves now. "You spent so long locking away and murdering anyone with powers, yet you had your own all along. You'd be nothing without them. You'd be a nobody."

"I don't need them to whip your pathetic bottom into submission, boy!" Davin yelled before lunging toward Kosar. His first blow was quick, and Kosar barely deflected it, but he managed.

Just like Syntha taught me, he thought. His cousin had trained him his entire life until he'd betrayed her in the Southern Reaches. She was the best fighter in that region, no doubt, which made Kosar the second-best. He was okay with that.

Their swords clashed. Even in his golden years, Davin surprised Kosar with his agility and strength. He drove Kosar back with powerful blows.

I've gotten rusty, Kosar thought. It had been three years since he'd trained, and in the safety of Davin's castle, he'd let his skills fade. A mistake, clearly.

"Let's end this worthless charade," Davin said just as Kosar took a step back and felt no solid ground beneath his foot. It came down hard on a step, and he realized too late that Davin had backed him into the stairwell. In his shock, Kosar didn't get his sword up in time to block the next blow, so he let himself fall back instead.

His ankle twisted as his foot landed on the top step, but he still managed to kick off with it, sending himself tumbling down the stairwell as Davin's blade swung through the air just inches from Kosar's face. As he slammed down on his back, he caught sight of someone running up the stairs, someone who had been on his mind just moments before.

"You!" he shouted.

CHAPTER 58
DENNY

Tchat-Challai soared over Capital City along with five other enormous falcons from the Realm Beyond. Denny watched them in awe for a few moments before realizing he had to act.

He peeled his eyes away from the birds and turned back toward the room. Jestan, Teyla, and the remaining warriors stood staring at the newcomers, transfixed by the sight. Was the curse on his friends gone? They still did not look like themselves, their familiar eyes glazed over, but at least they were not attempting to maul him or each other. Denny backed away from the window slowly, but nobody seemed to notice him. He dropped to his knees, then his belly, and slid back under the bed.

Serena Calvertson still lay in the same place, alive and awake. Pain contorted her distinguished features. She panted unsteadily and reached a shaking hand toward Denny. He grabbed it and held on as he closed his eyes.

Tchat-Challai, hear me, he ordered in his mind. He conjured a picture of the majestic creature, a vision of the soaring bird from the Realm Beyond. Denny had found it effortless to connect with the bird in that world, but this felt different. *Can you hear me?*

Nothing.

Denny opened his eyes and glanced at the dying woman beside him. He wanted to cry. His friend's mother, who could have safely stayed home in the north, had risked everything to fight for Aepistelle. She'd helped save Denny from captivity. She had no part in this conflict, yet she'd selflessly joined it.

When this was all over, if Gemma survived whatever Davin and Kosar subjected her to, how broken would she be when she learned of her mother's fate and how Denny could not protect her?

No.

He closed his eyes again, took deep breaths, held them, pictured the falcon, and released the breaths, over and over. As he did so, the sounds of the castle and the chaos faded away.

He was outside. In the air. Above hordes of people in the streets, so many dead or maimed, those who were still standing covered in the blood of their friends and neighbors. They all looked up, stared at *him* instead of continuing their mindless assaults on each other.

You found me, Tchat-Challai said.

You've come to help us. Thank you.

Just as you delivered hope to the Realm Beyond when you brought that man to us, Tchat-Challai replied. *He was the light that washed away the shadow. And your other friend, he was the hope that inspired them.*

Warmth filled Denny, knowing that Marzele and Arnem had helped secure the safety not just of this world but of another. The two men who had taken him in, dedicated themselves to his safety and growth.

And now we are here for you, Tchat-Challai assured him.

Denny continued to look out through the falcon's eyes as she glided over the castle walls with the others trailing behind her. The carnage on top of the wall was just as bad; the guards had used their weapons against each other. A couple of people remained in motion, the only folks seemingly unfazed by the birds' arrival. Tchat-Challai swooped toward them for a closer look.

Gemma stood motionless while two men parried with swords. Denny recognized the older man as King Davin, so he could only assume the younger man was Kosar, whom Gemma had told him all about before they'd visited the Realm Beyond. The falcons circled the scene, and Denny watched as Kosar tumbled down the stairs. If the man had been defending Gemma, she no longer had protection.

We must save her, he told the bird.

She must save herself. You can wake her.

How?

The same way you are speaking with me right now. Go to her, boy.

Denny's vision went dark for a moment before he awoke in the room under the bed. Serena's grip had loosened. Her life had left her body.

CHAPTER 59
KOSAR

"Hello, cousin," Syntha said as she approached the fallen Kosar. "Quite a situation you've created for yourself."

"Yes, well, I didn't have you to get me out of it. Perhaps losing you was my first mistake. My muscle, my armor, my coach."

Kosar reached out for her as she climbed the stairs to meet him where he'd stopped tumbling halfway down. He wasn't sure if she'd lift him to his feet or finish him off with her sword. Fortunately, she chose the former.

"If I'm really all those things to you, you have a funny way of thanking me for it," she said. He reached for his head and felt a knot the size of a stone. Dizziness washed over him, but Syntha supported him. "You left me for dead back in that barn, Kosar."

"I know, but—"

"All our friends, everyone who worked with you on that newspaper...all dead."

"I know, but—"

"Your brother—dead. Your father—heartbroken and powerless."

"Not my real father, but point taken, and I—"

"And me, Kosar. I dedicated my life to serving you, and you deceived me and everyone else who loved you and believed in you. And where did it get you?" Syntha gestured at the carnage that surrounded them. As he looked around, his eyes fell on the top of the stairs, where Davin stood glaring down at him.

"Another friend of yours I need to kill?" Davin called down. He pointed toward Gemma. "I still need to finish this one off first." He turned and strutted toward the statuesque Gemma.

"No!" came a male voice. Kosar wondered for a second if it was his own, if the concussion had caused him to feel so detached from himself that he couldn't even tell when he was speaking, but then a man pushed past him up the stairs. Kosar had seen him before, as had his spies when they'd trailed Gemma: Kieve Fallbrook.

Hatred and jealousy came over Kosar. This man had clearly been in love with Gemma as well, and she'd seemed to have positive feelings toward him. Nothing like the scorn she held for Kosar, despite everything he'd done for her.

Kosar looked down. His sword lay two steps above him. He bent forward and retrieved it.

"What do you think you're doing?" Syntha demanded.

Kosar kicked his right foot back, his boot slamming into Syntha's knee, and the woman stumbled back and plummeted down the remainder of the stairs.

"Sorry, cousin," Kosar called out. He leaped forward, following Kieve.

CHAPTER 60
GEMMA

*W*ake up, Gemma.

The voice pierced her thoughts, loud and yet not a sound at all.

Denny? she thought, and suddenly all the boy's emotions filled her mind. There was excitement over the arrival of Tchat-Challai and the other birds, which Gemma had noticed in her comatose state even if she couldn't react to it. There was also a profound sadness. Someone had died, and Denny had witnessed it. *What happened? What's wrong?*

Later, Gemma. You need to break through the cloud controlling your mind.

I can't, Denny.

You can. Move your head. Look to your left. Now.

She did. Her neck muscles flexed, and her head pivoted to the left. She caught sight of Davin strutting toward her, sword in hand. His cocky grin faltered when she moved, and he stopped in his tracks.

Behind him, two men burst out of the stairwell and darted across the wall.

Kieve!

And Kosar.

Davin saw the surprise on her face and turned around just as Kieve's sword came down toward him. Davin lifted his own to block it, but the blades never met. Kosar's sword pierced Kieve's shoulder, causing him to lose his aim and miss the king. While pivoting to face his attacker, Kieve stumbled and slammed into the ground at Davin's feet, dropping his sword.

Run, Gemma.

Gemma moved, breaking free of the invisible bonds that held her in place. She had no weapons, so she swung her fists. Punching a king, let alone an elderly one, wasn't a classy move, but here she was.

Davin stumbled forward at the blow from behind, nearly tripping over the fallen Kieve. From the ground, Kieve kicked up at Kosar, who had just turned around at the arrival of Syntha, cut, bruised, and angry. Gemma reached down and picked up Kieve's sword.

"I need to borrow this," she said, and Kieve smiled at her.

"Well, now it's a fair fight," Davin said as he took in the sight of Gemma with a blade.

"Nothing is fair with you in charge. Release your grip on these people," Gemma ordered as she and Davin circled each other, each waiting for the other to attack first. "Win on the strength of your skills, not your magic. Unless you're afraid you can't?"

"Okay, then." Davin smirked. He tilted his head up and bellowed to everyone within earshot, "The curse is lifted! You may move freely. Look around you and see what you have done to your friends and your families and your neighbors." His voice reverberated off the stone walls of the castle.

Gemma felt the fog that remained in her mind lift and dissipate. She launched herself at her king. Kieve's sword felt unfamiliar in her hands, but there was too much at stake to let that bother her.

Just as Syntha taught me, she thought. *Just as Teyla taught me in the foothills. And Richard. And Quincy. And so many others. This is for all of them.*

CHAPTER 61
DENNY

Denny rolled out from under the bed. He'd heard Davin's voice echo through the courtyard. He'd felt the change in the air and in his body. He got to his feet to see Teyla, Jestan, and the others mourning their fallen comrades. He walked to the other side of the bed, carefully stepping over the bodies of friends struck down unjustly. He hugged Jestan, then Teyla.

"I'm so sorry this happened," he told them. A glint caught his eye as sunlight peeked through the window and reflected off a blade—Gemma's machete, dropped by her mother. He bent down and retrieved it, then turned to the others. "Gemma needs this!" he shouted, and ran from the room.

The castle was massive, sprawling over several city blocks. Without Serena to guide him, Denny had no clue how to find the section of wall he'd seen Gemma standing on through Tchat-Challai's eyes. Up ahead, a door led to a balcony overlooking a courtyard. Denny pushed through it and stepped out into the warmth of the sun.

Come for me, Tchat-Challai, he pleaded.

The bird arrived within seconds, swooping low into the courtyard. Denny leaped from his perch and landed on a wing, then rolled toward the bird's back and held on firmly. Tchat-Challai flapped her wings and rose into the sky.

To Gemma, he said, pointing toward the spot where he'd last seen her.

As you wish, the bird thought back, and proceeded to fly toward the action on the wall.

CHAPTER 62
KIEVE

Kieve lay helpless, watching the duels on either side of him. Gemma held her own against King Davin, while Syntha warded off her pathetic cousin whom she had trained for years. He got to his hands and knees, trying not to draw the attention of his rivals or distract his allies. He looked around for a weapon and noticed the fallen guards farther down the wall. Slowly, he got to his feet and raced past Syntha and Kosar.

Kosar's blade swung for him, but he leaned away from it as he ran by, and Syntha deflected the sword before it could come any closer. Kieve went past the staircase and arrived at the bloody spot where two of the guards had been coerced into obliterating each other. One sword was missing, but the other remained. He picked it up and turned back toward the action.

CHAPTER 63
KOSAR

"It's time to end this petty squabble!" Kosar shouted at his cousin. His whole life, he'd been held back by the people he'd thought of as his family, and right now his cousin was keeping him from protecting the love of his life. "I'm trying to rescue Gemma, you dolt!"

"You're delusional," Syntha accused as she jabbed her blade toward him. He deflected it. "We're here to rescue her from *you*, you maniac."

"She seems to be doing fine on her own," came another voice. Syntha turned to watch Kieve's approach. The man had poached a sword from the fallen guards.

This won't do, Kosar told himself. *Not at all a fair fight.*

Kosar took advantage of Syntha's distraction and kicked his cousin. But he was still dizzy, and he lost balance when his foot connected with her already injured knee. He stumbled into her and grabbed her garments to steady himself, but she hadn't braced herself for his weight. She fell over the ledge toward the interior courtyard and pulled Kosar down with her.

But that wasn't the end of his story.

He felt as if he'd dropped his stomach along with his sword, but as he opened his eyes and looked around, he found himself floating in the air alongside his cousin.

"What the hell?" he asked as he looked down. The traitorous Royal Mystic Committee officer Palignon stood below. Alongside him were a woman and a teenager, both holding their hands out toward Kosar and Syntha.

They're freaks, he told himself. They were using their powers to levitate him and Syntha.

"What do we do now?" the girl asked her father.

"I'd say we should set Syntha down gently and drop the other one, but I don't want blood on your hands, baby," Palignon replied.

"Let's set them back on the wall," Palignon's ex-wife suggested, and that was what they did.

CHAPTER 64
GEMMA

Gemma was exhausted from the fight, but she couldn't give up. Her opponent was breathing heavily—wheezing, even. Davin's age was starting to show. She just had to persist. As she deflected his blows with the fallen guard's sword, she felt them getting less and less powerful, but her own strength was fading as well. She lost her grip on her sword, and it flew over the edge. Davin had backed her against the wall, where she could hear shocked murmurs from the citizens down below. She used her position and Davin's weakness to her advantage and pushed off the wall, slamming her body into the king and forcing him backward.

"Hey!" Kieve yelled from behind the king. He slashed down with the blade he'd acquired. Davin attempted to block it, but Kieve was faster. He lopped Davin's sword hand clean off. Kieve, Gemma, and Davin all stopped and stared in shock as the king's hand gushed not crimson but glowing emerald blood.

"What?" Kieve asked, but Gemma recognized the distinctive color.

"You've been consuming the mineral from Bahrun?" Gemma asked.

Davin turned to her and held up his stub of an arm. "I didn't need that runt of a woman to tell me how to make use of the stuff. I only needed to crush it up and swallow it. Wasn't sure it'd work, but would you look at that?"

The skin of Davin's forearm stretched and formed into the shape of a glowing green hand. Davin used his enemies' shock to his advantage. He swiped the sword from Kieve's hand without effort. Kieve and Gemma stepped backward with their arms shielding their faces, as if they could defend themselves from the blade.

"Gemma, look out!" came a voice from above.

Gemma glanced up to see Denny riding in on Tchat-Challai. He dropped something that clanged onto the ground next to her as the flapping of the bird's wings drove Davin back a few steps. When she looked down, she found her machete. She retrieved it.

"We've been over this, girl," Davin said with a sneer. "I can't be killed. I am immortal. Drop your weapon and surrender immediately."

"You're a stain on history," Gemma said, bringing the blade up. Unlike Kieve's sword, this weapon felt like an extension of her body.

"History is what I make of it," Davin said. "I shape what happens in this world. You are powerless to change that."

"Then why are you intimidated by what I wrote in that book? If I'm so powerless, then how can you explain why all those people gathered here today, ready to fight back?"

Davin laughed at this. "You mean that pile of bodies down

there? They've clearly lost, Gemma Calvertson, just as you have."

"You're wrong." Gemma lunged forward and sliced with her machete. Davin's green hand shattered into a cloud of mineral dust. He reached out his other hand, and she lopped that one off as well.

"No!" Davin screamed. He threw himself at her, weaponless. She hacked at him again, limited by the close proximity, and managed to slice into his stomach. Green blood squirted out, quickly stanched by a shell of glowing rock. He pushed her back, and she stumbled into Kieve. He reached over her shoulder and threw a punch into Davin's face, sending the man back two steps. It was all the space Gemma needed to swing at him. Her machete tore clean through Davin's neck. His severed head thudded to the ground at Kosar's feet. The king's body took a couple more aimless steps before falling backward, the stump of his neck spraying emerald liquid at the would-be prince.

"Recover from that," Gemma said.

"Father!" Kosar screamed. He turned his attention to Gemma, and she read hatred in his eyes. "He hadn't named me as his heir yet!" he yelled, as if all he cared about was power. Gemma shook her head in disbelief. Kosar bent down and retrieved the sword Davin had lost when she'd chopped off his hand. He brought it up to attack Gemma. She was ready with her own weapon, but it was unnecessary. Syntha came up behind him, weaponless but for her own body. She slammed into him and drove him toward the wall. Kosar tripped over a crenel and plummeted to his death on the cobblestones below with no gifted *freak* to rescue him.

Gemma and Kieve ran forward and held on to Syntha, preventing her from falling after her cousin. At the edge of the wall, Gemma scanned the shocked crowd.

"George!" she yelled down. A few bodies moved among the stunned onlookers as George, Quincy, and some of the crews of mercenaries and pirates she'd met over the years approached the nearest gate to enter the castle.

Gemma turned back to face the interior of the castle's perimeter. Tchat-Challai had landed on a stretch of wall and offloaded Denny. He patted the bird and made his way toward her. Gemma glanced down and saw Palignon hugging two women she assumed were his family. Through a door just behind that trio, Jestan, Teyla, and a handful of her warriors emerged.

There was carnage everywhere. Hundreds of innocent people had died. Gemma wanted to feel good about what had happened, but she couldn't. She dropped to her knees under the weight of it all.

CHAPTER 65
JESTAN

Jestan spotted Gemma up on the wall. Denny was standing over her, his hands on her shoulders. A man and a woman he didn't recognize also stood with them, clearly friends of Gemma's. At the foot of the stairs leading up to the wall, a man, woman, and girl around Denny's age stood, embracing one another. Jestan squeezed past them and ascended the stairs. When he was halfway up, George, Quincy, and the others appeared and started up behind him. He waited for George at the top.

"You're okay!" George said as he embraced Jestan. "I wish I could say the same for so many others. Le'Nelle..." He couldn't finish the sentence before the tears started, but Jestan didn't need to hear the words.

"Shh, it's okay," Jestan said as the man wept into his shoulder. "We'll get through this, my friend." His heart broke at the thought of telling George about the passing of his mother.

George stood up straight and wiped the tears from his face, then spotted his sister. He ran to her, and Jestan followed. Gemma and George held each other for a full minute. "It's over," they said to each other as Jestan watched the two of them, knowing the heartache was far from over.

When the siblings pulled away from each other, Jestan locked eyes with Gemma. She cleared her throat and spoke. "I don't know what to do now. We've defeated Davin, but now this kingdom is in shambles. Did we do the right thing, or did we make things worse?"

Below, cries of sadness and shouts of anger rose up from the crowd. Jestan walked to the edge and took in the scene of carnage. Hundreds had died down there, but hundreds more remained.

"Jestan the Just!" someone shouted.

"It's really him!"

Jestan took a step back, not wanting to be the center of attention for once.

A hand rested on his shoulder. He turned to see George; his face was shining with tears, but there was also hope. "What are you waiting for?" he asked. "This is what you've spent your life preparing for onstage. You've had an incredible impact on the people of Emyhrsen over the last few months. If anyone can comfort them, can talk them through this difficult time, it's you, Jestan."

Jestan stared at his best friend for several long seconds, taking in his words. Internalizing them. George was right.

Jestan stepped to the edge of the wall and lifted his hands. Raised his voice.

CHAPTER 66

HANNON, EIGHTEEN MONTHS LATER

It wasn't as if Gemma Calvertson were some sort of *chosen one* foretold by the prophets. At least not directly. She did fit the mold loosely described by some of them, such as the Solendaron. But it was her particular qualities and abilities that really set her apart. It was her just heart. Her passion for truth. Her bravery, which shone through clouds of doubt at just the right moments. And then there were, of course, her academic prowess and emotional intelligence, which were the reasons why Garrod Hannon had conspired with Telman Abernath to send the girl to Richard the Elusive five years earlier. The other qualities had revealed themselves later.

Hannon never could have predicted the events that had transpired after Gemma's initial meeting with the old hero, not in his wildest dreams. He had set out to absolve himself of the sins of helping the despot Davin rise to power and stay there, and Gemma Calvertson had more than undone that. She had given Aepistelle not only *freedom* but also hope and happiness and a future of peace.

Now, Hannon was on hand to present the keys to the Royal Library of Aepistelle to his former pupil and onetime underling. She had insisted on keeping the ceremony small—no special public unveiling of the restored institute of knowledge. Those who wished to learn would seek it out in their own time, and all would be welcome. There would be no gatekeeping, no censorship from a king fearful that his subjects would see through his lies. Not with Gemma Calvertson in charge.

As she walked up the steps toward the door to meet him, Hannon reflected on how she had changed since he and Abernath had orchestrated her first journey. He had seen her as a child all those years ago, though she had been twenty-three at the time. Her innocence and low self-confidence had made her seem incredibly young back then. But now she was different. She walked with purpose, held herself gracefully upright, showed no fear. Curiosity about the world around her still glowed in her eyes, her childlike wonder on display for all to see.

"We're back where this all started," Hannon said. He gestured for her to follow him across the landing. "To say you're the first person to step through these doors since Telman Abernath's death would be disingenuous—we've been restoring the building for quite some time, so tradespersons have been in and out, and I've been here to supervise the whole thing. However, I can say that you are the most deserving of these."

Hannon jangled a large ring of keys, then pulled the longest one out of the batch. He held that key between his thumb and forefinger and offered it to Gemma.

"Thank you," she said as she took it.

Hannon pointed to the keyhole under the knob on the

right side of the double doors. Gemma put the key in and turned until it clicked. Hannon pushed the door open.

"After you," he said.

CHAPTER 67
GEMMA

Gemma stepped inside the library, a place where she had spent hundreds of hours between her college days and her brief employment at University Press under Garrod Hannon. Researching and gaining knowledge from these books had been like breathing or drinking water: it was a part of who she was, a necessity of life. When she'd last been here, the head librarian had snuck a scroll into her bag, a part of the conspiracy between him and Hannon. Telman Abernath had paid dearly for the action—he'd been murdered by an assassin with the Royal Mystic Committee. Then a freak attack of birds had destroyed the glass dome that let sunlight into the library's many floors. The institution had been shuttered at that point, closed to the public and researchers alike.

Not anymore.

Gemma's breath caught as she looked around. The first thing she noticed was the scent of the books, overpowering even the smells of fresh paint and new wooden furniture. The light coming through the windows had a golden hue, giving the place the majestic feel it deserved. There were no patrons yet, but that wouldn't be the case for long. Gemma was going to open the place as soon as she and her staff finished cataloguing the vast archives.

"Well," Hannon coaxed, "what do you think?"

Gemma spun slowly, her eyes dancing across not only the shelves on the ground floor but also those visible on the higher levels.

"It's incredible. Breathtaking." She noticed the weight of the keys in her hand. She lifted them up to get a better look. "What are all of these for?"

"There are the archives in the basement reserved for academics. There are a number of offices on each floor for the staff and researchers. And then there's the top floor, where Abernath spent most of his time."

"The banned books and scrolls," Gemma said.

"Indeed. The religious texts, the spells and cantrips, the history books Davin rescinded from circulation."

"We're not going to need that key anymore," Gemma said. "Those books are going back down to the shelves. I'll get you the funding to reprint copies of them and distribute them across the kingdom."

"As you wish," Hannon said. "Well, I'll leave you to explore this place. You know where to find me."

"Thank you, sir," Gemma said.

"I'm not your boss anymore," Hannon replied. "It's the other way around, and that's how things should be. No need for the *sir*."

That reminded her of a question that had been nagging at her for quite some time. "A few years ago, I visited your office when I was a fugitive. Instead of protecting me, you threatened to call Davin's soldiers. Why?"

"As you'll recall, I said I'd give you thirty minutes. That

they came sooner was beyond my control. They must have been observing my office, waiting for you."

"But you still threatened to contact them," Gemma shot back.

"Yes, and I am sorry. As I said back then, I knew Davin had seers in his employ who watched for traitorous activity. I had to remain on his good side so I could continue to strike in strategic, clandestine ways. Furthermore, I had full faith that you could handle yourself. We're all glad to see that I was not misguided."

Gemma knew better than to get upset. She wasn't sure whether she could ever fully trust the man. But she would learn from history, just as she'd always been taught, in order to avoid repeating mistakes.

Gemma turned away and soon found herself lost in a volume she'd pulled off the shelf, one she remembered studying years ago about resource sharing among the individual kingdoms that made up the whole of Aepistelle. Once Hannon had left and the door clicked shut, Gemma put the book back in its place and climbed the restored staircase to its highest point. She leaned against the railing, once Abernath's perch, that overlooked the entire library and took it all in. It reminded her of everything she'd been through, all she'd sacrificed to help others gain freedom and truth.

After the death of King Davin, Jestan had given a speech to the surviving citizens assembled outside of the castle. He'd reassured them that after they had mourned, they would rebuild, that their lives would improve. He'd sworn that he and his companions would help to ensure that Aepistelle never fell into a period of darkness again, that the future would be bright. They had cheered him on, chanted his name for hours. Word had spread that Jestan had helped save their kingdom from the madness and depravity of King Davin, and soon he'd been asked by the majority to be the new king, as Davin had no heirs and no formal successor.

Jestan had considered it briefly. He'd realized that he truly did have a knack for helping people and solving big problems. He especially loved having an impassioned audience again, though he knew becoming king was not his only chance for that. He did have several years of new adventures that he could mine for new books and stage shows, after all. He'd agreed to be a temporary ruler, much as Richard had done in Emyhrsen.

Jestan had summoned the governors or surviving heirs of all the territories that made up Aepistelle. Some had understandably been suspicious of his intentions at first after what Davin had done to all their first-born children, but in a matter of hours, they'd come to trust him. Together, they had talked about their visions for the future of Aepistelle, and they had agreed to return to the way things had once been: each territory would be its own country. They had worked with scholars and experts to negotiate treaties ensuring that they would share resources and aid and coexist in peace. Even Bahrun Ik-Chalak Ghulem and Emyhrsen had joined the new union of nations.

Syntha had returned home to the Southern Reaches, where she took care of her uncle Joseph. Now that he had lost his sons, Kosar—whom he still considered his own flesh and blood despite knowing the truth of the boy's parentage—and Ysidro, Joseph had named Syntha as his heir to the throne.

After the battle at the castle, Teyla and her remaining warriors had taken their fallen sisters back to the northern mountains. The surviving crew of the *Ales and Sails* had transported them home, burying their fallen captain Le'Nelle at sea on the way.

Quincy and George had followed close behind them,

escorting the soldiers of Emyhrsen home and collecting the gifted refugees who had remained behind in Ferathan. It was now safe for them to come home, as Jestan had disbanded the Royal Mystic Committee. He had tasked Palignon with destroying the records that catalogued each gifted person and their abilities, as he believed such a database violated privacy and freedom. Palignon had accepted the assignment after taking a few weeks to reconcile with his ex-wife and daughter and moving back home from Pinedrop.

After the trip to Emyhrsen, Quincy and George had returned to Geoffrey and brought him to a facility that could best care for him. It was close to where Quincy lived, so he could visit his old friend often. Then George had found his way back to Capital City, where he'd taken on a role as Jestan's aide.

Denny had questioned his own place in Aepistelle following the battle. With his parents, Marzele, and Arnem all gone, he'd felt he had no purpose. He'd wanted to ride off on Tchat-Challai through whatever portal the falcons had used to travel into the realm of the living. Of course, Gemma had talked him out of it, and as soon as he had said goodbye to the bird, his girlfriend, Iyola, from Ferathan had run up to him and given him a passionate kiss. She had been one of the refugees who'd come down from the north with Jestan to attack the castle. George had described seeing her manipulate water to fight off attackers during the battle in Capital City. The pair had remained inseparable. Denny was glad to be with someone who was also struggling to learn to control her abilities. His wisdom and literal foresight were invaluable assets, and Jestan had employed him as an advisor, helping to set up programs for reintegrating the gifted into society. They had agreed that Denny could frequently take time off to be with the Wynstone women. They were, after all, his closest family.

Kieve had remained Gemma's partner even though they no longer served the defunct Royal Mystic Committee. He'd finally gotten Gemma to change out of her agent garb and into something a bit more appropriate for a date at one of Capital City's fine dining establishments. Their first outing had not ended in pursuing a suspect enrobed in a glass invisibility suit or anything of the sort, nor had any of their dates since. Kieve had received an offer to be the head of security for the newly recrowned king of Centeron, where he'd grown up, but he had turned it down to remain close to Gemma. He'd taken a less glamorous role under Palignon and couldn't have been happier.

And then there was Gemma herself. Her passion had always been for knowledge, using history to inform the present and plan for a better future. Jestan had named her the chief historian and archivist of West Aepistelle and commissioned the restoration of the Royal Library of Aepistelle. He had made her promise to consider other roles within the government as changes were made, and she had agreed. There was still much to do, corruption to weed out, injustices to fix, and it would take many more years to accomplish.

Now, as she looked around at the tens of thousands of books, Gemma knew she had all the tools within reach to make the world a better place for all.

NEWSLETTER

Please join the author's email newsletter at https://www. MacheteAndQuill.com for exclusive updates, behind-the-scenes content, and more.

If you enjoyed this story, please leave a review on Goodreads, BookBub, and your favorite online retailer so others can hear about it. Please tell your friends and librarians about the book as well!

Thank you.

BUY DIRECT

Please consider buying direct from the author. Signed, personalized books are available at MacheteAndQuill.com.

Direct sales help to not only to put a little bit more money into the funds to continue writing and publishing, but also to create a connection between the reader and writer in a way retail sales may not.

No matter where you buy or borrow, however, your readership and support is equally appreciated. We are supporters of bookstores small and large, as well as libraries.

Thank you.

We Are Not Alone in the Dark

A high school bully, quarreling friends, and an abusive father are the least of Bryan's worries. When night comes, so do the visitors, and he can't fight back. Who will rescue Bryan if nobody believes him? A coming-of-age alien horror novel.

Ditch of the Damned and Other Tales

A collection of five short stories by Ryan Hoyt.

Senior Class: A Raventree Hollow Story

Pearl and Rosemary are the last of their kind. At 90 years old, death calls for them. Who will be the left standing? A short story chapbook set in the town of Raventree Hollow, this can be read as a standalone tale or enjoyed along with *Raventree Hollow*.

Butterscotch: A Raventree Hollow Story

A family moves into an old home to find the previous owner has left behind a hutch with a candy dish. Aggressive neighbors, a trio of cats, and a hidden purple bag lead the family to seek out answers. "Butterscotch" is a short story chapbook set in the town of Raventree Hollow.

Ditch of the Damned

While traveling with her family across the American frontier, Eudora is pulled off the wagon trail by a sensation deep within her bones. She ignores a warning sign and proceeds toward a hole in the earth in the middle of the wilderness. "Ditch of the Damned" is a short story set in 1847.

The Hoarder's House

Erica's sister went missing in her own home. As Erica and her husband search for the lost woman, they find something luring in the depths of depravity.

Freddy Goodman (Ain't No Good Man)

His coming-of-age story was *so* twenty years ago. So why do the words of that old witch still haunt him? A short story of contemporary fiction with elements of magical realism.

ACKNOWLEDGMENTS

Well, it's done.

This series started life a decade before it was completed. Ten full years of imagining the world of Aepistelle, the events worthy of a story, and the characters to play it all out on the page. At the beginning, it was supposed to be an audio drama podcast. I wrote some scripts, recorded a couple test episodes, and then put it to rest.

In 2019, I revisited the story as a novel, completed in four months. I tinkered with it some more over the next couple years and finally released *The Forest of Despair* in 2021 along with the prequel, *The Witch of Ferathan*. It would be almost two more years before the sequel, *The Isle of Abandonment* (my personal favorite of the series), took the series to darker places. While less than halfway through that manuscript, I outlined what became this book, which helped me figure out where *Isle* would end, leaving the characters in some pretty dire places. I stuck pretty close to the outline for this one, and I hope you enjoyed the story.

I don't know where I go from here with my fantasy writing. It's hard to leave Aepistelle and these characters behind, but I'm pretty confident that this is the last of Gemma's story unless something really amazing comes to mind that is worth shaking up her *happily ever after* for. I have always wanted to go back and tell the story of "the great journey" with a younger Richard, Jestan, Arnem, and Maachel. Perhaps someday I'll get there. For now, I'm just grateful to have reached this milestone of a completed series. Thank you for coming along on this journey.

Huge thanks to Alison Cherry, the line and copy editor of this entire series. My writing can get messy. I screw up sayings, add in words that I think mean one thing but totally do not. I use far too many filler words. You don't see much of that because Alison cleans up my work. *Thousands* of words are cut without the sentences losing any of their meanings, and the whole thing reads so much better after she's slashed at it like Gemma with a machete.

Thanks to Tania and the design team at MiblArt for creating the newest covers for the series. It was heartbreaking to have to leave the old covers behind, but I'm happy to have a cohesive style across all four books in the series now.

Thank you to my family for supporting my writing endeavors and the time and money I spend on trying to make this something more than a little personal hobby. Love you guys!

To everyone who interacts on my Facebook page and makes me feel like a real author (am I a real author yet? Okay, maybe I am), thanks for being there for me. Your support lifts me higher than you know.

Finally thank you to the beta readers of this manuscript: Heather Sleeter, Angela Green-Carter, and Joan S. Smith.

Perhaps I'll see you all back in Aepistelle one day. Until then, please be good to those around you and always stand up for truth, justice, and freedom.

Best,

Ryan Hoyt

August 30, 2024

www.ingramcontent.com/pod-product-compliance
Lightning Source LLC
Chambersburg PA
CBHW021234190726
48289CB00005B/1315